ELEMENTAL

BROKEN PACT, BOOK TWO

ELEMENTAL

ASH FITZSIMMONS

This is a work of fiction. Names, characters, places, and incidents are products of the author's imagination or are used fictitiously and are not to be construed as real. Any resemblance to actual events, locales, organizations, or persons, living or dead, is entirely coincidental.

Print Edition ISBN: 978-1-949861-77-8

Cover design by MiblArt.

www.ashfitzsimmons.com

CHAPTER 1

Putting on a wedding is not a task for the faint of heart.

In the Pactlands, where I'd gradually made my home over the last four years, most folks just went to a judge—a quick trip to the Tribunal building in Beukal, a short ceremony, and boom, done. That cut to the chase, as the legal certificate was the important thing; anything else one might do to celebrate one's nuptials was gravy.

Some couples stuck to older traditions to make their wedding more of an event. For instance, I accepted an invitation to the wedding of one of my centaur colleagues before I realized that those were three-day affairs, big festivals out in the countryside that took place under the open sky, rain or shine. While severe weather was a true rarity in our magically created pocket world, our weather tended to reflect whatever was going on outside...and unfortunately for the happy couple, their wedding was held in a place roughly overlapping central Oklahoma during a nasty tornado outbreak. Pavilions blew over, the ground turned to churned-up mud under the hooves of the many family members and friends taking part in the old games and dances, and those of us capable of keeping off the downpour via spell made *good* friends with our less talented fellow guests. My shielding ability had grown considerably since my first fumbling attempts at casting, but whenever my considerably better trained fiancé, Yven, stepped aside to talk to someone, I found excuses to sidle closer to Ligh Birrid, a colleague from the Division of Laws and a water nymph, who seemed to have found themself all manner of new friends that wet weekend. "I love weddings," they told me as we huddled together, the rain curtaining around us as if we were standing beneath a glass dome, "but next time, I think I'll pack waders. Maybe galoshes," they muttered, pulling one caked shoe from the sucking muck. "The guest house's carpet is doomed."

Traditional elven weddings were sedate affairs by comparison, generally midafternoon ceremonies followed by partying long into the night. They were also increasingly rare events, as most younger elves didn't bother with the expense or the fuss, but I had been to one, and while it was different than the weddings I'd attended growing up in Virginia, it was more recognizable to me than, say, the wrestling matches between the bride's and groom's families at a centaur shindig. They weren't religious ceremonies—from what I'd gathered, the extent of theology for most elves was a vague concept of something unknown out in the universe, perhaps a larger force driving the "subtle energies," what everyone else less poetically labeled "magic." Rather, weddings were times to celebrate the binding together of families. At most such weddings, or so I'd been informed, while the officiant stumbled more or less poorly through the old High Elvish vows, he or she would create the illusion of massive trees on either side of the room, thin shoots labeled with ancestors' names that gradually wove around each other, forming stout trunks for the couple that would reach together and intertwine as a sort of canopy. It was an established tradition, Pop had informed me—hell, he'd had it done at his wedding to my great-grandmother in the seventeenth century—and naturally, I would have as much for mine.

Whether I wanted it or not, I was getting hitched in *style.*

There are worse fates than learning you're the next-best thing to elven royalty, but that doesn't mean it's not a complicated proposition.

For the first twenty-six years of my life, I was Rose Thorn, Richmond native, and eventually a small-business owner and decently talented portraitist and landscape artist. Aside from the sudden loss of my parents in a Valentine's Day car wreck, I was doing well by most metrics: I had a degree, I'd inherited my childhood home in the West End free and clear, and I rented studio space in Carytown, where I sold enough paintings to keep the lights on and my checking account in the black. True, my love life was often nonexistent, and the only family I had left was my Aunt Lily, the great-aunt who had been a grandmother to me, but for a twenty-something on her own, I was more than treading water.

Then Aunt Lily asked me to drive out to the mountains and watch her garden nursery while she left town to visit a sick friend. Turns out there was no friend—that was a code phrase, and she was in danger and on the run.

And also an elf, which I hadn't realized was a box one might check on a census form.

As it so happened, my grandfathers had been elves, my grandmothers human. All had died before I was born—my grandmothers passed of natural causes, while my grandfathers died a couple of decades after downing the aptly-nicknamed death draught, their one-way ticket to be with the women they loved, which also strangled their magical abilities. My parents had been talentless, as usual for children born in their situation...but the draught wasn't the most stable of potions, and instead of doubling itself in me, it left me untouched. I was a late bloomer, sure, since no one had ever let me in on the family secret, but I *was* talented—and more than that, a farseer, having inherited the wild talent notorious in my mother's family.

The poor agent from the Division of Plants and Potions who'd come out to inspect Aunt Lily's hidden greenhouse and stumbled into me instead had no idea what he was in for. Yven ti'Ansha was young for an agent—not quite fifty-three—the fourteenth child in a family from one of the lower-ranked elven Halls. He kept a meticulous bachelor apartment, had taught himself to make the most amazing buttermilk biscuits I'd ever tasted, and tended his orchids like they were his babies. He was in no way prepared for a stubborn civilian who refused to leave an active investigation. It was bad enough when he thought I was merely the unmentionable great-granddaughter of Lord ti'Cren, head of one of the Pactlands' wealthiest and most prominent Halls. That was just my dad's family—on my mom's side, I was the only living descendant of Lord ti'Dana, last ruler of the northern elven kingdom, who would surely never stoop to acknowledge a partly human great-granddaughter.

But Pop, who'd hidden me not out of embarrassment, but rather to protect me, did just that—and in public fashion. With news cameras rolling, he'd explained the circumstances of my existence while certifying me as a farseer before the judge overseeing my *other* great-grandfather's trial for a litany of crimes ranging from illegal production to murder. My acknowledgement into Hall ti'Dana set tongues wagging—genetically, I was ninety percent elven, while that other ten percent was scandalous—but it made me legally part of the family and gave me citizenship. And since Yven and I had fallen hard for each other by then, it cleared the way for our engagement.

I adored my fiancé, but I wasn't in a rush to get married. I'd had my life upended of late, been attacked by a siren, and had to hide from the ti'Crens and their operatives for more than two months. I had a life in Richmond that I wasn't sure I wanted to abandon, but I was also easing into a position at DPP, getting the remedial training I desperately needed under the watchful eye of Aunt Lily's uncle, Pateme ti'Tam. But as the months and years passed, I made my gradual transition into the Pactlands. I moved into an apartment in Pop's sprawling mansion, and Yven eventually worked through enough of his fear of my great-grandfather to join me. As I grew more confident in my uniquely oriented farsight, I stepped into my role as DPP's resident farseer, the person to call when Interdiction needed eyes on a target. Through it all, Yven remained steadfastly by me, fussing when I tranced too long and helping me discover new aspects of the world I was starting to call home, but never rushing me into marriage. Few people married until they were in their late thirties, at *least*, since schooling went to thirty-five. That I was gainfully employed instead of stuck in a classroom was odd enough without tossing an immediate wedding into the mix. But I was thirty-one now—still not fully of age but less alarmingly so—and when I told Yven I was ready to pull the pin, he jumped on board.

I finally had some friends of my own to invite, thanks to the weirdness of the intervening years. Annie Humphries had run in my circles back in Richmond, but she'd wound up in the Pactlands after being given a novel potion, married into the Wild Hunt, and snagged a job on the Interdiction side of DPP. Maya Mackay, a Carytown restauranteur and friend of ours, had likewise been stuck in the Pactlands for a time, but she'd been sent home with a memory wipe…which, until recently, only a handful of us had known hadn't worked. Jane Fortune was a sorcerer who'd been raised in Appalachian Georgia—also hidden from a homicidal family member, a fact that gave us plenty of common ground—and Pop had lured her into the Division of Intelligence about two years prior. Jane's confidante back home was Tabitha Bradley, a woman about twenty years older and wiser, an established pharmacist and longtime Wiccan without a shred of magical talent. Sure, she was solidly human, but Tabitha didn't panic in a crisis and rolled with whatever was thrown at her, and Pop respected that. The baby of the group was Maebe Amos, only twenty, who'd grown up in backwoods poverty near Jane before taking her place as Lady ti'Ammaas and pursuing an education in the Pactlands. And then there was

Canna Nerin, a healer at DOL, who was Jane's cousin and married to Yven's best buddy, Pars. Since she was nearly thirty years my senior, she'd become something of a den mom to our odd little sorority. While the higher-ups at the big Pact agencies were aware that Annie, Jane, Canna, Maebe, and I covertly slipped outside to brunch with the others on the regular, this fact went largely unmentioned by tacit agreement...though Pop occasionally sent his regards when he caught me on my way out the door.

We'd already survived one wedding in our group. The previous December, Jane and her fiancé, Connor Willow, had tied the knot back in Georgia. Connor was still the chief of police in the town next door to Jane's old stomping grounds, but he was also Maebe's cousin, and though he cringed whenever he was reminded of it, the head of one-man Hall ti'Catama. The two had been pressured on all sides once Connor put a ring on Jane's finger. Jane's young half aunt, Xila Aniap, had pushed for a big society wedding for the decent press; the fact that Xila's father had murdered most of his family by magical means had understandably tarnished their reputation. Connor and Maebe's kinfolk had wanted them to follow their little community's traditions—since East Branch had been scoured, surely an old-fashioned wedding was in order. Then there were people like Pop, who not so subtly suggested to Connor that a formal to-do in the Pactlands would be a smart move...and when was he going to quit his job and take a position at DOL, anyway?

Jane and Connor talked it over, wrestled with the matter, had a few bottles of wine, and then decided to hell with tradition or what anyone else thought best for them. Jane wanted a white wedding. Connor wanted to invite his fellow officers. They found a vineyard with an oversized glass-walled greenhouse as an event space, booked the place for the last Saturday of the year, and started planning a color scheme around the venue's Christmas greenery. The chaplain for the volunteer fire department officiated, while the rest of the Whitford PD served as Connor's groomsmen—even Sam, their K-9, who sat at the front with a festive red bowtie around his neck and was deemed a Very Good Boy by all and sundry. As for Jane, she'd been a lonely, homeschooled child by necessity, and as she hadn't made a best friend in college, she asked us to be her bridesmaids, with Canna as her matron of honor. Maebe and Sage Voln, another Georgia-reared teenager who'd found her family in the Pactlands, served as juniors, seeing as both had school to work around. Maya declined, citing the insanity of her holiday schedule, but she insisted on catering the wedding and offered Jane THC gummies the morning of to take the edge off. Since most of the county's law enforcement was in attendance that evening, no one went nuts, but there was ample champagne in the dressing room.

Not wanting to insult anyone, the couple extended plenty of invitations, most of which they assumed would be declined. After all, going outside the Pactlands required precautions—for instance, even Canna with her agency background didn't have official credentials, as she'd never had cultural training. But to the happy couple's surprise, the positive responses kept coming. The East Branchers were expected, but Jane was shocked by the number of her DOI colleagues who wanted to sneak out for canapés and cake. Annie's husband, Wylan, was a given, but as the couple knew some of Wylan's many brothers, they'd also invited the pack—and all forty-six Huntsmen attended. Even Morial, who passed as a troll most of the time, masked up and pretended not to know his brothers while surreptitiously greeting them. Gentle Breeze, his fiancée and the Interdiction chief, received an invitation in her own right, as she and Connor had bonded the previous fall. Xila and her mother came, as did Pars and many of the extended Nerin clan, and Wylan, whose terrifyingly broad skillset included sharing languages without the incapacitating potion generally used, had made the rounds in the days prior to the ceremony to ensure that the family could understand the service. (Canna had chaperoned, as the Hunter could be *a lot* to those who hadn't witnessed his goofier side.)

I wasn't surprised to see Pop, Pateme, and Kabno Erenani, the DOL director, in attendance, nor my great-uncle Teolm ti'Cren, who'd been helping Pop look after the East Branchers while they found their footing. Sage's father, Mirrik, came with the two judges who'd worked out citizenship for East Branch, though both were so heavily masked that I wouldn't have been able to recognize them had my life depended on it. Jane's adopted father, Yacovi Hewt, had invited some of his agency buddies from back in the day, and Connor had reached out to everyone who'd been part of their Unity Plan emergency road trip. (Annie's parents brought a lovely Waterford bowl and sat with their son-in-law, though I caught them in warm conversation with the Unity Plan abductees throughout the evening.) But one guest in particular made me smile: Ranarma Curain, Pop's cook and a favorite in my crowd. Pop had made sure he had an appropriate suit for the event and kept quietly checking on him, but Ranarma seldom met a stranger and was happy as a clam to hang out with Maya and talk shop. It was an odd crowd, some of whom were explained to Connor's colleagues as Jane's weird friends from Atlanta, and certainly not what one would expect from a high society wedding in the Pactlands, elven or sorcerer.

It was perfect. Jane was radiant, Connor insisted on his half of the wedding party renting tuxes, and Yacovi, overjoyed, barely held it together as he escorted his daughter down the aisle. He danced with her afterward, a little awkward on his feet but having practiced, and almost didn't make it through his speech. I slow-danced with Yven once my duties were behind me, tired, happy, a little tipsy and full of chicken, and wished our wedding could be so *easy.* Hell, there were plenty of vineyards in Virginia, and I knew half a dozen great venues in Richmond—I could throw together a decent wedding outside.

But that wasn't an option. Pop's had been the last main-line ti'Dana wedding in the Pactlands, since my granddad had sneaked off to get married in Virginia and my parents had likewise tied the knot in a simple ceremony. Several of Pop's nieces and nephews, and their children and grandchildren, had married during that time, but no one in the main line. Though I wasn't keen on all the fuss, Pop wanted to see me wed properly…and frankly, as he didn't ask for much, I didn't want to let him down.

Of course, seeing as my knowledge of how a high-end elven wedding was supposed to go was sketchy at best, I needed guidance—a wedding coordinator, someone experienced and capable of ensuring a flawless function.

And that was how I made the acquaintance of my dear cousin Calien.

Calien ti'Dana was Granddad's first cousin—my first cousin twice removed—but she was only seven years older than my mom. Pop's younger sister, Miral, had married a couple centuries before he got around to it, and she and her husband, Ceram ti'Har, had found themselves expecting about every fifty to seventy-five years—a little slow even by elven metrics, but they hadn't exactly tried to speed up the process. (Pop's brother, Jixan, and his wife, Galliama ti'Vir, were even worse, often going nearly a century between their six kids, the youngest of whom was only eight.) Calien was the baby of nine, and judging by her *charming* demeanor, she surely wasn't looking forward to relinquishing that crown.

I liked Miral. She reminded me of Pop in some ways, but she was easier-going and far more social, the sort of woman who'd never taken anything as gauche as a salary but kept a dozen charitable and artistic organizations running with militaristic precision behind the scenes. Born a princess, she had been taught the same lesson impressed upon her brothers: the circumstances of her birth were a happy accident, and with great privilege came great duty. Yes, her Hall was wealthy and carried more than its share of clout, and Miral didn't socialize with the "new Halls," the former commoners, but she wasn't an impossible snob. Her children, given their mother's or father's Hall in alternating order, had done well for themselves, mostly staying out of the spotlight and making the occasional appearance at functions.

And then there was Calien.

Had reality TV been popular in the Pactlands, Calien might have been a star, assuming that Pop wouldn't have stepped in and put the kibosh on it. She was pretty, gifted with the usual slender elven build, blonde and green-eyed—which, I'd heard through back channels, annoyed the hell out of her because hers wasn't the stereotypical ti'Dana look. Redheads were rare among elves, and gray-eyed redheads almost certainly had a connection to the Hall. Calien had her mother's surname, but she'd inherited her father's coloration, and he was a mere ti'Har cousin, not even close kin to its lady.

As the first girl born to her parents in two centuries, Calien had been a teensy bit coddled. She was never a great student, possessed no wild talent, and was middling with magic in general, but she was a natural socialite, the sort of person famous for being famous. After graduation, she'd told her parents she needed time to find herself, but in actuality, she and her well-heeled girlfriends had made the rounds and forged connections. By the time I was born, she'd convinced her parents to finance an extravagant penthouse apartment for her in Beukal, where she threw lavish soirees and chased write-ups. When Miral finally put her foot down and insisted that Calien do *something* besides spend the family fortune, she took up event planning—never full time, but enough to cover some of her expenses and keep her name in the press. Calien had coordinated several weddings for the rich elves in her orbit, though she had yet to marry, claiming that the available matches were beneath her.

Thus, when it came time to really plan my wedding, Pop had reached out to Calien to ask for her assistance.

At first, I'd been excited about the proposition of working with my connected cousin, but that had quickly fizzled. From the get-go, she and I butted heads, and when I pushed back, she never failed to remind me that she was doing me a favor. And then there were the looks she gave me, especially when she dragged me to her vendors for a fitting or tasting or selection. She might have been smart enough to hold her tongue, but Calien made clear in more subtle ways that she put me roughly on par with dog shit.

I think she believed I was too stupid to realize how much she loathed me. I'd tried to convince myself that our first meetings were just awkward, but then I'd done a little snooping.

The farseers at DOI lived by a code of conduct that kept them from randomly spying on people without cause. After one particularly grating session with Calien, I told myself that I was at *DPP*, then tranced to find her. When I located her a moment later, she was sitting in a plush white booth in a swanky bar in District 4 with her friends, lamenting the fact that she'd been drafted to plan my wedding. "It's bad enough that my uncle acknowledged the damn half-breed," she griped between sips of a pale green cocktail. "Now he wants all of this fuss over her and that nobody she's marrying?"

"Just back out," one of her friends suggested. "Come up with a scheduling conflict."

"*Right*," Calien retorted, "I can see that going over *so* well. You want me to tell my dear uncle no?"

"What's the worst that could happen?" the friend replied. "He can't un-acknowledge you."

"No, but he could complain to Mother, and she might be peeved enough to cut my allowance."

The others sat with that uncomfortable fact for a moment, then did their best to console Calien.

By the time I left them, I'd seen everything I needed to know about my cousin, and I was ready to fire her. Jane had been a big help when I was brainstorming wedding ideas, and I told myself that surely the two of us could pull this off...

And then I faced reality. I couldn't throw together the type of wedding Pop wanted on my own, and for all of her flaws, Calien *was* good at events. So, as stuck as she was, I sucked it up for Pop's sake and tried to play nice with her...mostly.

She didn't make it easy. We were six weeks out from my wedding day, and of late, the snide comments were worsening—not just from Calien, but from all of her little vendor buddies. I'd tried to be friendly and deferential, bowing to experience, but I saw how they talked to Calien instead of me and caught the weird glances they shot her when they thought I was distracted. And as Calien reminded me, the only reason that some of the top vendors were willing to work with me was as a personal favor to her. It didn't matter that I had a massive budget or that this was a chance to work on the first mainline ti'Dana wedding in centuries—as far as Calien and her ilk were concerned, I was a disgrace.

I'd have been lying had I said that didn't hurt.

Sometimes, I imagined the wedding I might have had back in Richmond, were things different. Had my parents not died, had Aunt Lily not called me for help, had I never peeked behind the curtain...

I could have rented space at the Virginia Museum of Fine Arts. My mom and I would have gone shopping for a gown together, perhaps with Aunt Lily or my mother-in-law or whatever bridesmaids I chose. My friends in town would have been there, some girls from college, my parents' colleagues... I couldn't quite imagine the groom in that scenario, but surely he'd have been a local boy, maybe the brother of one of the couples whose toddlers I painted, someone...normal. Mom would have fussed over me the day of, making sure my hair was perfect and my makeup flawless, and Dad would have escorted me with a twinkle in his eye that might just have been a happy tear, and at the end of the night, I'd have ridden off in a car with tin cans tied to the back toward a hotel room for a few hours and a honeymoon flight in the morning. It wouldn't have been a blowout wedding by any means, nothing worth an event columnist's notice, but at least I wouldn't have felt like half the guests were whispering behind my back. I'd have felt *pretty*.

And I wouldn't have ever had to deal with my freaking cousin.

But magic couldn't turn back time, and it couldn't restore the dead, so there was no way for me to avoid my fate that Saturday afternoon.

Besides, I told myself as I pushed open the door to the café Calien favored for our meetings, I'd much rather have had Yven than some nice boy from Richmond.

Our secret rendezvous spot was The Red Door, a small eatery in District 2 that, while superficially unassuming, was favored by agency personnel—a fact unknown to Calien, I surmised, as she had clearly chosen the place to avoid being spotted by anyone important. As a DPP agent, I was a frequent patron of Mangia Due, the café in our building that Maya had founded—the food was great, and you couldn't beat the location—but every so often, one needed a change of scenery and perhaps bacon, and The Red Door checked all the boxes.

Jatamin, the faun who owned the place and manned the grill, waved a spatula at me when I entered the largely empty restaurant—while the agencies were always staffed, the weekend was the ebb tide. "Back booth's open," he yelled over the sizzle. "You want a beer?"

"Please," I said, heading for the shadowed table.

"Filla, get Agent ti'Dana a beer," Jatamin called to the

lone waitress, his sister, who was already pouring at the row of bar taps.

She met my gaze and rolled her eyes, then trotted over to my table, her stained red apron bouncing against her goatish legs. "Here you are, dear," she said, sliding me the glass of pale ale I preferred. "Waiting for your friend?" I grimaced, and she chuckled low. "Thought so," she said, and pulled a pencil from its resting place in her tied-back mound of brown ringlets, where it perched between the top of her ear and her curling horn. "The usual?"

That would be a patty melt on garlic toast, no onions, with a side of homemade sweet potato tots—a bit different than my usual at the diner near Aunt Lily's home but in the ballpark nonetheless. Jatamin still hadn't taken me up on my offer to bring back Cajun seasoning for his fries, but I had no real complaints.

Filla glanced at the empty booth bench. "Any idea what I should put in for her?"

I sucked my teeth. "Is there a fish today?"

"Trout."

"Grill it and toss it on a salad, if you would."

"You've got it." She wrote up our order and bustled off to the kitchen, her stubby tail bobbing beneath her apron bow.

Our food was on the table, and I was a quarter of the way through my sandwich, by the time Calien strode in. "Hi," I said, raising my half-empty beer in greeting. "Traffic?"

She ignored the question. Calien could be late; I could not. "I cannot *believe* you're eating that garbage," she said, glaring at my plate. "Were you planning to wear a dress or a grain sack to your wedding?"

"Comfort food," I replied, and took a big bite. As she started on her salad, I asked, "What's on the agenda today?"

Out came Calien's purple notebook, which I'd slowly grown to despise. While we finished our meal, I mostly listened as she went through her list of to-dos and appointments for the coming week and wished Jane were there. My friend had told off the Forum—she'd have had no qualms about shutting Calien down. But Jane was stressed that weekend, and I didn't want to worsen her mental state.

Finally, as I paid Filla, Calien said, "We've got to talk about your dress."

I arched an eyebrow. We were using the designer of Calien's choice, a friend of hers whom she'd practically had to bribe to work with me, or so Calien claimed. "What's wrong with it?"

"The color."

Pactlands wedding gowns generally weren't white, and I'd opted for a deep blue off-the-shoulder design that worked well with my coloration and would be forgiving in case of spills. "What's the matter with blue?" I asked.

"It's out of fashion," said Calien. "The color of the spring this year is tangerine."

"Tangerine?" I echoed, and shook my head. "Yeah, no, not happening. I look horrible in bright oranges," I said, and held out a clump of hair for emphasis. "A muted orange, maybe, or something closer to terracotta, but tangerine's out."

Her eyes narrowed. "It's *the* color this season."

"And it doesn't work for me."

"Don't be difficult," Calien said with a sigh. "It's an easy fix. Just change your hair color. Brown would suffice."

"I've been a redhead all my life," I said, praying for patience. "Not changing that for my wedding day."

"Why are you like this?" she snapped. "It's not like you have the ti'Dana look, anyway. Just...darken it. Or go blonde, if you insist," she grudgingly suggested. "Personally, I don't think it would suit you."

You would know about lacking the ti'Dana look was on the tip of my tongue, but I bit it back. "Calien, I appreciate your input, but I'm not changing my hair," I said with forced calm. "And I don't even like tangerine. The dress is going to be the color I selected…and if it's not the right color the day of," I added, catching her little smirk as it started to form, "then I'll mask it. I'm *quite* capable of that."

"Are you?"

Masking being an innate skill for elves and one of the first I'd mastered, I knew how the comment was intended but let it go. "Yeah. My tutors have been great. Top-notch. DPP has handled everything except farsight, and I've had to go to DOI for that. Wild talents can be tricky, you know."

Calien reddened at the volleyed barb, then slid out of the booth—as usual, not even offering to cover her share of the meal. "You don't deserve my help," she said, then flounced out in a huff.

I finished my beer as Filla brought my change. "One to go?" she asked, nodding to my glass.

"Thanks, but I'm driving," I replied, and pulled a small vial of creamy liquid from my purse. The sobriety potion was expensive, but for my meetings with Calien, it had become a necessary part of my kit. I popped the cap and shot the potion, tasting orange and peppermint, and in about twenty seconds, my head was as clear as if I'd never tasted alcohol.

"Six more weeks of fun," I told Filla with feigned cheer, then shouted goodbye to Jatamin on my way out.

If the Pactlands were layered over the outside world, Beukal sat just west of Richmond, while Viratta was somewhere in central Pennsylvania. Thanks to the system of internal portals, however, I was home in less than forty-five minutes. I came in from Pop's massive garage, stopped by the kitchen to greet Ranarma, and headed straight for the greenhouse.

Personal greenhouses were rare in the Pactlands, largely because little but grass grew in the artificial dirt. But Pop could splurge, and as Yven made a point of bringing home bags of potting soil every time he went outside to do an inspection, the mansion's greenhouse flourished—particularly the corner where my fiancé kept the portion of his orchid collection that had outgrown our apartment. I found him on his knees beside a bed, carefully planting a pair of orchids that Aunt Lily had procured for him, and rapped on the frame of his sprawling vanilla orchid to get his attention. "Hey, there," I said, already growing uncomfortable in the greenhouse's warm humidity. "Those are pretty."

Yven stood and stripped off his gardening gloves, then brushed a stray platinum lock from his face. "How'd it go?"

"She wants me to change my dress to tangerine."

His face twisted. "*Why*?"

"Because it's in, apparently." Yven, I mused, could have gotten away with tangerine, though with his stunning turquoise eyes, I tended to prefer him in blues and grays. He'd already selected his formal robe for the wedding with his parents' help, and I'd chosen my gown's color to complement it.

"She thought I should go brunette for the wedding, and that would fix the problem," I continued.

Yven hesitated, then cautiously asked, "Do you…*want* to go brunette?"

"Hell, no."

"Oh, good," he said, and hugged me. "Six weeks, Rosie," he murmured into my hair. "Just six more weeks, and this'll be behind us."

I'd survived worse than Calien, I told myself, as I stood there, holding on to Yven, safe in the warmth of his arms, smelling potting soil and the woodsy cologne he preferred. For the moment, nothing could harm me. We'd outlasted bigger headaches than my cousin…and hey, at least she wasn't actively trying to kill me.

Well, I hoped not.

CHAPTER 2

Pateme didn't give me any pushback when I told him I'd miss work that following Monday. Then again, he and I were bound for the same location—the jewel of District 1, the white limestone edifice with the low dome where the Forum convened. The Forum's building was beautiful, appropriately grand to convey the gravity of the work done therein, and not a place I generally frequented if I could help it. But Jane had asked for me that morning, and so I pulled into the visitors' parking lot in my old Outback, straightened my robe, and headed in past the bronze double doors toward security.

Once cleared, I took the elevator upstairs to the representatives' offices and wound my way around the green-carpeted corridor toward the Hunt's suite. Latecomers to the Forum, as their father had never deigned to deal with the Pactlands' government, they'd been given only one suite and a fervent apology, as each representative generally had their own space. But Wylan didn't make a fuss. It was understood that the Hunt's three representatives were a voting bloc, and as the guys already shared a lodge, sharing office space was no true hardship. Besides, Wylan was more than capable of doing his own renovations, bending the space in the suite beyond all laws of physics, and those few who dared to visit found it a pleasant place, heavy on the leather upholstery and dark wooden furniture—decidedly masculine but not oppressive. Wylan had even stuck a pair of lamps made of deer antlers on side tables in the central sitting area, pieces he'd picked up one Saturday in Georgia while he and Connor had killed time waiting for us to finish brunching.

(There had, I understood, been several beers involved, and then the boys had gone wandering through Ragged Gap before spotting the lamps in a shop window. Wylan had held up the pair in place of his missing masked antlers, which both men had apparently been buzzed enough to find uproariously funny, and Connor had pulled out his Visa.)

I rapped twice on the suite door, which opened with a click, and nodded to the Huntsman on reception duty, a muscular, dark-haired guy in a lace-up shirt who could have graced the cover of many a bodice-ripper, had one airbrushed out his ten-point rack. For the life of me, I couldn't remember his name; that Annie managed to keep her dozens of brothers-in-law straight was no mean feat.

"*Finally*," Annie teased, waving from one of the couches with her travel coffee mug in hand. "Portal traffic?"

"As usual," I replied, and smiled at her companion. Tabitha had ventured into the Pactlands only a few times since her impromptu debut the previous fall, but if she was concerned to find herself in the company of a chunk of the Hunt, she gave no sign. Superficially, there was nothing about Tabitha to give one concern: she was a forty-seven-year-old African American woman who would have looked a solid decade younger if not for the gray threaded in her customary box braids, about average height and with an easy grin. She could rattle off the side effects of hundreds of drugs but also readily whip up a tisane that worked wonders against colds, or so Jane swore. Yet to the average Pactlands citizen, she was at least as concerning as the Huntsmen bustling among the suite's offices. Sure, plenty of folks consumed subtitled human media pirated from outside, and many in the agencies had interacted with humans, but to have one *present* and unguarded…

Let's just say there was a reason we'd arranged to meet in the Hunt's suite. The guys didn't flinch.

"Are you ready?" I asked Tabitha. "Not nervous, are you?"

She snorted. "Now, why would I be nervous? They know I'm coming," she said, then looked up as a brown-robed Huntsman brought her a cup of coffee. "Oh, thank you so much," she said in her accented Pactish, a little gift from Wylan. "Breakfast of champions right here."

He looked doubtful at the notion. "Have you eaten nothing more substantial?"

"Eh, I've got granola in my bag. Not really feeling it just yet," she said, rubbing her stomach with a grimace. "I'm not a huge fan of interrogation."

"Still, if you'd like…"

"You're sweet," she said, reaching up to pat his arm, "but for everyone's benefit, I'd better not."

"If you're concerned for your safety," he said, unconvinced, "you needn't be. We won't let harm come to you in there."

"I know, and I appreciate that—I do," Tabitha insisted. "It's just…cameras, right, and lots of eyes, and…"

"And the main meeting hall is *big*," I offered.

"Yes," she muttered, "that, too." Turning back to me, she asked in English, "Have you seen Jane?"

Before I could answer, someone knocked on the outer door again, which opened to reveal two people. Jane's blonde hair was neatly pulled back into a chignon, and her conservative gray robe was immaculate over a black blouse and tailored trousers—a fairly standard formal look for DOI but for the triple studs climbing her earlobes. But her face was tight, the tell of her anxiety. With her was Fellora ti'Mal, a young DOL agent and pyromancer of considerable talent—and considering the short flames rippling up Jane's hands, she hadn't just come for moral support. Fell and Annie were friends—Annie had saved her life, which had cemented their relationship—and once Jane started coming around, Annie made the introduction. A gifted pyro in her own right, Jane had taken to meeting up with

Fell in DOL's subterranean training rooms, where the two could fling fireballs at targets to each's heart's content.

Considering how stressed Jane had been over the last week, I almost worried that DOL was running low on targets.

Wylan emerged from the largest of the offices as the two settled on the couch opposite Annie and Tabitha's, his black robe identical to those of the other two of the Hunt's representatives but for subtle gold embroidery around the collar. "Welcome," he said, nodding to the newcomers and me. "Everyone all right?"

Jane grunted.

"I finally found out who's representing them," Fell announced. "Our counselors are pretty tight-lipped, but one of them let it slide. Eullan Bargem."

When this declaration was met only with polite bemusement, Fell pressed on. "He represented my father. One of the best defense counselors before the Tribunal in the last century. *Not* cheap."

The fact that Fell's father still had more than a hundred years to go on a penal farm for murder and attempted murder meant that the lawyer wasn't infallible, but if he was good enough for a wealthy ti'Pon...

"Where'd they get the funds?" Annie asked, her face scrunching.

Fell shrugged. "*Allegedly*, he's doing this as a public service. I'm not sure I believe that, but my counselor friend does. She says he thinks the Golden Children's treatment is a travesty."

Jane harrumphed at that, and Tabitha rolled her eyes.

I understood their perspective. About two and a half years prior, Katin Waughnn and her little family of sorcerers had rented a cabin in Whitford, a secluded place where they could continue their illegal brewing operation. Rather than do the drudgery, Katin had ingratiated herself to the local metaphysical community, the clique Jane dismissed as the "woo-woo brigade," who hung out at a shop in Ragged

Gap called Mystic Mountains and gave her the cold shoulder. Katin was pretty, a tall, blue-eyed blonde with a killer figure and excellent fashion sense, and she'd easily made friends with the local would-be witches through faux affability and a saleswoman's charm. They loved her, as "Katarina" sold them vials of a potion she called Oil of Life for dirt cheap, promising that it would make the talent within them grow and burst forth. Instead, she'd deployed a bait-and-switch tactic: the first two "levels" of Oil of Life were mostly Fingerflash, a harmless potion that made one's fingertips light up, while the final level for the most advanced of users was Velvet Leash, a potion that bound the drinkers to the brewer's will and left them in an almost zombified state. Katin had deployed her scheme and begun building her human drone army in several small towns across north Georgia, but she hadn't counted on finding Jane, who took Katin's actions *personally*.

Katin and the rest of the so-called Golden Children had been arrested and brought to Beukal to stand trial for illegal brewing, and DOL had done a thorough job of locking away the leaders and providing schooling and intensive therapy for the actual children in the group. But now this Eullan Bargem had finally convinced the Forum to consider their appeal, and Jane wasn't letting the Golden Children walk without putting up a fight.

As the hour drew near, the black-robed representatives and their brown-robed aides gathered their materials, and Wylan nodded toward the door. "Ladies, shall we?"

There are far less subtle ways to wander through the halls of the Forum building than in the company of the Hunt, but few more secure. The people we passed en route gave us a *generous* berth. It had been nearly three years since the Hunt finally joined the Forum, and Wylan had yet to kill anyone on the premises, but some folks just didn't take chances. We parted from our imposing escort only after entering the chamber—their tables were clustered together, while Jane and Tabitha had been asked to sit in a designated section near the dais, and Fell, Annie, and I joined them. As I took my seat, I turned to look behind us and saw the two balconies beginning to fill, particularly with media on the first.

Great.

Searching the wooden benches above us, I looked for the directors. Brown-haired Pateme could blend into a crowd, but he'd sandwiched himself between his chief deputy, Syvin Deop, a dark-haired faun in a purple robe, and Syvin's Interdiction counterpart, Gentle Breeze, whose pink robe stood out against her green complexion. In conjunction, at least to me, the mismatched trio were unmistakable. Across the aisle sat a far more coordinated contingent from Laws, the agents mostly in black shirts and pants, the counselors who'd come for the show in black robes. Their diminutive director, Kabno, was the only pop of color in the group, a white-haired, child-sized figure in a bright red robe. And then, on the other side of the DPP group, sat a cluster in gray robes I thought were from DOI...but then where was Pop? He hadn't mentioned sending a deputy in his stead...

I glanced around the floor as the representatives filed in, settling into their chairs and onto their padded mats, and then examined the dais above us. The Overseer's desk had been set up as usual on the far left, while a pair of long tables flanked another podium placed roughly in the middle of the stage. Both tables were equipped with a number of chairs, but the one closer to the Overseer had a mat as well, an indication that a centaur or naga was expected. Before I could really speculate, the door at the rear of the dais opened to admit the featured guests: a female sorcerer and male naga in black robes, both carrying DOL-marked bags, and then a male sorcerer in a more elaborate silver-trimmed blue robe with a brown leather briefcase. Behind him came a dozen black-clad people—all elves, sorcerers, and nymphs but for a lone troll, I noticed—interspersed with ten sorcerers wearing shapeless brown shirts and pants. The inmates took their seats in two rows beside their counselor, and their escorts, apparently officers from the penal farms, stood back at the ready. That was, I mused, overkill; anyone with the slightest bit of talent who ended up on a penal farm was given regular doses of the dampening potion, and if any of the Golden Children before us could so much as mask, I'd have been shocked. They weren't handcuffed, however, so perhaps the officers were present in case someone had any crazy notions about trying to crowd-surf over the representatives to freedom.

The DOL counselors spotted our group and nodded, then finished unpacking their laptops and binders just before the Overseer climbed to the dais. Ketling Tiramae was a fixture in the main meeting room, a gray-skinned metal nymph with piercing blue eyes and limited patience for grandstanding. She banged her wooden gavel on her desk to quiet the room, then cleared her throat and began, her face projected on the massive screen hanging at the back of the platform for the benefit of the spectators in the cheap seats. "On this the fifteenth day of April in the four hundred eighty-seventh year of the Pact, I call this meeting of the Pact Forum to order," she said, and faintly smiled. "Good morning."

A rumbled greeting answered that.

"We have before us today an appeal," she continued. "The Tribunal Committee has asked me to moderate this proceeding. Is that still your wish, Representative venDar?"

I glanced across the room at the naga representatives in time to see Kug venDar, the head of the Tribunal Committee, rise from her green and purple coils. "Yes, Madam Overseer."

"Very well," said Ketling, primly folding her hands on her desk. "Is our secretary prepared?"

The nymph at the designated desk on the floor nodded. "Yes, ma'am."

"Excellent." After a moment's consultation of her

computer, she said, "Mr. Bargem, the podium is yours."

The sorcerer in blue rose and took a slim folder with him to the podium, but it seemed merely for show, as he didn't open it before he began. "Madam Overseer," he said in a sonorous baritone, and offered a slight nod to Ketling. "Honored representatives. It is my privilege to be before you today. I'm Eullan Bargem, counselor for the petitioners. We thank you for hearing our appeal. I trust you've received our written petition."

"He's smooth," I whispered to Fell.

She grunted. "Not his first appeal."

Eullan swept one hand toward his clients. "While I am proud to represent all of these young people, I'd like to focus today on Katin Waughnn, as Ms. Waughnn was the primary target of the Division of Laws' illegal prosecution."

Jane tensed in her seat, and Tabitha reached over to pat her knee.

"Allow me to introduce Ms. Waughnn," Eullan continued as she slowly rose from her chair. Katin was still a stunner, even in her penal garb, though she seemed slumped as she stood exposed behind the table, her head bowed and hands clasped before her.

"Ms. Waughnn—Katin," Eullan said warmly—"is only forty-three years old. I'm sure that some of you remember your early forties—perhaps not all of you," he added to general chuckling from the representatives. "*I* do. Young, inexperienced, less than a decade out of school, learning to live alone, to negotiate romance, to provide for myself…to represent clients. I assure you, there are easier professions for a young man than law," he said, again to a smattering of amused noises. "But I had every opportunity and support. I was raised here in Beukal by loving parents, who spared no expense. Tutors, extra-curriculars, toys, anything I needed, anything I *wanted*—done. Even living on my own, working to pay my bills, I wasn't truly *alone*. And I see some of you nodding," he said. "You understand."

He paused, letting that settle, then gestured toward his client. "Katin had none of that. She wasn't born and raised here in the bosom of a loving family. Her parents were illegal brewers, and they and their companions in crime hid outside, where they could manufacture their wares and remain undetected. They actually brewed for Inade ti'Cren, and I'm sure I needn't remind you of *his* misdeeds."

That was putting it mildly. I didn't know the full tally of how many people my great-grandfather had killed, either himself or through his lieutenants, and frankly, I was okay with that.

"Anyway, this community of brewers began to have children," said Eullan. "First Dirk Vaniac here," he said, pointing to the dark-haired man beside Katin, "and then Katin. Twelve in total, boys and girls, all born near the Midland portal. For those of you who've never had a need to use that portal, let me give you an idea of what awaits outside. Midland is a city in the western part of Texas. Desert climate—flat, hot, dry. Oil country. The city itself is civilized, but beyond it, where the roads grow sparse and the population thins, there are places one can hide if one doesn't wish to be found. And that's where Katin and my other clients were born and raised. No contact with whatever kin they have here. No education beyond what their parents taught them—certainly no formal education in magic. Not much money, enough to get by, but not what one would consider true wealth. They had a few small homes, most of them old trailers parked on the property, and some dilapidated sheds where they brewed."

He paused, then said, "I can tell you in considerable detail what this place looked like because DOL took pictures when they raided. You see, when Katin was but sixteen, agents descended in the middle of the night and kidnapped her family—"

"*Excuse* me," interrupted the naga counselor, leaning past his colleague to glare at Eullan. "They were lawfully *arrested*, not kidnapped. Let's stick to the facts, eh?"

Eullan shrugged. "Truth is perception, and what your agency perceives as facts differs from what my clients perceived. As I said, poor Katin was sixteen. She awoke to shouting and crashing and flashes of light. Had she and Dirk not been camping with most of the younger children away from the buildings to see a meteor shower, they would have been snatched from their beds. As it was, two infants were taken…but no one knew that they had missed ten other children. Their parents never told their abductors, and since Katin woke the others, grabbed them, and ran into the night, DOL never realized there were more. Instead, they collected what evidence they needed, destroyed the brewing equipment, and seized all of the money and potion stock they could find.

"And *that* is what Katin and Dirk and the other children found the next morning when they sneaked back to see what was left of their home. Broken glass. Kicked-in doors. Smoldering fires. Tire tracks. No money," he said, looking over his audience. "No potions. No equipment. And not one adult in sight."

The representatives said nothing as Eullan let his silence hang for a moment.

"As I said, the eldest of them was seventeen—not even an adult by the standards outside. The youngest was five. They had no support, minimal education, and a healthy fear of the local government, which surely would have ripped them apart—and then, of course, whatever humans took them in would have discovered their talent as it developed. Katin knew she had no choice but to keep them together. To protect the younglings, to teach them what she could. But ten mouths to feed, living on scrubland with barely a vegetable plot to sustain them…that wasn't feasible. So, she and Dirk, and eventually the others as they came up, did what was *necessary* to survive. They're not proud of their actions," he said as Katin silently shook her head. "They stole—money, food, things to pawn. Slept in abandoned houses. Piled everyone into the few working vehicles they had and drove east, looking for shelter and sustenance. And before you condemn them, try to remember that these children would not have been able to live on the little they could have made from more…legitimate work."

I glanced at Jane, whose arms were tightly folded.

"Katin didn't have a full education, but she had learned enough to brew," said Eullan. "She and Dirk pieced together the equipment they needed. Found contacts near portals. Bought and bartered for ingredients, then began selling their wares. In time, they made enough to get by—and then their numbers began to grow. Remember, these children were on their own out there for the better part of twenty-five years. Some partnered off and had children of their own. After all, their families had been stolen from them—it was only natural that they make their own."

"Please," Jane muttered under her breath.

"Could they have found legal work as adults? Perhaps," Eullan continued. "Could they have found their way here and asked for help? Perhaps. But put yourselves into their position. Humans were a constant threat. DOL had practically orphaned them. They could trust no one but each other. Brewing kept them alive and together…but there were more children coming along, and so they needed to produce more to keep up the pace."

Turning to glance at Katin, Eullan said, "Today, here with you, they are not proud of what they did. But they're also not the people they were two years ago. Katin has had therapy during her incarceration. Tutoring to fill some of the gaps in her education. She's been a model inmate. One might even say that incarceration has improved her life."

Tabitha rolled her eyes.

"But my clients should never have been incarcerated in the first place," Eullan stressed, gripping the podium as he stared at the representatives below. "They were not born here, and they never even entered the Pactlands until they were arrested. They don't claim citizenship. Now, all of the rules we have about brewing and distribution and licensure, all of the oversight...that's for *citizens*. And the people affected by their actions outside, the ones caught up in that unfortunate, desperate mess that landed my clients here...well, they weren't citizens, either. They were human. So, let's recap," he said, beginning to count off on his fingers. "My clients, who do not claim citizenship, have never claimed citizenship, and harmed non-citizens *outside*, were hit with knock-out potions and dragged to Beukal. Their children were taken from them—none of my clients have even seen their own children since they awoke here. Can you *imagine*?" he said, his voice rising. "The pain and fear my clients and their innocent children have endured is unspeakable. They *must* be released, and they deserve compensation."

With that, Eullan turned again to Katin and nodded. "Go ahead, my dear. You wanted to speak?"

"Thank you," she murmured, keeping her eyes downcast. While her Pactish was intelligible, it was clearly accented. "What Mr. Bargem said is true. I...I know we did wrong. When you're brought up like we were, it seemed right—it made sense. But I realize now how wrong we were, and I'm grateful for the help I've been given. My parents are still incarcerated, and rightly so. They had every chance, they made their choices, and they're where they deserve to be. But please, if you could show mercy, we just want to go home. We're no risk to you. Just let us have our babies back and show us the way to Texas, and you'll never hear from us again."

When she'd finished and the flashes from the cameras in the balcony had subsided, the Overseer said, "Thank you, Ms. Waughnn, counselor. Rebuttal from the Division of Laws? Mr. vakHela?"

The naga's torso rose above the table as if he were standing, and he slithered to the podium. "Madam Overseer, honored representatives, I am Maugon vakHela. I led the prosecution of these offenders, and the Division of

Laws stands by that prosecution. For years, this band illegally brewed, bottled, and sold potions. The destination for those potions was the Pactlands. They *knew* they were making illegal product and selling it to our people—and I needn't list for you the many, *many* problems with the street drugs and other illicit substances that our agency and our colleagues at DPP continuously combat. Mr. Bargem says these offenders are too young to know right from wrong. *Look* at them," Maugon said, glaring at the other table for emphasis. "The youngest of their number is thirty-two. At thirty-two, our young people can marry. They can live on their own. Take side jobs when not in school. Sign contracts. No, they're not fully of majority, but we trust them to act as reasonable, civilized people. If you believe my colleague here," he said, gesturing toward Eullan, "these people are still little more than babes. With babies of their own, I should add."

He paused, then said, "And my colleague would also have you believe that they're not citizens—that Pact law does not apply to them. Their parents are citizens. They are citizens as well, no matter where they were born—that is their birthright. Now, I'm not without pity," he continued. "I wish our agents had found them during that raid. I wish they'd been brought here, educated, cared for, just as their children are being cared for now. I wish their parents had cared enough about their wellbeing to inform us of their existence." Maugon shrugged. "Obviously, we can't change the past. But they are precisely where they need to be now: housed, fed, educated, and given therapy. Their sentences are not unduly long—Ms. Waughnn here was sentenced as the ringleader of their operation, and she'll be freed before her seventieth birthday. Their judge showed mercy because of their youth and their unusual circumstances. But to stand before you and claim the law does not apply…no. Absolutely not."

Turning then to Ketling, Maugon said, "At this time, in an ordinary appeal, we would offer testimony from the victims."

The Overseer faintly smiled. "A complicated matter in this case."

"Correct. The offenders—the 'Golden Children,' if you like," he said with a roll of his eyes—"refused to name any of their contacts here, and so we can't know just where their products ended up. But we have with us today three witnesses to the events that led to the offenders' arrest, and their testimony will surely prove to the Forum that the Golden Children would be a danger to us all if allowed to go free."

"Very well," she replied. "Your first witness?"

Maugon peered down at the floor for a second, then spotted our group and beckoned with two fingers. "The Division of Laws offers Tabitha Bradley."

A rumble passed through the room, and the camera flashes intensified as Tabitha, who clenched her jaw as if she'd rather have been anywhere else but before that crowd, made her way up the stairs to the dais, past the Overseer's desk, and to the podium. As Maugon settled back onto his mat and Tabitha's face was projected onto the screen behind them, Ketling said, "Whenever you're ready, Ms. Bradley. What would you like the Forum to know?"

I saw Tabitha's chest rise and fall as she took a deep breath, but she maintained her composure. "Good morning," she said, her voice strong and even. "Some of you I've met. For everyone else, I'm Tabitha. Hi," she added, quickly raising a hand, and the representatives chuckled. "This, uh…this is quite a bit out of my wheelhouse…and I don't know if that translates," she muttered, "but…thank you for having me. On behalf of all the folks back in Georgia who will never know the full truth of what these people did to them, thanks for hearing me out."

She paused briefly, corralling her thoughts, and cleared her throat. "There's a store in the town of Ragged Gap called Mystic Mountains," she said, translating the name.

"It's a...hmm. Not sure of the word. Metaphysical?" she said in English, and looked down at Wylan. "Any idea?"

When Wylan spread his hands, Maugon provided the translation, and Tabitha thanked him. "It's a place for people who are open-minded about the supernatural or follow faiths outside of the mainstream," she continued. "Folks who believe in magic and want to learn to use it."

"Wait...*humans*?" interrupted one of the gnome representatives.

"I never said it was particularly powerful magic," Tabitha replied. "Do I believe that what I do as a practitioner has merit and efficacy? Sure. Does it look anything like what I've seen from, you know, the sorcerers in my life? Absolutely not. But that's beside the point—what you need to understand is that this store is a hub of sorts for people of this mindset, and if someone comes in talking about magic, they're not going to get laughed out of the building." Again, she cleared her throat. "Close to three years ago, a woman calling herself Katarina Weller started coming to Mystic Mountains. By all accounts, she was friendly and sweet, and...well, you see her right there," she said, nodding toward Katin. "Pretty blondes do have an easier time of it. Anyway, she managed to ingratiate herself to the owner of the store, who was so desperate to gain magical talent that she didn't ask too many questions."

I'd heard plenty from Jane about Stephanie Love, the proprietor of the shop and leader of the woo-woo brigade. Stephanie knew Jane had real talent—Jane had demonstrated when she was a teenager, hoping to make a cool older friend, but Stephanie had run her off and apparently never forgiven her for showing her up. Never mind that Jane was known as the person you went to when you needed something major in a hurry, like a violent spouse kicked out of town—she didn't kowtow to Stephanie, so she was never in with the Mystic Mountains crowd.

"Katarina—Katin," Tabitha amended—"told everyone that she'd developed this blend of essential oils that would unlock their potential. I assumed it was bunk—I mean, I've seen my share of charlatans, and who's ever heard of essential oils doing *that*?—but I was encouraged to sit in on one of her seminars, and I decided to give her a chance. She made her sales pitch for her stuff and got all the people who'd been using it to show off their glowing fingertips, and I asked what was in the blend. Obviously, she wouldn't tell me, but she gave me a demonstration. I'll never forget it," she muttered. "First time I'd seen *anything* like that sort of magic. She took one of the vials of her oil, tossed it up, and made it stop in midair before she put it down. Then there was this glass pitcher on a counter—iced tea, I think—and it levitated into her hands. She poured me a refill as I sat there with my mouth hanging open like an idiot. She told us that if we kept using her product, we'd all be able to do that, too. So, I bought a vial, and she promised me results."

"You used it?" one of the troll representatives interjected.

Tabitha shook her head. "Uh, *no*. I wasn't born yesterday. I've got a heavy science background—chemistry, biology, biochemistry, pharmacology, physics—so I decided to see whether I could figure out what was in the crap I'd bought. I wasn't planning to use it until I knew what was in it. I'm a pharmacist," she explained, "and adverse drug interactions is something I know quite a bit about. So, I tested what I could with the equipment I scrounged up. The substance did contain essential oils and alcohol, but there were some other components I couldn't readily identify. Given that there was, in fact, a *potion* in the mix, I don't feel so bad about my skills."

"Which potion?" he asked.

"Well, this is purely hearsay," said Tabitha, "but the sorcerers in my life told me it was something called Fingerflash...uh, *Fingerflash*," she amended, using the Pactish term. "But that was only in levels one and two of the oil. The final level was different, and there was a potion in there that left people...stupefied, I guess. Dazed. One guy told me he lost time—he came to work, and the next thing he remembered, he was vomiting, and he couldn't make his fingers glow anymore. I didn't know it then, but someone got to him with a neutralizer just before he was sick," she added. "But he was lucky. Folks started going missing, people I knew from Mystic Mountains. I was concerned, but since there was actual magic involved, I didn't want to just call the police. I went to Jane Fortune."

"Can you elaborate?" Maugon prompted.

"Sure. There were rumors that Jane had real talent. The Mystic Mountains crowd didn't like her, but I think they were more scared of her than anything. Jane had a small business, and so did I, so I'd mentored her a bit...and I buy moonshine from her father, so we were all acquainted."

Maugon smirked. "That'd be Yacovi Hewt?"

"Exactly. Best hooch in north Georgia," she replied. "I had no clue at the time that he was a *sorcerer*, mind you, but that man can distill. But back to Jane—there were so many rumors about her in the metaphysical community that I suspected some of them had to be true, so I caught up with her and told her about the oil I'd bought. Turned out she'd been at that seminar, just masked. I remember...we were in a restaurant at lunchtime, back in a booth by ourselves, and she confirmed my suspicions. Made the salt and pepper move on their own—something small, yeah, but *genuine*. She relayed to me that there was plenty she couldn't talk about, and that she couldn't teach me to do magic like hers, but we decided to team up and get to the bottom of that mess. We wanted a list of everyone who had bought the top-level oil, and we went to see a woman who owns another shop in town who was definitely using. Got there in time to find her having a seizure—she had a bad reaction to the potion. Neutralized her, and that stopped the seizure."

I knew damn well that Annie had been along on that

trip, but if Tabitha didn't want to drag her into her account, I certainly wasn't going to say anything.

"So, once she came around, I stayed with her, and Jane went off to investigate," Tabitha continued. "That night, she called me and asked me to babysit a bunch of neutralized victims as they woke up. They were scared…and queasy," she added, grimacing, "and furious with Jane for stealing their power. The owner of the shop finally came around and told them not to blame her, but I think that if Katin were to sashay back into town today, peddling potions, a good number of them would line up for whatever she was selling."

"You would consider Ms. Waughnn a danger to your community?" asked Maugon.

"Without question. I don't know everything that went on in that workshop of hers—I wasn't involved in the takedown—but I know she had absolutely no regard for the health and safety of my neighbors."

"And she publicly displayed magic?" one of the nymph representatives asked.

Tabitha nodded. "Craziest thing I'd ever seen…well, at the time. I, uh…I've had more than just a peek by now, you might say, and there's a whole lot of weirdness for a Georgian."

That time, there was soft laughter even from the media in the balcony. Tabitha's testimony at the Unity Plan trials had been thoroughly covered.

"But the Aniap girl also displayed magic, did she not?"

I cut my eyes to the sorcerer representatives, though I needn't have bothered. Elm Carinar was an annoyance of the highest caliber, and I'd heard her voice more than enough to last me.

Jane tensed and muttered, "*Fortune*," through gritted teeth.

Tabitha, at least, remained unruffled. "Yes, ma'am, but only to me, and I'd already seen what Katin could do. Jane and I were putting our cards on the table, I guess you could say."

The blonde sorcerer cocked her head. "I don't understand. Perhaps it's your accent."

"Jane and I were exchanging information," Tabitha tried again. "Building trust. Teaming up. She doesn't stroll through town, setting fires and levitating cars, if that's what you're afraid of."

"I still can't understand why no one has erased your memory," Elm snapped. "You're a danger to us all—"

The Overseer's gavel cut her short. "That is not a matter for discussion today, Representative Carinar," said Ketling.

"Ms. Bradley is here by invitation," Maugon added, "and her safety will be maintained."

I glanced back toward the representatives in time to see Wylan catch Elm's eye and slowly, pointedly, crack his knuckles.

Tabitha wrapped up quickly, and Maugon called Jane to the podium—and from him, it was "Agent Fortune" all the way. Jane reiterated much of what Tabitha had said, including her own memory of Katin's seminar, then briefly touched on the multi-agency raid that had brought down the Golden Children. "I went into their cabin," she said. "They held me at gunpoint, and Waughnn tried to sway me into joining them. 'We're practically gods here,' that's what she told me. She had absolutely no remorse about what they'd done. Brought up the woman who owns Mystic Mountains, who was obviously incapacitated, drooling where she stood. Waughnn told me that my neighbors were there for the taking, then said—and I remember this well—'Who gives a shit about humans?' And that's when I set the cabin on fire."

Maugon cleared his throat. "To be clear, you weren't an agent at the time?"

"I'd never even been in the Pactlands," she replied, "so no. And I had the fire under control—I was trying to drive them outside, where there was a cloud of knock-out waiting for them. It worked. Fair to say we all had gaps in our education. I didn't have much experience in brewing, and they couldn't fight me." She paused, then said, "Once they were out, I extinguished the fire and went searching for the victims. Those who followed my voice were like zombies. Found another two in the basement, still packing Waughnn's potions, despite all the commotion upstairs—they were that far gone. I got them outside, they hit the knock-out and dropped, and we got them neutralized. Once everything was secure, I dropped them off at Mystic Mountains and asked Tabitha to watch them. Figured they wouldn't want to see my face once they realized their power was gone."

"What condition were the victims in?" Maugon asked.

Jane's face tightened. "They were filthy, and that's before they threw up with the neutralizer. I mean, Waughnn had been keeping them enslaved in that house, dosing them with Velvet Leash, so she wasn't exactly running a hotel. And they weren't all from Ragged Gap. I didn't recognize some of them. She'd kidnapped them in other towns and brought them along. I don't know how long she'd held some of them captive."

"I think I know the answer to this," said the counselor, "but based on your observations, would you consider Ms. Waughnn and her followers a threat if released?"

Jane hesitated before answering. "Unless their therapy has been miraculously effective, yes. They had no regard for anyone but themselves when we met. And frankly," she added, giving Katin a strong side-eye, "I don't buy this apparent contrition for a second. Waughnn's quite the actress when she wants to be."

"Objection," Eullan protested. "The witness can't read minds, can she?"

Jane lifted her hands in surrender and ended her testimony.

The final witness was Liogh Birrid, the DOL agent who'd organized the takedown. I knew them decently well, as they'd been liaising with DPP since the 1960s...and since they'd been friendly with both of my grandfathers, they'd always treated me kindly. Considering Jane's patchy education and affinity for fire, it probably wasn't a bad thing to have had a water nymph involved in the raid.

Liogh was poised and collected at the podium, almost serene, their blue hair braided back and falling over a navy robe that flattered their green complexion. They had to mask considerably when they left the Pactlands—even without their striking coloration, their long, pointed ears, like an elf's on steroids, were impossible to hide. But Liogh was experienced and adept, a high-ranking member of their team, and they recounted the events in question with almost clinical precision.

When Maugon asked for Liogh's thoughts on any risk inherent in releasing the Golden Children, Liogh took a moment before answering. "I cannot fairly say whether Ms. Waughnn and her compatriots have changed," they replied. "I haven't observed them on the farms, and I'm not privy to their therapists' notes. But unless they have *significantly* changed, then I would have grave concerns about their release."

"Why is that?"

"From my observations of Ms. Waughnn," said Liogh, "she's savvy. Intelligent. She's not a helpless child, nor was she two years ago. My concern is that she's more sociopathic than she lets on. Her treatment of her victims evidences a disregard for others—"

"For *humans*, maybe," Elm interrupted.

Liogh cocked their head and stared at the representative until she slumped in her chair. "A symptom of a larger issue. In any case, she preyed upon weaker targets. I'm not a therapist, but I've been at DOL long enough to be concerned about recidivism from her, if not from the other offenders."

As Liogh exited the dais, Maugon said, "The Division of Laws has no further witnesses."

"Very well," Ketling replied, and peered at her computer. "A request was made for a recommendation from the Division of Intelligence as to future dangerousness. Is there someone here to deliver that—*ah*, Director ti'Dana," she said as Pop came striding down the central aisle. "Please."

I'd been in the Pactlands long enough to know that Pop's robes weren't cheap, but they weren't flashy—he preferred his fine wools and light silks with more understated ornamentation. Wealth whispers, after all. That morning, he'd dressed much like the DOI agents in the balcony, sporting a sleeveless charcoal robe over a black shirt and trousers, but tiny silver threads in the weave caught the light as he moved toward the dais, a small but costly detail. I tried in vain to figure out what was on his mind; Pop had a poker face that could make a lifelong blackjack player weep with envy.

He quickly climbed the stairs and nodded to Ketling, then walked behind DOL's table and took his place at the podium. "Madam Overseer, honored representatives," he said. "The Division of Intelligence was indeed asked for a recommendation. Unfortunately, we're split."

Low murmurs broke out around the room, and a few cameras flashed from above.

"Indeed?" said Ketling. "How so?"

"It is not agency policy to reveal the precise split when farseers disagree on an issue such as this, nor is it policy to identify individual farseers' opinions. But I can tell you that we are not in agreement as to the risk of releasing the offenders."

Ketling waited until the rumbling died down, then asked, "Could you tell the Forum *your* opinion, then?"

Pop faintly smiled. "With all due respect, Madam Overseer, that would defeat the purpose of making this a group endeavor."

"Question," whispered Tabitha, leaning over Jane so that I could hear her. "Why is this even an issue? Does that mean they're going to release Katin?"

"I don't know," I whispered back. "Pop hasn't said anything to me about this."

"Did you *ask*?"

No, I thought, kicking myself as Eullan made his final plea for his clients' freedom, I hadn't asked. I'd been pretty confident that this was in the bag for DOL...

Then the Forum voted.

The Hunt sided with DOL, as did Mirrik Voln from the sorcerers, Kug venDar, Lady ti'Ansha from the elves, and Foggy Lake from the trolls. I wasn't shocked to see Vinnorit Yentera, Evapi Shilg, Puln Berek, and Tennel Peolid on our side as well—all of them had had a loved one dropped outside by the Unity Plan, and I suspected that they thought they owed Tabitha a favor for looking after their kin.

But it wasn't enough, and when Ketling called the total, the Golden Children had won their freedom by a two-vote margin. As they screamed and cried and hugged their counselor, Annie gripped Tabitha's hand and said, "Come on, lady. Let's get you out of here before the fireworks."

They vanished, and I turned to Jane, who looked ill. "Maybe they *have* changed," I said.

"And maybe I'm the queen of England," she muttered, and rose from her chair. "If you see Diriem before I do, ask him what the fuck they were thinking, won't you?"

CHAPTER 3

That day wasn't my most productive. I couldn't focus at the office—even my tutor noticed that I was stumbling through my afternoon lesson and asked if I'd slept, a loaded question. Farseers who pushed themselves too hard, for too long, and didn't rest often began to hallucinate. Pop had orchestrated an ambush with a sedative once when I worked past all safe limits, and while I understood the need in retrospect, the incident still left a bad taste in my mouth.

I was trying to work as the afternoon wore on, but around four, a call from Annie interrupted my trance, and that was it. I locked up as soon as I could reasonably slip away and headed for my car. Yven's Mustang was still in its spot as I pulled out—he was much more punctual than I'd ever been—but I told myself I'd fill him in later. I navigated the portals back to Viratta and drove hard for home, then slipped into the mansion's massive garage and parked against a wall, far from Pop's more exotic sportscars. He'd sworn up and down that he wouldn't disown me if I dinged a door, but I didn't want to take that chance.

Scel, the house manager, was fluffing a flower arrangement in the foyer as I came in. "You're early, Miss Rose," he said, barely glancing up from his peonies. "Everything all right?"

"Hey, Scel. Not exactly," I replied. "Is he home yet?"

"His office."

"Thanks. Those are pretty," I added in passing, and made a beeline for Pop's sanctum.

The door opened at my knock, and Pop, who was working at his computer instead of trancing on the couch, arched an eyebrow. "You made good time."

"Traffic cooperated."

"Mm." He looked at the clock on the wall, then back at me. "You're home awfully early without cause…"

"We need to talk."

"*Ah.*" He gestured toward the couch in invitation, but I remained standing and folded my arms.

"Annie called with the scoop from Laws: the Golden Children are being released tomorrow."

Pop sat silently, waiting.

"*All* of them," I pressed. "She heard that they're getting their kids back tonight. Apparently, they're being released through the Midland portal in the morning with money and cars." When that didn't get a reaction from him, I demanded, "What the hell *happened*?"

"What do you mean?"

"I don't trust Katin as far as I can throw her. That little performance she put on today must have been good enough to convince a few representatives, but it was clearly an act."

One eyebrow rose. "You think?"

"I know," I insisted. "I was there when it all went down with Jane, remember? I saw what she did to those people!"

"She's had therapy—"

"A couple years of therapy isn't going to unwrap *that* package. She operates outside the law, doesn't care who buys what she sells, has *zero* concern for human life—"

He spread his hands. "Which, unfortunately, holds little weight with the Forum. If Laws had been able to point to particular buyers here who'd been harmed from her products, then maybe they'd have had more traction. But the fact that she duped a bunch of humans…they don't especially care. I mean, in all honesty, much of our agency protocols for working outside are concerned with fooling humans."

"But not *harming* anyone! Katin got herself some slave labor!"

"Which is reprehensible," said Pop with infuriating calm, "but not a major component of the Forum's calculus."

"If they're stupid enough to think she has more concern for them than she does for anyone outside, then they should be kicked out of office," I muttered. "Katin's a time bomb."

Pop just looked at me.

"Isn't she? What did you really see? And why couldn't your team come to consensus? This shouldn't have been difficult!"

While Pop had a well-honed blank face, I was learning from the master, and I held his stare in silence, waiting him out. Frankly, I suspected he could outwait me, but to my surprise, he glanced away first and huffed a soft breath. "You understand," he murmured, "that per DOI policy, I can't tell you everything."

"What *can* you tell me?"

"Between us and these walls…" He gave me an expectant look, and I nodded. "Very well. The reason we couldn't render an opinion for the Forum is that we had a holdout. They adamantly believed that the Waughnn girl will cause no problems and will settle into a quiet life outside."

"Are they *high*?" I scoffed. "Have they slept lately?"

His mouth tightened in faint annoyance. "They have a solid track record, and I couldn't discount their report."

"All right, and what do you think?" When he didn't answer me, I said, "I'm not asking the director, I'm asking my Pop."

"Rosie—" he began.

"Don't 'Rosie' me. You know damn well what happened in Georgia, and I've grown partial to Ragged Gap. Tell me she's not going to try something like that again—

maybe not in Ragged Gap," I allowed, "but there are tons of little Ragged Gaps all over the place. Towns that *don't* have a sorcerer keeping tabs on shenanigans."

Reluctantly, Pop said, "My gut instinct tells me that release is a poor choice."

"Your gut or your farsight?" I asked.

"The two are frequently in agreement, but…" He hesitated, then said, "I've had flashes of scenes that I don't understand yet. Some involving the Golden Children."

"Is there anything I can do to help? Are the locations throwing you? Something else?"

He shook his head. "If I thought you could clarify, I'd have come to you. It's more than that…but that's hardly unusual. Sometimes, I can focus and see matters clearly. Other times, it's like assembling a puzzle, and only about two-thirds of the pieces fit. So often, future farsight is a game of probabilities, and…well, omniscience would be useful, wouldn't it?" he added with a weary chuckle. "At least the things you see are actually happening, youngling. That must be nice."

"Not always," I said.

"Fine, when you're not hallucinating—"

"No, uh…"

It was my turn to pause and collect my thoughts while Pop waited me out, and when I didn't have my dander up, there really was something unnerving about being at the wrong end of that practiced stare. "So…I do see current events. That hasn't changed."

"Mm-hmm…"

"But sometimes, um…I get…nudges?" I said, failing to find a better word. "Like my spider sense is tingling, you know?"

One corner of his mouth curled. "Reference understood. Continue."

"It normally starts bothering me when there's something in progress that I need to focus on—you get flashes, I get flashes, same deal, or maybe it's an area that I've been concentrating on, and I get the sense that it's time to tune in. But...sometimes, not always, when I get a nudge, it's warning me about the future. Something to pay attention to."

"Go on," he said gently.

"Like, the mural I painted at Mangia—not the DPP Mangia, Maya's restaurant in Carytown," I clarified. "Back before everything. She wanted something sort of Mediterranean, and this landscape design just *came* to me, and it seemed to fit the parameters. Or I think so, at least. Maya hasn't painted over it yet," I added, grinning. "But, like, I did that a year or more before I met Yven, and the first time I took him to Mangia, he said I'd painted his family's estate. Made the trees way too big, but, you know, artistic license."

"And had you painted their house?"

"*Yeah.* When he took me out to meet his folks, I barely needed a tour of the grounds." After a moment's struggle, I said, "It's like...I get anxious sometimes for no good reason, and my mind starts wandering, fixating on places or people or what have you. And that's before anything important happens."

Pop nodded slowly. "That's not surprising, Rosie."

"It's not?"

"That you have a touch of future orientation? No."

I frowned. "But I thought farsight only goes one way. Past or future—"

"Or you," he finished. "You're the only farseer I've ever known to straddle the line, my dear, and that means we don't necessarily understand the full parameters of your talent. However," he said with a slight smile, "considering that you're a ti'Dana farseer, I'm not shocked that you would lean toward future over past. Most of the Hall's farsight has gone in that direction since...oh, I'd say at least the five or six generations before mine."

Considering elven longevity, I had no idea how far back in time that stretched, but then ours wouldn't have come to be known as the Hall that produced farseers if it were a recent phenomenon.

"I'll work with you," Pop continued. "Help you train your focus, learn to heed those nudges, decide which are most probable. Or I'll pair you with another farseer, if you'd prefer—perhaps someone who better recalls the learning period," he offered. "It *has* been a while…"

"Don't feel up to the challenge?" I teased.

He grunted. "My twenties and thirties were a long time ago, youngling. There are bound to be techniques I take for granted through experience that a younger farseer would remember to actually teach you. But that's not a matter we need to finalize this evening. Try to rest—and I assure you, there *will* be eyes on the Golden Children."

"Oh?"

His smile turned almost predatory. "Those vehicles they're being given…you didn't think they'd be handed over without trackers hidden in them, did you?"

"*Sneaky.*"

"This is Laws' doing, not ours," he replied, holding up his empty palms, "but yes. They're trainable."

"I won't tell Kabno you said that," I joked, and started to go. "See you for dinner—"

"Wait, Rosie."

"Sir?" I asked, turning back.

He stood from behind his desk and made his way to the couch, then patted the far end of the leather cushion. I sat, wondering what was on his mind. Pop didn't seem upset, but then he could be such a pain to read…

"Miral called earlier today," he said.

I bit back a groan.

"She said you and Calien had another argument." When I didn't answer that, Pop said, "Calien told her mother that you were rude and dismissive at your last meeting."

"Do you believe that?" I asked.

"Of course not, but I *would* like your side of the story.

It wouldn't do to quarrel with my sister without cause."

I tried to play it off. "We had a disagreement about my dress. I want it in blue, she wants it in tangerine. No big deal. Worst comes to worst, if the designer messes up, I'll just mask it."

Pop cocked an eyebrow. "What else?"

"Nothing major."

"Rosie," he murmured, "I know you better than that."

It really wasn't fair. I'd only known Pop for about four years, but he'd watched me grow up via farsight *long* before I was born, and he knew my tells more fully than I did. Seeing as there was no sense in lying, I sighed and said, "I told her my coloration doesn't work well with tangerine. She suggested I go brunette for the wedding."

"You've never been a brunette."

"Right? I like my hair color."

When I moved to get up, Pop gently gripped my wrist. "This isn't about changing your hair. Out with it, girl."

Reluctantly, kicking myself for how stupid it sounded, I told him, "Calien said changing my hair wouldn't be a big deal because I don't have the ti'Dana look. It's fine," I insisted. "We...push each other's buttons, I guess. Probably just stress from the wedding planning," I said, and tried to stand again.

But Pop didn't release me. "Rose Lea, sit."

And *that* was how I knew he was taking the matter seriously. Middle names were uncommon in the Pactlands, certainly among elves, but Pop had learned how to deploy them.

I plopped back onto the couch and held his gaze. "I'm okay—"

"You're not," he murmured. "And you need to understand something. Will you listen?"

I nodded.

"You are my blood. My heir. That's not up for discussion, and Calien's thoughts on the matter are irrelevant."

Glancing away—the wall behind Pop was much less intense—I muttered, "I know, I just—"

"You know," he said, tapping his temple, then pressed his hand to his chest. "But you don't *know*. Yes?"

After a moment, I nodded again.

"Little one, I don't give a damn what you look like. You're very pretty," he hastened to add, "but that doesn't matter. I don't care what color your hair is, what shape your ears take...none of that superficial nonsense changes anything about who and what you are. Now, that being said," he continued, leaning closer, "if my niece truly believes you don't have the Hall's look, then she's blind. You certainly have the hair," he said, tugging at a long red strand near his face, "and it's the rare ti'Dana farseer who doesn't have gray eyes."

"Mine are kind of bluish..."

"But not truly blue," said Pop. "And I'll tell you something else: there are times that you make a face or stand a certain way, and you look so much like your mother and grandfather, it hurts. Okay?" With a quick squeeze, he released my wrist, then coughed to clear his throat. "I asked Calien to assist with the wedding planning because of her reputation, but if she's being cruel to you..."

"Don't worry," I insisted. "We're both big girls, and I'm sure we can get along for a few more weeks. If experience is any guide, Calien will be back to her charming self by the time we meet up tomorrow."

"And what's the occasion?"

"Flowers. *Again*," I said, and stood. "Honestly, we should just truck over Yven's orchids and be done with it."

Pop cracked a smile. "You think he'd allow them to leave the house for something as inconsequential as his wedding? What if someone breathed on them improperly? Spilled wine in their pots?"

I gave him a long look. "Be nice."

"Of course," he replied, following me toward the door. "But I do worry, Rosie—were you to have a child with a pollen allergy, which do you suppose he would remove from the apartment first?"

"*Pop.*"

"I think it's a toss-up."

"*Sure.* And how many elves do you know with hay fever?" I retorted.

"None, which bodes well for your children's housing situation."

"Oh, good," I said, rolling my eyes, then gave him a brief hug and took my leave.

With dinner not until seven—Yven had a late meeting, and Pop, who'd been on his own for meals for decades, tried to be considerate—I headed upstairs, into the south wing, and up another two flights of the tower's spiral staircase to the apartment my fiancé and I shared for the last few years, our home inside the mansion.

Had someone told me five years earlier that I'd abandon Richmond to move in with my great-grandfather, I'd have had their head examined for a variety of reasons. My place wasn't exactly trendy, but it was paid-off and overly spacious for one person, and I'd grown up in that house. My parents' stuff was still there, squirreled away in closets and boxed up in the basement, and while I'd made progress in donating and otherwise divesting—largely with Yven on hand to keep me from strolling off down memory lane—the place was still in no condition to be put on the market. True, it had become a money pit, a mostly unoccupied home I maintained for no purpose but sentimentality, but I couldn't yet bring myself to sell it.

(Connor made me feel a little better about the waste. Like me, he'd lost his parents young, and he still lived in his childhood home in Whitford. At least I'd redecorated in part—his house had so many nineties interior design flourishes, from the big florals to the sponge painting, that the flatscreen TV came as a shock to the system.)

Besides, why would I have left Richmond? My business

was surviving, I enjoyed painting, and I could look after myself. I'd gotten pretty good at that, since the only family member I knew was my great-aunt, who lived out in the Blue Ridge.

But now there was magic in my life—the kind that let me open doors with a flick of my finger and change my face with a moment's concentration. I'd taken a job as more or less a remote-viewing spy, studying illegal growing operations and black-market brewers before Interdiction sent a team to take them down. I'd found love with a slightly fastidious guy who subscribed to an orchid fanciers' newsletter but would shoot to protect me. I'd also found family like I'd never imagined—some great, some iffy, some incarcerated due to my aforementioned spying. A mixed bag, really.

And while plenty of folks in the Pactlands lived on their own, for those in the main line of the old elven Halls, it was quite common to stick around the family manse. The mansions held by the heads of the wealthiest Halls were absolutely palatial. Top of the heap by square footage was Hall ti'Cren's estate in Kelomb, which was large enough that Aunt Lily, all of her siblings, and a good number of their children could have taken up residence in the suites. From what I understood, it wasn't even close to full—some of the siblings had moved out, a few were on penal farms, my grandfather had died in Virginia, and Aunt Lily wasn't crazy enough to return—but since a fair number of the main-line ti'Crens weren't thrilled with me for the black eye I'd given the Hall, I stayed away. Not that I needed a place to land—Hall ti'Dana's mansion was only slightly smaller and, in my opinion, better appointed, and since the only occupants had been Pop and the staff, I'd had my pick of the rooms.

Our apartment was in a quiet corner of the house, far from Pop's suite, and would have been plenty big enough for two even without the rest of the mansion's amenities. Yven and I had divvied up the space, and Pop, who had more furniture than he knew what to do with, had offered us whatever we desired. The entryway opened to a den just large enough to hold three leather sofas in a U-shape but still cozy—perfect for girls' nights. I loved the windows' stained glass, but for Yven, the true perk was the eastern exposure, which kept the many orchids scattered around the tables and shelves happy. To the right was a galley kitchen, nothing fancy—especially not compared to the main kitchen downstairs—but a convenient place to store my emergency Oreos and cheddar-jack cubes. Our bedroom and bathroom were in the far-right corner, and we hadn't protested when Pop outfitted the bed with one of his guest rooms' miraculously plush mattresses. On the left side of the den was a pair of rooms, his and hers spaces. Yven had made his into a home office, a place to plug in his computer and arrange his many horticultural books, but mine was my studio.

When I'd closed down my studio in Carytown, I'd schlepped everything to the mansion with the aid of a borrowed DPP Jeep. The agency had tricked out a number of inconspicuous SUVs, equipping them with hidden storage rooms big enough to hold dozens of passengers or entire labs, and while their use was monitored...well, Pateme was family, and I was a good driver. All of my gear had ended up in my home studio: easels, prepped canvases, boxes of paints and brushes, the digital camera I used to snap pictures of fidgety toddlers who refused to be sketched for oil portraits. At my request, Pop had taken up the ornate rug that had been in that room before I could ruin it, and though he insisted that just about any stain could be eliminated through the judicious use of magic, I kept drop cloths over the wooden floor. The windows in that room were clear glass, nothing fancy, but the lighting was excellent, and with my phone popped into its speaker dock, I could lose myself in my art.

Of late, I'd been working on a painting of my parents, a double portrait I'd sketched largely from memory, though

I'd consulted some old photos for the details. I'd painted them before when I was an experimental teenager, desperate for willing subjects, but though Mom had talked about doing a proper sitting once I opened my gallery, we'd put it off until it was too late. Eight years after losing them, I'd finally brought myself to do it, spurred by a push whose source I couldn't quite articulate. Part of that was an awareness of the passage of time; while I could still see and hear my parents in my mind, I'd realized that the details had begun to grow fuzzy around the edges. Painting them might not strengthen my memories, but it would freeze them in oils while they were still fresh enough to feel present.

But beyond that need for preservation, with my wedding drawing near, I missed them more keenly than I had in a while—and I'd had to fight Calien at every step to include even a nod to them at the ceremony.

It was Yven who'd told me about the traditional seating arrangements: the couple's parents in the front row, close to the central aisle, with the grandparents beside them, and any other close kin the couple wanted filling in the prime seats. If someone had died—a grandparent, a beloved sibling—their chair was simply left empty. In my case, that meant the first six seats on my side would be vacant, with Aunt Lily and Pop further down the row.

Calien had looked at me like I was nuts when I mentioned it to her, and she'd told me in no uncertain terms that I would *not* be leaving six empty chairs. That was the one time I'd broken down and gone to Pop for backup, and he'd assured me there would be no problem. I don't know what he said to his sister, but the next time I saw Calien, she begrudgingly told me I could have the chairs if I wanted them so badly.

I tried to choose my battles with her. As Calien repeatedly made clear, if she bowed out of my wedding, then all of the vendors would go with her—the event hall, the dressmaker, the caterer, the officiant, the photographer, the florist, the bard with the four-piece band, *everything*. Each of the vendors she'd selected was in high demand, and they were attached to my event only because she had made the pitch. None of them wanted to work with Yven and me. Thus, while I could push back to a point when Calien tried to drive over my plans with a tank, I had to make concessions. I couldn't *afford* to lose her. The wedding was in a month and a half, and the thought of starting from scratch made my guts knot.

Pop wanted a wedding, and I didn't want to disappoint him. More importantly, I didn't want to embarrass him. Calien had assembled a ridiculous guest list filled with people I'd never met: all of the heads of the Halls and their immediate families—even (though I was sure she'd held her nose) the heads of the recently reconstituted southern Halls—plus other prominent elves. Yven and I had fought just to get our friends and colleagues onto the list, and though Calien had been appalled at the notion of a bunch of middle-class agents and our faun and troll chiefs and the freaking *Hunter* in attendance at her soiree, she'd eventually relented. By then, the invitations had gone out, and nearly all the invitees had indicated they were coming. If the wedding fell apart because Calien got into a snit…

I couldn't do that to Pop.

But for an hour or so, I had peace. No Calien, no Golden Children, just me and the canvas and my parents as they'd been when they were about my age, with their lives spread out before them and no inkling of how short those lives would be.

In the painting, my mom was a smiling, gray-eyed redhead in a white boatneck top, which she'd accessorized with gold hoop earrings and the diamond solitaire she'd loved. Her smile was where I saw her mother, Grace, most strongly—it was wide and toothy, and Mom had inherited my grandmother's perfect cupid's bow. But the elven genes were strong—hell, I was proof of that—and Mom strongly resembled her father, Caradin, or at least the paintings I'd seen of him around the mansion. She had the Hall's coloration, if not the farsight; I'd wondered whether she'd have been a farseer as well had Granddad not been forced to take the potion that killed him and snuffed out his daughter's talent. Mom was also of a slenderer build than her mother, less curvy though not boyish. A mischievous twinkle had appeared in her eyes while I painted, a glint that spoke of poking a toe over the line. It was, I thought, the same look I saw in my grandfather's face in the gold-framed photo Pop kept on his desk in his home office: Caradin and Grace sitting together on a bench in a park outside of Richmond, beaming at the camera, with my three-year-old mother, in a watermelon-print sundress, straddling their laps. Sure, Caradin had been masked in that picture, but that only emphasized to me how much Mom had resembled him—and how I, in turn, could find myself in both of them.

Dad sat beside Mom in the portrait, one arm wrapped around her shoulders, sporting the beloved green polo shirt he'd worn to rags by the time I was ten. He'd been a little shy of six feet, a handicap to his dream of a basketball scholarship, but Dad had maintained his lean but toned physique long past high school. Having never known Dad's mother, Miranda, I'd found myself hard-pressed as a child to discern the resemblance. Aunt Lily swore that he had her temperament and burn-prone skin—notoriously in the Pactlands, thanks to a mocking ballad popular for a time after my paternal grandfather, Fradin, publicly took the draught and left, my grandmother was a beautiful redhead with lively blue eyes—but I'd always thought Dad was the spitting image of his father. Even having seen pictures of Fradin unmasked, I hadn't changed my opinion; cover up the ears, hide the sharper elven teeth, and the two of them could have been mistaken for twins. Dad had stayed blond—not Yven's platinum, but closer to gold—and while his hair had been cut progressively shorter, he'd never lost it. His brown eyes stared back at me from the canvas, and his head tilted slightly toward Mom, an expression I knew well: *You see what she's up to, Rosie?*

I studied the painting for a moment, still stuck on what the hell I wanted to put in the background—our house, a nondescript park, something abstract? It wasn't coming, and my parents were of no help.

"Y'all don't think I should wear tangerine to my wedding, do you?" I finally asked.

As expected, they made no reply, but I could almost hear Mom's scandalized voice in the recesses of my mind: *Rose Lea Thorn, don't you dare.*

"Thought so," I murmured, and started sketching a tree behind Dad.

CHAPTER 4

Two weeks later, all my resolve about Calien had been pushed to the limit. With the wedding nearing, she'd become ever more insistent that the only opinion that mattered was hers, and her insults had grown more barbed. Faking a migraine to end my makeup trial early wasn't my proudest moment, but if I didn't get out of the studio, I was going to shove a couple tubes of mascara in a place the sun didn't shine, and we didn't want *that.*

I'd told Calien that I didn't need a makeup artist. I'd been playing with cosmetics since I raided my mom's stash at the tender age of six and emerged from the bathroom looking like the world's tiniest clown hooker, and my skills had drastically improved in the years following. Hell, I'd painted professionally—I could freehand matching wings, no sweat. But she'd insisted, and so she'd retained the services of her dear associate Melinel Clunt, *artiste* to the glitterati. Melinel was a sorcerer of about ninety, old enough to know her trade but still young enough to rock hot pink hair and dark lipstick. Her features seemed East Asian to me, but I kept that thought to myself. The going hypothe sis among genetic theorists in the Pactlands was that the cluster of genes common to sorcerers had arisen at multiple points in human populations, which largely fit the data; on a genetic level, sorcerers and humans were indistinguishable but for a few key spots, and those variances in sorcerers themselves contained variations, with certain combinations arising more or less frequently along what humans would consider ethnic lines. But suggesting to the average sorcerer that she was kissing cousins with *humans* was considered fighting words, and so even the geneticists didn't discuss the issue in polite company—not if they wanted a social life outside the lab, at any rate.

Melinel wasn't Calien's friend—a sorcerer of average birth, much less one who had to *work* for a living, couldn't be expected to find a place in my cousin's rarefied social company—but since Calien dabbled in event planning to keep her parents at bay, she'd forged connections with most of the go-to designers, artists, and caterers for the rich and trendy, and Melinel certainly made the cut. She'd done Calien's makeup for a number of events, and the two had chatted cattily while Melinel studied my face. "You can't even see the elf in there," Melinel had decreed after practically peering into my pores. "This is like working with a sorcerer."

"Well," Calien purred, "you know *what* she is, right?"

"I'm trying to be polite," Melinel replied, and the two snickered. "And this is *not* my favorite coloration. That hair..." She lifted a chunk near my face with two fingers and scrunched her nose. "It's limiting. So are those eyes. Darker would be better. I could do something more dramatic."

"I keep telling Rose she needs to go brown for the wedding, but she won't *listen.*"

"Oh, absolutely," said Melinel, nodding emphatically. "Brown eyes would be better. What color is the dress?"

"Tangerine," said Calien.

"Dark blue," I snapped, glaring at her, then pulled away from Melinel. "And I'm not changing my coloration—my fiancé likes *this* face, you know?"

Melinel's lips pursed. "He might like another one better."

"He's hopeless," Calien muttered. "I mean, he chose *that*..."

Ignoring her, I kept my focus on the sorcerer. "If you don't feel comfortable working with me, that's fine. I've been doing my own makeup for years."

"But have you done it *well?*" she retorted.

"I used to make a living doing portraiture," I said, trying to emulate Pop's poker face. "Pretty sure I know how to contour."

I'd hoped that would shut her down, or at least sway her closer to my side, but it only opened up another avenue of critique. My bone structure was all wrong. I had fat in unfortunate places. My features were oddly shaped, my eyes too big, my brows too thick. Melinel even grabbed a pair of tweezers and plucked a stray hair from my jawline, which Calien watched with disgust.

"And *these*," Melinel concluded, pinching my pierced earlobes. "I can do nothing with these. This will have to be masked. Calien, could you—"

"I can mask perfectly well on my own, thank you," I interrupted, "but there's no need. I'll be wearing earrings."

That set off a round of horrified protestation from both women, and after another twenty minutes of Melinel trying shades and lamenting my stubbornness in not taking Calien's brilliant advice to go brown for the day, I excused myself with a headache, blaming my farsight.

As I waited at the portal building for my turn, regretting the leave I'd taken from work that afternoon, I rubbed my temple and tried to calm down. A few deep breaths helped with the tension, and a little head massage felt nice, but I couldn't shake the anxiety that had been gnawing at my stomach for the last three days. I'd chalked it up to the joy of wedding planning, but…no.

This was different. Much as I longed to blame my cousin, I *knew* this potential ulcer wasn't of Calien's making.

I was young for a farseer, and I had yet to do any formal training with my minimal future nudges, but this *was* a nudge. I just didn't know where it was prodding me.

Once I was through the portal and back in Viratta, I made the quick drive home, passed through the kitchen to let Ranarma know I was around if anyone came looking, then went upstairs and locked myself in my studio to work.

The one feature in my home studio that I hadn't had back in my shop in Carytown was a full-length couch, an overstuffed, tan-colored number that I'd brought from Richmond. It had been my parents' first "grown-up" couch, a hand-me-down from a coworker who'd been redecorating, and my mom had leapt at the chance to rid their place of Dad's broken futon. The couch was nothing special—and I kept one of the cushions covered with a throw pillow to hide a stain I'd made with a Capri Sun at seven—but it was worn in all the right places, and I'd gently declined Pop's offers to procure something nicer. He didn't press the issue—if anyone understood the desire to be comfortable while trancing, it was Pop—but he did remind me that the house was full of unused furniture if I ever wanted an upgrade.

As I kicked off my flats and stretched out on the couch, I mentally rehashed the lessons my farsight tutor had repeated dozens of times: *Close your eyes. Block your ears if you need to. Take deep breaths. Feel for your focus.*

Once he'd been able to publicly acknowledge me, Pop had done his best not to step on my toes as I figured out my upended life, but he'd insisted that I train with a farseer. Most of my remedial magical training took place at DPP, where a rotating group of agents taught me to defend myself, to create and destroy, to brew potions, and to not accidentally kill myself in the DPP greenhouse. Nearly four years in, while I lagged far behind my peers in formal thaumaturgy and theoretical magic, I could hold together a shield strong enough to qualify me for fieldwork and brew without creating accidental fireballs…assuming someone gathered the ingredients for me, that is, as the agent who oversaw the greenhouse practically broke out in hives every time I was escorted through the door. (Not that I blamed him. Yacovi, his predecessor, apparently hovered over Jane like a hawk whenever he allowed her into his greenhouse, and Aunt Lily certainly kept a watchful eye on me when I visited.) But no one at DPP could tutor me in farsight, so once or twice a week, I drove to DOI's windowless building for lessons with Fenna Coll.

Had she not been married to her work, Fenna would have been nearing retirement. She was a white-haired sorcerer of two hundred forty, a little shorter than me and soft with age, and even with the wonders of magically augmented medicine, she'd finally given in and bought a pair of green-rimmed reading glasses, which she only ever wore around the office. A past-oriented farseer of great repute, she'd started at DOI a couple decades before Ganti ti'Van and mentored him, and while he was the undisputed top farseer in their group, Fenna was the better teacher. There wasn't an ideal tutor for me because of my unique orientation, but Fenna was patient and encouraging, and she wasn't afraid to try different techniques until we found ones that worked for us. I enjoyed our sessions—Fenna never made me feel stupid, and unlike my lessons with Emarae ti'Mal and the Interdiction team, I never left with fresh bruises or worse.

With Fenna's guidance, I'd grown into a faster, more adept farseer, able to lock on and, more importantly, *hold* on without overtaxing myself. The recordings my granddad had left for me had given me the basics, but Fenna's lessons were a refining tool—and once Pateme realized how well I was improving under her tutelage, he didn't utter the first peep of complaint when I left work for a session with her.

At our last meeting, I'd mentioned my nudges to Fenna in passing, and she hadn't balked. "I can't help you with future matters," she'd said as I put my shoes back on, "but I'll make some enquiries and see if I can't come up with a few pointers. In the meantime, should you feel a pull toward something that's yet to transpire...treat it like you would a present matter, I suppose," she'd added with a little shrug. "Focus, connect, and see where it takes you."

Deepening my breathing, I sank into the familiar trance state where my farsight operated most readily. Visualization exercises seemed to work for me in general, so I imagined my anxiety as a spool of crimson ribbon in my hands and watched as the end flew off into the blackness of my imagination. When I gave the nearly empty spool a tug, I felt resistance, a fish on the line that might be worked up to the surface with a touch of luck. Focusing on the pull from the other end of the ribbon, I felt my mind spin around me until I opened my inner eyes and found myself in…a waiting room?

I turned in a circle, taking quick stock of the place. Commercial-grade gray carpet, the type that went down in squares and hid most stains. Six padded chairs, also cushioned in gray—vinyl, pleather, something in the "easily disinfected" family—and a long coffee table with a small fan of magazines and one of those wooden bead maze toys common to pediatricians' offices. A smaller, matching wooden table in the corner of the room offered a black Keurig, a spinning display of pods, and a selection of insulated cups and condiments. The only people in the waiting room were a young mother and a little boy of maybe five, who stared intently at an iPad.

The place appeared to be a shop. Plate-glass windows fronted the space, and as I peeked through the door, I saw a parking lot set atop a little hill. The building continued to my left—a strip mall, I decided. Around the parking lot and along the two-lane road below, the world was in full spring green—and since the trees were far taller than the gnarled, hip-high specimens seen in the Pactlands, I had to be outside. Drawing my attention back to the shop, I noted a black mat inside the door to catch dirt, a metal umbrella stand, and a baker's rack stocked with assorted products—lotion, hand sanitizer, lip balm.

But the central feature of the room was the waist-high counter that divided the waiting area from the back, accessible via a white wooden door with an AUTHORIZED PER-

SONNEL ONLY placard. There was a computer sitting on the counter by a credit card reader and a bulky black telephone. When I looked closer at the setup, I spotted a small business card holder full of cards for Ragged Gap Apothecary.

Before I could do more than register the name, I heard a familiar voice drawing closer from behind the counter. "All right, Mrs. Greer, you're set," said Tabitha, emerging from around a corner with a smile. She wore a white lab coat over a tan shirt and black pants, and her usual box braids were pulled back into a thick ponytail that bounced against her shoulders as she made her way to the computer.

The woman in the waiting room tugged the boy to his feet and proceeded to the counter, and I stepped aside to make room. It didn't *hurt* to pass through objects or people when I was in that state—while I could see myself, I was as insubstantial as a ghost to those around me—but I hadn't yet acclimated to the weirdness of finding someone's elbow deep in my stomach. "You think this'll work?" the woman asked Tabitha. "I heard prednisone is bitter…"

"Oh, no question," she replied, putting a plastic medicine bottle by the credit card machine, "but this isn't my first go-round with it. Here, have a whiff."

She opened the bottle, and the woman sniffed it before giving her dubious son a try. "Smells like orange," she said.

"Orange and vanilla," Tabitha replied. "And a sweetener. It's a winning combination nine times out of ten, and if it doesn't work, come back, and we'll try another."

"Mommy," said the boy, yanking at her shirt, "I wanted *chocolate.*"

Before he could throw a tantrum, Tabitha came out from behind the counter and crouched in front of him. "Hey, Jonas, can I tell you a secret?"

He glanced at his mother for reassurance, then nodded.

"The chocolate flavoring I have here for medicine? It's not great," she said, and stuck out her tongue in an exaggerated retch. "But that's not the only reason I don't like to use it. You know how you can eat too much of something, and your tummy gets upset, and then you don't want to eat it anymore?"

"Uh-huh," he mumbled.

"Well, sometimes, if you take medicine, your body doesn't react to it as well as we'd like. You might get an upset tummy. And if your medicine is flavored with chocolate, your body might start thinking that chocolate is bad—and I don't want to do that to you. Now, I am *not* saying that your new medicine is going to make you feel bad at all," she insisted, patting his arm. "It'll probably make you feel much better. But just to be sure—because I would hate it if you stopped liking chocolate—I did orange cream. Okay? And I promise you, if you get home and you can't stand the taste, I'll fix it. Deal?"

The boy left mollified, the mother grateful, and the door chimed as they took their leave.

Tabitha was a compounding pharmacist by trade, and while I knew she had a storefront in Ragged Gap, I'd never had occasion to visit. But there was nothing odd about the place—nothing that would set off warning bells, anyway. It was tidy and quiet, and only with the boy's iPad gone could I hear the radio Tabitha was softly playing in the back. I stepped into the waiting room for a moment, looking for clues, then noticed the sudden silence when the radio clicked off. A few seconds later, Tabitha came through the inner door and locked it behind her, then flipped a sign on the front door to CLOSED.

I glanced at the clock on the wall. It was only four…why was she leaving early?

Feeling the tiniest twinge of guilt at spying on a friend, I followed Tabitha out to her black Camry and slid into the empty back, assuming rightly that she'd put her purse in the shotgun seat. She made the brief trip in silence—decompressing, I figured—then headed up one of Ragged Gap's surrounding hillsides and pulled into the driveway beside her two-story home.

As far as my Georgia friends' houses went, Connor's was decently sized, Jane's was cozy but for the ridiculous bathroom she'd magically augmented, but Tabitha's looked like an adult lived there *and* took pride in the decoration. True, she didn't have a front lawn to speak of—the massive oaks that shaded her house prevented more than weeds from gaining a toehold—but she'd coaxed sweet-smelling honeysuckle vines up both ends of her long, tidy porch, and the flowerbeds were practically bursting with wildflowers, patches of planned chaos. Only if you knew what you were looking at did you catch the less ordinary touches. Off to the right side of the front walk was a twisting steel tree, its branches laden with an assortment of cobalt glass bottles. This was, Jane had explained, a trap for evil spirits, though whether it worked was anyone's guess. The other feature of the house that I hadn't understood at first glance was the color of the shutters and the porch ceiling, a pale, slightly greenish blue—"haint blue," Tabitha had told me, another supposed method of protection and a nod to her home and kinfolk down in Savannah.

That day, the door and windows were decorated with bundles of yellow flowers—pretty, I thought, but I wondered about the significance. Tabitha grew medicinal plants and made teas and such on the side—a less pharmaceutical offshoot of her day job—but normally, when she dried plants, she did so in her kitchen. Making a note to ask her later, I followed her up the porch steps, past the tinkling windchimes, and through the front door.

Tabitha sighed once the door was locked behind her, then sloughed off her sensible flats and dropped her white coat atop the washing machine. She padded into her kitchen, which looked like something out of a cottage showcase home: oak floor decorated with woven rugs in muted tones, a long window behind the farmhouse sink lined with potted ferns like a tiny hedge, pretty cabinetry in a distressed white finish, and a round wooden table with chairs for four. Bundles of dried herbs hung from a pair of clotheslines tied to hooks in the ceiling, ready for use. Tabitha opened the stainless steel fridge and pulled out a bottle of chardonnay, then poured herself a small glass and leaned against the counter as she closed her eyes and sipped.

"You and me both, sister," I muttered, wishing I were there in a more physical capacity. I'd have gladly joined her for an afternoon libation.

Suddenly, Tabitha's phone began to ring, and she dug it from her purse with a slight frown of annoyance. She glanced at the screen, then took the call on speaker mode and picked up her glass. "Hi, Stephanie."

"Hey, Tabitha," came a voice I didn't know, but the name gave me pause. Stephanie Love?

"What's up?" Tabitha asked.

"Just checking on everything for tonight. I *know* this is paranoia talking, but—"

"It's okay. Better safe than sorry."

"Thanks," Stephanie replied with a brief sigh. "Okay, you've got everything you need for the flower crowns?"

"Mm-hmm. Flowers are in the fridge, I've got thread, scissors…" She walked over to the table and peeked inside a tote bag sitting in one of the chairs. "Yes, scissors. And I've got some wire and wire clippers, too, just in case they need more structure."

"*Awesome.* Perfect. And you're going to be here…"

"Five-forty-fiveish, unless you need me sooner."

"No, no, that'll work. I've got you at a pair of tables in the back, put some chairs around…there's other tables closer to the café for refreshments…"

"Do you need me to bring anything else?" Tabitha offered. "I can swing through Ingles…"

"Thanks, but I think we're fine," said Stephanie. "My snack sign-up list is full. Incidentally, the maypole is up, and the fire pit is ready. I put the staff to work today," she added, chuckling. "Especially the boys."

Tabitha grinned. "Strong backs are always appreciated. Now, before I get there and everything kicks off, run me through the plan again, eh?"

"Sure," Stephanie replied as Tabitha sipped her wine. "Doors open at six. I figure we'll do the maypole once we have enough dancers…six-thirty, six-forty-five? Once that's decorated, we'll have our bonfire."

"And this is…in the parking lot?"

"Exactly."

Her brow knit. "Just how big a bonfire are we talking? I'm not trying to step on your toes, but if I put together a bonfire in *my* parking lot, my landlord would raise hell."

Stephanie made a hissing noise on the other end. "Calling it a bonfire is pretty generous. It's more of a nod to the idea that Beltane celebrations typically have fire, you know?"

"So…"

"Ernie has one of those nice porch fire pits, and I got some of the powder that makes the flames change color to keep the kids entertained. After our little debacle in Yancey Park, I don't want to give the fuzz any reason to start writing citations."

Said *little debacle* had been a party without a permit, an impromptu night out for the woo-woo brigade with a proper bonfire and plenty of booze…and once the liquor was flowing, a bunch of naked dancing. The Ragged Gap Police Department had had its hands full that night with inebriated witches and their buddies, but since Stephanie had thrown the party together to give Jane, Connor, Pop, and Ganti a chance to run a bunch of sorcerers out of town—and had woken up the next morning with a bad hangover and a criminal record—Jane was grateful and kept her criticism to a minimum.

"Sounds prudent," said Tabitha. "As long as the fire stays contained…"

"No worries there. But am I forgetting anything? Maypole, bonfire, flowers crowns, snacks…I've got a little talk put together about the holiday…"

"Well, it *is* a good night for fertility rituals, but since this is meant to be a family-friendly event…"

"That's something folks can do on their own," said Stephanie. "I've got no problem with sex magic as long as it's safe, consensual, and not in my store." She paused, then said, "I'm really glad you're coming tonight, Tabitha."

"Sure. Thanks for the invite."

"I mean, I know you're more of a solitary practitioner, but it's nice to have you around," she continued. "You're always welcome."

Tabitha smiled at her wine. "We could ask Jane to join us."

"Oh, um—"

"I'm *joking*," she insisted over Stephanie's stuttering. "Relax."

Stephanie coughed, clearing her throat. "Do you honestly think *she'd* come to a Beltane celebration?"

Making a face, Tabitha replied, "I'm not sure. Jane likes a good party, and that woman is *superb* with fire, but…yeah, this ain't her scene."

There was a longer pause on the line that time before Stephanie spoke again, and her voice was lower. "How much…*have* you seen?"

"What do you mean?"

"So, like, Jane's got power, right? *Real* power. You know it, I know it, half of my clients know it…hell, half this town might suspect with the way Ernie runs his fool mouth," she muttered. "The last time I saw her in action was when Warner Cavanaugh showed up that night last March…no, the March before. Gosh, it's been a year?"

Tabitha smirked at the phone. "It only goes faster."

"Ugh. But you were there, you saw how she broke his bones, and that fire all over her…and that kid with her, the brown-haired girl who threw an amethyst cathedral halfway across the store…"

The silence on Stephanie's end was a clear invitation

for Tabitha to jump in with an explanation, but Tabitha was more reserved. She sipped again, then said, "I remember. Warner hasn't been back, has he?"

"I haven't seen hide or hair of him since the ambulance carted him off. But..."

"Yeah?"

"So...I heard Jane got married to a cop over in Whitford late last year."

"Yep."

"Does *he* know?"

At that, Tabitha let out a full-throated laugh. "Oh, yes," she assured Stephanie, "he's *very* much aware."

"And he's...okay with it? He's not freaked out?"

"You know, it's not my place to tell tales, but let's just say he can hold his own."

"You mean—"

"I said what I said, and that's all."

"Huh." Fortunately, Stephane didn't push her for more. "Sorry, thought of one more thing for the party, wanted to run it by you. Since the veil is thin, I was planning to leave out an offering for the faeries."

Tabitha slowly nodded at the phone on the counter. "No opposition here. If I were doing it, I'd put out milk and honey, maybe coins—something shiny. Leave it in the flowerboxes out front."

"That was my idea, too. Glad we're on the same wavelength." Stephanie hesitated, then asked, "Just curious, but have you ever had a faerie encounter?"

"Can't say that I have, no, but don't let me be a wet blanket. Anyway, I've got to get myself together. See you in a bit."

Once they'd hung up, Tabitha finished her wine and put the glass in the dishwasher. "Faeries? No," she mumbled to herself. "*Elves*, now..."

"Can I have some cash?" I asked her. "I mean, if y'all are leaving money out..."

She couldn't hear me, I knew it, but sometimes, I carried on a one-sided conversation while trancing. Early on, I'd figured out the trick to talking through my physical mouth while the rest of me was occupied with farseeing—which, Pop had told me with pride, not every farseer could manage—but alone as I was, without someone sitting by me to take notes of my vision, I got bored of keeping quiet and made my own fun.

Having grown to know her, I didn't exactly *pity* Tabitha, but I understood that she was stuck in a weird place. She'd been a practicing Wiccan since college, and while I'd never seen her perform rituals or cast spells, I knew from Jane that she was a believer. What, I'd wondered, was it like for her to be exposed to actual physical magic—not sending intentions into the universe, but rather conjuring up fireballs and changing faces? From all accounts, Tabitha had handled the shock well; Pop, at least, was impressed at her stoicism in the face of magic. The rest of the Mystic Mountains crowd was a different story. Those in the Pactlands who knew the details of the debacle with Katin and her so-called Oil of Life couldn't believe how gullible and reckless Stephanie's crew had been, but coming at it from a more human perspective, I wasn't so quick to belittle them. These people believed in magic—*really* believed in it—and to have Katin's dangled in front of them must have been a trap they couldn't resist.

I remembered how it had felt the first time I managed to cast with Yven guiding me, how giddy I had been when I discovered the power to change reality at my fingertips. Never mind that those first magical fumblings had been small and awkward—I could *do magic*. Little old me, making a throw pillow float above the floor like it was bobbing on an invisible lake. A few gestures, the right frame of mind, and a whole new universe of potentialities lay open to me. But I'd grown up fairly well grounded in reality; while my parents had known that magic was real, they'd never let on, allowing me to think we were all just ordinary humans until the day they died. For the woo-woo brigade, however, who deeply believed in their craft and crystals, their meditation and mantras, Katin's promise of power must have seemed like an answered prayer. Desperate people don't always step back and consider the evidence, much less read the fine print, and Katin had reeled them in. Fortunately, Tabitha had a solid head on her shoulders, and her suspicion had saved her from a one-way trip to Katin's home brewery…and exposed her to a hell of a lot of magic of a sort she'd never expected.

But Tabitha hadn't run screaming. She hadn't fled when Pop dropped his mask and sprayed scent neutralizer all over her car before Jane climbed in, rendered invisible with a ring borrowed from Teolm's considerable vault of magical jewelry. She'd kept an eye on town when Jane wasn't around, surreptitiously checking for bad actors from the Pactlands. When Warner Cavanaugh, a local creep, had violated a restraining order against one of Stephanie's customers and tried to remove her from the store at gunpoint, Tabitha had kept her cool while Jane and Maebe…well, *neutralized* the situation. And just the previous September, when members of the Unity Plan—a sorcerer-heavy group that advocated for abandoning the Pactlands and making themselves known to humanity, and somehow thought that would end in anything less than violence—had kidnapped half a dozen people and tossed them outside, unmasked and unarmed, Tabitha had dropped everything to come to their aid, stitching wounds and trying to figure out antibiotic dosing for trolls and centaurs. Her aid was what had gotten her a peek into the Pactlands, as the agents with her had insisted that the humans who kept them alive be seen and acknowledged, *publicly*. I'd been allowed to come to the portal building for the triumphant return—having been forcibly sedated a few days prior after a long period of intense trancing and almost no sleep, I'd been feeling more like myself, and I'd still been cross enough with Pop that he hadn't protested my presence. There had been camera crews waiting, and suddenly, the story wasn't just about the kidnapped agents. Four humans were standing in Beukal in front of about half the Forum, a good chunk of several agencies, and every news outlet in our pocket world, and after a few confused minutes, several of the braver reporters had ventured close to them with microphones and a slew of question. Fortunately, three spoke Pactish—Dave and Maggie Humphries had acquired it from Wylan, their *very* protective son-in-law, while Maya had been given a language potion during her first, far less pleasant, visit, and the potion that was meant to have altered her memory to make her forget the Pactlands hadn't affected her fluency. That had left Tabitha as the lone member of their party who couldn't understand a word, but Yacovi had stayed close to his friend and neighbor, translating and keeping the worst of the press at bay until Wylan could get to them, apologize for not fixing the matter sooner, and then, in a matter of seconds, put Pactish in her mind.

No one in the Pactlands knew the full extent of Wylan's power—hell, I doubted that even he had a handle on it—but on occasion, it was really nice to have a friend who made your own abilities look more like card tricks.

Laws had quickly prepared to try every member of the Unity Plan they could find with so much as a toe dipped in that half-cocked scheme, and though they couldn't bring in the entire organization, they made a dent. The members not on penal farms had been oddly quiet since the previous fall—a good idea, as the public reaction had been horror when the details of their plot came to light. Kidnapping children from their beds and dumping them to be discovered by humans wasn't exactly a winning PR move.

As one of the farseers involved in that mess, I'd spent weeks testifying in tribunals, as had Ganti. All of the victims—even the children—were brought in to give their testimony, and Yacovi and Connor testified as well, though

Morial had been exempted. As far as most of Laws knew, he was just Moonless Night, the troll who helmed Channel 1's sports team, who'd somehow convinced a director to let him go outside after his girlfriend: DPP's Interdiction chief, who was larger than him, far better trained in weaponry, and more than capable of taking care of herself. It made for a cute story, especially as the two had become engaged during the craziness, but the counselors who tried the cases opted to put on agency witnesses whenever possible, perhaps fearing that the sports guy would flub it. *Kabno*, their director, knew damn well that "Moonless Night" was a Huntsman in disguise, but she didn't go blabbing to her legal team.

What was gratifying to me about the tribunals—and shocking to many—was that Kabno arranged for Maya, Maggie, Dave, and Tabitha to testify. She'd had to go to the Forum for permission, and the vote had been far from unanimous, but she'd been able to make a case for them…mostly. Maya had been a DPP employee and was no threat, while the Humphrieses wouldn't do anything to jeopardize Annie—that, and Wylan had not only vouched for his in-laws but also promised to keep an eye on them. Tabitha had no obvious reason to protect the Pactlands, but Pateme had stepped in to help Kabno and get her permission secured. Gentle Breeze trusted Tabitha, Pateme's old buddy Yacovi considered her a friend, and that was good enough for my great-great-uncle.

And the counselors *loved* her. Tabitha was poised in the witness seat, matter of fact in her responses, and didn't back down on cross-examination. Even without the spell that ensured truthful testimony by paining witnesses who lied, she came across as trustworthy: a rational, reasonable woman with a decent memory for detail. When the counselors pressed her about the odds of success for the Unity Plan's grand scheme to announce themselves and start over outside, she didn't mince words in shooting it down. "Look," she'd said to the judge at her first tribunal, an elderly troll who went by Smoke, "I grew up believing in the supernatural. I've believed in magic for a long time—nothing you would recognize as magic, I suspect, but let's say it primed me to not lose my mind when I saw what people like Mr. Hewt and Agent Fortune and, uh..."—she'd glanced toward where Connor was sitting in the audience with an apologetic wince—"Lord ti'Catama can do. But I'm an exception. If a bunch of you folks, even just a bunch of sorcerers, were to come out and show yourselves, especially with magic, it would be a disaster."

"And why do you say so?" Smoke had asked.

"Because we're not even good to each other," Tabitha had replied. "Human history is one long string of wars and worse interspersed with rest breaks. And since we're tribal on a good day, we're not going to be welcoming to people with the power to snap their fingers and change reality. And I'm sorry," she'd added. "I am. Indicting one's species isn't fun. But based on what I know of us, a big reveal of the Pactlands would end in absolute disaster."

Smoke's heavy violet brow had furrowed as he studied Tabitha. "But you're not afraid of us, are you?"

She'd thought before answering him, probably weighing politeness against the truth spell. "Sometimes, I get a little scared. I try not to let on, but...honestly, yes, sir." Cocking her head toward the rest of the room, she said, "I've seen what sorcerers and elves can do. Heard about nagas being able to swallow prey almost as big as they are. I've never seen a siren—or I don't think I have, at any rate—but I was told about the whole hypnosis thing. I'm, uh...I'm pretty confident that you could snap me like a twig. And...well," she'd said, shrugging, "I'm just me. What you see is what you get." Tabitha had paused for a sip of water, and while her complexion was sufficiently dark to disguise her flush, I'd suspected that her face was burning. "Now, back in September, with sorcerers on the loose and not too picky about collateral damage? That scared me half to death."

"But you assisted," Smoke had pointed out.

She'd nodded. "People were in trouble, and it was the right thing to do. And don't get me wrong," she'd added, "the folks with me were great. Not like I was sleeping with one eye open or anything." Quickly scanning the nearest benches, she'd said, "Chief there, Agent Berek, Ms. ti'Cren out in the mountains—I've got no quarrel with any of them. Good people. But, you know, sometimes...when objects start flying or, say, Wylan appears out of nowhere, it can all be a bit disconcerting."

At that, Smoke had leaned closer to Tabitha's chair. "Youngling," he'd murmured with a smile, the gold caps of his tusks sparkling, "I doubt there's a soul in this room who hasn't found the Hunter slightly disconcerting."

When Tabitha had finished and Smoke had called a recess, Gentle Breeze and I had met her at the carved stone boundary wall between the audience and the counselors. Tabitha had started to apologize, but the chief had shushed her. "The feeling is mutual," she'd said, "but you're okay. Hey, look how nicely this is healing up," she'd continued, lifting her black shirt to show Tabitha her scar, a brownish line against her green skin. "Your stitches were *straight*. The healers were impressed."

"Glad I didn't mess up too badly," Tabitha had replied, laughing.

"Not at all. And hear me," Gentle Breeze had replied, squeezing Tabitha's shoulder with a hand like a clawed catcher's mitt. "If there's *ever* anything I can do for you, give me a call. No questions asked. I owe you."

"No, no, there's no debt—"

"Bullshit," she'd replied in her best English. "And between us girls, even Morial has a healthy respect for Wylan. No one's insulted over *that*."

As Tabitha wandered into her room to freshen up, I sat in the kitchen and mulled over what little I'd gleaned about

Mystic Mountains' Beltane party. Nothing struck me as alarming—not unless the baby bonfire were to get out of hand, and Tabitha surely had Jane on speed-dial for such an emergency.

All of a sudden, a familiar touch of my shoulder yanked me back into my body, and I opened my eyes in my studio to find Yven looking down at me. "Hi, gorgeous," he said, flashing the pointed grin I'd grown to love. "Up to no good?"

"Just following a hunch," I replied, pushing myself upright.

Yven helped me ease myself toward verticality. "Powerball numbers, by chance?"

"Not this time. And what are you doing home?" I asked, taking him in. He hadn't even changed out of his navy formal robe yet, and it swept the ground as he stooped to pull me to my feet.

"I had a little vacation banked and thought I'd beat you back here. Figured cookies might help your mood after makeup."

I chuckled. "You're not psychic, are you?"

"No, merely attuned to the general pattern of your appointments with your lovely cousin," he replied. "So, how bad was it? Chocolate chip or a martini?"

Scrunching my face, I asked, "You think it'd spoil dinner if we did both?"

"Ooh. I think Ranarma will understand," said Yven, and escorted me to one of the couches in the den. As I sat, he kissed the top of my head. "I'll change clothes, and then cookies and booze it is."

"Have I told you I love you?" I called after him as he started toward our bedroom.

"You're just a sucker for my baking."

"Yeah, but I'm pretty damn fond of the baker, too."

He paused at the door and winked. "Play your cards right, and someday, I'll show you the hollow tree where I learned my impeccable skills."

I rolled my eyes. "You're incorrigible, station wagon."
"Let me have my fun, Rosie," he replied, and smiled as he headed for the closet.

CHAPTER 5

Dinner was lovely—one of the perks of a live-in chef who hadn't yet met a cuisine he didn't want to conquer—but not even the stiff drink I'd had ahead of the meal could calm my anxiety, and I only picked at my food for about ten minutes before excusing myself. Concerned, Yven started to get up, but Pop stopped him with a shake of his head. "Let her go," he murmured.

I paused, one hand on the back of my chair, ready to push it in. "You know what's going on?"

"I've seen flashes, and I believe you're connected with them," he replied.

"Can we be slightly more specific?"

Pop's lips barely curled. "No, we cannot."

"Cannot or will not?"

His carefully blanked face was the only answer I received, and, perhaps muttering a little more loudly than was warranted about know-it-all future farseers, I left the dining room and hurried back to my studio.

I made myself comfortable, took a couple deep breaths, and followed the thread of my unease, now more like a steel cable, back to Tabitha. I found her sitting at a long folding table strewn with flowers, guiding a pair of little girls as they wove flower crowns. People milled around her in the warm space, chatting in chairs, popping out the door a few feet behind the flower table, or loitering at the counter of what appeared to be a little café—the sign by the register proclaimed it to be "Mystic Munchies"—which had been lined with mismatched platters of food, pitchers of punch, and enough plasticware for a hundred. I turned to take in the rest of my surroundings. Yes, this was definitely Mystic Mountains. While I'd never been in the shop, I'd seen bits of the front part through the windows on my occasional stroll through downtown Ragged Gap, and the displays laden with geodes and polished points and crystal clusters were a dead giveaway. Heck, even if I'd closed my eyes, the faint scent of patchouli and nag champa from the incense bar along the wall would have told me I'd made it into one of northeast Georgia's finer metaphysical emporia. Midway through the shop, dividing the retail area from the event space where the party was going on, was a wooden sales counter, where I spotted Stephanie holding court with a knot of people, deep in a discussion of the Good Folk.

Nothing seemed amiss.

Anxiety made me study my surroundings. The ceiling in the front of the shop was considerably lower than in the back, and when I saw a door near Tabitha open and a woman emerge from a staircase, I surmised there was a second story—offices, maybe? Storage? No one was raising an alarm at the woman's return from upstairs, so I supposed it wasn't a forbidden place. With that settled in my mind, I poked my head out the back door to see the festivities in the parking lot. The maypole, which had perhaps been part of a basketball goal in a previous life, was wrapped with crepe paper streamers; judging by the haphazard weaving, I figured the kids had done most of the job. A group was standing around the promised fire pit, superintending the children taking turns tossing pinches of additives into the flames to make them sparkle and flare green—fun through chemistry, though quite possibly magical in the eyes of the elementary set. Everything seemed copacetic—the conversations were lively, the weather cooperative and clear, the kids decently behaved around an open fire. Back inside, the good vibes continued. Frankly, the only thing I saw that gave me pause was the plate of tofurkey sliders.

And then the shop's bell rang.

I glanced toward the front in time to see six people walk in—and leading the pack was Katin Waughnn, dressed in a flowy white tunic top, skinny jeans, and layers of thin gold necklaces. "Hello!" she called, all smiles. "How's everyone? Did y'all miss me?"

Proving that some people really are too dumb to live, a few of Stephanie's inner circle made a beeline for the front of the store, nearly toppling a display of singing bowls in their rush to greet her. Stephanie froze by the desk, staring, but Tabitha leapt from her chair and grabbed the little girls' shoulders. "Come on, this way," she murmured, and the girls followed her out of the shop. I ran after them and saw Tabitha push them toward the adults watching the bonfire. "Trouble inside," she said, her voice low but insistent. "Get the kids out of here. Go up to Mama Hen's, they're still open."

One of the men frowned. "What kind of trouble?"

"Katarina's back."

His eyes widened. "Wait, you mean—"

"Ernie, Goddess help me, if you don't get the kids the *hell* out of here—"

"Okay, *okay*," he said, raising his hands in surrender. "I'll, uh..."

"All y'all," Tabitha snapped, spinning one finger in a circle as if to encompass the bonfire brigade. "Mama Hen's. *Now*. Bitsy, get going."

"What about you?" Ernie asked as his wiser comrades hustled the children off through the parking lot toward the restaurant. "Aren't you coming?"

"I've got to help Stephanie," she replied, and strode back into the building before Ernie could press for details.

By the time we returned to the store, Katin—and yes, those were all Golden Children with her—was surrounded by excited would-be practitioners. "I *knew* it had to be a misunderstanding!" a gray-haired woman in a broom skirt practically trumpeted. "We're so glad you're back!"

But another group of people huddled in the rear of the building, the ones with common sense or at least a sense for danger, and Tabitha murmured to them to leave out the back as she headed for Stephanie. Before Tabitha could reach the desk, Stephanie managed to shake off her paralysis and clapped her hands twice for attention, a sound like a whip cracking over the garbled voices. "I'm sorry," she said once she had the Golden Children's attention, "but this is a private event. We can catch up later, Katarina."

At that, Katin smirked and unfolded a sheet of yellow paper. "Private? That's not what the flyer says."

"Stay!" exclaimed Broom Skirt, patting Katin's arm. "You're welcome here."

"I'm afraid you're trespassing," Stephanie tried again, a little more firmly. "You and your friends need to leave. *Now.*"

The Katarina Weller Fan Club turned and regarded Stephanie with irritation, but Katin just smiled her polished grin. "Don't be like that, silly," she said, her voice a honeyed drawl sweet enough to bring on diabetes. Gone was the contrite young woman from the Forum, head bowed and eyes downcast. *This* version of Katin was all confidence—no, triumph—and her blue eyes sparkled as she stared Stephanie down. "I'm so thrilled to see everyone again—I had to come by and bring my friends as soon as I got back to town."

"Where have you *been*, lady?" another woman asked.

"Here and there. Long story," she replied, waving off the question. "And y'all, I cannot *tell* you how sorry I am for how things turned out last time. We were interrupted before your power could truly bloom, and this other practitioner threatened my life if I didn't leave town. She's...well, she's what you might consider a warlock. Black magic. I've seen it before—"

"I knew it!" a man cried, slamming his fist against his

palm. "That Fortune bitch is no damn good—"

"I heard she stole your power from you," said Katin. "My sincere apologies, folks. It won't happen again."

"You need to *go*," Stephanie insisted. "This is my store, and you're not welcome here."

"Oh?" Katin cocked an eyebrow, then led the cluster of people away from the front door before muttering at the deadbolt, which slid into place. She turned back to Stephanie, her expression clear: *What are you going to do about it?*

"That...you have to get out of here..." Stephanie tried, but the show of magic seemed to have dampened her fire.

Ignoring her, Katin focused on her fans again. "I've got some *fantastic* news," she purred. "I've been working on Oil of Life, reformulating it. Remember how you had to go through all of that gradual dosing last time? Well, no more. It's a one-dose oil, and it works like a dream. And as a gesture of good faith," she continued, eyeing Stephanie like a wolf staring down a fear-frozen rabbit, "and to show my deep apology for any inconvenience you suffered last time by hosting me, I'm going to give you the first bottle—"

"Oh, no, you're not," said Tabitha, marching up from the back with her phone in hand. To my surprise, she broke into Pactish as she took up a stance between Stephanie and the Golden Children. "You're meant to be in Texas, *all* of you. So, here's what going to happen: either you leave now and get the hell out of this town, or else I'll call in reinforcements. You want to try me? I've got phone numbers for the fucking *Hunt.* Unless you want to deal with Wylan and his dozens of brothers, you need to leave. *Now.*"

I saw in that instant Tabitha's error. "Call them!" I yelled, momentarily forgetting that she couldn't hear me. "Stop bluffing and call Annie! She knows the way here—"

Katin's lips moved, and a bolt of force slammed into Tabitha's hand. Screaming in pain, she dropped her phone and cradled her hand to her chest—and that was all the Golden Children needed. Within seconds, two of them had grabbed Tabitha, and another two Stephanie, while the crowd looked on with bemused interest.

For an instant, I thought about ending the trance, finding my phone, and sending Annie and the cavalry myself, but things were moving too quickly in Ragged Gap, and I feared what I'd miss if I looked away. Katin surely wasn't going to try to force Velvet Leash on Stephanie and Tabitha—that had to be taken willingly to work. *Someone* with a modicum of magical education needed to witness this, if only to pass that information to persons more knowledgeable, and so I clenched my fists back in my studio and held on.

"This is perfect," said Katin, her smile wide and unkind as she took in her captives, Stephanie frozen again, Tabitha struggling. "A double demonstration."

With that, she pulled two small bottles of an iridescent silver liquid from her large canvas purse, followed by a pair of syringes.

"Let me go," Tabitha growled, squirming to break the hold of the sorcerers pinning her in place. "This is fucking assault. You're going to *pay*, bitch—"

"The only one paying is you," Katin sweetly interjected in her accented Pactish as she filled the syringes. "You know, if you can't say something nice about folks, you should keep your goddamned mouth shut. Let this be a lesson, hmm?"

"Walk away," Tabitha tried again, following Katin's linguistic switch. "I swear, even if you kill me now, they'll find your raggedy ass. You have any idea how many farseers I know?"

At least three, by my count, which wasn't a bad start.

But Katin snorted. "Like they're going to help you. They couldn't even keep us locked up, so what makes you think they'd see *this* coming? Now be a good girl and hold still," she said, passing one syringe to the last of the Golden Children before advancing on Tabitha. "Time to take your medicine."

I watched in horror as the needles went into the women's shoulders. As soon as the syringes had emptied, Katin and her partner withdrew, and then the four holding Stephanie and Tabitha in place released them. Tabitha had barely started toward the phone she'd dropped when she screamed like she was being burned alive and fell to the floor. Stephanie did likewise, narrowly missing a display of gem-studded athames on her way down, and wailed as she trembled on the old wooden floor.

The other partygoers, the ones who'd been so excited to see Katin's return, began to trade glances and back away as the women writhed in pain. I hadn't seen the original Oil of Life in action, but I assumed it hadn't worked anything like *this*.

And then the changes began.

Stephanie's hair, blonde with pink highlights, paled to snow-white, while Tabitha's dark braids turned a deep cerulean. A strange, sourceless wind began to whip around sobbing Stephanie, but Tabitha, who was clearly made of stronger stuff, dragged herself back to her feet as tears streamed down her face.

"So," said Katin, spreading her arms, "how does it feel? You've witnessed true magic, yes? How does it feel to have power of your own?"

"Are...are they okay?" asked Broom Skirt, who'd edged toward the locked door. "Oil of Life never hurt..."

"Oh, they're fine," said Katin, bestowing a salesman's smile on her. "It's like a quick growing pain. They'll be right as rain in just a minute."

Doubtful, I thought, wishing I could see what was going on in Tabitha's head. She clung to the sales counter, her fingertips almost bloodless with the strength of her grip, as she regained her wobbly balance...and then she glanced at Stephanie.

No, not at Stephanie—at the abandoned clear plastic cup of pink punch sitting on the counter between them, which began to bubble.

Well, *that* wasn't normal. I cut my eyes to Katin, but she seemed oblivious to the suddenly simmering drink, busy as she was with the spooked herd around her.

"While they're adjusting, who wants to be next?" she asked, patting her purse. "Plenty for everyone. By the time y'all leave here tonight, you'll have the power you've been waiting your whole lives for. I guarantee it."

More of the crowd seemed uncertain—the radius of the circle around Katin was widening—but a man asked, "How much?"

"How much?" Katin echoed, her pretty eyes widening. "Oh, goodness, not a cent. I let y'all down the last time I was here, and I want to make things right."

She was, I briefly registered, a decent actress, but that wasn't enough to overcome her marks' hesitation. Stephanie continued to cry in loud, pained sobs, and the others cast nervous glances at their leader, whose distress was clearly genuine.

"I promise you, she'll be fine," said Katin, raising her voice above Stephanie's. "It can hit a little hard when you do it all at once, but the result is *so* worth it. Why, everyone here with me took it, didn't y'all?" she said, turning to the other Golden Children.

"Sure did," said a brown-haired man—Dirk Vaniac, Katin's chief partner in crime. "Hurt for just a minute, but now…" He held out one hand and whispered, and a pink salt lamp unplugged itself and flew into his palm. "Easy-peasy."

Broom Skirt frowned at him. "Haven't I seen you before?"

"Don't think so," he replied, which I suspected was a lie. I didn't know if Broom Skirt had been one of the Oil of Life zombies, but if she had, then Dirk had been living at the cabin with Katin and the rest of her merry band.

"Come on," Katin cajoled, smiling at the partygoers, "who's next? Y'all want real magic, right?"

After a long moment punctuated only by Stephanie's

blubbering, Broom Skirt tentatively raised her hand. "Okay, I'll do it. If you're sure it's safe, Katarina…"

"I'd never do anything to harm you, Penny," she replied, lying through her pearly whites. "But if you're nervous about taking that oil, I do have an alternative—it'll be two doses, tonight and tomorrow, but it'll be a touch easier on the system. Want to try that?"

"Oh, that sounds perfect," said Penny, relief washing over her lined face. "Is it a shot, or…"

"Actually, it'd be better if you drank this version." Reaching into her bag, Katin produced a handful of tubes of a dark purple liquid I was confident was Velvet Leash. "Just knock this back, and then I'll give you the second dose tomorrow, and poof, magic."

A few of the others began to draw closer, reassured by the friendlier alternative. I prepared to break away and call Annie before the lot of them could be hauled off to the Golden Children's hidey-hole, but then I checked on Tabitha, who, though she gritted her teeth, had fire in her dark eyes. She fixed her gaze on Katin and grunted, and two seconds later, Katin dropped the glass vials as they began to shatter, breaking from the strain of the trapped, boiling potion.

Katin yelped as some of the hot liquid splashed her hands, and she stared at Tabitha in alarm as the shaking pharmacist glowered back at her. "How…" she whispered.

"*Run*," Tabitha growled, as the potion tubes in Katin's bag broke open, splashing the canvas with purple splotches like paintballs were being shot inside. Katin pushed the purse off her shoulder and practically threw it onto the floor, where it swelled and hissed like a bag of microwave popcorn. She looked at Tabitha for only another instant before throwing back the bolt and beating a retreat into the night, the rest of the Golden Children hot on her heels.

As their footsteps faded, Penny wheeled on Tabitha, hands on her hips. "What did you *do*?" she demanded. "Why on earth would you—"

"I'm saving your stupid ass," Tabitha ground out, pain etched on her face.

"Katarina said it wouldn't hurt—"

"It's not even the same damn color! If it were a milder dose, it'd still look like the crap they put in me, don't you think?"

The others stared at her blankly, and she groaned as she tried to straighten, leaning on the counter for support. "It's a trap, you fucking morons! Probably the same shit you drank last time she was around—you know, the potion that made you lose time? That stuff she gave you turned you into drones. She's a liar."

"You have no reason to say that," Penny protested. "You're just biased because Jane gives you the time of day—"

"Jane saved you," said Tabitha. "I *know* what really happened, and I know who and what your precious Katarina is. She ain't your friend, that's for sure—*oh*," she cried, nearly falling as she bent to collect her phone, then whispered, "Goddess help me, it hurts."

"Um...are you okay?" another woman asked, taking a tentative step toward Tabitha.

She raised her head, her mouth a tight line. "Do I *look* okay to you? Son of a bitch," she muttered, and staggered toward the rear door. "Get Stephanie out of here, take her home. The kids should be at Mama Hen's."

Penny frowned. "Why would they be—"

"Because I sent them there, away from this foolishness. Go collect them. I need to lie down."

I stayed by Tabitha's side, silent and invisible, as she unlocked her Camry and folded herself into the driver's seat. It took her a few minutes to muster up the strength to turn on the car and put it in drive, but she managed to make the trip home, albeit at an octogenarian's Sunday pace. She staggered up the porch steps, leaned against the door until she found her house key, then let herself in with trembling hands and flipped on a light.

With a long moan, Tabitha took a few steps into her cozy den and face-planted onto the couch. A couple of whimpering breaths later, she was unconscious with her shoe-clad feet still hanging over the armrest.

That was my cue. I opened my physical eyes and gave myself a second to reacclimate to physicality, then jumped off my couch and ran into the den, where I found Yven reading his orchid fanciers' newsletter. "Is everything okay, sweetie?" he asked as I tore around the room, looking for my purse. "What's going on?"

"Can't talk. Shit, *shit*, fuck, where did I—ah," I muttered, finding my bag beside the hall table where I'd dropped it. Annie was near the top of my list of recent contacts, and I squeezed the phone as I waited through three rings for her cheery greeting.

"Hey, lady," she said in English—despite our years in the Pactlands, it was comforting to hear our mother tongue on occasion. "What's up?"

"Golden Children are in Ragged Gap, they just stuck something in Tabitha and Stephanie Love, and I don't know where they went, but I think Tabitha made a bunch of potions boil—"

"*Whoa*, hold it, slow down. *What*?"

"Tabitha's hurt," I managed. "Fucking Katin Waughnn injected her with a potion, and she's passed out at home. We've got to get—"

"I'll grab Jane," she interrupted. "Do you have any pain potions handy?"

"Yeah, probably. See you in five?"

"Outside the mansion," Annie replied, and cut the call.

Yven followed me as I ran into the bathroom to ransack the medicine cabinet. "You saw the Golden Children?" he asked. "In Georgia? *Now*?"

"Yeah, but forget them. Tabitha—"

"Was given a potion, I heard that. Do you know what?"

"No clue. Iridescent, I think, but maybe that was just

the light. Injected. Must have hurt like the dickens," I said, barely conscious that Yven had kept the conversation in English. He knew my stressed mode far too well. "Her hair turned blue, and I think she made the rest of Katin's potions boil."

"*How?*"

"Hell if I know, but the Golden Children ran off, and—okay, that's three," I said, snatching the bottles of pale green liquid from their shelf. "I think Pop has a stronger painkiller, but I don't have time to go looking. Do we have any neutralizer?"

"Not here. Honey," he began, reaching for my arm, "calm down. Breathe. Let's find Diriem—"

"Tabitha's unconscious, and we've got to get to her," I interrupted. "I'll be back. Tell Pop where I've gone, okay?"

"Be careful!" Yven called after me as I snatched up my purse and ran from the apartment.

I sped down the spiral stairs, raced through the south wing, and had just flown down the wide main staircase when Pop marched into the foyer. "Rosie, wait."

"Can't," I said, running for the front doors.

"*Rosie.*"

I turned, impatient, and found him standing by the stairs with his arms folded. "She's not dying," said Pop.

"You don't know that—"

"I'm *positive*," he insisted. "But that's all I can give you."

"You knew this was coming?"

He looked like he'd tasted something bitter but was trying not to make a fuss. "Only in the last days. It's grown clearer."

There was no sense in chiding him for not warning me. I knew the DOI farseers' ethical rules, even if I didn't always follow them to the letter, and part of that code prevented future-oriented farseers from dropping hints if doing so might mess up what they perceived as the best outcome. The greater good had to be paramount, but the fact that a farseer could sit back and say nothing while a friend walked off a cliff—or in Pop's case, when his granddaughter and her husband took an ill-fated drive on an icy February night—made them the sort of people others regarded with a degree of suspicion, if not fear. They were useful tools, but they were also the sort that might blow up in one's hands.

"Can you tell me what they gave her?" I asked.

Pop shook his head. "All I know is that it's novel. Bring her to DPP." Pulling his phone from his pants pocket, he said, "I'll warn Pateme."

My thoughts flashed to Annie and Maya, who'd been carted off to the Pactlands after their own novel potion experience and hadn't been freed for a year and a half. I suppose my expression betrayed me, as Pop said, "I don't anticipate a long stay in quarantine, but she can't be left out there. Nor the other, but one at a time. Tabitha first."

With a curt nod, I took my leave and let myself out into the night. Before I'd reached the ground, Annie appeared a few feet away, the pavement softly illuminating in blue beneath and around her like the rippling of a bioluminescent tide. And she hadn't come alone. I recognized Jane immediately—ever so slightly shorter than Annie, with far lighter hair, though the most prominent detail that night was the fact that Jane's eyes, unlike Annie's, didn't glow like a cat's when they caught the light from the windows. With them were two hulking, antlered shapes that resolved into Wylan and Derat, one of Wylan's closer brothers and another Forum representative.

"She's still alive," I announced as I jogged toward them. "Pop says she's not dying—"

"I'd rather see that for myself," said Jane, grabbing my wrist, then linked up with Annie. "Let's go."

I barely had time to close my eyes before the world went black and the ground dropped away. Before I could do more than gasp, we were standing in Tabitha's dark kitchen, and Derat grunted as he banged into a chair.

Teleportation was not for the faint of heart.

"You didn't have to come," I said to the guys as Jane started flipping on lights and calling for Tabitha.

Wylan, nearly six and a half feet tall *without* the antlers, gave me an amber-eyed look of strong disagreement.

"Pop says we need to get her to DPP," I told them. "It's not like we're going after the Golden Children tonight."

"But they're here," he murmured, and shifted the heavy bow he'd slung over his shoulder. "The three of you are outnumbered."

"They don't know where Tabitha lives..." I began, then caught myself. I couldn't be sure. If Tabitha's address was public, then the Golden Children, who'd grown up in the States, were surely savvy enough to find her information and track her down—and if that failed, there were magical alternatives.

"Shit," I muttered.

Wylan and Derat nodded, and Derat said, "I'll take the front door. Is it secured?"

"Probably not," I replied, and headed into the den to find Tabitha.

She was lying where I'd last seen her, sprawled on her stomach, and Jane was busy calling her name and patting her face, trying to rouse her. "Um...why is her hair blue?" Wylan quietly asked me.

"Potion did it. I don't know if she's aware, so maybe don't mention it, eh?" I whispered.

He nodded, then joined Jane by the couch and said, "Let me." She made space, albeit warily, and Wylan gave the patient's shoulder a strong shake. "Tabitha," he said, his normal baritone infused with an almost indescribable thread of authority. "Wake. Come on, open your eyes."

With a groan, she started to rouse, but Wylan kept at it. "You can't sleep here, it's not safe. Tabith—*oh*, sorry," he mumbled as she yelped at the force of his touch.

The combination of power and pain did the trick, and her eyelids fluttered as she blinked up at him. "Wha'chu doin' here?" she slurred.

He crouched beside her. "Rose saw what happened. You need to come with us."

"Ro..."

"*Hey*," I said, waving from over Wylan's broad shoulder. "It's going to be okay, Tabitha, we're going to get you some help. Stay put for a second, I brought pain potions," I said, digging in my bag for the vials, then found one and thrust it toward her. "Here we go. Can you sit up? Drink this, you'll feel better."

She allowed Wylan and Jane to assist her into a sitting position, but she refused the pain potion. "What'd they give me?"

"We don't know," I admitted. "Pop thinks it's novel."

"Then I shouldn't take anything else. Don't know cross-reactions."

I looked at Jane, who knew more about potions than I did. "Never seen a bad reaction to a pain potion," Jane told her. "Annie, even you could take them after Roulette, right?"

"Yup," said Annie, "they just didn't work as well. That green one's like high-octane Tylenol."

Tabitha stared up at her, unmoved. "You mean the one with *codeine*?"

"No, I...um..."

We weren't getting anywhere arguing potential potion interactions with a pharmacist. "It's okay, let the healers handle it," I told the others, and nudged Wylan aside to get in front of Tabitha. "Here's the deal," I said, gently taking her hands. "We need to get you to DPP. They'll be expecting you."

Annie grunted, but she didn't argue with me. "For how long?" she muttered.

"Pop wasn't sure," I replied, which seemed like the safest answer. "So, what we're going to do now," I said to Tabitha, "is pack a bag and close up the house. Guys, why don't you check the doors and windows?" I said to Derat and Wylan. "Jane, Annie, give me a hand."

With the three of us, we could have transported Tabitha to her bedroom by magical means, but I decided she'd had quite enough of magic already that night. Instead, I slung one of her arms around my shoulders, Annie took the other side, and Jane ran ahead of us to get the lights and doors.

Though Tabitha was obviously hurting and still somewhat out of it, she told us where to find her suitcase in the closet, then curled up in a knot on the bed and mumbled as needed to help us locate her things. In five minutes' time, we'd almost filled the bag with clothing and shoes—Annie, who'd been through this before, insisted on grabbing multiple seasons' worth—but as I was tossing Tabitha's small jewelry box into the suitcase, Wylan yelled, "We have company!"

"Golden Children or woo-woo brigade?" Jane called back.

"Don't know, not risking it with the four of you," he said, and I caught the lights dying as he and Derat hastily joined us. "Let's go. Are you ready?"

"I...guess," said Annie, giving the untouched bathroom a frustrated glance, then zipped the suitcase, threaded her arm through the plastic pull handle, and reached for Jane. "Babe, could you—"

Before she'd finished, Wylan had scooped Tabitha off the bed like a child, and Derat grabbed his wrist.

As the doorbell rang, Annie said, "DPP. Let me drive."

We landed in the parking deck beside the elevators. A pair of Interdiction agents leaving late froze in their tracks, then slid out of our way as Annie, dragging Tabitha's suitcase, hurried to punch the up button.

Officially, guests to the building were meant to be logged at the desk in the lobby, but we ignored that regulation and headed straight for the fifteenth floor, where the healers' suite and the quarantine wing were located. Wylan cradled Tabitha all the way upstairs, and he trailed Annie and me down the white tiled hallway until we reached a pair of sliding doors with a badge scanner in the middle, a half-dome of milky glass. I held my badge in place, and the glass flashed red as the doors opened for us. Behind them, the walls were pale blue, a distinction between quarantine and the rest of the medical floor—well, that, plus the locked doors.

At the end of the hall, we turned right and approached the first control station, a lockable booth behind thick windows. Two technicians were on duty, a gnome and a troll in black scrubs, a pair that might have been comically mismatched were I not so frazzled.

"Agent ti'Dana, Agent Humphr—" the gnome began, but Annie's name ended in a squeak as Wylan and Derat came around the corner. He swallowed hard, then continued. "Um…hello. The director said to expect you…"

By then, his companion had already unlocked the booth and emerged, ducking slightly to fit his massive frame through the doorway. "Here," he said to Wylan, extending his arms.

Wylan shook his head. "I've got her. Where to?"

The technician led us down a short hallway and through another set of locked doors—and there it was in all its glass-enclosed glory, the quarantine room. Set within a larger space with an observation desk and room for healers and technicians to maneuver, the quarantine room was designed like a summer camp cabin from hell. Two rows of twin beds faced each other from either side of an aisle, all visible from the desk. Anyone larger than a standard human would have to shove the beds together to get comfortable, and I had no idea whether any were strong enough for, say, a healthy centaur. The only part of the quarantine room with any privacy was the pair of multiperson bathrooms. I was pleased to see that some of the accoutrements from the Roulette victims' stay seemed to have lingered—the booth in the back for smokers, the projector for a television, and even a small coffee urn on the side counter, which a sorcerer technician was setting up. She looked toward the doorway at the commotion and stiffened, then hastily completed her work and left through the vestibule—without the decontaminating shower, I noticed.

"This way," said our escort, letting his colleague skirt our group, then ushered us into the quarantine room.

"Place gives me the willies," Annie muttered, as Wylan gently placed Tabitha on the nearest bed.

"You can step out," I offered, but she shot that suggestion down with a glare. Annie might have had a touch of residual trauma from her time in quarantine, but she was tough.

"*There* you are!" announced a muffled voice from outside our enclosure, and I caught a flash of swishing black lab coat as Vinla ti'Gata, the lead research healer on the Roulette team, strode into the room. She looked to be in her late twenties, a blonde, brown-eyed elf with two centuries' experience at DPP, and Annie, who'd been poked and prodded far too much by the researchers, tensed as she approached the vestibule. Since our last quarantine experience, someone had realized the utility of a speaker system, as Vinla picked up a black item that looked suspiciously like a CB radio's microphone, which was tethered to the wall with a coiled cord. She tapped a button on the wall panel, and the hum of an open line sounded within our enclosure. "Hi, sorry, have you been here long?" Vinla asked. "I was about to pack up for the night when the memo came from the director. And what do we have here?" she continued, peering at Tabitha.

"This is Tabitha Bradley," Annie shouted. "You're going to be on her case?"

Vinla winced, then nodded. "No need to yell—quarantine is miked. And all of us in the Roulette group are working on this. Getting the squad back together," she weakly joked. "Novel potion...*yikes.* I love an identification challenge, but not when the potion's already working. Are we sure it's novel?"

"So says Diriem," Annie replied.

The healer cut her eyes to me, and I nodded.

"All right, then. Wait there," she said, and headed for a wardrobe near the door. Quickly, she exchanged her coat for a black moon suit, checked the supplemental air supply, then let herself in.

"This isn't contagious," Jane protested. "She was given a potion, not a disease."

"Assume nothing, youngling. You'll live longer," Vinla replied, and approached the bed to see the patient up close. With a grunt, she turned to the troll who'd come in with us. "Let's do a blood draw and quick analysis, and—" She paused as Tabitha moaned. "Is she in pain?" she asked Annie. "And can she understand this? The director said the victim was human..."

"I understand," Tabitha muttered from the bed. "Not my first trip here."

"*Huh,*" said Vinla, and I wondered how often she saw daylight, or even a newscast. "That's convenient. Scale of one to ten, how bad is it?"

"Solid nine."

The healer swore in Low Elvish. "Okay, priorities. Let's get a pain potion going—"

"Drug interactions," Tabitha reminded her.

"We're going to monitor you," she promised. To the technician, she said, "Blood draw kit, neutralizer, pain potion...and you're not going anywhere. Be right back."

Jane, Derat, and Wylan watched warily as Vinla sealed herself in the vestibule and was showered with a green cleaning agent. "Is that really necessary?" Derat muttered.

"Protocol," the technician replied. "The whole point of quarantine is to keep whatever's in here from escaping, you know?"

"So...how badly will that stuff sting on the way out, do

you suppose?"

He blew out a long breath behind his tusks. "It doesn't hurt, but we're bound for decontamination after this."

"Come again?" said Wylan.

"Decontamination," the technician repeated. "Probably overkill in this particular instance, but again, protocol. A long shower, a broad-spectrum neutralizer, and then a little rest to make sure the neutralizer stays down."

The Hunter eyed him suspiciously.

To his credit, the technician didn't run, though he did retreat a pace. "The neutralizer hits hard," he explained. "It's nauseating."

"It's *awful*," I muttered, and Annie, who'd had her own fun in the decontamination suite with her fellows in Interdiction, groaned her agreement.

"But necessary," the technician insisted. "Look, in case whatever was given to your friend here is at all transmissible, we've been exposed. This is a matter of public safety."

Wylan looked down at Annie, his mouth tight. "You agree?"

She hesitated before answering. "Reluctantly. Sorry, hon. Please don't bolt."

"No one's bolting," he said, wrapping an arm around her shoulders. "And if you've been through this and survived, then I'm confident we'll be fine."

"Sorry," Tabitha whispered from the bed.

"You did nothing wrong," said Jane, carefully pushing Tabitha's blue braids from her face. "Don't worry. Just—oops, sorry," she mumbled as even her light touch made Tabitha yelp in pain.

Vinla hurried back, a tray of implements and bottles in her hands, and the vestibule doors opened with a warning siren to admit her. "Still hurting?" she asked Tabitha.

"Uh-huh."

"Okay. Let me draw blood, and then we'll see what we can do."

The technician helped hold Tabitha down, as the needle in the bend of her arm made her scream and jerk. But Vinla was skilled and hit the vein on the first try, and once the technician had bandaged the wound, she injected a pain potion into Tabitha's shoulder, followed by a shot of dark green liquid I knew all too well.

"Just wondering," I said, "but won't the neutralizer stop the pain potion from working?"

"The neutralizer is slower to act if given intramuscularly," Vinla replied. "With any luck, she'll start feeling some relief…at least for a while. I'm really sorry," she said to Tabitha, "but once this stuff takes hold, you'll probably be sick. I'll get a bucket from the bathroom."

"Or you could knock her out and let her sleep through this," Annie suggested. "That's what happened when I got stuck in here, anyway."

"Not exactly," said the healer. "We didn't give your group the neutralizer—there wasn't good data on how humans would react, and we didn't want to make matters worse, especially with fatalities among the exposed. Post-Roulette, we've got better data, and I don't see any reason why we can't try it now. I'm not especially hopeful, but it's worth the attempt."

"You could still sedate her," Annie pressed.

Vinla shook her head. "Not going to risk aspiration. How are we feeling?" she asked Tabitha. "Any relief yet?"

"A little," Tabitha managed.

"Good. Stay there, try to remain on your side, and I'll get that bucket for you."

Once Tabitha was equipped and the technician had placed a large bottle of water beside her bed, Vinla said, "All right, I need to get this sample to the lab. Everyone else, decon."

Jane looked anxiously at Tabitha, who'd uncurled slightly but seemed to be only marginally more comfortable. "One of us should stay—"

"Not unless you want to remain in quarantine," said the technician. "There's a time window on the neutralizer—the sooner, the better."

"I'll be fine," Tabitha told Jane, and gave her hand a weak squeeze. "You go."

"And if she's still hurting after the neutralizer, I'll sedate her," Vinla promised. "Right, cleaning spray, then down the hall. You know the rules."

We passed through the vestibule in groups of two, closing our eyes against the shower and holding our breath when a cleaning gas blew over us, then followed the grim-faced technician out of quarantine, past the elevators, and down the hall to meet our fate. Once we reached the decontamination area, the technician gestured toward three sets of double doors. "Men's room on the right, women's on the left, unisex down the hall. Take your pick," he said, and headed into the men's room.

"See you on the flip side," Annie muttered to Wylan and Derat, then helped me steer reluctant Jane into the women's room to get the party started.

CHAPTER 6

I'd had my share of unpleasant potions even in my few years in the Pactlands. The invisibility potion, kept in the standard field agent kit, was notorious: useful for a short period, followed by inevitable vomiting. The neutralizer used in the decontamination suite didn't have quite as violent a finish as the invisibility potion did, but it was disgusting. Dark green and thick as pond sludge, it went down with a taste I could only describe as the smell of hot garbage rendered into liquid form, and it left most drinkers nauseated for hours. Unfortunately, if you threw up too soon, you had to take another dose, so the three of us lay back in our terrycloth bathrobes on the recliners provided for the experience and prayed for our stomachs to chill out. With all of our clothing, jewelry, and other possessions having been sent for cleansing, it wasn't as if we could just up and leave, anyway—well, except Annie, who stuck with Jane and me, sipping a can of cherry seltzer for dear life.

"Y'all?" Jane mumbled as we neared the hour mark.

"Yeah?" I replied, wishing I could sleep.

"This shit doesn't happen at DOI."

"That's because your agents get brought over here for decon," said Annie. "You just haven't had the joy yet."

Jane groaned and closed her eyes. "Remind me to put in for a desk job, okay?"

Before I could respond, someone knocked at the outer door, then cracked it open but didn't enter. "Girls? Are you decent?" Pop called.

"Hey," I called back, not bothering to get out of my chair. If I didn't move, my guts were less inclined to invert themselves.

Pop risked a peek into the lounge, then let himself in and closed the door. "Sorry, this isn't entirely appropriate, but under the circumstances..." He took us in, frowning. "Oh, you don't look good."

"Why has no one developed an alternative to decon?" Jane grumbled. "So many research healers in this freaking place, and this is the best we can do?"

"It's an uncomfortable process, I'll grant you that," he said, and helped himself to a seltzer.

"Did Pateme call you?" I asked.

"He did," said Pop. "I told him this was unnecessary, incidentally, but I don't get a veto in matters of DPP policy. Anyway, I gave Yven the update. He sends his love and wants you to know your bed is waiting."

"Tell him it's going to be a while. I'd text him," I said, "but my phone's being cleaned."

"Again, unnecessary." Huffing a quiet sigh, Pop sank into an empty recliner. "How long until you're cleared to leave?"

Annie squinted at the clock on the wall. "Been about an hour, so we *can* go—if we throw up at this point, we don't have to re-dose. But experience suggests we're going to feel like shit until midnight or so. Have you checked on the guys?"

"Not yet," said Pop. "You're not overly concerned, are you? Wylan's a big boy."

"It's not Wylan I'm worried about," she replied, closing her eyes. "He doesn't even really get indigestion. But Derat's not so lucky, and...well." She raised one hand and let it flop back to the armrest. "Last time any of the boys come out with me for a suspected novel potion."

"By the way, while you're here," Jane interjected, "whichever of you had the bright idea to free the Golden Children needs to have their head examined, or at least their talent recertified. Someone's off their game."

"Noted," Pop said dryly.

"Who thought they wouldn't be dangerous, anyway?" Annie asked.

A soft grunt answered *that.*

"Come on," she wheedled, "who do we need to punch on Tabitha's behalf?"

"I'm afraid that's not information I'm at liberty to share," said Pop. "Besides, we all have off days. I've been wrong."

"About something like this?"

"No," he admitted after a moment's thought, "but that's not to say any farseer is ever one hundred percent accurate."

"Fine," said Jane. "Then answer me this: did you see this coming?"

"Bits and pieces, which only began solidifying in the last days."

Her brow furrowed. "What do you mean, bits and pieces? You saw the shit at Mystic Mountains go down?"

"Not until this afternoon. I saw Tabitha with blue hair once, a few weeks ago, but nothing of the context. More of a feeling, odd flashes of late…" He hesitated briefly, then spoke again, his voice lowered. "There are forces in play that are occupying much of my farsight's attention. Honestly, I thought it was a fluke that I saw Tabitha at all. Didn't know why she'd opted for that apparent dye job, but it wasn't any of my business."

That seemed to mollify Jane. "Any idea what she's been given? Rose said you thought it was novel."

Pop nodded. "And that's the best I can offer, truly. If I knew the potion, I'd have told Pateme. There's nothing to be gained by leaving Tabitha in quarantine to suffer if there's an easy antidote. Now, what about the other woman?" he asked. "The blonde with the pink in her hair—"

"Stephanie Love," Jane volunteered. "That's her store."

"*Ah.* So that's the notorious Stephanie," he murmured.

"I saw what the Golden Children did to her but not what happened after they left the premises. Any insight, Rosie? Pateme wants to know whether he should send a crew to retrieve her. I *told* him this isn't communicable, but…" He shrugged, muttering, "The man can get hung up on protocol."

"He's cautious," said Annie. "That's not a terrible thing…"

Pop didn't disagree, but since I knew he still hadn't entirely forgiven Pateme for kicking me out of the Pactlands that once on the chance that Yven would take the death draught, he didn't need to say a word for me to know where his thoughts had strayed.

"Let me see if I can find Stephanie," I told the others. "I think my stomach's calm enough for the moment."

"Are you certain?" said Pop. "We could ask someone else—Yacovi Hewt is in town, isn't he? If Pateme asked him, I don't think he'd mind a brief search."

"Dad's in Nashville this week," muttered Jane. "There's a homebrewers' conference this weekend, and he and his moonshiner buddies are having a get-together in advance."

"What are they doing, strategizing how to run from the IRS?" joked Annie.

"I think it's something to do with still optimization, but he was sketchy on the details. Told Con and me that we should have plausible deniability."

Considering the percentage of law enforcement around Ragged Gap that purchased Yacovi's very smooth yet very illegal wares, I didn't think he had to worry too much about his cop son-in-law, but better safe than sorry.

"I can manage," I said. "Just give me a few minutes…"

Closing my eyes, I focused on the sound of my breathing, tuning out the low voices in the room, then called to mind Stephanie's face and held it steadily before me until my inner eyes opened.

I was standing in a bedroom, a modest space with slate-colored walls and carpeting that had perhaps once been cream before time and traffic had pushed it closer to oatmeal. The centerpiece of the room was a pine four-poster bed with an honest-to-God crocheted canopy—presumably once white, now a dingy yellow. The bed was made with a matching crocheted coverlet, which had been pulled cockeyed along with the more substantial blankets beneath. Buried beneath them on the left side, curled in on herself like an overcooked shrimp, was Stephanie, whose hair was the whitest thing in the whole room. It lay snarled on the pale pink pillowcase, and Penny, she of the broom skirt, was smoothing it from Stephanie's sweaty forehead.

Many of the partygoers who'd been all over Katin had migrated to Stephanie's bedside, and judging by their hangdog expressions, they were waking up to the fact that they just might have been bamboozled. One woman emerged from the master bathroom with a wet washcloth in hand, and Penny began sponging off Stephanie, who moaned but didn't stir.

"Y'all think we should try some arnica?" the washcloth bearer asked. "It helps—"

"Not for this," said one of the men who'd been by the fire pit—Ernie, I recalled. He leaned against the dresser with his arms folded, staring tight-lipped down at Stephanie. "What's keeping Bitsy?"

"She lives on the other side of town," said Penny. "Wonder if she ran into anyone…"

An uncomfortable silence fell over the room for a moment, punctuated by the swishing of Stephanie's old ceiling fan.

"Katarina doesn't know where Bitsy lives, does she?" asked Ernie. "*I* sure never told her—"

"About the only thing you never told her," grumbled Penny.

"Do y'all really think that was her who drove by?" another woman asked.

An old, bald man in faded camo pants, who stood by the door, nodded. "Going way too slowly to be a normal driver, and I bet she knows damn well where Stephanie lives. Guess all our cars out there spooked her, but…" He turned and called down the hallway, "Anything, y'all?"

"Just Bitsy!" another man hollered back. "She's pulling up."

"All right, well, keep alert, and keep your guns close." To the bedroom crowd, he muttered, "Can't believe you morons were ready to welcome that bitch back. Why did no one *shoot*?"

"Because we don't all go around expecting violence, Jerry," Penny said reprovingly. "Especially not at a place like Mystic Mountains…"

"Translation: not a one of you was armed," he snapped. "Least Ernie had sense enough to call me. Shit," he muttered, the profanity rendered polysyllabic by his thick drawl. "Here's the plan: we keep watch here all night and shoot anything that ain't one of us but tries to come in."

"Or we could call the law," Washcloth Woman suggested. "Tell the cops someone's stalking Stephanie—"

Jerry cut her off with a snort. "You think that'll do any fucking good? Whatever else Katarina is, she's the real deal, and I'm not banking on the PD and their peashooters." Giving the others a sour look, she said, "I ain't the only one here who lost *days* the last time she was around. What the hell got into you numbskulls?"

"You don't have to be mean," Penny protested.

"You don't have to be stupid," he retorted. "If Katarina meant no harm, then Fortune wouldn't have run her out of town."

"Oh, so you trust *Jane*," Penny countered with a disdainful sniff. "That snobby little—"

"Fortune saved my baby girl when her no-account husband was using her as a punching bag," Jerry interrupted, his voice low with warning. "Y'all don't have to like her, but you ain't going to speak ill of her with me here. Got it?"

"It's a free country," Washcloth Woman began, then shrank beneath the glare Jerry shot her.

"Sure is," he said. "Like I tell y'all every Veterans Day, you're welcome. But look, I've seen some shit. I don't know what the fuck Fortune really is, if she's a witch or what, but she's a good neighbor, and Stephanie swears she saved our asses. Y'all think Stephanie would lie about that, after all the crap she's said about Fortune over the years?"

A few around the bed mumbled in the negative.

"Then why the *fuck* did you morons think Katarina was up to anything good tonight?" Jerry demanded. "Swear to God, some of y'all are too dumb to live. Did your mamas drop y'all on your heads?"

"That's not helpful," Penny icily replied.

Before she and Jerry could worsen their spat, I heard the front door open, and in jogged a petite woman with a head of red corkscrew curls, another person I recognized from the fire pit. "Here you go," she said, thrusting a Ziploc baggie toward Penny. "Left over from my gallbladder surgery last fall. It should still be pretty potent."

Penny pulled a pair of pill bottles from the bag and read the labels. "Oxy and Ambien?"

"Give her a painkiller, then let her sleep," said the redhead—Bitsy, I assumed. "Worked like a charm for me."

But Penny hesitated. "Should we call someone first? I'm not sure we should be giving Stephanie *this* without a doctor weighing in…"

"Who'd you want to call?" asked Ernie. "No doctor's going to okay using someone else's meds, and Tabitha…"

He fell silent, but Jerry perked. "That's not a bad idea, get the pharmacist on the phone. Did she not come to the party?"

The bedside crew exchanged glances, and Penny cleared her throat. "Katarina got her, too."

"*What?*" Jerry yelped.

"Yeah. Whatever she stuck Stephanie with, Tabitha got a dose. She was going home to rest—"

But Jerry was already cussing a blue streak and marching for the door. "You two, with me!" I heard him call. "We're going to see about Tabitha. Get your guns."

Ernie ran after him. "Hey, wait now, we need y'all here—"

"Is *anyone* looking after Tabitha?" Jerry barked. "Does Katarina know where she lives?"

The best Ernie could do was stammer, and the old man slammed the door behind him as he departed.

After another moment's silence, Penny opened the pill bottles. "Someone get me a glass of water. Stephanie, hon, wake up. You've got to take some medicine."

I left then, though I didn't particularly want to; the chance to ignore my physical body and its nausea was a perk of farsight. "Stephanie's home, and she's got babysitters," I announced. "Some with guns. Sounds like the Golden Children made a drive-by but got scared off by the number of cars at Stephanie's place. Uh…some old dude named Jerry is heading to Tabitha's with a couple others to check on her. He's *pissed* that no one accompanied her home. Also, he's a fan of yours, Jane."

She chuckled softly. "Jerry's a codger, but he's all right. What do we do about Tabitha's house? Car's in the driveway, no one's home."

"There's not much we can do tonight," said Pop, "unless you'd like to have Wylan waiting for them to explain the situation, which I can't imagine would go well."

While Wylan was impervious to bullets, he claimed they stung. Besides, I didn't want to be responsible for giving Jerry a heart attack.

"They'll probably assume Katin got her," said Jane.

"We can deal with that later," muttered Annie. "And you said there's folks with guns at Stephanie's place, Rose?"

"Yep."

"So, maybe a pickup wouldn't be ideal tonight. We'd have to knock everyone out…"

"How's Stephanie?" Jane asked.

"In pain," I said. "They were giving her Oxy when I left. Ambien, too."

"Good shit," said Annie approvingly.

Pop grunted. "Not ideal for a novel potion, but...well, one problem at a time. She should be secure enough for the night."

"Especially if I can find Katin's hiding place," I added, shifting in my recliner. "If I start tracking her now, maybe we can get a location on her by dawn. Even if she's driving around, she's got to hole up eventually, and *someone's* babysitting the Golden Children's kids. If Laws could be on standby for retrieval—"

"Wait."

I glanced quizzically at Pop. "What for?"

"We don't want to bring them in yet."

"Why not?" Jane protested. "They're a danger to my hometown—"

"But they're not acting alone," he said in a low, quiet voice that tolerated no argument. "This isn't merely the Golden Children at play. They're part of it, certainly, but not the root."

"You've got to kill all the hydra's heads," Annie murmured.

Pop nodded. "Something like that."

"Then what are we dealing with?" asked Jane. "Give Rose the names, let her find them, *boom*..."

"Unfortunately, this will take a more delicate touch. Rosie, if you can, find Katin and her fellows, and keep an eye on them. I want to know where they're hiding and whether they'll try to run. But for now," he said, pulling his phone from his pocket and glancing at the screen, "Pateme wants to speak with you as soon as you're confident that you can avoid being sick in his office. Are you up to it, or shall I make your excuses?"

I smirked. "Pateme doesn't want to join the party in the ladies' lounge?"

"That's a firm *no*, my dear, and I should probably be on my way before anyone gets the wrong impression." He stood from his recliner, took another sip of seltzer, and tossed the can into the garbage. "Well? Do you need a hand to get upstairs?"

"Tell him I'm on my way," I grumped, abandoning my comfortable chair, and paused for a moment to be sure that my stomach was feeling cooperative before I followed Pop into the hall, padding along in my DPP bathrobe and gripper socks.

Once we'd reached the elevators and were clearly alone, he quietly said, "I know you want to haul in Katin and her people. Don't let Pateme or Kabno do it yet."

"Can you give me anything concrete?" I whispered.

"No. I need you to trust me, Rosie."

"Could you, say, slip something to Jane that just happens to reach my ears?"

His mouth quirked. "Do you truly believe that's how DOI operates?"

"I mean…maybe?"

Pop sighed. "Say the word, little one, and you'll have a job. You could see for yourself that way."

"But that smacks of nepotism," I teased as the descending elevator announced its arrival.

"*Please*," said Pop, stepping aboard. "And working for Pateme doesn't?"

He had a point, I acknowledged, as I climbed into the elevator heading to the top floor. Of the three most prominent agencies in the Pactlands, I was kin to the directors of two. Perhaps I should have tried to work my way into Laws to cut off any whispers that I was receiving preferential treatment, but frankly, I *was*. People my age—Annie's age, certainly Jane's age—were meant to be in school, end of discussion. All of the East Branch survivors were attending North Lake to make up for lost time. But the three of us, adults by every American metric, even business owners, had been granted dispensation to work and remedial tutoring through our agencies. Annie, who couldn't cast to save her life, needed to know only the rudiments of how magic worked, plus a ton about the plants and other potion ingredients DPP regulated. Jane, who'd received a decent if incomplete sorcerer's education from her father, had only patchy spots to cover. As for me, however, I worked as hard with my tutors as I did running down suspects with farsight for DPP and anyone else who came knocking. While I'd come a *very* long way in only a few years, I knew damn well that anyone my age in school would be able to run rings around me in magical theory, Pactlands history, cultural studies, and a dozen other topics useful to the well-schooled Pactlander. Pop and Pateme knew my shortcomings, but they'd opted to focus on practical skills and let me pick up the rest piecemeal—and considering that my practical education included tidbits like creating fireballs, that was *fine* by me.

The elevator chimed when it reached the twentieth floor, the most opulent in the building. Regulatory's floors were fine, and Interdiction leaned toward the utilitarian, but for the executive and administrative heads of the agency, something a touch nicer was in order. My great-great-uncle wasn't a flashy man, but he knew quality...and on occasion, he liked a crystal chandelier as much as the next guy with a decorating budget.

As befit the director, Pateme had one of the corner offices, which put my spacious room on the nineteenth floor to shame. Floor-to-ceiling windows, a beautiful wooden desk on carved feet, plush guest chairs that looked practically new, a personal tea bar with a dozen loose-leaf varieties in glass jars—Pateme's office was lovely and might have been deemed immaculate if not for the bookcase cluttered with reference manuals, treatises, brewing guides, and journals he'd read once and squirreled away for later perusal.

Judging by his robe, a gorgeous piece in spring-weight green silk that probably cost a trainee agent's monthly salary, he had yet to go home for the evening, though he'd unbuttoned his brown shirtsleeves and rolled them nearly to his elbows, the only indication that he was somewhat off the clock. "Sit, Rosie," he ordered, pointing to one of the blue guest chairs, then placed his small trash can beside me as he headed to the tea bar.

"I'm feeling better," I fibbed.

"While I *can* remove vomit from the rug, I'd rather not," he replied, and began measuring leaves into a filter bag while the water in the kettle came to a boil. He assembled the brew, added a sugar cube, and brought the white ceramic mug to me. "Here, this won't hurt."

I cautiously sniffed the steam. Mint.

"It's just tea?" I asked.

"A tisane, technically," he replied, using the English term, "but yes. If that doesn't settle well, I also have a ginger blend, but the mint is a less aggressive starting point."

The tea wasn't as sweet as I usually took mine, but considering the neutralizer still hard at work, that wasn't a bad thing. I tucked my bathrobe around my knees and sipped, enjoying the comforting warmth for a moment as Pateme settled into the chair beside me.

"I'm sorry you're going through decon," he said as I drank. "Never a fun experience. Now, I hate to make your life more complicated while you're suffering, but I need details."

"What do you want to know?" I asked, cradling the mug in my hands.

"Let's start with everything," he replied, faintly grinning. "If it helps narrow your focus, I'm sending a team to the attack site tonight. Gentle Breeze is making the calls and selecting people, so while she's strategizing, what can you tell us?"

I closed my eyes, trying to replay what I'd witnessed. "The attack was in Ragged Gap. Do you have any familiarity with the place?"

"Just for Jane and Connor's wedding. I stopped by

Yacovi's house the day before."

"*Right*," I sighed. "Okay, uh...so, Ragged Gap is in a valley, yeah? Yacovi lives up on one of the surrounding hills, but the downtown area, so to speak, is in the valley."

"What do you mean, 'so to speak'?"

"Calling it 'downtown' is a stretch," I explained. "If there are a thousand people living in Ragged Gap, I'll be shocked. The downtown area is just a few blocks of shops and restaurants, a town square, a couple old churches...an overpriced gas station," I added, reviewing the layout with my mind's eye. "Mystic Mountains is the attack site. It fronts the town square, but if I were you, I'd approach from the rear of the building."

"Oh?" asked Pateme.

I nodded. "There's a parking lot. Unless someone stuck around to clean up, you'll find a maypole and a fire pit, and the back door's right there. *Probably* unlocked, but I can't guarantee it."

"Not a problem. What's the camera situation?"

"Per Jane, Mystic Mountains has none because Stephanie's weird about that. Uh, Stephanie Love, the owner. She's the other person who was dosed tonight."

"Where is she?"

"Home, being looked after. She's got friends with guns on the property, since apparently, the Golden Children are out cruising. Folks are spooked. If you're set on bringing her in, you'll probably have to use knock-out, and there's a crowd to deal with."

"Noted," he murmured. "As long as she's being monitored, she can wait. Tell me about the store layout."

I sipped, buying time while I assembled my thoughts. "It's two-story, but I've never been upstairs. All the activity seems to be on the ground level. Merchandise in the front, a big check-out desk about midway back, and in the rear, there's a multipurpose space on one side and a café area on the other. It's not huge." Recalling my first visit to the town, I said, "Yven and Pars have been to Ragged Gap. So has Annie—"

"But she's out of commission for the rest of the night," said Pateme. "Who else?"

"Liogh Birrid, I think, if you want to make this a multi-agency affair."

"Not yet. Pars Mera, you said?"

"Yes, sir."

"Mm. I suspect Gentle Breeze has already been in touch with the boy, but that's good to know."

Pars, a father of four who'd recently celebrated his fifty-eighth birthday, wasn't what I'd think of as a "boy," but age became relative *really* quickly when you were dealing with immortals, and Pateme had been around since the late fifteenth century. The fact that Yven was nearly fifty-eight and I was freshly thirty-one was one of the few facets of our impending wedding that Calien hadn't seen fit to criticize.

"And this store's wares?" Pateme asked. "Anything dangerous?"

"It's a metaphysical shop," I told him. "Like, uh…geodes, polished rocks, drums, books, some jewelry…there's an incense bar…honestly, I think the only thing dangerous in there is a handful of ceremonial daggers, and they're probably not the sharpest."

His brow furrowed. "Dare I ask?"

"That's a question for Tabitha. I know I'm a Pisces, and that's about as far down that road as I go."

As Pateme methodically prodded for details, I reviewed with him what I'd seen that night. After a time, as he refreshed my tea, he said, "The team driving out there will try to get traces of any and all potions out of the floor for analysis. The floor was…carpeted?" he asked hopefully.

"Wooden," I replied, shaking my head. "Is that going to be a problem?"

"Marginally more complicated but not impossible. Now, this potion that you think Tabitha made boil—tell me about it. It wasn't the same one that she was injected with?"

I waited until he'd returned with my mug and took a long sip. Mint wasn't magical, but my stomach approved. "No, definitely not. The one they gave to Tabitha and Stephanie was...kind of like an oil slick," I said, rolling my eyes to the ceiling as if I could see it painted above me. "Pale pinks, purples, blues, a silvery base—iridescent. I haven't seen one like it. The one in the tubes they were going to give the others was dark purple. Katin told them they'd need to drink two doses, one tonight and one tomorrow, to get the full effect, but I think that was bullshit. My best guess is Velvet Leash."

"Why do you think so?" he asked, studying my expression, and I wondered whether this conversation would end up on my annual performance evaluation.

"The color, first of all. There aren't that many drinkable dark purple potions."

"But there *are* others."

"Sure, but think about Katin's purpose. That whole 'Oil of Life' business ended with Velvet Leash so she could make herself a workforce. The first two concoctions she sold them had Fingerflash in the mix so they'd be tricked into thinking they were getting power, and it was growing. They had no reason not to trust her when she offered them Velvet Leash, so they took it willingly, and then they fell under her control."

Pateme, who'd opted for a bracing cup of black assam, nodded between sips. "Mm-hmm."

"This time around, she comes back, apologizes for having to run away from mean old Jane, and promises them power again. She had a number of them on the hook—I could see it in their faces."

"I thought they'd been warned..."

"According to Jane, Stephanie came around and finally told them that Katin was no good, but I don't think some of her people ever truly believed it."

His eyes narrowed. "Do they not understand that they

lost time? And didn't some of them have partial memories of what happened once they were with Katin?"

I shrugged. "Remember who you're dealing with. They want power, and it's always been out of their reach. Katin's products were the closest they ever came."

"Fingerflash is a glorified party trick."

"Not if you're human," I reminded him. "Come on, you wake up one morning, and suddenly, you can make your fingertips glow on command? That's *impossible.* Amazing. And these folks have probably been laughed at a little all their lives. Witchcraft and crystal healing and reiki and auras and stuff—that's fringe, see? But now they're gaining power, and they're *right.* So, not only is this promised power something beyond their wildest dreams, but it's also vindication. Some of them are clinging to it, I guess," I said, and drank. "No one wants to admit that they've been taken for a fool, you know?"

But Pateme remained perplexed. "It was just Fingerflash, yes? Nothing else? Why would they imagine that everything would change with the third dose?"

"Because Katin demonstrated her power for them, remember? Humans can't do magic, here's one who can, ergo, power can be acquired if you do what she did." I paused, thinking, then said, "You don't remember a time before you could cast, do you?"

He smiled slightly over his mug. "It's been quite a few years. No."

"Okay, well, *I do.* And that first moment when it clicks and the world changes in some subtle way, and *you* did it...that's insane. It's overwhelming. Ask Yven if you don't believe me, but I'm pretty sure I giggled for a solid five minutes because the alternative was hyperventilation and running around the house. So...I can't entirely blame the Mystic Mountains folks," I said. "Katin lied to their faces, but she made it convincing enough that they were desperate to believe her. And so, seeing as she got a warm welcome at the shop tonight, why not deploy Velvet Leash again when she had people on hand willing to take it?"

"It makes sense," Pateme allowed, "but for the attack."

He had a point. Katin could have walked into the store that night, passed out tubes of Velvet Leash like shots at a bachelorette party, and had at least half a dozen people under her control within days. Why had she gone after Stephanie and Tabitha first? Revenge? Stephanie hadn't done anything to her the last time, so had Katin turned on the woman when Stephanie found a bit of spine?

"Katin told everyone that she was giving Tabitha and Stephanie real power," I said, mentally reviewing the footage. "But then the potion obviously hurt them, and folks got scared, and Katin went into 'happy saleswoman' mode…" Frowning at Pateme, I said, "I don't think Katin knew what that first potion was going to do. Or maybe she thought she did, but it didn't work right. People started backing away. She could have lost her chance…well," I amended, "she did lose it once the potions started boiling and exploding, but I bet she wasn't expecting *that*, either."

"And she's only had her freedom for two weeks," Pateme pointed out. "So, where did this novel potion come from? Don't tell me she developed it—there are plenty of practical skills taught on the penal farms, but brewing isn't one of them."

"She's had time to think about it…"

"But I strongly suspect she lacks the theoretical background. Oh, I'm sure she can follow a recipe," he clarified, "but so much experimental brewing ends in explosions or worse. How did she do it? Where did she get the ingredients, the equipment?" He leaned back against his chair and drank his tea in silence for a moment, contemplating the night-darkened city through the windows, then asked, "Can you tell me whether the Golden Children are still in the area?"

"Other than the possible drive-bys at Tabitha's and Stephanie's, I don't know," I admitted, "but I'd assume they're close. There were only six at Mystic Mountains, meaning the rest of the group is holed up somewhere with all their kids."

"Mm. And by now, Diriem has told you not to help me bring them in quite yet, correct?"

I froze, trying to blank my face, but Pateme wasn't a novice. "Don't worry, little one," he murmured, "he already warned me."

"Do you…want to bring them in tonight?" I hesitantly asked.

To my surprise, he shook his head. "No. It's premature."

"So, you agree with Pop?"

"Diriem's reasons are his own, and he has not deigned to share them with me," replied Pateme with a snort. "I won't ask what he's told you—you're in an awkward enough position as it is. But coming at this from an angle of practicality, it's too early to round up the Golden Children."

"Why's that?" I asked.

He flashed a brief, predatory smile. "Because to this point, all they've done is assault humans. If we want to make a case for terrorism as we did with the late, unfortunate Goobers," he continued, pronouncing the rogue sorcerer's nickname as if it pained him to do so, "then we need more evidence. Something Laws can use. With that in mind, here are your instructions," he said, holding my gaze. "Find Katin and the Golden Children. Monitor them. I want a daily dossier, understood?"

"Can do," I said, "assuming they're unprotected." After putting my mug on an end table and pushing myself from my chair, I paused for a second to be sure my stomach was feeling merciful, then nodded to Pateme. "I'll get to work."

"Tell Yven to stay close tonight, hmm? If he's late in the morning, I won't count it against him."

"I would, but I won't be seeing him," I said, and smiled tautly. "Tabitha's stuck in quarantine. Surely someone down there can drag a couch into the viewing room so I can babysit her."

He frowned. "There's staff on duty with English fluency, and I *know* she's conversant in Pactish—"

"She's alone, she was in pain when I left her, and she's going to be scared when she wakes," I said. "She should have a familiar face around, yeah? I can trance from there."

His mouth tightened, but he gave me a curt nod. "Just don't exhaust yourself to the point that Diriem steps in. I can't afford to have my one farseer out of commission right now."

"Aw," I teased, heading for the door, "you do care."

"I never said I didn't, Rosie," he protested. "And there's a decent couch in the technicians' break room. I trust that you can float it where you want it."

CHAPTER 7

Pateme was right—the couch was decent, but nothing more. I caught naps between trance sessions, but by five Thursday morning, I hadn't seen more than Katin continuing to drive around wooded backroads. Three problems impeded my search. First, I didn't know the geography on an intimate level so as to pinpoint where she was going. I *assumed* Katin was still near Ragged Gap only because I hadn't any signs indicating otherwise. Jane might have been able to tell me whether Katin had left the county, but I couldn't exactly loop her in and share my trance. Second, of all the Golden Children, Katin's was the face I knew best, and I wanted to get copies of the others' dossiers from Laws to help me focus on them. And third...well, I was nauseated from the neutralizers until the early morning, and after two or so, I finally caught a couple hours of deep sleep before waking to trance again.

When Tabitha began to stir, I'd just seen Katin at an Exxon station, heading for the bathroom, and I'd decided to retreat for a bit. Sipping a cup of strong coffee from the technicians' old pot—apparently, they liked their coffee concentrated enough to cause heart palpitations—I walked over to the glass wall around quarantine and watched as Tabitha opened her eyes and groaned.

I plucked the microphone from its holster on the wall and opened the line. "Morning," I said. "How're you feeling?"

"Been better," Tabitha croaked, but managed to sit up in bed and rub her face. "What happened?" After blinking at her surroundings, she spotted me outside the thick glass, her expression quickly edging toward panic. "*Rose*?"

"It's okay, you're safe," I insisted, coming as close as the mic's cord and the glass would permit. "You're in quarantine at DPP, remember? We brought you over last night."

She stared at me for a moment longer, and then her face relaxed as her memory cleared. "*Right*," she sighed. "That's why I feel like shit."

"Probably the neutralizer they gave you. I had to take it, too. Leaves you queasy as hell."

"No, I'm not queasy…"

"Are you hurting? You were in a lot of pain when we got to you."

Tabitha paused, taking stock. "I'm hurting a little," she replied, "but I've had worse discomfort the morning after a long hike. This is nothing like it was. I just feel…I don't know, strange," she finished lamely, flopping one hand onto the covers. "Do they know what I got stuck with?"

"Not yet—or if they do, they haven't told me," I said. "I overnighted in here, and I haven't heard any triumphant commotion from the techs, so…probably not."

"Great," she muttered. "Guess I'm not going home today, eh?"

"I wouldn't count on it. But I texted Yacovi after I got my phone back," I said, pointing to the small pile of my belongings on the floor. I'd put my clothes on after that delivery and used the borrowed bathrobe as a makeshift blanket. "He's aware of what happened, and he said he'd put a note on your shop this morning saying you're sick."

Tabitha flashed a half smile. "He's good people."

"No complaints here. So," I asked, "are you hungry? Does anything sound good? There should be coffee and water on the counter over there," I added, pointing out the drinks, "but if one of the techs brewed the coffee, you might want to *cut* it."

"High octane?"

I grimaced. "And burned. But Mangia Due's open by now, and I'm happy to put in an order. What's your preference? Pastry, bagel, something more substantial? They do a good bacon, egg, and cheese sandwich off-menu."

"Ooh." She paused, her face scrunched in thought, then said, "That sounds great, actually. I didn't eat much before the party last night, and once I got there, it was nothing but flower crowns until Katin showed up..."

By then, I'd pulled out my phone. Mangia Due had launched an app a few months prior, and it was a thing of beauty for the chronically underslept in the agency. "Let's get two of those sandwiches, then," I said, making a note in the custom entry, "and...what else?"

"Hash browns?" she asked hopefully.

"Not on the menu—they're not a big thing here. But there's this sweet side dish...take something like gnocchi, deep-fry them, toss them with powdered sugar, and add a warm berry compote on the side."

She regarded me dubiously. "*Gnocchi*?"

"It's something in the gnocchi family. I don't know what's in the dough, but they're delicious."

"All right, I'm game. And something with espresso?"

"Naturally. How many shots were we thinking?"

"Double-shot latte a possibility?"

"Yup." I input the rest of our order and scheduled it for immediate pickup, then waited for the app to give me a total. The sandwiches had to go to one of the staff for approval, and while I'd never been denied, it always took a minute in the busy café.

"Excuse me just a second," said Tabitha, pushing herself off her rumpled bed. "Uh..."

I pointed to the pair of bathrooms on the other side of quarantine. "Right there. The part that *doesn't* have glass walls."

"Small mercies," she said, chuckling, and shuffled away.

About three seconds after Tabitha hit the bathroom, I heard a piercing scream so loud that the speakers on my side of the room wailed. "Tabitha?" I demanded, clinging to the microphone. "Are you okay? What happened?"

She stomped out of the bathroom, now fully awake, and jabbed her index fingers toward her head. "Why the fuck is my hair *blue*?"

"Oh...crap," I muttered. "Guess you didn't notice that last night..."

"No, I sure as shit did *not*."

Suddenly, I was grateful for the wall separating us. Judging by the look on her face, Tabitha was ready to make someone pay, and I didn't want to risk that. "It happened shortly after you were injected," I explained. "You went blue, Stephanie went white."

"It's not just this!" she continued, tugging at her braids. "Look at my arms! My eyebrows! My freaking *eyelashes*, Rose!"

"I know—"

"How do I fix this? I can't go around looking like a freak of nature!"

In that moment, I wished Annie had spent the night—surely she would have known what to say. Instead, I offered Tabitha the best comfort I could: "The old Roulette team is working on your case. They're some of the best in the agency, and DPP's research side is second to nothing in the private sector. But they don't have answers, and *I* don't have answers, so...I'm really sorry, but it's going to be blue for a bit."

Huffing a sigh, Tabitha stormed back to the bathroom.

"I don't think it's going to wash out," I called after her.

"Yeah, but I've still got to pee," came her exasperated response.

My phone chimed with the payment screen from Mangia Due, and I completed the transaction while waiting for Tabitha to reappear. When she did, she looked no happier.

"It's blue *everywhere*?" I guessed.

"Carpet matches the curtains," she said through a fake smile. "Lucky me!"

"God, I'm sorry," I said, leaning against the glass. "Look, worst-case scenario, you don't have to have actual talent to use masking jewelry. We'll get you a pendant, ring, whatever you need. Have you looking like yourself again in no time."

Relief smoothed some of the tightness of her expression. "Really?"

I nodded. "My great-uncle has the keys to the vault of possibly the best jewelry store in the Pactlands. Plenty of masking pieces in that collection. He helped Annie, and I can't imagine that he wouldn't hook you up…once you're cleared, I mean."

Tabitha's face fell. "How long will *that* take?"

"Don't know. That's a question for the team here. But they're going to be monitoring you pretty closely at first—you know, one of the fun features of Roulette was that it screwed up almost every other potion and magical item Maya and Annie tried to use. Annie had some *horrible* side effects, and no one wants that for you. So, uh…try to chill for now," I said. "I'm going to go pick up breakfast, and I'll be right back."

I hung up the microphone, grabbed my purse, and headed for the exit. Before I left, I looked over my shoulder and found Tabitha staring after me as if I were walking out of prison and leaving her to rot in solitary.

Of course, for her at that moment, the comparison wasn't far off.

It took about fifteen minutes for me to go down to the lobby, wait for our food, and return to quarantine, and Tabitha had kept herself busy in my absence. She'd made her bed, redone her ponytail, and pulled clean clothes from the suitcase we'd hastily packed, though she'd left her shoes off. As I triggered the microphone, she said, "There's a bin of toiletries in here. Thanks for grabbing my stuff last night…you didn't raid my bathroom, did you?"

"Sorry, we got interrupted before we could. We think the Golden Children made a drive-by."

She grimaced, then nodded to the oversized paper sack in the crook of my arm. "That's two breakfasts around here, huh?"

"Not exactly," I replied, and having figured out how to leave the mic on without holding it, I docked it to begin unpacking. "The Mangia crew wanted to know what I was doing here so early, and I mentioned you were in quarantine, so they sent up"—I peered into the bag—"looks like a good chunk of the day-old discount stash."

"Nice of them," said Tabitha.

"I think Maya told them some horror stories about her time in here. Anyway, they hope you feel better soon, and if you need more coffee during business hours, it's on the house."

Tales of quarantine's resident brewmaster and the burned coffee had apparently reached the lobby.

I put my things in a small pile, then located the drawer in the quarantine wall—another addition since the Roulette days—and put Tabitha's goodies inside. When I closed the drawer, my side sealed, and the drawer popped open on her end for retrieval. She lined up her food and snacks on the counter, then plopped onto a nearby bed and sipped her coffee. "Not bad at all."

"Korek was born to work an espresso machine," I said, pulling up a chair on the other side of the glass. "I've never even seen him use the cheat sheets Maya put together for Annie."

With the microphone on, our conversation was no more difficult than it would have been using a pair of phones on speaker mode—useful, as we rediscovered our appetites within a couple of bites, and I needed both hands to manage my oversized breakfast sandwich. Tabitha deemed the sweet gnocchi worth getting again, and as she was wiping the grease from her sandwich on a wad of paper napkins, she looked past me and sat up straighter. I turned, mouth full, and quickly swallowed as Enva Orafer walked in, escorted by a technician. I knew the detective relatively well, as she led the team at DOL that liaised with DPP—that, and almost dying by siren together tends to bond folks. She wasn't quite middle-aged for a sorcerer, though she looked a few decades younger, with flawless dark skin and a short Afro that never seemed to have a hair out of place. As detectives went, she was highly respected down the street. Her only real handicap that I knew of was her severe allergy to an ingredient in the language potion. She'd taken it once, early in her career, to get English prior to an assignment in Kentucky, and it had almost killed her. Enva was the only seasoned bilingual agent I'd met, as most acquired a variety of languages as their suspects' preferences dictated. She wore a burnt orange robe over a crisp white blouse and black pants, looking far more presentable than either of us did that morning.

"Thank you," she said as the technician left, then started toward us, a purple tote bag slung over her shoulder. "Good morning," she said in her accented English, raising a hand to Tabitha. "Nice to see you again."

"Circumstances could be better," Tabitha replied, but she grinned. "What's up, Detective? Did they rope you into this mess, too?"

Enva spread her hands. "Potion crimes are my turf, and my director is *not* a happy woman. I told her I'd be here first thing."

A wise move, I thought. Kabno might be small, but gnomes were incredibly strong for their size, and most of DOL knew better than to cross her.

"Director ti'Tam called my boss last night to fill her in," Enva explained, "and since I worked on the Roulette case, I got tapped."

"Not your first 'weird potion' rodeo, huh?" said Tabitha.

She paused, parsing that, then chuckled. "Exactly.

They're feeding you okay?"

Tabitha nodded. "Rose went downstairs for grub. I've got some cookies and stuff in here if you're hungry…"

"Thanks, but once it's in quarantine, it's not supposed to leave."

"*Right*," she muttered, and put her coffee on the floor. "Did they tell y'all how long I'm going to be in this box?"

"No, and that's a question for DPP," Enva replied. "We don't have any say. But, uh, having spent a week in quarantine myself," she continued, opening her bag, "I thought you might need some of these."

I watched with interest as Enva loaded a selection of bottles, a pair of combs, a pack of tiny elastics, and a satin bonnet into the drawer and sent them through. Tabitha glanced at the labels as she pulled them free, then looked back at Enva, her expression softening. "This is too much. You didn't have to—"

"It's no trouble," Enva assured her. "The toothpaste and such in there is perfectly serviceable, but the shampoo…ugh. I was a dry, frizzy *disaster* when they let me out. All of that is highly moisturizing," she said, pointing to the largest bottles, "and there's a leave-in conditioner, that's an oil I like, that spray bottle is a nice moisturizer…I don't know when you're planning to wash, but if there's something particular you need, let me know, and I'll do my best."

"I'll pay you back—" Tabitha began.

"Absolutely not. After everything you did for Taug, and our counselors, and DOL more generally—shoot, that's nothing, lady. No reason to ruin your hair just because you're stuck in here."

She pointed to her braids. "Any chance of dye?"

"If the staff here wouldn't kill me, I'd sneak it in," said Enva, "but I think they want you as natural as possible for now to watch for side effects. It's…not a bad shade of blue."

Tabitha gave her a *look* through the glass.

"I know, I get it. If it makes you feel any better, I dyed mine bright pink for my hundredth birthday, and *that* was a mistake. Looked like cotton candy, know what I'm saying?" Shaking her head at the folly of her more youthful self, Enva pulled a notepad, a pen, and a small voice recorder from the tote and asked, "Would you mind giving me your recollection of events last night? The counselors will be ever so grateful down the line if I can get a statement from you while things are fresh."

"Sure," said Tabitha, tucking one foot beneath her. "But be straight with me: y'all aren't going to prosecute Katin's crew for what they did last night." When Enva hesitated, Tabitha said, "Y'all don't have jurisdiction. I saw how things went down with East Branch—folks can attack humans with impunity as long as it's all done outside of the Pactlands, yeah?"

"We're in a difficult position," the detective admitted, "but I'm not giving up hope. The guy who came up with Roulette did it outside in an unlicensed brewing facility, and yes, he only attacked humans, but we were preparing to go forward on a couple of theories. One, if there'd been any indication that he planned to release the potion here, we'd have tried him for terrorism. But there's also a catch-all: if one of our citizens does something outrageous out there, we can call it a threat to the safety of the Pactlands. I've seen that charge stick before."

Tabitha picked up her coffee and considered that as she drank. "And that was the problem with prosecuting the Golden Children: they weren't citizens."

"Exactly. Or they didn't claim citizenship. You ask me, a child born to two of our citizens has citizenship by default, but what do I know?" said Enva, rolling her eyes.

"And we're right back in that position," Tabitha replied. "Non-citizens attacking non-citizens in Georgia."

"For the moment, yes," Enva admitted, "but this investigation is just beginning. So, what do you recall?" she asked in Pactish, starting the recorder.

Tabitha sipped again, then followed her linguistic lead. "I'm happy to tell you what I remember, but you should know there's a *big* gap between me getting stuck and waking up here. I tried to piece it together before breakfast, and I've got snippets, but my memory is patchy."

"If it helps," I interjected, "I saw the whole attack go down, and I watched until Tabitha got home."

"Sorry, you *what*?" Tabitha demanded, staring at me.

"I just got a feeling!" I blurted, holding up my hands as if to stop her from lunging through the glass. "Something told me to tune in, my intuition or whatever, and I caught you at the party a few minutes before the Golden Children showed up. It's not like I make a habit of spying on you," I insisted. "But I was anxious and didn't know why, and…well, I guess we know why *now*, but that's all."

"And you didn't try to intervene?" Enva asked.

"No," I mumbled. "It happened too quickly. I thought for an instant about breaking away to call Annie and see if I could get her there, but I was afraid of what I'd miss…"

"It's okay," Tabitha said as I fell silent. "But next time you get a tickle about me, how about a little heads-up, huh?"

"I'll do what I can."

She grunted, then looked back at Enva. "Okay, then between the two of us, we should be able to put together a timeline for you. Where do you want to start?"

"Well, since we've got a farseer involved," said Enva, "when did this anxiety begin, Rose?"

"Uh…" I thought back over the previous week, then said, "I started getting anxious about four days ago, but I couldn't pinpoint it until yesterday afternoon. I saw you in your pharmacy," I told Tabitha, "just before four, with your last customer—the lady and the little boy?"

Tabitha nodded.

"And then I followed you home. Stephanie called you about the Beltane event, and I left after that conversation."

"Hold it," Enva interrupted. "Beltane?"

I deferred to the expert with an open hand, and Tabitha said, "It's an old festival. Roots in Europe, and it's one of the eight Sabbats on the Wiccan Wheel of the Year. Holidays, if you like," she offered. "Other pagan traditions recognize some of the Sabbats, too, but the Wiccan tradition is the one I know best, so…" She paused to adjust her position on the bed. "Beltane marks the transition from spring to summer. It's about vitality, fertility, all that fun stuff. Whatever rituals you do, there's almost always fire involved. Some folks get *very* into the fertility aspect, if you catch my drift, but that's not what we were up to last night. Family-friendly Beltane, no funny business."

While Enva's expression suggested that she didn't quite follow, she moved on, coaxing us into recounting what we remembered of the previous afternoon and evening. She took notes as she listened, though the recorder continued its work, and she doubled back whenever she was unsure of a point.

As Tabitha and I told her about the Golden Children, she asked Tabitha, "Why didn't you run? If there was a back door, then why didn't you flee? Surely you didn't think you could take on six sorcerers by yourself," she added, almost chiding.

But Tabitha didn't shrink away. "Those were my people in there. Some are weird, some are misguided, a few have their head up their ass, but that's my tribe. I didn't run *because* I know what the Golden Children are, and I wasn't going to leave Stephanie and the others to face them alone. They were defenseless."

"So were you," Enva pointed out, not unkindly.

"Hey, I do have phone numbers for the Hunt. If I'd been a little quicker on the draw, things might have gone a whole lot differently."

Enva's dark eyes widened. "Your plan was to use the *Wild Hunt* against the Golden Children? In the middle of a crowd of humans?"

"Desperate times, desperate measures," said Tabitha.

"And you know the boys would have enjoyed it."

"I...don't doubt that, actually, but that's beside the point."

Finally, as Tabitha and I wound down, Enva asked her, "How did you make the potions boil?"

The best Tabitha could offer her was an unsure grimace. "Beats me. I just...*felt* it, I guess. I was pissed and scared and aching all over, and I kind of sensed that the potions could be an outlet. I'm sorry, but I don't have a better answer," she said, weakly chuckling. "No ritual I've ever done has allowed me to do what I pulled off last night."

Enva put her notepad aside. "Think you could do it again?"

"What, now?"

"If you feel up to it."

"Guess I could try," said Tabitha, and rose to pour a glass of water at the counter. She held her palm over the glass for a few seconds, and then, as we watched, the water floated out of the glass and toward her, levitating for a moment before splashing to the floor.

"Holy shit," I muttered.

Enva cleared her throat. "That, um...that's certainly unexpected."

"Still don't know what I'm doing," said Tabitha, returning to the bed. "It's not like I've been experimenting in here, and frankly, I'm not sure that's safe."

"Mm." Enva turned off the recorder and packed her gear away in her tote bag, then stood and approached the glass. "I'll get this typed up into statements for both of you and bring them by later today, if that's all right."

"Sounds good," said Tabitha, and I nodded.

"Excellent. And as for your new abilities," said the detective, cocking her head as she studied Tabitha, "I think I know someone who may be able to help. Are you feeling up to having company?"

Two hours later, as Enva was going over Tabitha's statement with her, Liogh walked in with an escort, clad in sweats and pulling a black weekender suitcase. "Hello!" they said in English, lifting a hand in greeting. "Ah, quarantine. Nothing says 'fun' like a few days in forced isolation, eh?"

"Especially not when you're isolating with your whole team," Enva replied.

"Mandatory fun," I quipped.

Liogh made a face. "Emphasis on *mandatory*. So," they said, approaching the glass, "I hear you have a new party trick."

"Something like that," said Tabitha. "Um…you're the company, I take it?"

Liogh looked questioningly at Enva, who nodded. "I'm not sure that you two were formally introduced during the trials," she said. "Tabitha, this is Liogh Birrid. They're part of our liaison team with DPP—"

"You were at the Golden Children's hearing, right?" Tabitha interrupted. "You testified."

"Precisely, and while I feel slightly vindicated now, I'm so sorry they came after you," they replied. "But we *have* met—last December, Jane and Connor's wedding?"

Her eyes narrowed as she studied the nymph, but Liogh laughed it off. "It's not like half the guests were masked or anything," they said, and reached beneath their shirt to trigger their masking pendant. Suddenly, the green-skinned, blue-haired detective had shifted complexions to an ethnically ambiguous tan, with long black hair and black eyes to complete the disguise—and far smaller ears, naturally. While Liogh's disguise leaned masculine, they maintained their willowy physique, a few inches over six feet tall and built like a well-toned rail.

"*Oh*!" Tabitha cried. "I remember you! Yacovi's buddy, yeah?"

"The same," he said with a grin, and disengaged the mask. "And he's had nothing but good to say about you.

Now, what's this Enva tells me about water powers?"

Tabitha poured herself a fresh glass of water, placed it on the counter, and took a few steps back. When she beckoned with a crooked finger, the water floated out in a neat cylinder, which then shifted into a sphere as it drifted toward her. She caught it in her palms, cradling it like an unusually melty snowball, then tossed it twice before dumping it back into the glass.

"Not bad," said Liogh. "And this started last night?"

"Yep. I'm not really sure what I'm doing," she admitted. "Been playing around a bit this morning, but it's not like this came with an instruction manual…"

"Well, then," they said with a smile, "you called the right nymph."

Liogh didn't even have to gesture. The water in Tabitha's pitcher rose in a spiral and formed a thin circle, which widened as it spun until it was large enough to pass around Tabitha like the world's wettest hula hoop. As it retreated to the pitcher, Liogh said, "I don't know anything about the potion you received, but I *do* know water manipulation. If it's all right, I'll join you in there, and we'll see what we can do, eh?"

"Oh…oh, no, I can't ask that," Tabitha protested. "I'm okay, you don't have to—"

"You are *not* okay," they said gently. "I'd be stunned if you were. And considering all you've done for my colleagues, not to mention Yacovi and Jane, I'd be happy to try to return the favor. My director's already cleared it. Besides," they added, cocking their head toward me, "the youngling looks tired, and the TV options in quarantine aren't great. I brought playing cards."

At that, Tabitha grinned. "You bring enough for canasta?"

"Mm. Not quite…"

"I'll have a few extra decks sent up," I promised. "And earplugs. That's the only way you'll sleep with them around."

"I had surgery in January!" said Liogh. "The nose has been fixed!"

"And we are *so* pleased with the result," Enva added. "Really, the healers did good work."

I arched a brow. "No more chainsaw?"

"Barely a peep, I swear."

"*Thank you*," said Liogh, and with a dramatic sniff, they dragged their bag into the quarantine vestibule. Once inside, they chose a bed near the back, giving Tabitha plenty of room, then helped themself to the coffee urn. "How's the brew?" they asked her as they poured.

"Sub-par. Mangia has offered to help."

They took a test sip and recoiled. "Oh, good," they said, putting the mug back on the counter. "I brought a phone, and with any luck, they'll deliver." Liogh hesitated for a moment, absently gnawing their lower lip, then said, "I don't mean to bring up what's perhaps a sensitive point, but your hair wasn't quite so blue the last time I saw you."

Groaning, Tabitha flopped back on her bed. "Potion effect, or so they tell me. I take it yours is natural."

They made a show of tossing their long hair over their shoulder. "Yeah, it grows in this color. Pretty common for water nymphs—you'll see anything from green to purple. I've got a cousin with the most *striking* deep violet coloration, hair, eyes, skin, everything. She's gorgeous, models. Me? Average." They paused, then said, "The sudden color change has to be distressing."

"It's not the end of the world," Tabitha replied, though she didn't sound convinced.

"Hey, you're not going to hurt my feelings," said Liogh, and patted the foot of her bed. "May I?"

She sat up and nodded, and he took a seat. "Look," he said quietly, "I've been masking for most of my career. It doesn't really bother me anymore, but the first few times…few *hundred* times…were disconcerting, and I had full control over my appearance. You don't, and when you add sudden talent to the mix…it's okay to not be okay,

Tabitha."

For I moment, I thought she was going to claim she was fine—Tabitha had never been the weepy sort, in my experience—but then her jaw began to wobble, and she sniffled.

Liogh jumped up to grab a wad of paper napkins off the counter and handed them to her as she fought to maintain control. "It's going to be all right," they said after she'd blown her nose. "Most likely not today, but I've got faith in the research healers here—they're the best of the best," they assured her. "They found an antidote to Roulette, yes? It took a while, sure, but they did it. And for now," they added with a little grin, "at least you don't have antlers, right?"

Tabitha sniffed again but swallowed back her tears. "Small mercies."

"And until the team here clears you to mask, maybe we can find you a nice hat. Something fetching."

"Old lady church hat," said Tabitha. "Wide brim, big-ass bow."

"Satin?"

"Absolutely. Maybe some silk flowers. My grandmother had one with a whole fake dove on it." Ligoh snorted, and Tabitha cracked a smile. "Okay, maybe no birds."

"Well, while you're making millinery decisions, let me just say that blue's not a terrible shade on you. I mean, I'm a *tad* biased," they admitted, "but your hair's not hideous."

"You are absolutely not objective."

"But I'm not blind, either." With that, Liogh rose and headed for their bed. "Let me get unpacked and settled in, and then we'll see what you can do."

"Want to order more coffee first?" she called after them.

"Ooh. *Yes*."

With Liogh moving in, Tabitha calm and somewhat caffeinated, and Enva equipped with our signed statements, I started packing my things, as I was craving my bed after the wakeful night. Enva waited, offering to walk out with me and save a technician from having to escort her yet again, and I was just about to return the couch to the break room when Annie came in with Jane, who carried a loaded hiking pack and a pair of bulging canvas tote bags.

"Heard you'd overnighted," Jane said to me. "Get any rest?"

"Not enough, and what're you doing here?"

She nodded toward quarantine. "Joining the party, what's it look like?"

"You went through decon," I began to protest, but Jane shut me up.

"I slept on it, and I felt like shit for not being here, so I'm not leaving Tabitha to deal with this on her own. Annie was nice enough to give me a lift," she added, and Annie raised her travel thermos in weary morning salute.

Tabitha, who'd been listening in through the microphone we'd kept engaged, rapped on the glass to get Jane's attention. "Hon, you don't have to do this. Sweet of you, and I appreciate it, but you don't need to be stuck—"

"I brought snacks," Jane interrupted, hoisting one tote, "a computer with better TV access than whatever they've got in there, and an external hard drive full of movies. Also, some face masks, because why the hell not?"

Liogh waved from the back of the room. "Come on in!" they called. "No shortage of beds. But do you think you could make a run down to Mangia first?"

"I'll handle Mangia," said Annie. "Jane, go get settled."

I gripped her shoulder before she could get to the vestibule doors. "Is Connor aware of what's going on?"

Jane smirked and patted my hand until I released her. "I filled him in first thing this morning, he's on standby, and he's available for house checks or anything else needed while Tabitha is indisposed. So's Dad. Now, scoot," she ordered. "You know you trance better after a good night's sleep, and I *want* Katin."

"Nice to know you care, Jane."

"Duh," she said, giving me a brief hug. "Okay, slumber party time!" she announced, marching up to the vestibule doors. "Annie, there's room..."

"I'm far more useful to y'all making deliveries," Annie pointed out.

As Jane went in, I muttered to Annie, "And still slightly traumatized?"

"You know, you never quite get over waking up in Neverland with antlers growing out of your skull," she replied in kind. "I'm happy to bring food, but I ain't going in there for any sort of indefinite stay. No, *thank* you." To Enva, she asked, "Ready to head out? We should get Rose on her way before I have to sic Diriem on her."

"You wouldn't," I grumbled.

"As I see it, friendship means keeping each other from hallucinating," said Annie, and waved at the trio in quarantine. "Someone text me your order!" she called. "I'll be right back."

Yven and Pop were long gone by the time I walked into the house in the previous day's clothes, but Scel was waiting in the foyer, impeccably dressed as always and with his trusty clipboard of tasks in hand. "Ah, Miss Rose," he said, and glanced at his watch. "Right on schedule."

One fun feature of the blinding potion that all DOI farseers and I took quarterly was that it hid us from other farseers' prying eyes...with one hitch that seldom arose. The blinding potion had a weakness that allowed farseers in the target's bloodline to peek around with sufficient concentration. I'd used it to great effect to bring down one of my great-grandfathers and his criminal enterprise.

My *other* great-grandfather, who had zero qualms about exploiting the potion's weak point, occasionally kept an eye on me.

"He gave you a heads-up, did he?" I asked Scel.

The house manager smiled. "Mentioned it on his way out this morning. I took the liberty of having your room refreshed, and your bed awaits," he added with a pointed glance toward the staircase.

"Thank you, Scel." Even after living in the mansion for several years, I had yet to fully adjust to the presence of a staff that regularly changed the linens and picked up after me, but it was *nice*. "And I'm fine, really. Not hallucinating."

"Let's keep it that way."

"Pop nags me enough," I said, beginning the ascent. "You two don't need to tag-team this."

"*Three*. You're forgetting Yven," he called after me.

Grumbling about the men in my life, I trudged to my apartment, which I found tidied and smelling vaguely of lemon. I spared a glance for Yven's many orchids, which were enjoying their morning sunbath, then investigated the bedroom. The bed was turned down, the white linens looked crip, and someone had spritzed them with lavender. On my nightstand, placed atop the charging pad for my phone, was a small glass bottle containing a golden potion and a folded piece of paper, a note in Low Elvish written in a neat hand that I knew well: *Rest. You will need it.*

Yes, it bothered me on occasion that Pop could be nosy and overprotective, but he wasn't *wrong*.

The sleeping potion he'd left for me was one of the more pleasant options, as it went down like minty mouthwash, minus the alcohol burn. I tossed my clothes in the hamper, slipped into my pajamas, then slugged back the potion and snuggled into my clean sheets. The potion was an easy way to ensure that I didn't toss and turn while I tried to turn off my brain, but it wouldn't keep me asleep longer than I needed, and I guessed I'd be awake again before Yven came home.

I didn't see my fiancé until early Friday morning, when I

rolled over in the unexpected darkness and found him sleeping beside me.

Easing out of bed so as not to wake him, I tiptoed into the bathroom, then grabbed an afghan off one of the couches in the den and curled up on my studio couch, where I could address my pressing urge to trance without fear of interruption.

My eyes had barely closed before my inner eyes opened to show me Katin.

She was sitting in a wooden rocking chair on what appeared to be a deck overlooking an expanse of trees...or so I thought, given the night around us. The only illumination on the porch was a camping lantern at her feet, and with no moon above, the stars shone brightly—though not as impressively as they did in Ragged Gap, I thought. Wherever Katin was, the light pollution had worsened. As my vision adjusted, I could make out the silhouettes of peaks against the skyline, patches of black pocked with the pinpricks of security lamps or insomniacs' windows, but I could spot nothing familiar.

Katin clearly hadn't slept. She hugged one knee to her chest, while her free hand clutched a white mug half-full of a tea blend heavy on the lemon. She wore black leggings and an oversized plaid shirt, its sleeves rolled and cuffed just below her elbows, and her hair hung limply around her face. If she'd showered in the last day and a half, I'd have been shocked.

Unable to read minds, I settled for studying Katin's face in the low light, the shadows beneath her eyes and the tightness in her jaw. Occasionally, she sipped her tea, but for the most part, she slowly rocked and stared out at the warm night.

But where *was* she? The mountains suggested Appalachia, though could she have driven west to the Ouachitas? Possibly. If the Golden Children had left Ragged Gap at some point on Wednesday night or Thursday morning, they could have made it to western Arkansas with time to spare. Unfortunately, my knowledge of the Ouachita Mountains was worse than my familiarity with the southern end of the Appalachians, and nothing on that porch was giving me any hints.

I'd just decided to leave Katin until daylight when the glass door behind her slid open with a squeal and Dirk stepped though. "Hey, Kitkat," he murmured, bending to kiss her neck. "I got you some dinner."

"I'm not hungry," she replied, continuing to rock.

"You've got to eat, babe," he insisted, crouching beside her. "Keep up your strength."

"What's the fucking point?"

Dirk sighed and gripped the arm of the chair to freeze its motion. "Honey, look at me."

Though she took a sip of tea first, Katin slowly turned her face toward his.

"We're *fine*," he said. "No one's going to find us."

"There are freaks in the goddamn Pactlands who can see the fucking future," she muttered. "Of course they're going to find us. And I tell you true, I ain't going back to prison. Not there, not here, *nowhere*."

"Kitkat—"

"Stop. That hasn't worked since I was a teenager." With a soft huff, Katin stared out at the mountains once more.

"Katin," Dirk tried again, "it'll be okay. No one's going to prison. Now, come on inside," he coaxed. "You need to eat, and then maybe you and I can have a little time to ourselves, eh?"

Apparently, she wasn't in the mood for his advances that night. "We're screwed."

"Babe—"

"You think they'd chase us into Canada? Mexico? What if we made it down to South America, you think they'd follow?"

"You're dreaming up the worst," said Dirk. "They ain't going to chase us over two damn humans. DOL learned its lesson."

"Maybe, maybe not. You don't know that." After a long sip and a glare at the trees, Katin said, "This wasn't supposed to happen. No one said *anything* about the potion doing…that."

"Ain't your fault—"

"And that bitch, the pharmacist," she continued, as if Dirk had never spoken, "I should have known she'd be trouble from the start. She was suspicious at my demo, you know? Thinking too hard. Now she's got *connections*," Katin said bitterly. "She'll call her little friends, and DOL will hunt us down."

"If she's still alive," said Dirk.

Katin spared him an impatient glance. "She made it home, didn't she?"

"And she wasn't there. We searched the whole place—"

"Then someone must have come to get her, genius."

"Or she slunk off into the woods to die," he suggested, but even he didn't sound convinced.

"More likely she's in the Pactlands," said Katin.

"So what if she is?" Rising, Dirk stood in front of Katin's chair so that she was forced to face him. "DOL has no case. Even if they did, our lawyer's *good*. But if you're worried, honey, we'll keep moving until you feel safe, okay? I promise," said Dirk, and kissed her forehead. "We'll get a place and figure things out, and we'll make it. *All* of us."

"I don't know how far we'll have to run," Katin whispered.

"That's something we can talk about tomorrow, once you've had a bite and slept. Come on," he said, offering her his arm, "you'll feel better after a cheeseburger."

Katin let him pull her to her feet, picked up the lantern, and followed him back into the house. "And hey," said Dirk, locking the glass door, "before you go worrying, remember that we've got a friend at DOI. Yeah?"

"I guess," she mumbled, then sniffed the air. "That

smells good. Onion rings?"

"Only the best for you, Kitkat."

She rolled her eyes. "Where'd you go this time of night?"

"Cook Out—they're open late. Got you a milkshake, too."

Katin kissed Dirk properly that time, then settled in at a rustic pine table and finished her tea as he made a show of unpacking her food in the kitchen. As he carried the loaded dinner plate to the table, I looked over the detritus on the counter, searching for a clue, something unique…

And then I spotted the restaurant receipt. He'd crumpled it, but I could still make out the address.

Pigeon Forge, just a few hours over the Tennessee border from Ragged Gap and into the Smokies.

They hadn't run nearly far enough.

CHAPTER 8

I spent the morning at home, gathering information. A call to Enva had netted me penal headshots of the elder Golden Children, and just before lunch, she sent along a file with pertinent details about the younger generation—names and ages, but most importantly, faces. Alone in my studio, with Yven working on reports in the den in case I needed anything and keeping the coffee warm, I dipped in and out of trance, cementing my findings.

The Golden Children had rented half a dozen tourist cabins in Pigeon Forge, the kind of places with decorative ON MOUNTAIN TIME signs, wonky Jacuzzis on the back porch, and a selection of brochures for Dollywood and themed dinner attractions. Early May wasn't peak season, but still, the fact that they had sprawled around town suggested that the Forum's payout had been substantial—that, and they were paranoid. Much more challenging to round up everyone if they'd scattered. I peeked in on small groups of adults, on adults with kids, and then back on Katin and Dirk, the former of whom seemed increasingly ill at ease in her love nest.

They'd move on soon, of that I had no doubt, but for the moment, they seemed to be decompressing. Some of the adults slept in, the children watched TV and ate sugary cereal, and I quickly excused myself from one cabin when I caught a couple making up for their long separation on the penal farms. As the other couple in the cabin was doing the dishes with earbuds in, I assumed the situation wasn't unexpected, if thoroughly awkward for me.

When I emerged around eleven, blinking in the sunlight, Yven put aside his computer and held me as I readjusted to corporeality. "Good hunting?" he murmured into my hair.

"Uh-huh."

"Are you hungry, Rosie?"

I paused to consider the question. "Yeah, I think so. But I need to check on Tabitha—"

"Shower first," he said, gently steering me toward our room. "She's not going anywhere. And I'll ask Ranarma to send something up, okay?"

There was, I mused, letting the hot water ground me, truth to the in-flight warning to put your own oxygen mask on first.

I was feeling almost normal when I left our bedroom, flushed and shower-damp and wrapped in a fluffy bathrobe, and Yven was waiting in the den with a tray of soup and sandwiches from the main kitchen, which tasted practically gourmet to my famished stomach. I hadn't eaten in nearly twenty-four hours—not unusual when I was deep in an investigation—and as I tore into a turkey sandwich, I was grateful that Yven loved me and my weirdness enough to remind me to care for myself.

Babysitting me was a role he'd willingly taken on. Early in our engagement, after his second or third all-nighter spent making sure I stayed hydrated and keeping a pain potion at hand for the odd headache and a willing ear tuned to listen to my mumbled commentary on my visions, Pop had taken him into his office for a chat while I was out of the house. "We're not easy partners," Pop had told him—or so Yven recounted to me months after the fact. "Farseers can be distant, distractable…prone to forgoing baths and forgetting dinner engagements. I speak from long and sometimes embarrassing experience. But just because you love Rose does not obligate you to tend to her when she's trancing. She will learn, she'll make mistakes, and eventually, she'll understand how to keep herself healthy and mostly civilized."

"Eventually, sure," Yven had replied. "I have every confidence. But until then, as long as she needs someone...as you said, I love her."

He never complained. When I hid away to scratch the mental itch to trance, when I had to beg off from an evening together because Interdiction was desperate for a lead, when I worked for days with barely a nap and turned feral, Yven was by my side—and when I was too far gone to know what I needed, I could trust him to hold my hand. On those days when he was outside doing inspections, I missed him dearly, but I didn't suggest that he quit his job. Yven didn't *have* to work—between my DPP salary and my access to the ti'Dana fortune, I could keep the two of us afloat, and Pop wouldn't have batted an eye had Yven become my full-time caretaker—but he'd made a good career at DPP, and he worked well in Regulatory. Besides, Yven's job was what had brought the two of us into each other's orbit—I couldn't ask him to resign, nor did I want him to. But I *did* appreciate his ministrations, and eventually, Syvin had given him blanket permission to work from home when I needed minding.

I had no idea how I'd been so fortunate as to find him, and in less than a month, we'd finally be official. There was, I'd decided, quite a lot I'd put up with from my delightful cousin if it meant I got to say my vows with Yven.

While I stuffed my face, he said, "I went ahead and called Jane to tell her you'd be by."

"Thank you," I mumbled around a mouthful of bread. I didn't know what Ranarma put into his sourdough loaves, but they were next to magical. After a hard swallow, I asked, "How're they doing?"

"Not great," said Yven. "Tabitha's still hurting, and complications have arisen."

"Complications?" I echoed.

He shrugged. "Jane said they'd fill you in once you get there. So, want to carpool to the office?"

I threw on some clothes—Yven might have opted for a respectable brown robe, but as far as I was concerned, DPP was lucky to get me in pants that day—and we drove to Beukal in his beloved red Mustang, an import modified to never need gasoline or trigger police radar. We parted in the elevator at the tenth floor, and Yven kissed me before disembarking. "I'll check in at five, yeah? Won't strand you here," he promised, grinning, before heading for his cubicle.

Alone, I continued up to the fifteenth floor, then scanned myself into the quarantine wing and proceeded to the control station, which was staffed by a pair of sorcerers that afternoon. "Hi," I said, beginning to open my badge, but one of the technicians cut me off.

"You're expected, Agent ti'Dana," she said quickly, and pressed a button to unlock the rest of the doors between us and quarantine. "Go ahead."

I hesitated, considering her tone. "Is everything all right?"

"Not exactly. See for yourself."

My stomach knotted as I hastened down the hallway, and I was jogging by the time I hit the quarantine room. There was another technician on duty, a naga, who had curled his tail beneath him at the desk outside of quarantine. He gestured to the microphone in invitation, and as I neared the glass wall, Jane and Liogh joined me on the other side.

"Hi," I said, clutching the mic. "How's Tabitha?"

Jane thumbed one hand over her shoulder. "Sleeping. She got a sedative about an hour ago. Poor thing's been miserable all morning."

"What's hurting her?"

"Everything," said Liogh. "And that's not the worst of it."

"Yven said something about complications…"

They moved toward Tabitha's bed, and as Jane eased back the blankets, Liogh lifted her hand.

I stared in disbelief. Tabitha's fingers had become translucent.

"What the hell?" I muttered.

"Question of the hour," said Jane as she and Liogh tucked Tabitha in. "The researchers have no clue. That started last night, and it's spreading."

"How far?"

"Fingers and toes for now," Liogh replied. "The researchers are perplexed—they've never seen anything like this. Now, they managed to isolate the potion in her blood, but all they've told us is that it's novel and complex."

I groaned. "Fantastic."

"At least the research healers have a shiny new puzzle," they said, which was answered by a grunt from the technician. "And none of the support staff are getting much sleep. But on the positive side, Tabitha can still control liquids, and she's getting better at it."

"That's...something," I allowed.

"It's pretty amazing, actually," said Jane. "And she's intuiting," she added, to which Liogh nodded their agreement. "She was practicing as a distraction most of the morning, but the pain got to her, and Vinla knocked her out to give her some relief."

Depending on what Tabitha had drunk, she could be out for hours. "Tell her I stopped by, okay? And if things get worse or weirder, would you give Yven a call?"

"Yeah, sure." Jane slung her arm around Liogh's back—they were too tall for her to comfortably reach their shoulders—and said, "We'll hold down the fort."

"Any luck with the Golden Children?" Liogh asked.

"Eastern Tennessee, last I checked," I told them, and pointed to the ceiling. "Going upstairs to keep spying. If you need something—"

"We're fine," Liogh said firmly. "And we'll give Tabitha your best once she wakes."

As I left quarantine, I tried not to think about Tabitha's ghostly fingers. I had no idea what that meant for her, and if she'd stumped the research healers…

They found an antidote for Roulette, I told myself as the elevator rose toward my office. *They can fix this, too.*

I hoped.

The truth was that not every potion had an antidote. Most could be undone, but a few—the language potion was an easy example—were permanent.

Trying not to dwell on that disconcerting possibility, I let myself into my office, stretched out on the couch, and forced my racing mind to focus on Katin.

Yven had to drive home alone that evening, as the director called a meeting for five-thirty and asked me to stay. "I'll get a ride with Pop," I'd told my fiancé. "No need for you to sit at your desk, twiddling your thumbs."

"I don't mind," he'd replied.

"I know, but that's silly. Go home, eat whatever spread Ranarma has put out, and think of me and my sad desk crackers."

He'd promised to save me a bite—unnecessary, as Ranarma's dinners could usually feed ten or more—and left on time to navigate the portal traffic back to Viratta with the radio for company.

As I'd anticipated, the meeting was a multi-agency affair. Pop and Ganti had come over from DOI, Kabno and Enva had joined us from Laws, and Syvin and Gentle Breeze flanked Pateme at the table. I pulled up a chair and was settling in when Vinla swept through the door with another healer, a brown-haired sorcerer who appeared to be about my age—early sixties, I estimated. "Sorry, *sorry*," she said, and plopped her bag on the table. "Have we begun?"

"Breathe, Ms. ti'Gata," said Pateme, and underhanded her a small bottle of water from the tray at his end of the table. "Kabno, Diriem, have you met Mr. Parritin?"

"Um, hi," the sorcerer said, awkwardly raising a hand.

"Dante Perritin."

"He was my second on the Roulette team," Vinla added, "and he's helping out again."

I briefly studied him as he took a seat beside her, then asked, "*Dante*?"

He made a face. "My mother has an unhealthy fondness for medieval European literature. Got permission to study in Italy and everything. You should meet my siblings, Virgilio and Beatrice."

"*Oof.*"

"Right?" said Dante, then slid over at the table to make more room for his boss.

As Vinla unpacked, Gentle Breeze said, "Rose."

"Ma'am?" I replied.

"How's Tabitha?"

There was no point in lying to her. "Not great. She's translucent from the elbows and knees down."

Gentle Breeze's eyes widened. "What do you mean, *translucent*? I thought her hair turned blue!"

"Oh, it did. This is new," I said with a joyless smile. "They've kept her doped up all afternoon so she can rest—"

"We're weaning her off tonight," Vinla interrupted. "Pain's a useful metric of how this is progressing—"

"If you don't give that woman every damn pain potion she wants," rumbled Gentle Breeze, staring the healer down, "then you and I will have a problem."

Vinla was an excellent research healer, and I was sure she'd had all the training in magic customary for a young elf...but Gentle Breeze was better than eight feet fall and a solid three hundred pounds, and if her sharp tusks weren't warning enough, then surely the claws she was drumming on the table made her point for her.

"She'd probably like company," I said to Gentle Breeze, breaking the standoff. "Once she wakes, I mean. Jane and Liogh are with her, but I bet she'd be happy to see you."

The troll grunted, and Vinla hurriedly turned on her tablet.

"We'll return to the matter of the victim. *Victims*," Pateme amended, rubbing one temple. "I understand we have an identification of the potions found in the store?"

"Yes, sir," said Dante, consulting his own tablet. "I received the findings from the lab about half an hour ago. Velvet Leash, the technicians are positive."

"So, the Golden Children have picked up precisely where they left off," said Kabno, and glared at Pop. "Care to explain?"

"As I told the Forum, there was a difference of opinion," he calmly replied.

"*And*?"

Pop stared back at her, closed-lipped and blank-faced, and Kabno nearly growled—impressive, considering her small stature and high-pitched voice. Before she could throw hands, I said, "I've got some intel."

"Please," said Pateme, shooting his colleagues warning looks.

"They're on the move. Left Ragged Gap hours after the assault," I said as the eyes of the table turned to me. "As of this morning, they were in Pigeon Forge…uh, about three or four hours north in Tennessee. Tourist area in the mountains. They packed up and headed northeast early this afternoon, and I believe they're overnighting in the Tri-Cities area."

"Sorry," said Vinla, "where?"

"Bristol, Kingsport, Johnson City. They're in Tennessee, close to the Virginia line," I explained. "Actually, there's a Bristol on both sides, but whatever. The important thing is that they're putting distance between themselves and Ragged Gap."

"Not much, all things considered," said Kabno. "If they'd driven hard, they could be back in Texas by now."

"Sure," I replied. "But they're traveling in a group with kids, and Katin's freaking out that they're going to get caught. I think they're trying to avoid the places DOL might naturally look for them...and since they know where some of the portals are, it's probably a safe bet that they'll avoid those locations, too."

"How many portals do they know?" asked Gentle Breeze.

"Beats me, but they used to sell their product via the Tampa portal, so I assume they've heard of others." I paused then and looked at Pop, whose expression remained an unreadable mask. "Early this morning, I spent some time with Katin and Dirk—her boyfriend," I added as Vinla's mouth opened. "He mentioned that they have a friend at DOI. Look, I'm not trying to stick my nose where it doesn't belong, but I think you've got a real problem, Pop."

"I'm aware," he murmured.

"Then what are you doing about it?" demanded Kabno. "If DOI is giving bad information—"

"These are serious accusations," Pop protested. "I can't act with less than certainty."

She gestured to Ganti. "Can't his team poke around?"

"I'd be happy to, ma'am," Ganti replied, "but it's not that simple. All of our farseers are protected, if you'll recall. Conceivably, we could neutralize the blinding potion for the entire team, but—"

"That would be a terrible idea," finished Pop. "The plan, Kabno, is to allow matters to marinate for a time. The Waughnn girl is paranoid, and assuming the Golden Children have an ally in my agency, he or she is likely paranoid as well. Give them a chance to settle, to lower their guard. The longer this goes without overt agency action, the more likely it becomes that someone will grow too relaxed, get cocky, and blow their cover."

"Or we could grab the Golden Children now," suggested Pateme. "Apply pressure, see who cracks."

Kabno shook her head. "We have nothing to hold them on yet—they've assaulted two humans, nothing more. I don't like it," she said, raising her voice as Gentle Breeze started to protest, "but I want to *keep* the little assholes this time, so we need to wait and allow them to hang themselves."

"Agreed," said Pop.

"Any idea how long this is going to take?" she asked him.

"Nothing I can share." Turning to Vinla and Dante, he said, "And the patient? Any idea what she was given?"

"It's definitely novel," Vinla replied, consulting her tablet, "and the preliminary tests aren't promising. This thing is *complex*, whatever it is. We're working on it," she stressed, cutting her eyes to Pateme, "but this isn't a problem with an overnight solution."

He nodded. "And…you intend to rouse Ms. Bradley this evening?"

"Carefully, sir," she replied, surely feeling the weight of Gentle Breeze's stare. "Very carefully."

Yven was a one-car man, but Pop had been collecting since the early days of the automobile, and he rotated among his favorites. That night, I rode shotgun in his black Corvette Z06 convertible, his latest acquisition. There was a *strong* market in the Pactlands for modified human-made vehicles, and for the right price, dealers savvy enough to use shell companies and hide their tracks could get just about anything. In my opinion, the Corvette was a ridiculous ride for a guy who mostly drove to and from the office, but there were largely uninhabited stretches far outside of Beukal where one could go in a souped up sports car to blow off steam, and he was thoroughly enjoying his new toy.

That I still drove my trusty preowned Outback pained him on a spiritual level.

Pop barely spoke that night as he navigated out of the city toward the portal building. The evening exodus had slowed but was still congesting the outward portals, and we idled in line, awaiting our turn. I kept sneaking glances at him, trying and failing to gauge his mood, then took the plunge and asked, "Are you angry with me?"

He jerked as if I'd woken him from an unplanned nap, then frowned as the question registered. "No. Why, did I give you that impression?"

"I wasn't sure."

"I'm not angry," Pop told me. "Not with you, anyway. Just...thinking."

Satisfied, I settled back in my seat, and Pop inched forward.

"The ramifications of these developments may be farther reaching than I'd initially anticipated," he murmured after a moment.

"Come again?"

"There are pieces in play I don't yet see," he replied, "and sitting in traffic isn't helping the matter."

"Something I can do?"

"No," he said, and reached over to pat my knee. "You've done enough for now. Rest well tonight—you'll have a big day tomorrow."

I frowned at that pronouncement. "Are we expecting something weird from Katin? Can you give me a hint?"

He chuckled low. "Not Katin, dear. You have a dress fitting with Calien in the morning, do you not?"

Groaning at the reminder, I leaned back and closed my eyes as we moved closer to the portal home. "How about I blow that off and work on the Golden Children instead?"

Despite Pop's suggestion, I stayed up late, first stealing a few hours with Yven, and then slipping off to my studio to look in on the Golden Children before going to bed. As I'd anticipated, they'd made camp near the Virginia line at a Holiday Inn, and aside from Katin, who sat up in the lobby, taking nips from a single-serving bottle of Jack in her purse, they seemed to be sleeping soundly. Satisfied, I joined Yven in bed, and he woke just enough to spoon behind me and pull me close before drifting off again.

Saturday dawned gray and drizzly—a front was pushing through the Mid-Atlantic, bringing rain to Viratta and Beukal alike—and when I checked on the fugitives, they appeared to be in no hurry to drive off in the downpour. Thanks to the weather-dampening properties of the Pactlands, the thunderstorms outside were merely an unpleasant shower for us, and so I didn't build in much extra time to get to the capital. A leisurely breakfast was just what I needed to fortify me for the morning's appointment.

After I showered, I called Jane to check in, planning to stop by on my way to the dress shop, but she told me not to make the trip. "Tabitha just got to sleep around five," she reported, her voice low and weary on the line. "It's been a hell of a night."

"What happened?"

"They weaned her off the sedatives, that's what happened. The pain potions she was taking weren't doing jack, and Liogh and I finally convinced Vinla to authorize something stronger. Once she got a little relief, she conked out." Jane sighed. "Everyone's exhausted. Annie brought breakfast, and Gentle Breeze was here at six to check in, but we're in no shape for company. I'll call you," she promised.

"Is Tabitha still see-through?" I asked.

"Yeah," Jane muttered, "and it's spreading. Arms and legs are fully translucent. We don't know if that's causing all the pain or what, and the healers here have no fucking clue how to help her, so…you know, if you've got some positive vibes to send our way, we'll take them."

Thus, I wasn't in the greatest of moods when I left the house, and that only worsened when I neared the portal and saw the wreck. Viratta's portal wasn't large, only an inbound and outbound lane, and some well-meaning but misguided parent had taken a kid with a learner's permit driving in the rain. The sedan hadn't left enough room on approach to the portal and had plowed into the back of an SUV, and while there were no injuries, traffic was backed up until the investigator from DOL could assess and clear the scene.

Twenty minutes later, delayed and damp, I sloppily parallel parked half a block from the dress shop in swanky District 4 and speedwalked down the street for my appointment, clutching my umbrella against the sneaky gusts.

Black Swan was the couture house Calien had chosen for my gown. I couldn't fault her for that—Black Swan was a name frequently whispered at galas—but the particular designer Calien had convinced to work with me, Tiami ti'Dir, left me cold. Tiami was only a little older than Calien, barely eighty, and she'd designed for all of Calien's circle as her reputation grew. My cousin had proudly informed me that she had no fewer than four of Tiami's frocks in her wardrobe—not that she would ever be caught re-wearing a dress, mind you—and she'd stressed to me what a favor Tiami was doing for her by deigning to design my wedding gown.

Since our first appointment, Tiami and Calien had been as tight as sorority sisters, conversing almost exclusively with each other and barely answering my questions. Given Calien's image-consciousness, I wasn't sure why she was buddying up to a ti'Dir—in the Hall hierarchy, they were somewhere down around ti'Ansha, and Tiami was nowhere near the main line—but the two made it clear that I fell somewhere far beneath their notice.

The doorbell tinkled as I entered the shop, and I willed my dripping umbrella dry before leaning it against the wall. Before I could pat my hair into place, Calien stood from one of the plush violet chairs, arms folded and eyes narrowed. "You're *late*."

"I'm sorry. I've had a work emergency, one of my friends is in quarantine, there was an accident at the portal this morning, and it's only two minutes past the hour—"

"The appointment was at ten," she snapped. "Not two minutes past ten." She looked at Tiami, a tall, sylphlike woman with raven-black hair, and shook her head. "You see?"

"I'll do what I can," Tiami replied, and pointed me toward a large dressing room, its gray velvet curtain pulled back in invitation. "Take your clothes off, and make sure you're dry—I don't want water spots on the fabric."

Fortunately, I'd had training enough to manage that, and once I'd wriggled into the blue gown, I alerted Tiami. She ordered me out and onto a raised platform before a trifold mirror, and I stood still while she popped a pincushion on her wrist, grabbed a piece of chalk, and began to work. To my dismay, Calien joined her, offering her oh-so-helpful critique.

"You know," said Tiami, marking up the back of my dress, "I always imagined that the first ti'Dana wedding I designed for would be yours, Calien."

"It will be, don't worry," my cousin replied, smirking at my reflection.

Tiami pulled the fabric so tight that I almost lost my breath. "Oh?"

"Well, this one hardly counts—consider the couple."

The two laughed, and though I held my tongue, my cheeks flared.

After another minute of tugging and pinning, Tiami scowled. "The gown is tighter than I'd expected."

"I *warned* Rose to watch her diet," said Calien, "but you see how she ignores my advice."

"Honestly, I'm not sure it would have made a difference," Tiami replied. "She's chunky for an elf. I'll have to redo these seams if we don't want her to look like an overstuffed pillow. Or she could mask, I suppose..."

"Imagine having to mask to fit in a gown," Calien scoffed. "While you're fixing Rose's mess, don't you agree that the gown would look better in tangerine?"

Tiami nodded fervently. "*So* much better. This color is

all wrong for the season—I'm embarrassed to be working with it. Right, then, I'll try to let out the back, and I'll change the color—"

"The gown will be blue, thank you," I said with as much dignity as my scarlet face would afford me.

Calien's fists went to her hips. "Don't be difficult, girl. You have no idea what you're doing—"

"It will be blue," I said, turning to stare down Tiami, "or I'll take my business elsewhere."

Tiami gasped like I'd slapped her. "*Excuse* me?"

"She didn't mean it," said Calien, swooping in. "Stressed, I suppose. And Rose, we've already put down the deposit. You can't get that back. Now, behave yourself and let us work—"

"I'll buy a dress off the rack before I wear tangerine to my own damn wedding," I said, glowering at my cousin. "And I don't want to hear one more word about the color from either of you, is that clear?"

Calien and Tiami shared a look, and Calien took the lead. "Who do you think you are to threaten *me*," she said, "let alone poor Tiami? This woman is a genius, and you wouldn't know fashion if you spent a century doing nothing but reading look books."

"I don't care," I said, frustrated and struggling to hold back tears. "It's *my wedding*."

"And if you don't listen to us," said Tiami, "you'll look like a fat rube. Is that what you want?" Shaking her head, she said to Calien, "I'm risking so much of my reputation already on this commission. If she's not willing to give me creative control…"

"She will," Calien insisted, and glared up at me on the alteration pedestal. "You are ignorant and uncultured," she said through gritted teeth, "not to mention ungrateful, and I'm doing my best to save you from yourself. So, you can either do as we say or—"

"Excuse me."

I looked over Calien's head at an older elf, one who

would have seemed perhaps thirty had she been human but was clearly closer to Pop's age. She'd pulled her blonde hair into a messy updo, and unlike Tiami, who worked in a fuchsia formal robe, she wore a white T-shirt over slim jeans. "Ms. ti'Dana," she said calmly, "would you kindly remove that gown and join me in my office?"

Tiami stiffened. "There's no need. I have this under control—"

"Clearly, you do not. Give me a moment with the bride."

I returned to the dressing room and stripped off the gown, then quickly redressed and followed the woman to a small office on the upper floor of the shop, which overlooked the action below via a pair of windows. "Please have a seat," she said, gesturing to two gray velour chairs facing a clear acrylic desk, and locked the door. "I don't believe we've met. I'm Jevva ti'Cel."

Jevva—*swan* in High Elvish, an old name. I realized she was the chief designer, quite likely the founder of the house. And since Hall ti'Cel was one of the smaller new Halls, less prominent than even ti'Gata and ti'Van, I could only imagine how irked Tiami had to be at the interruption. "Rose," I said, forcing a small smile.

She took the other chair, her brown eyes softening. "Will you tell me what's wrong?"

I plucked a tissue from the box on the low table between us and dabbed, trying not to smear my makeup. "No one is listening to me."

"So I heard." She stood again and glanced out the window, then frosted the glass to opacity with a flick of her finger. "They're still down there, whispering like schoolgirls."

"I'm not trying to be difficult," I said, "and they're right, I don't know fashion here, but—"

"My dear," said Jevva, "this is *your* gown. It doesn't matter what Tiami or anyone else thinks. You're the one who's planning to wear it, and your wishes are paramount.

End of discussion." Taking her seat once more, she said, "You're unhappy, and that's unacceptable. If you want your deposit back, I'll give it to you, but if you're willing to work with me, then *I* will make your dress, and I'll make it to your specifications."

I nodded, sniffling. "Okay."

Jevva smiled. "Wonderful. Would you stand up, please? Let me get your measurements."

Rather than pull out a tape measure, she used a spell, which created a headless mannequin of my proportions and skin tone. Jevva circled it with a notepad in hand, periodically nibbling on the end of her pencil, then pulled a fat binder off a bookshelf and opened it on her desk. "Let me show you some of my work," she said. "I have ideas about what would be flattering, but if you're set on a particular style, we'll start there."

"I, uh…I'm not married to anything," I mumbled, joining her. "The one Tiami was working on was pretty…"

"But tainted," she said gently. "Am I right?"

"Yes, ma'am."

"Then we'll start fresh. When's the wedding?"

"June first. If that's not enough time—"

She waved one hand dismissively. "I've thrown together gowns overnight, Rose. We have *weeks*. Now, why don't you flip through here and see if anything catches your eye?"

Jevva did lovely work, I mused, slowly paging through the binder and its photos of dressed-up women—celebrities, I assumed, though I could only name a handful. Work and training had left me little time to catch up on Pactlands pop culture. I paused on a picture of a brunette in a strapless crimson ballgown with a sweetheart neckline, then tapped the page. "What about something like this?" I'd been drawn to a similar dress early in the process, which Calien had immediately vetoed.

"Oh, I love that one," said Jevva. "Did that about ten years ago for a charity gala."

"I like the silhouette..."

"You've got a good eye. That would look beautiful on you."

"You think?"

In response, Jevva gestured at my mannequin until a copy of the dress hung upon it. "Absolutely. You've got the curves to carry it off," she explained. "That's not a dress I'd choose for, say, a nymph—they're far too stick-like, and dresses like that end up wearing them, know what I mean? But this would complement your figure—and you are not *fat*," she added, holding my stare. "You've got more of a sorcerer's build, but that's hardly a demerit, youngling."

My smile that time was warmer.

"As for the dress," she continued, circling the mannequin, "may I make a suggestion? I like to do this for my brides," she said, and with a little gesture, the back of the dress switched from a zipper to laces. "I build a little extra fabric in this piece here, you see," said Jevva, pointing to the layer behind the crossed ribbons, "and the laces are forgiving. That way, if you gain or lose a bit, or if you're swollen, or if you just want to enjoy the party after the ceremony, the dress will still fit perfectly."

"Brilliant," I replied.

"And how about a train?" Another gesture lengthened the back hem until it stretched across the office. "Makes a dramatic entrance, and then you can—"

"Bustle for the reception," I finished.

"*Precisely*. I've got a whole system for bustling worked out, so that won't be a problem. Do you like the length? Longer, shorter?"

I considered the back of the gown. "Maybe a little shorter and wider?"

It adjusted itself accordingly, and Jevva nodded. "I like it. Now, before we go any further, let's talk color. I don't think this would be the most flattering shade for you..."

"My mother would roll over in her grave if I wore a

crimson wedding gown."

"We can't have *that.*" She twitched a finger, and the gown turned ivory. "This is the customary shade for human gowns, is it not?"

"For Western weddings," I said. "White, cream, ecru, something in that family."

"It could suit you. Not stark white—that would wash you out—but ivory would work with your complexion. Your hair would certainly pop," she added, smiling.

The dress was gorgeous, even in preliminary form, but I couldn't commit to it. "My cousin told me that white gowns aren't common for weddings here, and I want to do this correctly…"

Jevva placed her hand on my shoulder. "There is no *wrong* color," she said, "and I've certainly seen white in wedding attire. If you love it, wear it." She paused, eyeing me shrewdly, then said, "I take it that Calien is helping you plan this wedding."

"Yes, ma'am."

"Mm. And I assume she's not taking your preferences into account." When I didn't immediately disagree, Jevva said, "I've seen her at work, and the woman is like a gale. The end result is usually lovely, but since this is *your* wedding we're talking about…"

"I don't know how to throw a big society wedding," I mumbled. "She does. And I appreciate her help, I do, but—"

"She isn't listening," Jevva finished. "If I may?"

I nodded.

"My brides come to me from all manner of traditions, and seemingly every culture, clan, and family has its own rules for weddings. I tell my brides to honor their traditions but not to be *bound* by them. This is your event—make it a reflection of you and your fiancé."

"I would," I said, "but my great-grandfather wants us to do it right, I guess, so…probably best not to do a white gown. It'd just call attention to the obvious." I sighed as I considered the mannequin. "What's traditional for elven weddings? Please tell me not tangerine."

"Heavens, no, *especially* not with your coloration," said Jevva, appalled. "I mean, I've seen brides in orange, but it's not required. There's no set color palette. That blue you'd selected for the dress Tiami was working on was quite nice, actually. Do you like that?"

"Yes, but Calien doesn't."

"It's not Calien's wedding, is it?" she retorted, and gestured the gown from white to deep blue. "What about some gold accents? That would be lovely with your hair."

A knock at the door interrupted Jevva's detail work, and with an irritated grunt, she waved it open. "Yes?"

On the other side stood Tiami and Calien, the designer pink-cheeked, my cousin glowering. "I've got this under control," Tiami began. "You don't need to trouble yourself with—"

"Oh, but I do," said Jevva, her tone clipped and cold. "*I* will be handling Ms. ti'Dana's gown. And were I you, Tiami, I would endeavor with future clients to ensure that the person wearing the clothes is satisfied with your work. The opinions of any friends"—she said the word with evident disdain—"who accompany the client are immaterial. Do I make myself clear?"

"Yes, ma'am," she muttered, and, shoulders hunched, she slunk off, leaving angry Calien in the doorway.

"We may be a while," Jevva told her. "Why don't you run along, dear? I'm sure Rose can call you when we're finished."

But Calien wasn't so easily cowed. "I'm the one planning this wedding—"

"Which does not give you total artistic control."

She began puffing up. "Just who do you think you're speaking to? My friends and I pay for you to keep your little shop—"

Jevva's deep, throaty laughter cut her short. "Girl," she finally said, wiping a tear from one eye, "I designed your *mother's* wedding gowns. All of them. I designed for the late queen. Do you honestly believe that you can intimidate me?"

Apparently, no one had mentioned this to Calien, as it momentarily shut her up.

"You followed Tiami into my house," Jevva continued. "She's but my apprentice. If you take your business elsewhere, I won't starve. And if I were to inform Lord ti'Dana of what I witnessed on the floor today," she said, lowering her voice, "he would be exceedingly displeased. I've designed for him as well," she added with a smirk.

Calien stared back at her, floundering.

"We need some privacy," said Jevva, and closed the door in my cousin's face.

After a few seconds, I heard an enraged shriek, followed by rapid, angry footsteps on the staircase. Jevva glanced toward the door, shaking her head, and waited until the shop's front door slammed before resuming. "So, what are we thinking for the color of the lacing? Blue or gold would work…or perhaps a different shade of blue…"

"You've been at this for a while, huh?" I said, smiling as my stomach began to unclench.

"Since I was a girl. I grew up in the shadow of Hall ti'Dana—the fortress, I mean. Her Majesty sent for me when I was thirty and had begun making a name for myself, and I started designing for the family—the queen and the princess in particular, but also for cousins and anyone else hanging around. I didn't know the full contours of the family," she said with a shrug. "But His Majesty kept me around after his parents' deaths—Lord ti'Dana, that is—and once the Pactlands opened, his sister financed my first shop. I've designed for ladies and lords, for chieftains, representatives, actors, musicians, all manner of people. And while I am quite fond of the princess," she said, "her youngest leaves much to be desired." She gave me another long, assessing look, then said, "You seem overly anxious for a bride. Most of my clients are excited. I don't mean to pry…"

I sank into my chair again. "Honestly?"

"We're alone, dear," she replied, taking the other chair. "And I've heard a bit of everything in these situations, so don't be shy."

Still, I hesitated before speaking. "I'm not sold on a society wedding," I quietly confessed. "It's not my scene, and I don't know what I'm doing. At all," I muttered. "This is for my great-grandfather, and I don't want to embarrass him."

Jevva nodded. "Hence the helpful cousin?"

"Calien doesn't like me—she's made that crystal clear—and the closer we get to the event, the more the gloves are coming off…"

She frowned briefly, then seemed to understand what I meant. "More of what I saw today?"

"Yeah. And look, I want to be grateful—she's done a lot to get this wedding off the ground. I mean," I added, laughing weakly, "I know the only reason I got a dress appointment here is because Calien pulled some strings—"

At that, Jevva snorted and shook her head. "Perhaps with Tiami, but for anyone in this house with *sense*, a simple, 'Rose ti'Dana is looking for a wedding gown' would have sufficed."

"You say that," I told her, "but you're the first designer, vendor…whatever…to give me the time of day."

Jevva's pause was longer, and I kicked myself. Sayings rarely worked in exact translation, and while I was spoiled to have surrounded myself with people who had English as at least a tenth, if not second, language, most folks outside of the agencies had no reason for fluency. But she caught the gist, and her mouth tightened. "These vendors, your cousin selected them?"

"Exactly—connections from her work. I wouldn't know where to begin."

"Mm. Perhaps she needs better partners," said Jevva.

"I'm sure they're great, they just don't really want to

work with me."

"Then Calien never should have retained them. And on that subject, I will be having a serious conversation with Tiami concerning her future here. It's acceptable to turn down a commission, but I will *not* have my customers treated like that."

"I…I'm not asking for her job," I quickly began.

"Oh, no, this is about me, dear. I have a standard, and she didn't meet it. Perhaps better supervision until I'm convinced that she knows how to act." Shaking her head, she said, "Between us, I took on Tiami out of obligation. I've designed for her mother for years, and when the girl expressed an interest, I agreed to allow her to apprentice. She has some talent, but I think her designs are overdone…and *tangerine*?" she said, arching a brow. "With your coloration? Absurd."

"Calien says it's fashionable and wants me to dye my hair to make it work."

Jevva looked at me like I was insane. "This isn't a fashion show, it's a wedding. And let me tell you, youngling, I've worked my share of society weddings, and there's no need for *every* trend to be represented. This is lovely," she said, gesturing to the mannequin. "A classic shape, conservative but flattering colors. You won't embarrass anyone in that gown." She hesitated, then said, "The one Tiami was doing has a rather different silhouette. May I ask why?"

"That's what Calien told me I needed to choose," I explained. "She said something like this one looked too, um…"

No elf with the slightest bit of taste would be caught in that, was what she'd told me. *You already look odd—don't draw attention to it.*

I didn't finish my thought, but Jevva nodded. "It's not a shape many elves favor for the same reason that it doesn't work on nymphs—it's too much dress," she said, waving one hand up and down her slim frame. "Something with a form-fitting cut is often more flattering. And you could certainly wear a dress like that—you're not *fat*," she said again—"but it would fit you differently. That's not a bad thing."

"Unless you're trying to pull off an elven wedding with defective goods," I joked.

Jevva didn't laugh. "You know," she said, leaning toward me, "some people are petty. Some will always look for the flaw in others that makes themselves seem less imperfect. But I recall watching the news a few years ago and hearing how the greatest crime boss in the Pactlands was brought down by a barely trained farseer with a funny accent—which, incidentally, has improved."

The corner of my mouth began to twitch.

"You're different, dear. That doesn't mean defective. Now," she said, glancing at the mannequin again, "is this what you'd like to wear?"

"I think so, yes."

"Wonderful," she said, beaming. "I'll have it ready for your final fitting in a few days. Could we say Sunday week?"

I found Calien waiting outside the shop, sulking on one of the delicate iron benches that dotted the sidewalks in District 4, perfect for the fatigued shopper or the personal assistant left to guard the bags. The bench in front of Black Swan had been fit with a wide awning, and Calien huddled beneath it in the rain, dry but peeved. She looked up from her phone when I emerged with my umbrella, then grabbed her own and marched over to intercept me before I could make it back to the safety of my car.

"I have never been so humiliated in my *life*," she hissed. "And I cannot believe you were so rude to poor Tiami—"

"Save it," I snapped, moving into her space, and Calien retreated a step. "Jevva and I designed my gown, and it's lovely, and it sure as hell isn't tangerine. Are you going to tell me that I'll ruin everything by wearing a dress by the house's founder? Or am I only good enough for your little apprentice friend?"

Calien flushed. "Tiami is at the forefront of the next generation of designers—"

"And if she wants clients, maybe she should learn to stop insulting them to their fucking faces."

"She's a visionary!"

"Yeah, well, Jevva designs for your mother," I retorted. "Surely you're not going to tell me she's not good enough for my wedding gown." As Calien sputtered, I said, "Enjoy the rest of your weekend. I've got places to be."

I managed to reach my car without interruption, and when I glanced over my shoulder, I saw that Calien had disappeared. With a sigh of relief, I slipped behind the wheel and dropped my wet umbrella on the floor, then leaned back and closed my eyes.

Eloping was sounding better by the day.

I was reaching for my phone, planning to check for messages, when the phone began ringing. Grabbing it, I checked the screen: Jane.

"Hey," I said, "how's it going?"

"Not good," Jane replied tersely. "You need to get to quarantine. *Pronto*."

CHAPTER 9

The streets of District 4 might have been busier than usual on Saturday morning, but District 2 was dead, and I raced through them at reckless speed, willing the traffic lights to stay blue as I approached each intersection. I slammed my Outback into park once I reached the DPP garage—I'd taken Syvin's reserved space, but I didn't care—and I paced in the elevator as it rose with maddening slowness to the fifteenth floor. Once the door opened, I sprinted for quarantine, stopping only long enough to flash my badge at the lock.

There was only one technician on duty at the control station, a sorcerer who saw me coming and opened the doors in my path.

When I reached quarantine, I found a cluster of technicians and healers squeezed around the glass walls and elbowed my way toward the front. "Jane! I'm here!" I yelled, and the startled technicians in front of me made a path. Finally, I reached the glass and leaned against it, almost pressed in by the crowd behind me, and looked for my friends.

Jane was sitting on an unmade bed, clutching her phone. Liogh was sitting cross-legged on the floor in a pair of gray sweats—their pajamas almost certainly. There was no sign of Tabitha.

"What's going on?" I called, and banged on the glass. "Jane!"

She looked up, her expression grim.

"Where's Tabitha?"

In response, she pointed to the floor…and that was when I noticed the large puddle in front of Liogh.

"*What*?" I yelped.

Jane nodded. "She kept getting more translucent all night. Collapsed into that about half an hour ago, and now we're a goddamn side show, so…" Glaring out at the quarantine staff, she said, "More solutions, less gawking! You're not helping!"

"Patience, youngling," Liogh murmured with surprising calm, then asked, "Could you hand me a hair tie, please?"

Jane did as they asked, avoiding the puddle, and Liogh braided their hair as they considered the strange liquid, which seemed to me like oddly viscous water. Once their hair was out of the way, they rested their hands on their knees and gently said, "Tabitha, I know you can hear me. You're aware of your surroundings, and you must be so scared. Do not panic. I'm not going anywhere."

I don't know what sort of response I'd been expecting from a *puddle*, but I was disappointed.

"You have control over liquids," Liogh continued in the same soft, measured cadence. "You know that—I've seen it, Jane's seen it, Rose has seen it. She's here, too," they added, barely flicking their eyes toward me. "You're not alone. So, what I need you to do now is push your fear aside and work with me. Let's figure out how you can pull yourself back together."

"Do you think she's still alive?" one of the techs behind me whispered.

"How could you tell?" whispered another.

If Liogh could hear them, they ignored the commentary. "You're all right, Tabitha. You've just phased into a different form, and now you need to learn how to become solid again. You can do this," they said firmly. "And until you work this out, I'll be here. I won't allow anything to happen to you, okay?"

"What if we got a sponge?" the first tech muttered.

Liogh leaned a little closer to the floor. "Can you move

nearer to me? Just a twitch."

Around me, the room held its breath, and the staff pushed so close to the glass that I felt the first stirrings of claustrophobia.

And then, ever so slowly, the puddle began to shift toward the detective.

"Heavens," one of the healers remarked, "she *is* alive…"

"That's fantastic," Liogh told Tabitha. "Excellent progress. Now, as I suspect you'd rather not stay on the floor, let's see if we can't speed this along…" They climbed to their feet and took up a steady stance, then closed their eyes and exhaled.

The puddle rose, elongating and twisting until it formed the rough approximation of a bipedal body, though the face was as smooth as a still pond. When Liogh opened their eyes again, they smiled. "There we are—that's better. I'm holding you together," they explained. "We're going to work on recalling your shape and what solidity feels like, but I *can* catch you. See?"

Tentatively, the faceless construction raised her mitt of a hand and held it up as if examining it. *How* she managed that trick, I had no clue, seeing as Tabitha was still entirely liquid and had no eyes.

"It's weird, I know," Liogh soothed, "but I have all the time in the world, and we'll make this work." Turning to Jane, they said, "I don't mean to kick you out of the quarantine party, but this might be easier for Tabitha if she and I had some privacy."

"Are you sure?" Jane asked.

Tabitha's head dipped in a slow nod.

"Um…well, okay, then. Let me get my stuff…"

She packed quickly, and then, after an uncertain glance at Tabitha, approached the door to the vestibule. "What next?" she asked the crowd outside. "Decon?"

Vinla pushed her way closer. "No, you can go without it."

Jane's eyebrows shot up. "Seriously? No sewage potion?"

"No. We don't have a full breakdown of the novel potion yet, but we've agreed that the effects aren't communicable. You two have helped considerably in that regard," she said, and then, sounding almost hurt, added, "And the neutralizer is *not* sewage."

"Huh," said Jane. "So...why all the security?"

Vinla pointed to Tabitha. "Probably safest for her right now, yes? We don't want anyone *stepping* in her."

Jane grunted, then said to Tabitha and Liogh, "If you need me, call. Day or night. I'll come back."

"We'll be fine," Liogh assured her. "Get some rest—one of us should."

With that, the doors were opened, and Jane escaped quarantine without so much as a decontamination shower. She hadn't had a recent regular shower, either, I deduced, seeing her greasy hair up close.

At Liogh's request, the room cleared—the last thing Tabitha needed was an audience, they insisted—and I walked Jane to the elevator. "What's your plan?" I asked.

"Well, I'm parked back at DOI, so I figured I'd bum a ride over there and nap."

All agents in the big Pact agencies could expect to keep odd hours on occasion, but DOI's could be some of the worst, and Pop had planned accordingly. While there were guest rooms in the building for people who needed temporary government protection, there were also a number of small apartments for agents to use as crash pads—nothing fancy, a bed, a bathroom, and a sitting area, but they served their purpose. And since Pop budgeted for twenty-four-hour on-premises catering, overnighting agents didn't even have to cook. Because Jane still commuted home to Geogia on the weekends—Connor was reluctant to quit his job, and neither of them had had the inclination to work up a suitably impressive house for Hall ti'Catama yet—she'd been assigned one of the apartments until she took the plunge and got a place closer to the office.

"Or," I suggested, "you could come home with me."

"Mm," she said, stroking her chin. "Tempting."

"Laundry, hot shower, ridiculous mattress, and you know Ranarma wouldn't mind putting out an extra plate. Come on," I cajoled, "no reason to stay alone at work. That's *sad*."

"So, you're suggesting I bunk up at my boss's place instead?"

"If he needs you, he'll find you either way."

"Fair." She grinned as the elevator arrived. "Should we warn him?"

There was no need to do more than shoot Pop a brief text. Though it wasn't the largest private home in the Pactlands, the mansion was cavernous, and it didn't lack for guest accommodations. I'd never pried as to *why* Pop had felt the need to construct such a massive house—even when his siblings lived with him, they'd had thousands of unused square feet—but I suspected it was partly an echo of how grand the original Hall ti'Dana had apparently been and partly a reflection of his hopes for a family. Pop had never considered remarrying after losing his wife, and with one child, one grandchild, and now one great-grandchild, he had a long way to go if he wanted to fill the place.

In the meanwhile, the rules of hospitality had practically been codified among the northern elven aristocracy, and their move into the Pactlands had done little to change that. When winter storms threatened travelers, say, or bands of unfriendly humans posed a threat, one could always seek shelter in the fortified Halls, and it was expected that unless a guest offered grave offense to the host, he would be welcomed for as long as necessity dictated—or longer, as such was a sign of the Hall's wealth. The old Hall ti'Dana had been home to a pack of courtiers, advisors, servants, scholars, soldiers, and an odd assortment of people who'd seemingly flitted among the Halls, staying for a few weeks or months at a time, trading gossip and banter for lodging. Its modern counterpart was empty by comparison, and as Pop had never been overly social, he'd seldom had cause to entertain anyone from outside the family for more than dinner since my grandfather was a boy.

But then I'd blown into the mansion with all the calm and subtlety of a tornado, ignorant of the etiquette and unsure of my footing, and Pop had been *delighted.* Move Yven in and surrender the greenhouse? Absolutely. Hide a slew of folks from the Hunt? Of course—and the culinary grads were more than welcome to play in the kitchen. Host Jane, Connor, and all the survivors of East Branch? Why not?

"You're young," Scel had told me with a knowing smile, "and he enjoys the occasional chaos."

Thus, when Jane followed me into the house from the garage, Pop was waiting in the kitchen, doctoring a cup of coffee. "It's palatable," he said, nodding to the pot. "Ranarma is shopping, and I did my best."

"Thanks," said Jane, "but I'm going to pass out, if it's all the same to you. Haven't slept much since Wednesday, so..."

"Your room is being prepared—south wing as usual. I hope that's satisfactory."

She smirked. "Honestly, a rug would be satisfactory right about now, so thanks, boss."

"Of course." Gesturing to me with his mug, Pop asked, "How is everything?"

Groaning, I headed for the warm carafe. "Let's see, I've pissed off Calien, and now Tabitha is a freaking puddle, but other than that...guess the rain's lightened up."

"A *puddle*?"

"Yeah, she phased into a sentient liquid this morning," said Jane. "Liogh Birrid is trying to help her, but...yikes."

"What of the other woman...Stephanie?" Pop asked.

I shook my head as I dumped a considerable volume of sugar into my drink. "Haven't checked lately. I've got to look in on the Golden Children, and if Stephanie's gone full puddle as well…"

"She had people with her after the attack, right?" Jane pressed.

"Yes…"

"Okay. Her posse's not going to leave her unattended, and even if she were to dissolve into goo, they wouldn't call a doctor. Most of her inner circle has little use for Western medicine. She'll keep," she said while I took a test sip. "Worry about that bitch and her little buddies, eh?"

I glanced at Pop, whose expression gave away nothing, then raised my mug to Jane. "Roger that."

Having followed my eyes, Jane turned her attention on Pop. "What do we need to do for Tabitha?"

He shrugged. "She's in capable hands, I should think. The quarantine team, plus a water nymph…I doubt you or I could do anything more for her."

"Is she going to survive this?" Jane demanded, holding his stare.

Pop blinked slowly but didn't look away, and his face remained a careful blank.

"Damn it, Diriem…"

"As I said, she is in competent hands," Pop murmured. "I can offer you nothing more than a bed right now."

Jane regarded him suspiciously, then surrendered to the promise of rest. "You'll tell me if that changes, right?" she asked, and started toward the foyer with her backpack.

"I make no promises," Pop replied.

"What? Can't hear you!"

He shook his head. "Is that so?"

"I'm going to take that as a yes!" she called.

Pop and I shared a look, and I sipped my coffee. "You hired her."

"I did," he said, and shooed me on. "Happy hunting, youngling. I'll tell Yven you're hiding upstairs."

It was Yven who managed to coax me out of my studio Sunday morning for breakfast. I'd skipped dinner, as to my dismay, when I started trancing on Saturday, I'd discovered that the Golden Children had split up. All afternoon and evening, I followed their cars, taking breaks to try to plot their positions on my computer's map and keep tabs on them. Some hadn't stopped until after midnight, while others had begun moving again before dawn.

"You have to eat, Rosie," said Yven, tugging me off the couch as I groaned at the obnoxiously bright sunlight. "They won't disappear if you leave them for a few hours."

"They might."

"Rose Lea."

"That only works for Pop," I muttered, but I allowed him to help me to my feet.

Jane was already at the table by the time we made it, Yven in a tidy rugby shirt and chinos—about as close as he came to slouchwear—and me in the previous day's clothes. She glanced up from her latte as we entered the dining room and winced. "Rough night, huh?"

"Long night," I croaked, and waved as Ranarma peeked in from the kitchen. "Morning. Anything strong on offer?"

"Coming right up. Yven?" he asked.

"Please." My fiancé sat next to me and grabbed a pastry from the platter, then nudged the plate of bacon my way. "You need the protein."

"That's a lot of cholesterol…"

"You're fine," said Jane, pushing a covered bowl toward me. "Eggs. They're even cheesy."

While Ranarma knew how to pull off a number of traditional elven dishes and more than his share of Pactlands standards, he'd done his best to make me feel welcome—first with an alarming variety of gelatin salads, then with a growing selection of recipes that Jane and Maya kept sneaking him. But my favorite of his efforts was his weekend breakfast spreads, much of which wouldn't have been out of place on a country grandma's table. For good or ill, Ranarma had discovered grits, and he liked them with bacon grease and cheddar.

I filled my plate and tucked in, realized after a few bites that I was famished, and picked up the pace. As Ranarma brought in coffee for Yven and me, Jane asked, "So, where are the little darlings now?"

I didn't answer her until I'd had that first hit of caffeine. "They've split up."

"Oh?"

"Yep." Turning back to my eggs, I said, "They were in the Tri-Cities Friday night. Katin's paranoia must have gotten the best of her, since the group had already splintered when I got back to them yesterday afternoon."

"It's not paranoia if someone is actually stalking you," Jane pointed out.

"True," I allowed. "Anyway, some have turned west to Nashville, one car made it as far as freaking *Dallas* early this morning, and the sane ones—or at least the ones with kids—are hanging out around Roanoke. Katin and Dirk are together, and they've tracked south to Highlands."

She frowned. "North Carolina?"

"Bingo. It's about a three-hour drive, so they haven't gone *far*. Managed to snag a rental cabin back in the woods. Katin was up late checking in on the others, but she's sleeping in today," I reported. "Seemed to be more relaxed."

"She *does* know that we can find them even if they split up, right?" said Yven.

I paused to wash down a bite of biscuit—Ranarma had borrowed Yven's recipe, but he hadn't perfected it yet. "Yeah, but I think she knows damn well that if we go after any of them, we'll grab her first. Look," I explained, "the only people she cares about are the Golden Children. That's it. She and Dirk practically raised the other adults. I'm guessing that her thought process is that if they're not with her when we find her, then maybe we'll leave them alone."

"Unlikely," said Jane.

"She's doing what she can," I replied. "And unless someone out there is selling blinding potion…"

Jane had left her phone on the table, and its ringing cut me off. She flipped it over and said, "Liogh," then quickly opened the line. "Hey, I'm here with Rose and Yven," she said, and turned on the speaker. "How's Tabitha?"

"Well, good morning to you, too," came Tabitha's voice.

I goggled as I leaned across the table. "You're back to normal?"

"Uh…*no*," she replied, drawing out the word, "that's not what I'd call this, but I *am* both solid and opaque again, so…progress?"

"She's doing much better," came Liogh's voice from the background. "Come see."

"On our way," said Jane, and hung up, only to immediately call Annie. "Hey, Tabitha's no longer goo," she said without preamble. "Want to give Rose and me a lift?"

The doorbell rang, and I made a brief gesture to unlock it.

"It's open," Jane told Annie. "Dining room."

A few seconds later, Annie jogged in wearing an old Flying Squirrels T-shirt from a giveaway night at The Diamond and a pair of hot pink leggings. She hadn't bothered with shoes, and she padded right past us to poke her head in the kitchen. "Hey, Ranarma," she said, "any chance of getting coffee to go?"

Tabitha laughed when we trooped in a few minutes later. "Y'all could have dressed," she said, rising from her bed to approach the glass—I saw that someone had gotten smart and left the microphone on. "It's not like I'm going anywhere."

Jane glanced at Annie and me. "The important bits are

covered. How the hell are you?"

She spread her arms. "Like I said, progress. The hair is still *off*, but the rest of me is more or less as I remembered..."

"She's done beautifully," said Liogh as they joined her, their expression speaking in equal measure of pride and exhaustion. "We worked all yesterday afternoon and into the night, and around, um..."

"Midnight-ish," Tabitha volunteered. "Something just clicked. Don't ask me how, but I figured it out. Want to see?" she asked us.

"Uh, *yeah*," said Annie.

Tabitha grinned, then sat on the floor. "Okay, give me a sec..." she said, closing her eyes.

As we watched, she liquified into a form indistinguishable from water but for its viscosity. The puddle seemed too thick for an ordinary spill, and it slid out from Tabitha's abandoned clothing until it had formed a neat pool by the foot of the bed.

"Holy shit," Annie whispered.

Jane nudged her in the side. "Told you."

"Yeah, but...whoa. Does that hurt?"

The puddle flowed back the way it had come, then rose, forming into a vaguely humanoid shape and taking the clothes with it before the details solidified into Tabitha's features. "Nope. Tingles a bit, but it's not painful...and my damn shirt's on backward again," she muttered, pulling her arms out of the sleeves to fix the problem. "There are still kinks to be worked out..."

"You're doing *really* well," said Liogh. "Let's maintain our perspective here, yes?"

"It's true, there are kinks," Tabitha replied.

"Yes, but for a human who liquified yesterday, your performance has been marvelous. Also, the fact that you're not curled up under the blankets is shocking."

Tabitha shrugged. "What good would that do?"

They regarded her strangely. "This has to have been

traumatic…"

"Oh, yeah, I'm sure I'll have nightmares eventually, but I ain't got time for that now. By the way, has anyone bothered checking on Stephanie?" she asked, searching our faces. "If she's gone full puddle…"

"That's on the to-do list," said Jane.

Tabitha's mouth tightened. "I know y'all aren't buddies, but *today*, please. If she's going through anything like I've been through this week, then she's a mess right now…"

Her voice faded, and hearing footsteps behind us, I turned to see Vinla, Dante, and Pateme approaching, the healers in their black lab coats, Pateme sporting a pair of jeans that, given the creases, seldom saw daylight.

Annie smirked. "Ooh, are we expanding our casual wardrobe, Director?"

"We need to do laundry," Pateme replied, and nodded to Tabitha. "Ms. Bradley. I'd say it's nice to see you again, but the circumstances could be better," he began, switching to English.

She gave her arm a pinch. "Hey, I'm solid. Better than yesterday."

"So I heard," he said, turning to the healers, only to find Vinla regarding him blankly. Perhaps, I mused, Dante's literature-loving mother had passed along a few languages to her son. "Oh, uh…sorry," Pateme continued in Pactish, "I was just saying that Ms. Bradley has improved."

"Right," she said. "And if you authorize it, I'm prepared to release her from quarantine."

Tabitha stood a little straighter. "Yeah?"

"You're not contagious—the effects you've experienced obviously haven't been transmitted. Since you can maintain your structure, I think it's safe to allow you out of there."

"So…I can go home?" she asked, looking back and forth between Pateme and the healers.

Pateme winced. "That wouldn't be ideal. Please believe me, I'm not trying to hold you here unnecessarily, but—"

"You were exposed to a novel mutagenic," Vinla interrupted, "and we still don't have a good understanding of its mechanism or how to reverse it. *Could* you leave and be safe outside? Possibly, maybe even probably, as long as you can keep yourself intact. But I understand that your hair color is a concern—"

"I've got masking pendants at home," said Jane. "We can hook you up—"

"No masking," Vinla said firmly. "Not yet. Until I'm convinced that she won't end up like Annie did, we can't risk it."

"I'll assume the risk," said Tabitha.

But Annie shook her head. "I get it, I *do*, but renal failure's no fun."

"I've got a business to run," Tabitha protested. "Prescriptions to fill."

"And I'm sure we can make up the financial loss," Pateme soothed, "but for now, perhaps you could come down with a long illness."

"Mono?" suggested Annie. "And hey, if there's stuff you need to do back in Ragged Gap, maybe I could take you under cover of darkness. Wait for nightfall, sneak you to the store, you put in whatever calls you need…"

Though she didn't seem happy, Tabitha nodded, resigned. "That…could work, yeah. If you could take me back tonight, let me make the arrangements, I'd appreciate it."

Vinla frowned. "Is that safe? Allowing her to go outside in her condition?"

"We'll make it safe enough, and it's non-negotiable," Annie replied. "I was yanked off the face of the earth with no chance to handle my affairs. We're going to do right by Tabitha."

"If you're concerned, I'm sure Gentle Breeze wouldn't mind coming along to babysit," I said.

"That sounds like an excellent idea," said Pateme before the healers could argue. "I'll call her later this morning. For now…" He gestured, and the quarantine doors unlocked. "Agent Birrid, I'm sure you're ready to see your own bed. Thank you for your assistance. Ms. Bradley…hmm." Folding his arms, he looked at Annie and said, "The apartment we used for you two could be set up again. It's available."

"Or, for now," she countered, "Tabitha, you could come home with me. We've got tons of room, and you would double the number of women on the premises. You know Wylan wouldn't mind."

"Unwise. I can't get to the Hunt's territory in case of emergency," said Vinla.

Annie's brow knit. "We can bring her back and forth, it's no trouble—"

"Plan C," I interjected. "Come with me. Jane's already sleeping over, and Pop's not going to complain about one more."

Pateme eyed the healer. "Is Viratta close enough?"

"I mean, preferably, she'd remain in Beukal," said Vinla, "but…I suppose."

"Works for me," said Tabitha, heading for the bathroom. "Just let me pack, eh?"

I followed her into quarantine, then slipped into the bathroom while she gathered her few toiletries. "If this doesn't work," I said softly, "if you're uncomfortable, no pressure. There's a hotel not far from DPP, and I bet we could find a way to put you there if you want."

"Oh, no, this sounds great," she replied, grabbing a bottle from the shower stall she'd claimed. "Look, I like Annie and Wylan, but *how* many guys are in that house?"

"Several dozen."

She whistled low. "That's what I thought. Thanks, hon."

Though Pop seldom had cause to engage the wards on the mansion that would keep even the Hunt out, Annie tended to err on the side of manners and materialize in the driveway.

As Jane steadied Tabitha, our newest houseguest said, "Aw, man, that doesn't get any less weird with...holy *shit*," she muttered, and stepped back to take in the house. "Rose, is this..."

"This is the place," I said, heading up the stairs. "Come on, let's get you moved in."

She followed after me, with Jane carrying her bag, and stared wide-eyed as she took in the foyer. "Damn, girl," she said under her breath.

In fairness, I'd had much the same reaction the first time I visited the place. "Let me find Pop—"

"Ah, right on time," he said, emerging from a sitting room, robe on and dressed for the office. "Good. Jane, I asked for Tabitha to be put in the room beside yours, so if you wouldn't mind orienting her..."

"Not a problem," said Jane.

Tabitha cleared her throat. "Um...sorry to drop in on you, uh—"

"It's Diriem," he offered, and smiled. "No need to apologize, and welcome back to the Pactlands, as it were."

"One of these days, I'm going to have an uneventful visit."

"Perhaps. Unfortunately, I need to be at work," he said, "but I'm sure the girls can help you settle. Lunch is generally around noon, but if you're hungry, just let Ranarma know—he does special orders. Rosie, I'll see you tomorrow."

"Tomorrow?" I echoed as Pop headed across the foyer. "Are you camping at work tonight?"

"I'm keeping a full schedule, and so are you, youngling. Have fun in Ragged Gap," he added, and disappeared around the corner.

"Know-it-all farseers," I grumbled, and gestured Tabitha's suitcase off the ground. "All right, Tabitha, we're heading for the south tower."

As promised, her room had been prepared—the bed was even turned down—and she sighed as she put her bag on a luggage rack. "This is the nicest place I've ever stayed," she said. "No joke. I'm kind of afraid to touch anything…"

"Don't worry, you can't be any worse than we were," said Annie. "Diriem's numb to us."

"And just about everything is fixable, so relax," I told Tabitha. "Why don't you take a hot shower, wash the quarantine away?"

"That's actually not a bad idea." She dug in her bag until she found a pink shower cap—a gift from Enva, I assumed. "Um…question," she said, clutching the cap to her chest. "Would one of y'all mind waiting here while I rinse off?"

"Sure, no problem," said Jane, and Annie and I nodded. "Not worried about getting lost in the bathroom, are you?"

"This probably sounds stupid, but just in case I end up going down the drain…"

We assured her that we'd wait there and check on her in ten minutes, and with a degree of trepidation, Tabitha steamed up the bathroom.

She seemed to feel better when she emerged, wrapped in the fluffy white robe left on the back of the door, and I showed her how the TV remote worked while Annie filled a glass with water for her nightstand and Jane set the alarm for lunchtime. Before we could see ourselves out, however, a knock at the door heralded the arrival of one of the staff, a young sorcerer named Cirat who smiled with apparent relief to find me in there. "Hello, Miss Rose. Sorry to interrupt," she said, and nodded toward the bed. "I forgot to put this on. If I could have a few minutes to redo the linens…"

"Oh, sure. Hi," said Tabitha in her accented Pactish. "Thanks so much. What did you forget?"

Cirat extended the bundle in her arms. "Plastic sheet,

miss. Lord ti'Dana suggested it. In case you were to lose control in your sleep, you wouldn't be absorbed by the mattress."

Tabitha retreated to the bathroom to dry off, and the rest of us gave Cirat a hand, making quick work of the sheets. Once she'd left, Tabitha emerged in her pajamas and carefully sat on the edge of the bed. "So…is your great-grandfather *always* right about the future?" she asked me.

"He didn't say you were absolutely going to liquefy in your sleep," I replied. "Just a precaution."

"Yeah, and that's a whole new fear unlocked," she mumbled. "If y'all don't see me for lunch, come find me, okay? Maybe send up a mop."

CHAPTER 10

With Tabitha comfortable and dead to the world, we could finally turn to the problem of Stephanie.

Technically, were we following protocol, DPP would have sent a team in to conduct reconnaissance and potentially extraction. But Annie, having been the target of such measures, was wary to drag in backup, and Jane claimed it would be a bad idea. "This is Ragged Gap we're talking about," she said. "I know that town like the back of my hand. This ain't peak tourist season, and a bunch of strangers with weird accents are going to set off alarms, and I *really* don't want to have to explain away freaking DPP to the local cops."

"Too bad Stephanie doesn't live in Whitford," I muttered, grabbing a few imported Cokes from my apartment's fridge. I'd insisted on changing clothes before we departed, and Annie had made a quick trip back to the lodge for pants in a non-neon shade and a pair of shoes.

"Right? And thanks," said Jane, snatching one of the plastic bottles before I could offer it. "Okay, who wants to drive?"

After a brief discussion, we decided that none of us wanted our cars anywhere near suspicious activity, so Annie blipped us over to DPP and checked out one of the agency Jeeps with an app on her phone. The vehicle was forgettable, just a dusty black Grand Cherokee with cloth seats and Virginia plates, but hidden in a physically impossible pocket accessed through a trapdoor beneath the trunk's carpet was a storage space large enough for a few kayaks, an ATV, or at least a bedroom's worth of furniture. Once the app sent confirmation, the driver's door unlocked, revealing a nondescript keyring on the dashboard. We piled in, with Jane riding shotgun to direct, and Annie wrapped her arm through the steering wheel before linking hands with Jane and me, the better to ensure that the Jeep arrived with us. "Ready?" she asked.

I closed my eyes. "Do it."

My stomach lurched as the world fell away, but gravity returned an instant later, and I opened my eyes to find that Annie had dropped us in Jane's front yard. "Hope no one saw that," Annie mumbled, peering out the windows.

Jane waved off her concern. "It's Sunday morning. Half this town's at church, and the other half is sleeping in until brunch. Or fishing," she allowed. "We should be good."

She directed Annie down the mountain toward downtown Ragged Gap, then guided us to Mystic Mountains. "I don't want to barge in on Stephanie without cause," she explained on the way. "Especially not with a crowd. Let's swing by the shop and see if she's around."

"You really think she's okay?" I said, arching a brow.

"Could be like Roulette," said Annie, stopping to let a jogger pound through the crosswalk. "Remember, it didn't do anything to most of the folks who took it. Tabitha could just be *lucky* like Maya and me."

"Maybe, but I saw Stephanie's hair change color, and that sure as hell doesn't bode well."

We parked about a block from Mystic Mountains, and Jane led the way down the quiet sidewalk. I'd expected to find the store locked—my experience suggested that boutiques in tiny towns didn't open before ten, and it was quarter past nine—but Jane pushed the door open, and we walked into an asthmatic's nightmare of patchouli incense.

Once we made it through the haze at the front of the shop and coughed our lungs clear, I saw a small crowd in the multipurpose space in the back, filling several rows of chairs that faced the café. Someone had set up a wooden podium, and Penny, sporting a gray broom skirt and loose black T-shirt, was in the middle of her remarks. Spotting us, she froze, then jabbed one finger at Jane and yelped, "*You*!"

Jane lifted her hands to keep the crowd at bay. "Whoa, now," she said calmly, "what's going on? Where's Stephanie?"

Penny's eyes were puffy and red, and I suspected it had nothing to do with the incense. "Wouldn't you like to know?"

Jane coughed again—that incense was strong enough to kill a house full of fleas, even at the rear of the store—and glanced toward Jerry, who'd come to town that morning in a camo jacket and slightly stained Dickies pants. "What's all this?"

The old man stood and nodded a curt greeting. "Stephanie disappeared. Don't know if she's gone or dead or what…" He paused as Penny wailed, his expression suggesting that wasn't the first time he'd been thus interrupted that morning. As she honked her nose into a handkerchief, he said, "Wish you'd been here for Beltane. Katarina Weller came back, and she stuck Stephanie and Tabitha with some shit. Tabitha wandered off alone, and I *think* she made it home—her car's there—but she's gone."

"I heard about what happened," Jane replied. "Tabitha's safe, don't worry. She needed a specialist, someone with better training than mine, so we got her out of town."

A look of relief crossed Jerry's wrinkled face. "She's okay?"

"Getting closer to it. I don't know when she'll be ready to come home, but she's not dead—my friends here will back me up on that," she added, and Annie and I nodded. "Now, what's this about Stephnie disappearing?"

Penny started to speak, but Jerry cut her off. "Whatever she got injected with Wednesday night must have hurt like a mother—we had to give her opioids to get her to sleep.

Her hair turned white, too. Didn't know pain could do that."

"It can't," said Annie. "What happened next?"

"Well, we had to keep her knocked out all day Thursday—she woke up in pain, and we didn't want her to suffer. But that night...it was the damnedest thing..."

"Her fingers vanished!" Penny blurted.

"Vanished, or just became translucent?" asked Jane.

"Translucent," said Jerry. "You could grab 'em, but you could see right through 'em. And then more of her got like that, arms and legs, then her torso. Her head was the last to go, and that was early Saturday morning."

I traded glances with Jane and Annie, then asked, "Was she sedated all that time?"

"Had to be," said Jerry. "She wailed like a banshee when the drugs wore off."

"Uh-huh." Folding her arms, Jane said, "So, she was home in bed when this happened, I take it."

"Yep. And once she went fully translucent, she just disappeared."

"Clothes and all?"

"No, those were left behind where she'd been lying. Like she got raptured or something."

"Unlikely," Jane muttered under her breath. "Okay, weird question: did anyone see an odd puddle at Stephanie's? In the bed, maybe?"

The mourners shook their heads.

"And is anyone at her house now?"

"No," said Penny. "We locked up yesterday in case she ever comes back..."

"Get a grip, woman," said Jerry, sighing, as Penny started to sniffle again. "Jane, any ideas?"

She looked at us, questioning, and I took the lead. "I don't believe she's dead," I told the woo-woo brigade. "Tabitha's alive, after all. But it may take some time for her to, uh...reappear."

Jerry eyed me warily. "And you are?"

"Friend of mine," said Jane, intervening. "She's got the gift, too. And I agree—we'll find Stephanie, but this may not be an immediate thing."

"Can we help?" asked the woman with the red curls—Bitsy, I thought. "Is there a ritual or—"

Jane shut that down in a hurry. "No. Y'all keep Mystic Mountains open for now. If anyone asks, Stephanie's gone out of town. And if you see the slightest sign of Katarina, you call me. *Immediately.*" Looking at Jerry, she asked, "You have my number?"

"Yessum."

"Great. Pass it around. We're going to get to the bottom of this," she promised them. "But y'all do me a favor and stay away from Stephanie's house for now. There may be clues, and we don't want to contaminate the scene."

As the three of us turned to go, Penny called, "What *are* you, anyway? I think we have a right to know!"

Jane stopped, her shoulders hunching. "Why? You've never wanted anything to do with me. Why do I owe you jack?"

"Because Stephanie's hurt, and it's all because of you—"

"Stop it," I snarled, wheeling on her, and marched toward Penny until I was up in her face. "I saw the whole damn thing happen, princess, and you were right there, welcoming Katarina back. Remember? Stephanie told her to leave, and you got pissy."

Penny backed off, her eyes widening. "That's…how…"

"None of your business, and don't you dare blame Jane for this mess."

Before I could continue, Jane gripped my arm and pulled me away from Penny. "All you need to know is that I'm on your side," she told the would-be witch. "I've been trying to protect y'all, but you're not making it easy. Just…don't drink any strange liquids, all right? Please?"

With that, she steered Annie and me out of the store

and back toward the Jeep.

As we climbed into the vehicle, Annie asked, "You ever think of coming clean with them? Showing them what you can really do?"

"It's tempting," Jane admitted, "and very much against both Pact law and common sense." She leaned into her seat and released a long sigh. "Okay, what's the plan? Stephanie disappears, no puddle…"

"Maybe she was absorbed into the bed," Annie suggested.

"If that were the case, surely she'd be out of it by now. Tabitha could move on her own as a puddle."

"What if she's not a puddle?" I mused. "Remember, Tabitha's hair went blue, but Stephanie's went white. What if she got a different power?"

"Roulette again," Annie murmured. "You think?"

"Give me a minute." I closed my eyes and tried to visualize what I'd witnessed after the Golden Children injected that potion. Stephanie and Tabitha had screamed and collapsed, their hair had changed color, Tabitha had made nearby liquids boil…

"There was this sudden wind around Stephanie," I said. "Localized. It couldn't have been a draft."

"Tabitha got water power, Stephanie got air," said Jane. "Color-coded to boot. Shit," she whispered. "What do we do? You want to get Maebe over here?"

While Maebe was a talented aeromancer, she was also very green. "I think it might be a better idea to get an air nymph," I replied, "or at least a fully trained aeromancer. Do we want to drive over there and see if we can find her first?"

"If she's turned to air, good luck with that," said Annie, and glanced at Jane as she pulled her phone from her bag. "Who're you calling?"

"Liogh."

"Weren't they going home to sleep?" I asked.

"They'll forgive me," said Jane, and slipped into Pactish. "Hey, there. Sorry to wake you," she said, and grimaced to herself. "Know a good agent with air abilities?"

When we rendezvoused in the DPP deck before dawn Monday morning, we needed a second vehicle.

"Feeling better?" Liogh asked Tabitha as she slid out of the one Annie had borrowed the day before. "You look whole."

"I didn't dissolve in my sleep, so I'll count that as a win," she replied, smiling. "And I held it together through a ride back to Ragged Gap with Annie."

Their brows rose. "Teleportation?"

"She's tough," said Annie, clapping Tabitha on the shoulder. "We closed up her pharmacy, and she made all the necessary calls for her customers."

"Let the extended mononucleosis recovery commence," Tabitha added wryly.

"No issues at all," Annie told the detective. "Gentle Breeze was *bored*."

"I bet," they replied, then looked past her as the fifth member of our party squeezed out of the Jeep. "*Ah*, youngling. I'd wondered if you'd be along on this jaunt. Good experience for you, I suspect."

Maebe, still sleep-puffy around her eyes and nursing one of my imported Cokes, croaked, "Morning, Detective."

They chuckled. "Little early?"

"Sun's not even up," she grumped. "I don't know if I can help you, but…" She perked as an elf with short black hair stepped from the passenger seat of Liogh's car. "Orten!"

He spotted her and grinned. "Well, now, Lady ti'Ammaas. It's been a while—look at you."

Maebe flopped her empty hand as if showing off her white tunic top and green polka-dot leggings. "Only the finest. You're coming with us?"

He gestured to his own jeans and black T-shirt. "That's the plan."

Before the two of them could ramp up, Liogh stepped in with introductions. "Ladies, this is Orten ti'Gata, one of our investigators in Violent Crimes. He's a well-trained aeromancer."

"Trained me," Maebe piped up.

That was why he looked vaguely familiar, I realized—he'd been sent out to Viratta to give Maebe the crash course when her wild talent explosively revealed itself.

"Orten," Liogh continued, "this is Annie Humphries with DPP, that's Jane Fortune from DOI, I trust you've met Rose, and the lovely lady with the striking hairdo is—"

"Tabitha Bradley," she interrupted, extending her hand. "Hi."

The investigator shook it. "Liogh briefed me yesterday. I'm so sorry to hear about your, uh..."

She released him and let her hand drip onto the cement floor before recalling it into place. "I mean, it could be worse."

"That's the spirit," muttered Annie. "So, here's the plan: I'll get us to Jane's house, and Liogh, you caravan behind us while we drive to Stephanie's. Don't know what we'll find once we're there, but I suspect one of us can pick a lock. Okay?"

Orten cleared his throat. "You, uh...you're the Huntsman, right?"

"Officially?" Annie wiggled one hand. "I'm not as proficient with weapons as the boys are, but I can get us where we need to go. All right, load up, mask up, and let's do this."

Maebe joined Liogh and Orten to make room, and Jane, Tabitha, and I piled back into the borrowed Jeep. Annie gripped the door handle, and after that awful jolt and blackness, we landed in front of Jane's cabin, bathed in the glow of her security light. Before I could open the door, Annie vanished, only to reappear a few seconds later with Liogh's car. Their passenger door swung open, and Orten practically fell out onto his knees, where he clung to the weeds for a moment before brushing himself off and tentatively returning to his seat.

"First-timer," Annie remarked, turning the key.

"To be fair, it's weird as hell," said Tabitha. "Not that I'm complaining about the shortcut."

Seeing as the nearest portal was an hour away in South Carolina, none of us minded terribly.

Liogh followed closely as Jane directed Annie down one mountain, around the center of town, and up another hillside, and we pulled into the driveway of a ranch-style house that might have been unassuming but for its canary yellow paint and bubblegum trim. The flowerbeds were clean and tidy, and despite the oaks on her neighbors' properties, Stephanie had managed to cultivate a thick, green lawn. Whatever else could be said for her, she took pride in her yard. Much as Tabitha had done at her home, Stephanie's front door and windows bore garlands of yellow flowers, though even in the blue predawn light, they'd seen better days.

"The Beltane decorations are just sad now," said Tabitha, who'd taken the back seat with me. "Think we should remove them?"

"No," said Annie. "If someone does report Stephanie missing, that might be considered evidence tampering." She opened her door, listened briefly for signs of life, then climbed out and unkinked her back while Liogh parked behind us. Leaning into the Jeep, she asked, "So, do we know anything about a spare key, or do we need a little hocus-pocus?"

Jane snorted as she unbuckled. "*Wow*. Should I be offended?"

"Hey, I thought I was among friends."

"Yeah, but…hocus-pocus, my ass," she said, and slammed her door.

Tabitha and I followed, and Liogh, Orten, and Maebe

met us at the door. Muttering under her breath, Jane cast a quick spell to turn the latch, and we hastened inside before any stray joggers could notice our crowd.

Though the windows were closed, the house was cool—even in the mountains, air conditioning was a way of life from spring through fall, and recent afternoons in Ragged Gap had been edging toward the eighties in a brief heat wave. I assumed that Stephanie's posse would have left the air on even after her disappearance, just in case she were to return to a miserably warm house. But the temperature outside was low enough to keep the system shut off, and the ceiling fans were still…

Yet there was a draft.

An odd current of air passed behind me, then to my right, but I couldn't pinpoint its source. I flipped on the overhead light in the den, and I felt the current move again, almost circling me before it disappeared.

"Does anyone feel a breeze?" I asked.

Jane nodded. "Yeah. Do we think…"

"Probably," said Tabitha, and stepped into the middle of the room. "Stephanie?" she called, keeping her eyes toward the ceiling, and switched to English. "It's okay, hon. We know what happened, or we've got a pretty good idea, anyway. I dissolved, and I'm guessing you…sublimated? Close enough. Everyone's worried about you. Jane stopped by the store yesterday to check in, and she heard you'd vanished. We're here to help."

"May I?" Liogh murmured, touching Tabitha's arm, and she ceded the floor. "Good morning, Ms. Love," they said calmly as the breeze rushed past me again. "You can call me Leo—I'm a friend of Coby Hewt's. Let me fill you in," they said, their English too clipped to be southern but their generic American accent eerily good. "The woman you know as Katarina Weller is a sorcerer…like Jane here," they added, nodding toward her.

"Uh, should you be saying that?" Orten interrupted in Pactish.

"She's heading to Beukal momentarily—there's no sense in lying," they replied in kind, then slipped into English again. "Katarina didn't just skip town. She and her family, for lack of a better term, have been incarcerated since the time Jane freed you from that cabin. I was there, incidentally, but I'm sure you don't remember—the potion she'd used on you is potent stuff. Unfortunately, Katarina and the others were released from custody in mid-April and returned to Texas. We'd hoped they'd learned their lesson, but that was a mistake." They folded their arms and stood still as the strange breeze ruffled their long ponytail. "Hello, there. I know you can understand me, and I know you're frightened. There's a place we can take you—the place where Tabitha was taken—where you can get the help you need."

"Here's the sitch," said Jane. "You and Tabitha were injected with a novel potion. There's a team working around the clock to figure out how it works and how to reverse it, but until then, you're not safe here. Also," she said, glancing at me, "Katarina and her buddies are on the move. They're not in the area, but they're not too far away, either. We need to get you out of here."

Maebe, who'd been poking around the kitchen, returned with a large mason jar, the kind with a hinged lid. "Um, excuse me, Stephanie?" she said. "Hi, I'm Maebe. We met at your store one night when Warner Cavanaugh came by, remember? Jane broke his arms and shattered his knee, and you let me have a piece of amethyst? It's really pretty, by the way. I keep it on my desk," she said, faintly smiling. "So, um, I'm what you call an aeromancer. It means I'm particularly good at moving gases around. Orten here is much better trained than I am," she continued as he raised a hand. "I think, if you hold still, we can get you in here for transport," said Maebe, patting the jar.

"It's weird as hell, I know," said Tabitha, "but it's the only way to get you where you need to be. Cooperate."

The breeze made a few more agitated laps around the

room, but then the air seemed to still. Maebe held the jar steady, and Orten murmured to her in Pactish, "Feel it? That odd energy?"

"Mm-hmm."

"Good. Let me do the tricky bit, youngling…"

He gestured, and a sudden wind blew toward them. Maebe slammed the lid of the jar and latched it, then gripped the jar tightly to her chest as it began shaking in her arms.

"*Hey*," said Jane, tapping on the glass, "calm the fuck down, Stephanie."

"Not helpful," Tabitha muttered, and took the jar from Maebe. Holding it in the crook of her arm, she said, "No one's going to hurt you. Now, this next bit may feel weird, but it's going to save us a road trip, so…you know, I don't think you can throw up in that form, so that's one perk."

The jar rattled more violently.

"I'll explain later," Tabitha promised. "Turn the lights off, y'all, and let's beat it."

We didn't bother loading into the vehicles. Annie had us join hands in a circle and dropped us in the hallway just outside the quarantine wing, then returned to Georgia for a minute to retrieve our rides. "I checked the Jeep in, and Liogh, you're in a visitor space," she said, tossing them their keys. "Okay, let's go complicate Vinla's morning."

The healer, who'd been forewarned of our retrieval expedition, was waiting by the glass-walled enclosure, sipping a cup of burned coffee, with groggy Dante beside her. "That was fast," she said as we showed ourselves in.

"Aeromancers," said Liogh, thumbing both hands at Maebe and Orten, then disengaged their mask and said in English, "Victim number two is in the jar."

Vinla frowned, unable to follow his linguistic switch, but Dante asked, "You're sure?"

"Positive," said Orten in kind. "And I'll be staying in quarantine with her until she improves."

The jar almost shook out of Tabitha's grip at the news.

"I can stay, too," Maebe offered. "If that'd be okay, Stephanie."

The shaking calmed somewhat, and Tabitha smirked. "Think that's a yes, kid."

"Whoa, now, hold on," said Dante in Pactish, eyeing Maebe, "what's your affiliation?"

"Um…I go to school at North Lake," Maebe replied, "but I can miss a few days—"

"You're *underage*?" Vinla interrupted. "How the heck did you get permission to go outside?"

Jane wrapped her arm around Maebe's shoulders. "This is Lady ti'Ammaas, my husband's cousin," she told the healers. "Trust me, she's got permission."

Vinla's brow furrowed as she considered Maebe. "She's…what…"

"She has authorization," came Pateme's voice from the far side of the room, and I wheeled around to see him walk in, impeccably dressed for the office despite the hour. "And I was asked to convey to her that the arrangements have been made with her tutors," he added. "So, why don't you two make yourselves comfortable?" he said to Maebe and Orten. "I'll have your things delivered."

While Maebe took the jar from Tabitha and followed Orten into quarantine, I met Pateme's eye. "Got an early wake-up call, huh?" I asked.

"As grateful as I am for the occasional tip," he said, "I do wish Diriem were better at sleeping in. Now, what of you?" he asked, pointing to Annie and me. "Should I anticipate seeing either of you around the office today?"

"Oh, sure," said Annie, covering a yawn. "All things are possible through caffeine."

But I shook my head. "I'm going to work from home. Assuming you want me to keep an eye on the Golden Children…"

"Absolutely," said Pateme. "I'll call for a report tonight."

We borrowed Annie for a few minutes more, first to

get all of us back to the mansion, and then to ferry Jane to DOI, where her truck was still parked. Once the two of them had departed, I gave Tabitha an apologetic shrug and said, "Trancing's pretty boring to everyone except me. Think you can entertain yourself until lunchtime?"

"Hell," she said with a snort, "I'm going back to bed. I am *convalescing*, I'll have you know."

I grinned and headed for the wide staircase. "Bed's okay?"

"Is it magical? I'm pretty sure mattresses aren't designed to feel like that."

"You'd have to ask Pop. I've never pried too deeply into the furnishings," I replied.

"Mm." Trailing me by a step, Tabitha asked, "You think he'd notice if I took a mattress with me?"

CHAPTER 11

I spent the rest of Monday going in and out of trance—checking on the Golden Children, who continued to spread out, but also peeking in on quarantine. When I collapsed around ten that night, Stephanie still hadn't solidified, but Maebe and Orten appeared to be in decent spirits.

Yven woke me on my studio couch Tuesday morning. "Rosie," he said gently as I mumbled a greeting, "do you think you should shower?"

"Shower?" I croaked, blinking my gummy eyes.

"Yes. Remember our appointment with the officiant at noon? In District 4?"

I groaned as the gears clicked. "Shit, that's today?"

"It doesn't have to be," said Yven. "I can call Calien—"

"*No*, no, don't do that. She's pissed at me." I sat up and rubbed my head, then focused sufficiently to see that my fiancé was already dressed for the office—and wearing a robe I'd picked out, a deep blue with delicate gold accents. Yven's taste skewed conservative, especially for work, but he admitted that I had an eye for robe design. Pop, who was glad to see Yven branch out beyond his first post-graduation business attire, had practically pushed us out the door to visit the tailor and assured me that money was no object.

Clearly, a shower was the bare minimum I needed to accomplish that morning.

Yven escorted me to the bathroom—I could be a bit wobbly after a long stretch of trancing, especially if I'd skipped meals—and turned the shower on while I stripped off my wrinkled clothing. By the time I emerged, pink and swaddled in terrycloth, he'd made me a cup of tea and brought up a tray from the kitchen. "Eat. Rest. Enjoy," he said, and kissed my forehead before he took his leave. "Meet me at the office at eleven?"

The protein helped my farsight hangover, and I managed to make myself presentable in a knee-length green silk dress between peeks at the Golden Children. When I rapped on the wall of Yven's cubicle, I felt almost like myself—well, the version of myself fit for polite company.

He signed out and drove us to the meeting, following the address plugged into his phone. As he maneuvered through the lunchtime traffic in District 2, he asked, "What's this fellow's name, again?"

I chuckled. "Feon ti'Grell."

"And *why* are we skipping work to meet with him?"

"Because Calien says he's the best in the business," I replied. "He's the go-to guy for high society elven weddings. And I've seen some videos—he does beautiful work with the family trees. They almost seem alive, and the names on the trunks and branches flash and glow as they link up."

Yven reached over and took my hand. "As long as you're happy."

"This is less about happy and more about getting through this mess, but thanks, sweetie." I squeezed his hand and leaned back against the seat. "Calien told me all her friends have used him for their weddings, so he comes highly recommended."

"Well, he's had a few weeks to look over our ancestral notes. I hope he doesn't have too many questions."

Yven and I had spent a long, laborious weekend assembling the data the officiant would need to make our trees work during the ceremony. My ti'Dana and ti'Cren sides were well-mapped, but I'd had to dig through my parents' basement and its many storage boxes to find the crumbling family Bibles that guided me back a few generations. As for Yven, while I'd given myself papercuts and chased away spiders, he'd been on the phone with his grandparents, picking their brains. Yven could trace all of his family back before the Pact, and while I could only get my human family to the late eighteenth century, we had enough to work with. I'd made careful notes and put everything into a binder, which I'd handed off to Calien to pass along to Feon.

Yven parked on the street in front of a narrow three-story building fronted in white marble and lined with spiraling columns—gaudy to me, but then parts of District 4 had more money than taste. We climbed out, and Yven, smiling reassurance, offered me his arm as we headed in through the tall gray doors.

Calien, decked in a confection of tangerine taffeta and tulle, almost leapt from her chair in the sumptuous waiting room as we entered. "*There* you are," she snapped, smoothing her poofy skirt. "About time!"

Yven glanced at his wrist. "We're five minutes early."

My cousin ignored him. "What are you *wearing*?" she asked, giving me a disapproving once-over. "And your face is swollen. What's wrong with you?"

"Work emergency," I replied, not bothering with the details—I doubted Calien would have cared. "I haven't been sleeping much."

"Well, pull yourself together, and try not to embarrass me this time," she said, and flounced off up the steep marble staircase.

I met Yven's eyes, and he wrapped his arm around my waist as we followed after her.

The second floor of the building was entirely open but for a pair of closets, and the furnishings were gloriously overdone: brass chandeliers, curving white couches, wooden ebony tables, eight-foot framed mirrors, white rugs with pile so thick it bordered on shag. The side tables were decorated with crystal vases full of fresh-cut flowers—an expensive extravagance in the Pactlands—and placed behind the sleek white desk, as if flanking the man in the matching leather swivel chair, was a pair of boxwood topiaries shaped into short towers of green balls. Though the plants were only about two feet high, their presence spoke of a ridiculous sum spent on the imported soil, fertilizer, and supplements necessary to keep them alive. Yven's orchids grew in small pots outside of the greenhouse, but the dwarf topiaries perched in pots large enough for me to have curled up inside, a clear show of wealth.

Then again, the owner of the topiaries didn't seem like the minimalist type. The elf I took to be Feon was leaning against his desk, sporting an all-white ensemble—long-sleeved silk shirt, tight trousers, and an embroidered silk robe, white on white, that ventured beyond formal into couture. It trailed behind him as he straightened and slowly approached us, appraising. Feon was pasty, with washed-out gray eyes and barely even a hint of a flush. The only part of him that screamed with color was his hair, bright orange and twisted into an immobile topknot.

Tangerine. Of course.

"Calien," he said, taking her hands in greeting, his voice as smooth as oil. "So good to see you, dear."

"Likewise." She pecked his cheek, and when he released her, she perched on the edge of a couch.

Feon returned to his desk, leaving Yven and me standing awkwardly there, but we sank onto the couch beside my cousin and waited as he settled in.

"So," said Feon after a moment, steepling his bloodless fingers, "let's go through the logistics. The venue is secured?"

"Absolutely," said Calien, pulling her purple notebook and pen from a pocket within her massive skirt. "Reserved, paid, mine."

"Excellent. And you have my specifications?"

She consulted her notes. "Looks like your usual contract, but I did notice the strawberries."

"A new addition. I'll need a generous bowl."

"Of course. What are your thoughts on the linguistic problem?"

"What problem?" I interrupted.

The pair of them glared at me before turning back to their conversation. "Pactish would be best," said Feon. "Were the guests of a uniform caliber, perhaps I could do Low Elvish, but considering some of the rabble on the list you showed me—"

"Excuse me," Yven firmly interjected, "but are you referring to our guests?"

That time, my fiancé bore the brunt of the others' annoyed glares. "I told you my guest list was better, but you didn't listen," said Calien. "It's a mixed crowd. Pactish is the only option."

Though Yven kept his voice level, I could hear the frustration thrumming through it. "I've been to plenty of weddings with mixed guest groups, and they've all been conducted in High Elvish. Put the translation in the program as usual. Where's the issue?"

Calien and Feon traded looks, and he said, "We can discuss this later."

"There's nothing to discuss," Yven began, but I put my hand on his arm to grab his attention, then tried to steer the conversation to a less fraught track.

"I see you received our ancestry notes," I said, nodding to the black binder on Feon's desk. "Did you have any questions? Yven and I had to do some creative phonetic rendering on a few of those," I added, forcing a smile, "but we both speak High Elvish, so I think we're close enough to make this work."

Feon eyed the binder, then looked back at me. "I'm not doing trees for this ceremony."

"Why not?" I demanded, surprised by the flat refusal. "You've done such a beautiful job at other weddings—"

"Exactly. *Other* weddings," he replied. "I'm only deigning to touch this one because Calien is a darling, and I owed her a few favors. But if you think I'd sully myself by going into the details of a *ti'Ansha* tree…and not even a main-line tree?" He laughed incredulously. "What do you want next, a ti'Van wedding? And don't get me started on your messy lines," he continued, smirking at me from the other side of the desk. "I could mention the ti'Dana and ti'Cren branches, I suppose, but certainly not the rest."

I felt the blood rush up my neck and into my face. "We've done the research for you," I said, wilting under his scorn. "All you need to do is label the trees. Please."

"Absolutely not. You really want me to show off *human* ancestry? Disgusting. We'll do without."

I sat there for a few seconds in silence, humiliated and trying to find a way around the problem, but Yven beat me to it. He pushed himself off the couch and plucked our binder from the desk, then said, his voice a veneer of ice over controlled fury, "In that case, your services are not required."

Feon stared up at him, frowning. "*Excuse* me?"

"Did I stutter? You're fired."

As Yven helped me up and Calien sputtered, Feon jumped from his chair and marched around the desk. "*No one* fires me! You need me! Who do you think you are, you—"

"The client," said Yven, not even looking at him as he gave me the binder. "You refuse to do the ceremony as we want it, so the contract is void. We'll expect our deposit back by the end of the week. Come on, sweetheart," he murmured in English, then escorted me down the stairs.

We'd barely made the foyer when Calien caught up to us, almost tripping over her feet in her haste. "What are you doing?" she hissed. "You can't fire Feon! He's exactly what this wedding needs in order to be—"

"Are you blind and deaf," Yven interrupted, "or do you just hate us?"

My fiancé typically maintained an even keel—useful for an agent whose primary task was checking growing facilities for irregularities—and while he occasionally revealed flashes of temper, I rarely saw his anger. The tone he was taking with Calien, however, was the one I'd last heard when he told Pateme to go fuck himself, and it stopped my cousin in her tracks.

"That cretin insulted me to my face," he continued, pointing to the second floor, "and he insulted Rosie to her face, and I will *not* have my wife insulted at her own wedding. Do you understand, or shall I use smaller words?"

As Calien appeared to be on the precipice of an explosion, I tried to mediate. "Maybe we can reason with him," I said to Yven, rubbing his back. "If not…I mean, I can deal with it for Pop's sake."

Yven gently cupped my face in his palms. "Diriem wouldn't want this. You know that—"

"Excuse me," said Calien, her voice whiplike in its sharpness. "Remember your place, boy. You will speak of my uncle properly—and how dare you presume to know what he wants?"

He didn't so much as flinch at her venom. "I *live* with the man. I see him almost daily. And I'm speaking of Diriem as he told me to address him. Now," he said, stepping closer to Calien, "I certainly don't pretend to know every detail of your dear uncle's thoughts, but I do know that he adores Rose, and he would never stand for the absolute disrespect we just experienced. Do you disagree? Because if you do, I'd be *thrilled* to call him right now and let him weigh in."

Perhaps realizing she wasn't going to win that fight, Calien went in another direction. "I don't have another officiant lined up. Feon is the best in the business, so if you want your damn wedding to look at all respectable, then you need to march back upstairs this instant and grovel. I cannot believe you ingrates would insult my friend like that—"

"I can't believe you would allow your friend to insult your *cousin* and me like that," Yven retorted. "So, no, there will be no groveling. We'll find an officiant on our own, thank you."

Leaving Calien to steam, Yven shepherded me out of the building and into his car, then quickly put it in gear and took off. Two blocks later, once he could pull into the relative privacy of a small parking lot for a strip of boutiques, I broke down, clinging to our binder for lack of a better idea.

"Rosie," he murmured, pressing a handkerchief into my fist that hadn't existed a moment prior, "sweetie, I'm sorry."

I blew my nose.

"Do you want me to go back and punch him? Because I'll do it, and I'm fairly confident that Director Erenani will let me out of the cells."

I started to laugh at the mental image and ended up in a coughing fit. As I pulled myself together and dabbed at my eyes, I managed, "I just want this to be *right.*"

"And you're stressed and miserable. I just want to be married. If it'll make you happy, I'll drive us to the Tribunal building right now and find a judge."

"I'm a mess," I replied, sniffling.

"You're beautiful. Seriously, want to run back downtown and make it formal?"

Tempting as the offer was, I shook my head. "Pop wants a real wedding. If not for him, we wouldn't even be together."

"No, we wouldn't be together *legally,*" Yven amended. "You're stuck with me, Rosie." He leaned over and kissed me, then rested his forehead against mine as I calmed. "I'm so sorry, honey, I didn't realize Calien was that obnoxious."

"She's gotten worse of late."

"Lovely," he muttered. "Why don't we talk to Diriem tonight, hmm? Fill him in. He wouldn't want you struggling with this mess on top of the damn Golden Children, and I suspect he wouldn't mind having a word with his dear little niece."

"I know, but I don't want to turn this into more of a family mess than it already is," I said, and sighed as I pulled down the visor to check the damage to my mascara in the mirror. "What are we going to do about an officiant? Do you know any? Do they need, like, a license or something?"

"No, all the officiant needs to be able to do is keep the ceremony going and make the trees. There are plenty out there...but I have an idea," he said, and produced another hanky. "Here, this one's clean."

I licked my finger and dabbed at my smudged makeup, then tried to wipe off the worst of the streaks. "Thanks. Who'd you have in mind?"

Yven grinned. "Tell you when we get there."

Independent growers and producers working outside the Pactlands were only some of the operations DPP regulated. Equally important—and generally overseen by teams of senior agents—were the large-scale producers within the Pactlands, those businesses or cooperatives that had managed to gain access to land sufficiently connected to the outside world to grow more than grass and knee-high trees. Those magical supports weren't cheap, and so domestic producers not working for the Pact needed significant funding to keep their companies in business.

One of the wealthiest of the bunch was Dashom Brothers, located a short drive outside of Beukal's city limits. The eponymous Dashom brothers, a trio of sorcerers, were long dead, but their company lived on. While it produced a small selection of conventional foodstuffs, Dashom was known for its experimental greenhouses; some were testing grounds for soil additives and fertilizers, but others were dedicated to growing new and better strains of plants for use in potion production...and Aunt Lily's big brother, Teolm, headed the potion unit. A gifted floramancer like his sister, Teolm had made a name for himself as an experimental botanist, eschewing his father's legitimate and criminal businesses alike. (In fairness to Teolm, he hadn't known that his father was the crime boss known as Silver—of the ten ti'Cren siblings, only my grandfather, Fradin, a DPP agent, had been fully privy to *that* horrifying little factoid.) But with his father's incarceration had come a few changes for Teolm: the finest jewelry store in Beukal to keep afloat, a mansion and squabbling siblings to superintend, and a title that still, nearly four years on, hung from him like an ill-fitting coat.

I'd never had cause to visit Dashom, and judging by the two wrong turns he took, neither had Yven, but he parked in a visitor spot near the front door of the facility's long brick office building and led the way inside.

A pretty receptionist in a conservative eggplant robe sat at the desk separating the nicely appointed waiting area from the pair of brass elevators. "Good afternoon," said the sorcerer, smiling politely. "Could I see your identification please?"

That took me aback, but Yven seemed unbothered by the request. "Certainly," he replied, and handed her his DPP badge. I followed suit and waited as she held each next to a milky square of glass, a scanner that flashed blue at each presentation.

"Agent ti'Ansha," she said, passing Yven's badge back to him, "and Agent…ti'Dana?" She eyed me with evident surprise but kept any personal questions to herself. "How can I help you? DPP hasn't scheduled an inspection for today unless my calendar is wrong…"

"Oh, no, this isn't an inspection," said Yven. "I was wondering if we might steal a few minutes with Lord ti'Cren."

"*Ah*," said the receptionist, glancing at me again, and I could almost see the tumblers fall. "He's in today. Let me call him for you. Have a seat, please," she offered, nodding to the chairs.

We only waited a few minutes before Teolm strode in, streaked head to toe with a bright red substance I sincerely hoped was an exotic pollen. Like Aunt Lily, he was undersized for an elf, perhaps an inch shorter than me and wiry, and I saw hints of his sister in his face—the shape of his dark eyes was a tell, but the resemblance came through most strongly when he flashed a dimpled smile just like hers. "Rosie!" he said, grinning. "Yven, hi! Please tell me you're leaving agency work and want a job," he added in a stage whisper.

"Not just yet, I'm afraid," said Yven, chuckling. "And if that's what I think it is, I hope you'll understand if we keep our distance."

"Oh, it's *exactly* what you think it is," Teolm replied, rotating his stained arms as if showing them off. "But the anti-inflammatory is good for another few hours, so no need to panic yet."

I didn't follow, but I wasn't surprised. While Yven wasn't a floramancer like my great-uncle, his knowledge of regulated species was nearly encyclopedic, and his ability to grow plants in the Pactlands had left more than a few of his colleagues wondering whether he might have a late-blooming wild talent.

Under ordinary circumstances, a young agent from a low-ranking Hall would have had no reason to cross paths with the head of a Hall as prominent as ti'Cren, but Yven's circumstances were anything but ordinary. I'd introduced him to my great-uncle following my great-grandfather's trial, as Teolm was then one of the two members of that Hall who'd deign to speak with me. (Technically, Aunt Lily was a ti'Cren, but having grown up knowing her as the sweet old lady in the dirt-stained apron who sold flowers and sneaked me candy behind my parents' backs, I had a hard time envisioning her as an elven aristocrat.) Yven had been shy—he'd still been coming to terms with the fact that Pop was on board with our relationship, and he was treading *far* outside his usual social circles. But later, after

Yven had moved to Viratta with me, Teolm had come out one evening to talk to Pop, Pop had lured him back to the mansion's greenhouse, which had largely become Yven's domain, and Teolm and my fiancé had spent *hours* going through the details of Yven's orchid collection. Teolm respected DPP's work, but he wasn't above poaching, and he'd made clear to Yven that should the time come to transition into the private sector, the door was open at Dashom.

Catching my confusion, Yven explained, "Dashom Brothers is the biggest producer of fire lilies, period. Looks like someone has been hand-pollenating."

"Hand, arm, shoulder…" Teolm paused to scratch a glob of stuck-on pollen off his ear. His hair, dark and short, had snarled into red-tinged clumps. "Head. Leg. Everything, really."

"The flowers are about this long," said Yven, stretching his arms out wide, "and they grow in thick clusters. You pollenate one, you pollenate them all, unless you're using a collector on a stick."

Teolm shook his head. "Doesn't work nearly as well. I'm not touching you, Rosie, because the pollen is sticky as honey and makes skin swell on contact. These clothes are a biohazard," he said, gesturing to his long-sleeved green T-shirt and jeans, both of which were horribly stained. "Three washes before I'll put them on again—learned *that* lesson the hard way."

Yven winced in sympathy.

"Anyway, what brings you kids out here?" Teolm asked, in remarkably good spirits for a guy one potion away from blowing up like he'd been attacked by supercharged bees.

"Is there somewhere we could talk in private?" I asked.

Teolm nodded and led us into the elevator, taking pains to touch neither us nor the walls. We disembarked on the third floor, and he led us to a fairly utilitarian and not at all coordinating office—a metal desk, two wooden chairs for guests, a long table loaded with equipment and bottles of plant specimens, and a wall-spanning bookshelf sagging beneath the weight of its contents. He made a rapid gesture to turn on the overhead lights, then another to coat his desk chair in a plasticky film. Clearly, this wasn't Teolm's first filthy foray to his office.

We sat, and Teolm gestured the door closed and latched. "Go ahead," he said, crossing his legs. "What's on your mind?"

I glanced at Yven, who took the lead. "Strange request. You're planning to come to our wedding, right?"

He smiled. "Of course."

"Well, as of today, we're missing an officiant. The one our delightful planner selected was…"

"An asshole," I volunteered.

"Yeah. Apparently, our wedding isn't good enough for him to pull out the High Elvish text, and he refused to do our trees."

Teolm's jaw dropped. "He *refused*?"

"Got all snippy about it, too," I said. "I'm not sure what was more offensive to him, my grandmothers or Yven."

"Oof. Have you told Diriem?"

"Not yet. We kind of have a situation with the Golden Children…it's under control," I fibbed as his brow furrowed. "Pop and I have been working some odd hours, that's all."

"Nothing new there. So," said Teolm, looking between Yven and me, "an officiant, eh?"

Yven nodded. "Here's the thing: the one we fired is known for his tree illusions."

"They're really pretty," I added.

"But since he's out," Yven continued, "I was thinking…what if we had real trees?"

Slowly, Teolm began to smile.

"I know my share of floramancers," said Yven, "but only two are particularly suitable for this, and Liliol will be helping Rosie that morning."

"Naturally," said Teolm. "She's coming over a few days in advance, just in case."

"So I heard. I know it's a big request," Yven told him, "but I also know you speak High Elvish. We got it from Diriem around the same time, so—"

"The script wouldn't be a problem," he assured us, then turned and gestured at a large pot beneath the window behind his desk. The tiny plant in the center of the pot began to grow like kudzu on steroids, sprouting vines and leaves and swelling exponentially as it raced to cover the surface of the potting soil. Within seconds, it had produced a purple blossom the size of my hand, which bobbed with the force of its rapid development and release.

"*Nice*," I said.

Teolm grinned. "A little floramancy, a little illusion—you'd need both to achieve the effect you want. But I'd be honored, and I'd certainly practice before the big day."

The bands of tension wrapped around my chest started to loosen. "Really?"

"Sure!" He beamed beneath his pollen coating. "Now, I've not done this before, so I can't guarantee perfection—"

"'Close enough' would be great. And we have all the names for the trees," I said. "I left the binder in the car, but we've put everything together."

"Great. Tell you what," said Teolm, "you two come out to Kelomb for dinner one night, and we'll go through the details. Would that work?"

I hesitated before answering him. The last time I'd been to the ti'Cren mansion, I'd been brought in undercover as a portrait-painting sorcerer, forbidden by the previous Lord ti'Cren to reveal my true identity. In the weeks that had followed, I'd helped send my great-grandparents and three of their children to penal farms, and I suspected that the youngest of my grandfather's siblings, Mafora, probably hadn't forgiven me for the way her brief marriage had ended. "Are you sure that's a good idea?"

"Absolutely," he replied with a reassuring smile. "You're welcome, little one. And should anyone protest, I'll remind them of whose house it is." Glancing at the clock on the wall, he said, "What about tonight? I've finished pollination for the day, and I should be able to clean up by six."

Yven and I thanked him, and then we rose to go. "Don't want to keep you from your shower," I said. "We'll see you for dinner—"

"Hold on, dear. Before you go, would you like to see my greenhouse?"

A smile broke across Yven's face, an expression not unlike that of a child discovering a bike, a gaming system, and a puppy under the Christmas tree, and I was suddenly *very* glad that I'd worn comfortable shoes.

I'd learned a fair bit about magical plants since coming on at DPP, but I couldn't name most of the species that filled Dashom Brothers' massive experimental greenhouse. The humid building was probably the length of two football fields, and it was packed from floor to peaked glass ceiling with flowering plants, shrubs, trees, and trellised tendrils. Hearing a familiar rustling, I peeked beneath a bench a few minutes into Teolm's grand tour and spotted a thick green vine moving beneath, its tip following us as we passed down the stone walkway.

"Amazonian slithertrap?" I asked.

Teolm turned back and nodded. "Yes, but it's not in the friendliest of moods right now. Broody, frankly. I wouldn't try to pet it, were I you."

Having seen what Aunt Lily's giant slithertrap could do when peeved, I kept my distance. Sally liked me, but this slithertrap was a stranger.

"What's upset it?" asked Yven, crouching for a better

look.

"It flowered two weeks ago."

He straightened, grinning. "*Really*."

"I know! They rarely flower," he explained to me. "But they self-pollenate, and this one's got a seed forming. I've seen it from a distance—the slithertrap won't let anyone get close. With any luck, we can catch it once it's mature, and then we'll see about germinating it."

Under the watchful non-eyes of the slithertrap, Teolm escorted us around the facility, pointing out his favorites and talking shop with my *delighted* fiancé. I didn't have much to contribute to the conversation, so I mostly observed, keeping my hands well to myself and trying to spot plants I knew among the artificial jungle. I paused before a strange flower the size of a teacup's saucer, which burst forth with layers of purple and green petals. "Teolm? What's this one?"

He spotted the flower and turned to Yven. "Bet you know."

"Dashom calavaria," he replied without hesitation, and leaned closer to examine it. "Gorgeous. I've never seen it live..."

"That's because we don't license it—this property is the only place in the world you'll find it growing. It's mostly in the regular greenhouse, but we try to improve on it here."

Yven chuckled. "I think you did a fine job the first time."

"Eh, there's always something to be tweaked." To me, Teolm said, "Calavarias are used in a number of potions. *This* strain was developed here a couple hundred years ago through selective breeding and dumb luck—"

"Surely not," Yven interrupted.

"Oh, yes. I was part of the team—I can say that. The leaves of a calavaria contain a number of chemicals that are particularly potent in combination. Our strain has about double the potency of the others on the market, so we grow it exclusively."

"And it's never escaped?" I asked.

"The slithertraps in the greenhouses are highly effective against burglars, and I've never heard of it being loosed elsewhere. That's not uncommon with companies like ours," he explained. "Most of us have proprietary strains, and we make our money from selling top-of-the-line product. And since the only monetary value of this plant is in its leaves..." He grabbed a rubber glove from one of the many dispensers mounted on the support columns, then plucked a flower and carefully tucked it behind my ear. "There. Lovely."

CHAPTER 12

The call I'd been hoping for came from Maebe around three on Wednesday afternoon. "Stephanie's stable," she reported—in High Elvish, I noted, and guessed she wanted ours to be a private conversation. "Not happy in the slightest, pretty scared, but she's solid again."

"Are they releasing her?" I asked in kind.

"The director says she can leave as soon as he receives confirmation that she has a place to stay. Obviously, she's in no state to go home."

"Right. I'll have Pop give Pateme a call," I said, "and I'll drive in to get her."

About an hour later, once Stephanie's accommodations were arranged, I pulled into the DPP garage with Tabitha riding shotgun in my Outback. Stephanie, Tabitha, and I had similar builds, so I'd brought a duffel bag of some of my athleisure pieces and a new pack of underwear from the quick-shop store in Viratta—nothing fancy, but I figured it'd get her out of the building with her dignity intact.

"Gird your loins," Tabitha muttered as we started toward the elevator. "This could get messy."

Quarantine was expecting us, and Vinla met us at the control station. "How's the patient?" I asked.

"Eh." She made a face. "Physically, she seems whole. The aeromancers have been coaxing her to shift between phases, and she can manage it."

Tabitha grunted. "And emotionally?"

"There...have been tears," Vinla admitted. "I gathered she was uninformed of our existence..."

"*Absolutely*," said Tabitha.

"Bit of a shock, I'm sure. But the Roulette bunch recovered nicely, yes?" she said, brightening. "I bet she'll be fine once she's out of quarantine."

"Speaking of Roulette…" I hinted.

Vinla sighed and absently massaged her shoulder. "We're working on it, I swear to you, but this potion is complex. My team has some hypotheses but nothing ready for dissemination." Turning to Tabitha, she asked, "You're still stable? Any new side effects?"

Tabitha cupped one hand under the other to catch the drips as the second liquefied, then recalled it into place and wiggled her fingers. "Nothing new. No pain, at least."

"Well, that's a relief." Pointing down the hallway, she said, "Shall we release your friend?"

We followed her into the quarantine area. As soon as Stephanie saw us, she ran to the glass wall and frantically waved. They'd given her the yellow shirt and pants typical of hospital attire in the Pactlands, but her feet were bare, and the wide-eyed look on her face suggested she feared we'd leave without her.

"Hey," said Tabitha, raising a hand in greeting as we neared. "We came to spring you."

"We're going home?" Stephanie asked, her voice rendered slightly tinny by the speaker.

"Not quite yet." Tabitha stepped aside while Vinla unlatched the doors, and when they opened, Stephanie staggered free and fell into Tabitha's arms, sobbing.

I locked eyes with Maebe and asked in High Elvish, "Did you beat her or something?"

"It's been a long couple of days," she replied, and stifled a yawn. "Orten deserves a raise."

The agent waved wearily and shouldered his bag, and Maebe grabbed a tote stuffed with clothing. "Please tell me you two are taking the rest of the day off," I said, switching to Pactish.

Orten nodded. "And tomorrow—my director's feeling

generous. Liogh's on their way to give us a ride."

"I don't want to go to class in the morning," Maebe muttered.

"Then don't, youngling," Orten told her. "What are they going to do if you stay in bed, drag you by your ankles? You've earned a recuperation day." To me, he explained, "She's been working hard."

"I can handle it," said Maebe.

"You're very gifted, but you're also very young," he replied. "Give it another couple of decades, and I think you'll find Director Erenani on your doorstep with a job offer—*if* you ever feel like working, I mean," he quickly added, backpedaling. "I wasn't meaning to imply—"

"I grew up in a cabin with no plumbing," Maebe interrupted. "If I ever start putting on airs, someone smack me, okay?"

As a technician escorted them out to wait for Liogh, Tabitha awkwardly rubbed Stephanie's back while she cried. "Hey, Stephanie," I said in English, and waited until she raised her flushed, wet face. "I'm Rose—I'm a friend of Jane's and Tabitha's. Brought some clothes in case you didn't want to walk outside in hospital pajamas."

She sniffled and wiped her nose on her bare forearm. "Where are we going?"

"You're coming home with me," I replied, trying to sound upbeat. "Tabitha's staying over, too. Thought y'all wouldn't mind each other's company until the researchers here figure out how to fix you."

"And where's your place?"

"Uh...it's in a town called Viratta. Look, I'd take you back to Ragged Gap in a heartbeat," I said, "but the stuff Katarina's crew stuck you with is new, and the folks here aren't sure how it works yet. In case of complications, they want you close by."

"*Complications*? I disappeared!"

"You phased into a gaseous form," Tabitha corrected. "I went liquid. At least neither of us ignited, right?"

As Stephanie began to tear up again, I handed her the duffel bag. "Here, why don't you get dressed?" I suggested. "I'm sorry about the underwear—best I could do on short notice, but it's new."

With promises that we wouldn't leave her, Stephanie hurried into to the quarantine bathroom to change clothes and emerged in wash-faded black leggings and a purple tunic top. I'd forgotten shoes, but she seemed to feel marginally better and followed Tabitha and me out of the building unshod.

Stephanie climbed into the back of my car with the clothes and her wadded-up pajamas, and with Tabitha situated, I started for the surface. "The drive's not too far," I said, slipping into the role of de facto tour guide. "Well, it *would* be, but we've got a portal system in here to make things simpler."

"What do you mean, portal?" asked Stephanie.

"So, uh…we're basically a little west of Richmond right now. Virginia, I mean. Viratta would be in Pennsylvania, and that'd be one heck of a daily commute, so we use portals to get back and forth."

"Like an artificial wormhole," Tabitha offered. "Or a rip in the Veil, if that makes any more sense."

"They're painless, don't worry," I said. "But since it's just about quitting time in Beukal, we may have a bit of a wait at the portal building."

Stephanie frowned behind me. "In *where*?"

I guessed Maebe and Orten hadn't had the bandwidth to explain. "You're in Beukal. It's the capital city of the Pactlands. We're leaving the Division of Plants and Potions…once the light turns," I muttered at the passing cars. "DPP has the primary quarantine facility for all of the agencies, so that's where we stuck you Monday morning."

Glancing behind me as I pulled into traffic, I caught Stephanie staring open-mouthed at the city and thought she was admiring the architecture until she gasped and blurted, "What the hell is *that*?"

To our left, two trolls in formal robes were crossing the street, holding hands—a couple, I assumed, probably off for after-work drinks. "They're trolls."

"*Trolls*?"

"Please don't stare. Folks here are already twitchy about humans."

She sank lower in her seat but watched them until they were out of the crosswalk. "I can't believe this is real," she mumbled.

"You get used to it," said Tabitha. "I've been over a few times now, and the shock wears off."

"It was a surprise to me, too," I told Stephanie. "I fell into all of this headfirst and had to tread water for a while, but it's getting to feel more like home. I'm originally from Richmond," I added, hoping that would put her at ease.

"Do you dissolve or whatever?" she asked in a small voice.

"No, you and Tabitha are unique on that front."

She paused, then asked, "Do you have *power*?"

I chuckled softly as I pulled up to the next red light. "Yeah."

"Rose can see what's going on in other places," Tabitha told Stephanie, turning toward the back. "She saw what happened to us and called for help, and she's been keeping an eye on the Golden Children ever since."

"The what?"

"Katarina and her buddies...well, actually, her name's Katin. That's what they call themselves, the Golden Children. Long story."

"They were released from prison a few weeks ago," I said. "Swore they'd leave y'all alone and keep their noses clean, but we see how *that* turned out." I peeked back in time to see Stephanie's jaw tremble.

"Hon, it's going to be okay," Tabitha told her. "They'll fix us."

"Absolutely," I said, trying to sell it through inflection alone. "Look, this isn't the first time DPP has had to deal with humans being dosed with a novel potion, and it's not the worst, either. The pros are on it, and they'll figure it out. Probably not in the next few days," I allowed, "but you're not going to be living on the street or anything in the meantime."

"And hey," said Tabitha, "you've got power now. Might as well enjoy it while it lasts, right?"

Stephanie's voice wobbled when she spoke again. "I…I've always wanted real power, yeah, but…but not like *this*!"

"It's overwhelming, I know," Tabitha replied, "but there's plenty of space to practice where we're going. You'll get the hang of it, and maybe once the folks here are convinced that you're not a danger to yourself, they'll let you leave. Hell, at least your hair's a normal color."

"It's *white*!" she wailed. "I look like an old woman!"

"Oh, please. Call it platinum and put some pink highlights back in it, and no one will notice."

"My eyelashes are white, too! And my eyebrows! And—"

"*Makeup*, Stephanie. You're pasty to begin with, and you can cover a lot with mascara and brow gel." Pushing up her sleeve, she held her arm toward Stephanie and said, "Even my body hair is blue now. I can't go home looking like this. You might just pass if you can keep your head on straight."

"I'll get you some cosmetics, promise," I said. "Not tonight"—frankly, I was exhausted after spending most of the day tracking Katin's wayward band—"but we can go shopping later this week, okay?"

"Okay," Stephanie murmured.

"And Tabitha's right, there's plenty of practice space at the house," I continued. "Maebe was staying over when she discovered her aeromancy, and…well, let's just say that windows are fixable. There's very little that you can break beyond repair."

"This is magic?" Stephanie asked. "Really?"

She sounded surprisingly depressed at the notion, given what I'd heard about her from Jane.

"As far as we can tell, yep," I replied.

"I never imagined it would be like this. I mean, I envisioned something more...all-purpose, you know? Like, making things fly or change colors or what have you, not just moving air around."

"Assuming your power is like Tabitha's, then you have a quasi-nymphic talent. They only have power over one element—air, water, metal, you get the picture—but they can do crazy stuff. They *can't* phase into their element, however, so you differ there. And I know it's not crystals and intentions and"—I barely stopped myself from saying *shit*—"stuff like that, but it *is* magic."

"Careful what you wish for, right?" said Tabitha.

"Now, here's the big wrinkle," I told Stephanie. "Until now, it was understood that it's impossible to give someone magical talent who wasn't born with it."

"Jane's been telling you the truth," Tabitha added.

"Right. But you two got dosed with this mystery potion, and DPP has its hands full figuring out what happened to you."

"So...how long are we going to be here?" Stephanie asked. "Like, a week? Longer?"

I chose my words carefully before answering her. "I don't know. The last time DPP had to deal with a situation like yours, it took months to work out the potion and an antidote. But like Tabitha said, you look close to normal, and once you're not a threat to yourself or anyone else, I bet they'll let you leave."

"They don't have the right to keep me here," she protested. "Y'all kidnapped me and brought me—"

"We saved your ass," Tabitha shot back, "and since you don't know jack shit about this sort of magic, you ain't going nowhere yet, and neither am I. Just think of it as being spirited away to Tír na nÓg for a bit," she muttered, turning to face the front again.

"Permanently, don't you mean?"

I slowed to let a delivery van into my lane. "Come again?"

"This is Tír na nÓg, and I ate the food. I…I shouldn't have, I know that, but I was so hungry, and—"

"This isn't *actually* Tír na nÓg," Tabitha interrupted, then caught my bemusement and clarified, "The Celtic Otherworld. And Stephanie, the food's safe. It won't trap you here," she added impatiently.

Stephanie wasn't buying it. "Uh-huh. And you're going to sit there and tell me I didn't see faeries back in that place?"

Laughter escaped me before I could bite it back, and I tried to disguise it with a cough to be polite. "Sorry. No, no faeries, and this isn't some mystical land—it's an artificial pocket world. Created by magic, yes," I admitted, "but believe me, you're not going to get stuck here if you eat a sandwich."

"Then what did I see in quarantine?" Stephanie prodded. "Maebe sure as shit ain't human, and that guy with her…you saw their ears, right? And you're going to tell me they aren't faeries?"

"Elves," I said. "Faeries don't exist, or at least not that anyone here knows of."

"And…you've interacted with these elves?"

Tabitha's laughter left her wheezing, and I reached over to thump her between the shoulder blades. "Pretty extensively in the last few years," I said between Tabitha's coughing spasms. "I, uh…I'm about ninety percent elf, so…I'm guessing we have a lot to discuss tonight."

"You're *what*?" she yelped.

"Jane really didn't tell you much, did she?" I muttered, and slowed to join the line at the portal building.

As soon as the door to the garage closed behind us, Ranarma hurried out from the kitchen, still wearing a dishtowel over his shoulder. "Just who I was looking for," he said—and in English, to boot. "Yven's upstairs changing clothes, and it'll be the four of you for dinner tonight."

"Where's Pop?" I asked.

"Eating privately. I think he has work to do or something," said the cook, then pointedly cut his eyes toward Stephanie and back to me.

Ah.

I sniffed the air. "Fajitas?"

"Yes, ma'am. Thought that'd be easy." To the others, he said, "Tabitha, I know you're not a vegetarian. And you…Stephanie, yes?"

"Uh…no, I just don't like beef," said Stephanie, taking him in. "Um…"

"That's fine, I'm making chicken, too. Ranarma Curain," he offered with a smile. "Any food allergies I should know about?"

When she regarded him quizzically, I explained, "Ranarma is our cook. He's fantastic."

"You have a *cook*?" Stephanie replied, wrinkling her nose.

"There's a full staff here. You did see the size of this place when we drove up, yeah?"

"Yeah, but I thought you said you had an apartment."

"An apartment *in the house*. But it's much nicer to eat down here than to put together something upstairs. Come on," I said, "let me show you to your room. Ranarma, do you know—"

"Uncle was having it readied half an hour ago," he replied. "Next to Tabitha's."

"Thank you." As Tabitha led the way, I locked eyes with him and mouthed *Sorry*, and he grinned.

By the time we'd escorted Stephanie into the south wing, her mouth was hanging open. "This ain't an apartment complex," she marveled, taking in her room. "This is, like…"

"It's a mansion," said Tabitha. "You're going to love

the bed, trust me."

As Stephanie stood on the threshold of her guest room and Tabitha tried to coax her inside, Yven emerged from the tower's spiral staircase and joined me. "Hello, gorgeous," he said, and kissed my cheek. "Success?"

"Something like that," I replied in Low Elvish for privacy. "She's twitchy as hell."

"Mm. Do I need to mask?"

Before I could answer, Stephanie glanced our way and yelped in surprise. Backing off with his hands raised, Yven hastily said in English, "Sorry, you're fine, didn't mean to startle you. Stephanie, I presume."

She nodded, hugging herself.

"This is Yven, my fiancé," I said, stepping in to diffuse. "He doesn't bite."

"Hard," he added, and cracked a smile when I shot him an impatient glare. "Ranarma said it's fajita night."

"So he told us," I replied. "Tabitha, um…would you mind showing Stephanie the way back downstairs when she's ready?"

Dinner was an awkward affair. Though the food was excellent—Ranarma had tried his best to put something familiar to our guests on the table—Stephanie was underslept, traumatized, and more than a little wary of Yven, who gave her plenty of space. I didn't see a hint of Pop all evening, and I figured he was trying not to exacerbate the situation. By the time we retired, Stephanie seemed more comfortable with Ranarma, who looked human and was only too happy to provide cake and a variety of hot beverages. I left her sitting at the table with Tabitha and a mug of lightly spiked decaf, begging off so that I could check in on the Golden Children before getting a few hours of sleep.

Yven left early Thursday morning, but I decided to work from home, partly for the comfort of my studio but mostly to keep an eye on the patients. They joined me about ten minutes after I sat down for breakfast, and Stephanie seemed to be in better spirits after a shower and a decent night's sleep. "I still can't believe you didn't tell me about this," she groused to Tabitha after Ranarma popped in to take coffee orders.

Tabitha shrugged and reached for the fruit bowl. "If you hadn't been such a bitch to Jane, you might have learned on your own."

She scowled but didn't argue. "Where *is* Jane, anyway?"

"Presumably back at work. She has an apartment at DOI, and the commute's a lot shorter if you're camping in the building," I said, and took the fruit from Tabitha. "Thanks. Ooh, blueberries."

"At where?" Stephanie asked.

"The Division of Intelligence. She's an agent now."

"Which doesn't leave her much time for making soap," Tabitha added. "Didn't you wonder what happened to Fortune's Fancies?"

"I…I guess I thought she wasn't making any money," said Stephanie. "Especially after Bitsy kicked her out of the Mercantile…"

"She was doing fine," Tabitha replied with a hint of reproach. "And she sold at my place and The Robin's Nest after Bitsy had her little snit fit."

I'd heard enough from Jane to know why Stephanie ate quietly after that. Bitsy, a member of the woo-woo brigade, had been furious when she lost her "power"—never mind that she'd been given a neutralizer because the Velvet Leash she'd unwittingly consumed made her seize. As Stephanie had refused to tell her flock that she'd been wrong about their beloved Katarina and that Jane had saved their sorry asses, Bitsy had turned on her friend, and Jane, who'd been selling her wares on consignment in Bitsy's popular store for years, had been kicked to the curb. Apparently, Bitsy had made apologetic overtures since then, but Jane kept her distance. Considering that the Mystic Mountains crowd had shunned her since she was a kid, however, I couldn't blame her. And while Stephanie and Jane had worked out their own sort of truce, I doubted the two would ever be best friends.

Ranarma had just stepped in to ask about refills when Scel appeared from the far doorway. "Question," he said to his nephew, "is there any chance that you could work up a clear soup this morning? Cirat is unwell."

"Of course," Ranarma replied. "Is she…" Scel put a hand to his chest and made a subtle gulping motion, and Ranarma nodded. "No problem. I've got chicken stock, and I'll take it to her momentarily."

"Thank you. Feltha is assisting her, so just knock."

Once Scel had departed, I asked Ranarma, "What's wrong with Cirat?"

He leaned toward me and whispered, "Morning sickness. It's hit her hard."

Overhearing him, Tabitha said, "If she's vomiting badly, she's going to need fluids and salt."

Ranarma smiled tightly. "Hence the stock."

"Sure, but what's the local equivalent of Gatorade?"

The term being unfamiliar to him, the two stepped into the kitchen to discuss the matter while he heated Cirat's breakfast, leaving me with my toast and irritated Stephanie. "What was that all about?" she demanded.

Crap. With everything else on my plate, I'd forgotten that Stephanie couldn't speak Pactish.

"One of the staff is feeling bad, and Ranarma is making her some soup," I replied.

Stephanie looked aghast. "You make your staff work even if they're *sick*?"

"She lives here. Most of them do." When Stephanie's expression morphed toward confusion, I said, "It's common in the larger houses. Room and board come with their salary."

"So you can bother them at all hours of the day and night?"

"*No*, and why the hostility?"

"It's just weird," Stephanie protested. "There's what, three of you? Why do you possibly need all of *this*?"

"I...think it's less of a *need* and more of a *want* situation. This is what my great-grandfather's accustomed to, and it's normal for the heads of the top Halls to live in this fashion, so...I mean, I'm not complaining." As Tabitha returned to the dining room, I asked in Pactish, "Is she an 'eat the rich' sort, or is something else wrong?"

"Stressed, I imagine," Tabitha replied in kind, and took her seat. "Stephanie, hon, whatever it is, you need to chill," she said in English. "Eat your breakfast."

She looked between Tabitha and me, her brow furrowed with consternation. "What were you saying?"

"Just asking about Cirat," Tabitha fibbed, her stare willing me to play along. "So, what's the plan?" she asked me. "Gym?"

"It's all y'all's today," I said. "I'll be working in my apartment if you need me before lunch."

Stephanie huffed. "Of course you have an in-home gym."

"I'll show her the way," Tabitha told me, offering an out, and I took my coffee to go.

But that still left the matter of Stephanie's presumed monolingualism to deal with, and I knew damn well that the research healers would have my hide if I tried to slip her a language potion. The alternative plan was preferable, in my opinion, because the language potion's effects varied from flulike symptoms to several days of unconsciousness, whereas Wylan could do the trick in a matter of seconds.

I didn't want to bother him if the Forum was doing something important, however, so I called Annie instead.

"He's working from home, the bum," she said with fondness. "Which probably means he's playing with the guys instead of reading the committee reports he'll gripe about tonight."

"I don't mean to be a pest—"

"You're not. What time do you want him there?"

Wylan might have been a deep well of poorly understood power, but his wife had his ear.

I was on my way to the front door at eleven when, right on time, the bell rang, and Scel gave me a look as he hastened to answer it. "No need to run, Miss Rose," he murmured, and drew back the bolt. "Ah, sir, good morning," he said, stepping aside to admit Wylan. "Will you be staying for lunch?"

"Hi, Scel. No, thank you. I've got plans at home—"

"Oh, come on!" called Ranarma, peeking in from one of the hallways. The look Scel shot him could have curdled milk, but the younger Curain was of a less formal bent than his uncle.

Wylan waved, chuckling. "It's not that I don't love your food, man."

"*Sure*, it isn't. Come see me on your way home," Ranarma added. "There's a new coffee bean out of one of the greenhouses, and I think you're going to like it. Kona-adjacent."

"Mm. I'll be the judge of that."

Trolls might have had the most sensitive noses, but the Hunt's weren't far behind. Now that he'd finally developed a taste for coffee, Wylan had become something of a bean snob.

"Thanks for coming," I told him as he followed me upstairs to the gymnasium. "I hope I'm not interrupting too badly..."

"Not at all. I've had enough archery practice for one day, anyway," Wylan replied, rotating his shoulder. "Annie said the other potion victim is...coping?"

"She's twitchy."

"Well, I suppose being taken to the Pactlands without warning would leave one disoriented. And she turns to gas?"

"Yeah. We brought her over in a mason jar."

"She's probably had better weeks," he replied with more generosity than I was feeling toward Ragged Gap's mystical maven. "We'll make this quick, eh?"

Once we'd reached the gym—frankly, getting up to it was workout enough some days—I knocked and cracked the door open. "Hey, Stephanie? Brought someone to help you with Pactish."

After a few seconds, she solidified atop a stack of mats and slid to the floor. "Oh?"

"Uh-huh. This is Wylan…"

In retrospect, I should have handled the introductions better. Sure, *I* knew Wylan, and Tabitha had waved as he walked in, but he was a lot to absorb at first glance. Wylan was a big guy, not counting the impressive rack of antlers, and he'd come dressed in what passed for casual attire among his brothers: an off-white lace-up shirt and leather leggings (the latter of which, on him, I suspected suited Annie *just* fine). True, his ears were pointed, but they were smaller than the elven variety, almost hidden in his shoulder-length brown hair. And yes, his eyes were an unusual shade of amber and shone like a cat's in the dark, but that certainly wasn't on display in the late-morning sunlight.

No matter. He barely got out a greeting before Stephanie shrieked, tripped over a mat, and went sprawling on the ground.

Tabitha hurried over to check on her. "Breathing, no blood. Do it now before she wakes, okay?"

Wylan rubbed his scruff. "Should we wait?"

"Ordinarily, I'd say consent is important, but, uh…nah, hit her. And hey, you," she said with a lopsided smile. "Welcome to the madhouse."

He knelt beside Stephanie and put his fingers to her temples for just a couple seconds, then retreated. "Offer stands," he murmured to Tabitha. "We have room for guests."

"Appreciated, but I'd better not," she replied, glancing at her unconscious companion. "See you around, okay?"

I escorted Wylan out of there before Stephanie could come to and freak out again. "Does she know about us?" he asked me as we headed for the staircase. "Annie has told me some of the stories about the Hunt outside…"

I hesitated, then said, "You know how Tabitha's a Wiccan?"

"So I've heard. I'm sorry, I'm not well versed in it."

"Neither am I, and I don't think Stephanie is a full-fledged Wiccan, but she's familiar enough with it to celebrate their holidays. Uh…"

"Yes?" he prodded.

I came to a stop by a little-used sitting room and dug in the pocket of my leggings for my phone. "There are two deities in Wicca, a female and a male. And, um…" A quick image search later, I showed him the screen.

His eyes widened. "*Oh.*"

"That's the Horned God."

"Huh." He peered down at the phone, his head slightly cocked. "You think she may have mistaken me for—"

"It's possible."

"I see. And…does Tabitha…"

"She's doesn't believe that you're at all divine."

"Oh, good." He cleared his throat and stepped back. "So…coffee?"

"Seems like the safest plan," I replied, and led the way.

Stephanie was not happy when she awoke in the gym, even when Tabitha revealed she was now fluent in Pactish. She wasn't happy at lunchtime when I joined them for salad and quiche Lorraine. And she definitely wasn't happy around two, when Tabitha called me to let me know that the day's practice was over. "She's sulking in her room, I think," she told me as I groggily reoriented myself to my body. "Flounced out after she got frustrated and vanished for a moment."

"Is she normally like this?" I asked, pushing myself into

a sitting position on my studio couch.

"No. But here's the thing: in her sphere, Stephanie has been something of a guru for years. It's a *small* pond, right, but she's a big fish. Knows how to cleanse crystals and do reiki and read tarot cards, you follow?"

"Sure…"

"Well, all of a sudden, she's way out of her depth and grappling with not being seen as an expert in anything magic-related—"

"She's *not*," I protested.

"Not in magic as you understand it, no," Tabitha diplomatically replied. "Stephanie…she's wanted real power as long as I've known her. That's what made her such an easy mark for Katin, yeah? Her and most of her inner circle. Now she has power, and she's freaking out." With a sigh, Tabitha said, "I told her to get a grip—we're safe, there are people trying to fix us, and we're hanging out in a freaking mansion. That went over about as well as you'd imagine."

I thanked her for the update, and then, for the second time that day, I called Annie.

It was about four by the time Annie could finish up at DPP, and I met her at the door when she appeared in the driveway. "How're we doing?" she asked, keeping pace with me up the staircase.

"Not great." I glanced at the canvas tote slung over her shoulder. "What's in there?"

"Little help. Don't you worry," she replied with a wink, then gripped her masking pendant and hid her Huntsman's features.

I led Annie to Stephanie's room, and she rapped twice before letting herself in. "Hey, there," she said before Stephanie could tell her to go away. "Sorry, I don't think we've met properly. I'm Annie Humphries."

At least she muted the television, though she didn't rise from the couch. "Stephanie Love. Didn't you…"

"I handled transportation to and from your place. And

four and a half years ago, I got dosed with a novel potion at my friend's Halloween party and ended up here. Oh, no, I got better," she clarified as a look of horror crossed Stephanie's face. "The research team at DPP cobbled together an antidote."

"So...you..."

"I stuck around for love. Think you met my husband earlier today," she added with a little smirk. "But that's neither here nor there. I woke up the morning after the party with fucking antlers," she said, tapping her scalp. "My friend Maya had wings. Most of the other guests were unaffected, except the three who died, so on balance, it could have been a lot worse for us. But that didn't make it *easy.*" Reaching into her bag, she extracted a bottle of rosé. "Local winery, I love this stuff. Tell me you're not a teetotaler."

"Uh, no," said Stephanie—and if my eyes weren't deceiving me, she appeared to be thawing. "Sweet?"

"Nicely balanced. I also brought brie and crackers," she said, patting the tote, "because I'm fancy like that. Mind if I use those?" she asked, pointing to the glasses set out by the snack tray atop the table in the corner. "And this thing has a screwcap, so we're in business."

As Stephanie rose to grab the glasses, Annie turned to me and murmured, "We'll be fine. Tell Tabitha I'll see her later, okay? This is a one-on-one sitch."

"I think she'll understand."

Seeing myself out, I closed the door, then knocked on Tabitha's. Like Stephanie, she was watching TV, and I asked, "Want to take this to my place? I've got booze."

Tabitha turned off the television. "Do you think Vinla will object if I drink?"

"Not if she doesn't find out about it."

"Good point," she replied with a faint smile, then stood and unkinked her back. "Yeah, I think I could do with a little company."

CHAPTER 13

I was breakfasting early Friday morning with Yven before he left for the office, debating whether I should put in an appearance myself, when Tabitha and Stephanie wandered in. "Hey," said Tabitha, pulling out a chair. "Did y'all sleep well?"

"Can't complain," Yven replied, "but as for this one…"

I patted his hand. "You can learn a lot when you peek overnight. For instance, two of the Golden Children just started north after spending a couple days in Tampa."

Stephanie frowned. "They…went to the beach?"

"Probably not. There's a portal near Tampa."

"I doubt they're trying to return," Yven explained before she could press me. "Some portals tend to attract illegal producers—they don't want to risk coming through, but they need a market for their goods. They'll arrange to meet buyers near portals, make the trade, and go on without chancing interference by the Portal Authority."

"That bastion of competence," I muttered. "Anyway, the Golden Children used to buy and sell through the Tampa portal, so they're likely up to their old tricks. Katin and Dirk are still holed up in North Carolina, and I wouldn't be surprised if they have company soon. Bears watching—"

"Indeed," Pop interjected, emerging from the kitchen with a large mug, "but could I borrow you first? I have a project that requires your assistance."

"Uh…sure," I replied. "Do I need to come down to

DOI?"

"No, no, I'm confident that you'll be effective from here. Or were you planning to go to the office? Are you scheduled with Pateme?"

"Not today—"

"Who're you?" Stephanie blurted.

Pop eyed her, the corners of his mouth barely twitching. "Your host, Ms. Love."

"This is my great-grandfather," I began, but Stephanie cut me short.

"*Please*," she said, laughing incredulously, then asked Pop, "You're what, thirty? Thirty-five?"

He paused for a sip of coffee. "Six hundred ninety-seven. Ninety-eight in August."

Stephanie turned to Tabitha, who nodded.

Her jaw dropped. "*How*?"

"Good genes and a fantastic skincare routine," Pop deadpanned, then beckoned to me with two fingers. "Rosie, dear, could we speak in private?"

I followed him into his study and closed the door behind me. "Sorry about Stephanie. She's kind of a handful right now."

"Trust me, little girl, I've seen worse." He settled onto the couch, taking pains not to wrinkle his black robe or spill his drink, and I joined him. "Here's what I need from you. I'm planning to have a conversation with one of our farseers around eight, and I'd appreciate it if you could sit in remotely."

"Can do, but unless this farseer is a cousin"—not impossible, as many of the future farseers had at least a distant ti'Dana relation—"I'm not going to be able to see anyone but you. Takes a blood connection to get through the blinding potion, remember?"

At that, he smiled—not a warm expression, but rather one much closer to predatory. "Of course. Which is why I've waited so long to have this conversation."

"I don't follow."

"This farseer is part of the group having their blinding protection reapplied on Monday. Between us, the potion is always spotty at the end of the quarter, and with this person in particular, I know that his potion tends to degrade a day or two early. It hasn't caused a problem before now, but...well. Would you mind eavesdropping?"

I grinned. "My pleasure."

"Excellent," said Pop, and sipped. "Better finish your breakfast, Rosie—you have a long day ahead."

"Really?" I mumbled.

He nodded. "Sorry, youngling."

Somehow, in the confusion of the last days, we'd neglected to mention to Stephanie that elves, nymphs, and Huntsmen were functionally immortal, but with a kiss for Yven on his way out the door, I left Tabitha to handle the fallout of Stephanie's revelation while I made myself an egg sandwich and retreated to my studio to work. Safe in the sanctuary of my apartment, I put on a pot of coffee, poured myself a glass of water, and arranged a notepad, pencil, and voice recorder by my couch, tools for just about any contingency. I kept an eye on the clock as I finished my breakfast and tidied up, then settled in around ten of eight, closed my eyes, and focused on Pop.

Time and practice had made me much more adept at sending my farsight after a particular target, and I could usually lock on with ease. The problem came when my target was protected with the blinding potion and spell—when I tried to focus on someone thus shielded, all I could see was white, like I was walking through a blizzard. If I focused on someone unprotected and there was a protected person with him, I'd see a white splotch where the protected person was, and his words would be inaudible to me. But there was a known weakness to our blinding protection, one I'd employed to great effect to track and stymie my *other* great-grandfather: a farseer related by blood to the target could see through it. It didn't come automatically—I had to concentrate—but though Pop was well-protected, the whiteout soon dissolved into his office at DOI, and I found him checking his email. He worked steadily on his inbox until a few minutes past the hour, then locked his computer and murmured, "Now, Rosie."

I tracked him as he stepped into the hallway and followed him past a line of open and closed doors until he paused before a cracked one and knocked. "Cudda," he said, poking his head into the gap, "would you mind coming to my office for a moment? There's a matter I'd like to discuss with you."

Cudda's response was faint but audible—a simple, "Yes, sir"—which boded poorly for the state of his blinding protection.

I stepped back as he emerged from his office. While it didn't hurt if people walked through me in my incorporeal state, something buried in my psyche insisted it was *unpleasant.*

I didn't know Cudda personally, but that wasn't a great surprise. DOI had the pick of the litter of farseers, and most were too busy to hang out with the undertrained kid with the weird present orientation. But I'd heard Pop mention a number of his agents, and the only Cudda I knew of was Cudda ti'Ren. He was a future farseer, relatively young—only about a century and a half, give or take—and from what Pop had said, he was rather gifted.

He also wasn't hideous, though with the potion in his system, he seemed a little fuzzy around the edges to me. Tall and slender, with large green eyes and a honey-blond ponytail that hung nearly to his waist, Cudda cut a striking figure and stood nearly a head over Pop. His voice, though softer to me than it must have been in person, was pleasantly low and smooth, and he conversed with Pop as he accompanied him down the hall, pale blue robe swishing behind him.

I didn't know much of Hall ti'Ren. Pop spoke well of

its lord, but they didn't run in the same circles—ti'Ren was a mid-ranking Hall, old and long-established, though far outclassed by ti'Dana. But as Pop had told me, a farseer's family was the *last* thing he considered in deciding whether to bring on a trainee. After all, Ganti ti'Van was the best past-oriented farseer Pop had ever known, and his Hall scraped the bottom of the elven social hierarchy.

Unsurprisingly, Pop's corner office was the largest and presumably the best appointed in the building. While DOI had no windows as a security measure, a spell created the illusion of a floor-to-ceiling window behind his heavy mahogany desk, which offered an accurate view of the city's doings beyond the thick walls. The furnishings wouldn't have seemed out of place had they been transported a century back in time but for the few electric lamps and the pair of large monitors sitting atop the desk—Pop wasn't always on the cusp of the newest technology, but neither was he a late adopter. The entire left wall of the office was covered by an overburdened bookshelf stacked with texts in a dozen languages. While the rear of the office was Pop's working space, the front was for company: to the left, a navy leather couch, armchairs, and a coffee table for more social visits, and to the right, an ornate mahogany table and chairs for eight, a more intimate collaboration space than the large conference rooms.

Pop gestured to the couch in invitation. "Have a seat, please."

With a look of mild bemusement and anticipation, Cudda carefully sat, and Pop gestured the door locked before he took an armchair.

After an uncomfortable few seconds of silence, Cudda cracked. "What's on your mind?"

"I need you to be absolutely honest with me," said Pop in a low, almost conversational tone that I suspected was anything but.

Cudda frowned. "Of course…"

Leaning forward, his arms resting on his knees, Pop

asked, "Why did you believe that Katin Waughnn and the Golden Children would behave themselves if they were released outside?"

The younger agent looked back at him. "Uh…well…"

Not letting him finish, Pop continued, "They've already wreaked havoc in Georgia. Went right back to the town where they were last operational out there and attacked some of their former victims. DPP currently has two humans in protective custody because they were exposed to a novel, mutagenic potion."

That wasn't entirely accurate, seeing as they'd been freed from quarantine.

"All attempts to locate the Golden Children following that attack have failed," said Pop. "They're protected from farsight now, and they're in the wind."

Another fib, I noted.

"So, tell me," he said, holding Cudda's gaze, "did you *truly* see this ending well?"

Whatever else his virtues and vices may have been, Pop was the master of the poker face and pointed silence, and he barely twitched as Cudda squirmed, first repeatedly clearing his throat, then shifting in his seat. Thanks to the degradation of his potion, I could just make out the droplets of sweat forming along his hairline as his face flushed.

Finally, after nearly a minute beneath Pop's unflinching stare, Cudda broke. He jumped off the couch and began to pace, running one hand over his head in agitation, then blurted, "I didn't, all right? I didn't."

"Then why lie to us?" asked Pop, calm in the face of Cudda's burst of frenetic energy.

"My girlfriend insisted it was the right thing to do. She said they deserved to go free—"

"*What* girlfriend? You're in a relationship?"

Cudda nodded miserably. "We've been keeping things quiet while we get to know each other…"

Pop allowed that to hang for a moment, then sat back in his chair and shot Cudda a look of deep skepticism.

"Come, now, surely you're not so stupid as to turn in a false report on a Forum request based on a *partner's* preferences. Give me the truth, ti'Ren."

Cudda stopped a few feet away from Pop, seemingly poised to speak, then clamped his mouth shut.

"You know," Pop murmured, "this meeting is a courtesy, and I *will* find the truth, one way or another. This is my agency," he said, his tone dipping dangerously low, "and my people do *not* keep secrets from me. Do you understand?"

"It's not your agency!"

The two regarded each other, Pop with the tiniest flicker of satisfaction, Cudda with a look like he was poised to either fight a brawl or vomit on his shoes.

"It's not yours," Cudda said, bowing up. "And it's long past time for someone else to take the helm."

Pop crossed his legs. "Is that so? And…you thought lying to all of us and the Forum would accomplish that?" He smiled as Cudda began to deflate. "Besides, even if I were pushed out, what makes you think you'd be named the next director? You're far too junior an agent. But that *is* your goal, is it not? Surely you haven't gone to these lengths on someone else's behalf."

Though Cudda stuttered for a moment, he managed to regain his spine. "What makes you think you're the only one who can run this agency? You can't even control your own Hall!"

"I never said that I alone could superintend DOI," Pop replied. "And what do you mean, I can't control my Hall?"

"Come on," said Cudda, smirking, "the mongrel's proof of that."

The silence stretched between them again, and Pop barely moved a muscle until he said, his voice soft but razor-sharp, "I assume you mean Rose."

"Who else?" he scoffed, folding his arms. "She's not even a proper farseer."

"What gave you that impression?"

"If she were, you'd have her here," Cudda replied with a note of triumph.

Pop chuckled low. "If Rose wished to be here, boy, I would give her an office today. But her talent is particularly useful to DPP and DOL, and I dare say that if I were to attempt to force her, I'd find myself in a fistfight with Director ti'Tam. Fair warning, he's scrappier than he seems," Pop added as lightly as if he were discussing the weather. "And were Rose to tire of DPP, I *know* Director Erenani would make a strong bid for her. As it is, she's cleared dozens of cases for those agencies. Her talent isn't defective," he said, flashing a smile with too many sharp teeth. "It's *extraordinary*."

Cudda suddenly seemed less sure of his footing.

Perhaps seizing the opportunity, Pop rose and stalked toward him. "And if I *ever* hear of you referring to her as a mongrel again, I'll leave you with the healers for a week. Understood?"

Seldom had I seen Pop angry, and he wasn't the explosive type. But he was quietly seething, and though Cudda had six inches on him, the agent retreated a pace.

"Now," said Pop, closing the distance, "just what did you intend to do, hmm? Did you think you would embarrass me in front of the Forum for offering a split opinion?"

Cudda tried to recover. "No one knows who the dissenting voice was, do they? It might have been you who was so very wrong…and with the right whispers—"

"It's merely tradition that keeps us from identifying the predictions of particular farseers when we're asked for an opinion," Pop interrupted. "In this case, if need be, I can break with tradition. There's nothing to stop me."

"Except it's your word against mine, and if the Forum thinks you're strong-arming a junior agent into taking the blame for your mistake…" He grinned, letting the threat hang.

But Pop smiled back at him. "You might imagine so,

yes. However, when is your blinding protection due for reapplication? Monday, am I correct?"

"What of it?"

Pop's smile widened. "I asked Rose to observe this meeting. If I'm right, your protection has degraded enough that she can see and hear everything in this room. Now," he continued as the blood drained from Cudda's face, "it might be unseemly for you and me to go before the Forum and ask for the truthfulness spell to be applied so that they might arbitrate an agency dispute…but I'm not above that, and now there's a third witness. I told you her talent is extraordinary."

As Cudda flailed, Pop moved in for the kill: "With all of that said, tell me why I shouldn't fire you right now."

Panicking, Cudda said, "It was my girlfriend's idea, I swear—"

"Her name?"

He hesitated, then shook his head. "I can't. She's…I can't."

"You're ensorcelled? Chaining potion?"

"No, but—"

"Then give me her name. *Now.*"

Still, Cudda refused. "I can't do that. I won't."

Pop stepped back, gave him a long look, then sighed. "Very well. You're suspended, ti'Ren, effective immediately. Go home."

"For how long?"

"Until I can appoint a disciplinary board and summon you back. Go," he said. "Don't even think about touching your computer. You have your car keys?"

"Uh…on my desk…"

"Then let's retrieve them together."

I followed them as Pop marched Cudda down the hall and into the agent's much smaller office. Pop watched as Cudda picked up a leather satchel, then reconsidered and said, "Sit there," pointing to Cudda's visitor's chair. "I want you present while IT locks down your system in case they have any questions."

With that, I yanked myself back into my body and, groaning, sat up. My head spun like I'd come off a carnival ride, but I took a few breaths until the vertigo cleared and my limbs felt like they were attached to me once more, and I grabbed my phone.

Jane picked up on the second ring. "Hey, there. Is Stephanie being a bitch?"

"Dunno," I croaked, then cleared my throat. "I need you to plant a tracker on Cudda ti'Ren's car."

"Huh?"

"*Now*. Please. It's important. I'll answer questions later, but you've only got a few minutes—"

"On it," she said, and the line went dead.

First task completed, I turned to the second and called DOI's main line. "Good morning," I said to the receptionist's greeting, "this is Rose ti'Dana from DPP. Could you connect me to building security, please?"

Despite my agency affiliation, my surname carried clout at DOI, and the receptionist obliged without a fuss. A moment later, a low, gruff voice said, "Security."

"Hi. Rose ti'Dana," I said without wasting more time on pleasantries. "The director needs a favor."

He paused for only a second. "Yes, ma'am?"

"Cudda ti'Ren will be leaving soon. He's one of the farseers—"

"I'm familiar with Agent ti'Ren."

"Great. Please stall him for a few minutes…and should you see someone approach his vehicle, that's also part of the favor."

He grunted. "Can do. And if the director asks about this conversation?"

"Responsibility is mine."

"That's what I like to hear. Very well," he said. "Have a nice day, Agent…and I'm sure we can give you a moment."

About ten minutes later, as I was finishing a cup of coffee, Jane called me back. "Tracker's in place, my boss probably thinks I'm nuts, and what's going on?"

"Cone of silence?"

"Yeah, sure..."

"There may be a mole in DOI."

"This Cudda guy?"

"Right," I said. "I'm going to be watching him, but in case I lose him, I want to have a backup way to know where he goes. Can you keep an eye on him?"

"Oh, sure. The tracker's synched to my phone, so we're in business. Let me know if you need help, okay?" She paused, then asked, "Does Diriem know about this?"

"He's aware," I replied, which wasn't exactly false. "Thanks, Jane."

After I hung up, I slipped into the bathroom to wash my face, mentally preparing for the next round. But as I returned to my studio, my phone began to ring—Pop, I saw, tapping the screen. "That was fun."

"You saw it?"

"All the good bits."

"Mm. What's your assessment?"

"Don't be upset..."

Pop chuckled. "Oh?"

"I, uh...I'm going to follow Cudda once he's out of the building, but just in case, I got Jane to put a tracker on his car. We need to know where he goes so maybe we'll figure out who his girlfriend is."

"I see. So, you're giving my agents orders now, are you?"

"No," I protested, "I'm using the tools at my disposal to get the intel you want, and right now, that means leaning on the Brunch Club sisterhood."

"Is that so?" Pop laughed again, then said, "Just know that there's always a spot for you at DOI, my dear. Once you grow bored of DPP..."

"*Goodbye*, Pop," I said, and quickly ended the call.

Stretching out again, I closed my eyes, thought of

Cudda's handsome face, and let my farsight lead me back to him.

Unfortunately, Cudda proved to be a boring subject. He didn't reside downtown, as I'd anticipated, but rather in a bungalow in Old Farm, a more family-friendly district on the outskirts of Beukal. Plenty of agents lived in the area, including Gentle Breeze and Pars, Canna, and their brood, and while it wasn't stylish, it was unobjectionable—a former agricultural district with stubby trees, modest homes, and low crime. Old Farm was the sort of place where children played in the winding streets and no one batted an eye, and were I not living rent-free in Pop's palatial home, I'd probably have encouraged Yven to look for a starter house for us there.

Cudda's place wasn't anything special—a two-bedroom floorplan with mismatched furniture, a large television on the den wall, and a surprisingly well-appointed kitchen for a bachelor. As soon as he locked the front door, he made a beeline for the liquor cabinet, poured himself a healthy triple of a local rum, and settled on the couch with the TV on. And there he stayed all day, making the occasional foray back to the kitchen for a refill or to the bathroom to unload, but otherwise becoming one with the cushions as he moped and made himself drunk. He didn't even bother removing his formal robe as he vegetated.

I spent the afternoon jumping between Cudda and the Golden Children, particularly the two making the trek north from Tampa. They were driving decently hard, and by the time I checked in on them, they were stuck in traffic just north of Atlanta. Another two or three hours to Highlands, I calculated, assuming the roadway gods smiled upon them…and then, shortly after one, I found them pulled over on the side of the road with a steaming radiator.

Well, *that* wasn't good.

Unexpectedly, I saw Dirk and Katin driving away from

Highlands. They'd been in a nice, private cabin for close to a week—where were *they* going?

As I learned close to dinnertime, the answer was back to Pigeon Forge. The couple had found another secluded mountain rental, one with three bedrooms upstairs and a large bonus space below. The downstairs part of the cabin wasn't particularly well furnished, offering guests little more than a futon, an air hockey table, and a powder room convenient to the whirlpool tub on the lower deck—not my choice for a vacation stay, but then I wasn't on the run.

I was about to take a break and let the two settle in, but I decided to check on Cudda one last time. Just as I focused on him, his phone began to ring, and he fumbled with the screen until he answered it. "Hi, baby," he said, slurring his words. "I'm in trouble."

To my frustration, he kept the phone pressed to his ear, and I couldn't hear the other end of the conversation.

"Director kicked me out. Suspended," he said, and groaned as he flopped back on the couch. "Cornered me this morning. Whore-get knew I lied…No, *no*, I didn't mention you."

Not by name, at least.

"No, baby, he doesn't know anything about you. I'll keep you safe, I just…*ugh*…" He paused, then said, "So what if I am? Been there almost ninety fucking years, and security walked me out! I'm allowed a drink!" Cudda huffed as his apparent girlfriend answered that, then said, "Don't be bossy. I need your *support*, baby…Why not? What's going on?…Okay, then, can you come here after that?"

The pause that time was longer, and I suspected Cudda was getting his ear chewed off.

"Fine. See you tomorrow," he said, and cut the call. Dropping the phone on the coffee table, he managed to stand, then wobbled to his bedroom with all the grace of a tired toddler. Still dressed—even his shoes—Cudda collapsed face-down on his bed and closed his eyes, and in minutes, he was softly snoring with his hair falling over the pillow.

He was, I feared, going to have one hell of a hangover in the morning.

My dinner break would have been brief had Yven not insisted that I sit and converse with him, Tabitha, and Stephanie. "You know you focus better when you're not famished," he reminded me.

In truth, I had missed him of late, as my frequent bouts of espionage had severely cut into our couple time. So, I lingered at the table and drank coffee, and talked to my fiancé about the goings-on in Regulatory, and fielded a few of Stephanie's odder queries—and for a few stolen moments, I almost forgot about the work awaiting me that night.

But duty called, and around eight-thirty, I pried myself away from the others and their impromptu game of Yahtzee to check on Katin.

The minute I found her, even my physical body muttered, "Oh, *shit*."

Katin and Dirk had unpacked in their new cabin, and their two minions had finally arrived from Tampa in a rental car. Their malfunctioning vehicle, I took it, was toast, abandoned on the side of the Interstate. But they'd managed to bring all of their luggage with them, including four big cardboard boxes filled with the sort of equipment that had become all too familiar to me through my potions lessons—not the nicest of equipment, and judging by the scuffs and dings, certainly not new, but just what a home brewer would need to set up a modest operation.

And then there was the Publix bag, an insulted green tote of the sort I'd used hundreds of times to schlepp home frozen goods before Ranarma came into my life. It wasn't full of ice cream and single-serving pizzas, as I'd briefly hoped, but rather packed with jars and bags brimming with dried botanicals and a variety of colorful liquids.

Well, with that, there was no chance in hell that the Golden Children had acquired a set of burners to make indoor s'mores.

I left them as they began setting up in the cabin's sparsely furnished lower level and opened my real eyes, then grabbed my phone.

My first call was to Pateme, who sounded unsurprised to hear from me after hours on a Friday evening. "Rosie?"

"Katin's brewing again," I announced, rubbing my forehead as I grounded myself. "Some of her little buddies just drove in from Tampa with gear and ingredients, and they're setting up as we speak."

"Delightful. Any idea what they're making?"

"I, uh…I didn't take inventory," I admitted, feeling a mite foolish. Of course my boss at the freaking *plants and potions* agency would want to know the specifics.

But Pateme wasn't the sort to explode at his people for errors. "Mm. Think you can assemble a list?"

"I'll do my best." Chuckling weakly, I said, "This would be much simpler if I could loop Yven in when I trance."

"Could you not draw what you see?"

"I can try, but he's so much better at the subtleties than I am."

"Ti'Ansha is well-trained, youngling. You are not…*yet*," Pateme replied, not unkindly. "A partial list and some fair guesses would be better than nothing. See what you can do, eh?"

"Yes, sir."

Promising to call Pateme before morning if I noticed anything else particularly alarming, I hung up, then called his counterpart at Laws.

Under ordinary circumstances, it would have been absurd for a junior agent at DPP—particularly one still underage—to have the DOL director's cell phone number. But I'd done my share of work for our sister agency, and since DOL usually came to me only if something was both pressing and *big*, Kabno had wanted a direct line to me to get developments from the horse's mouth, so to speak. And because I didn't abuse the privilege, she almost always took my calls.

"Golden Children?" she asked without preamble when the line connected.

"Yes, ma'am. Preparing to brew."

"*Shit.*"

As Kabno's voice was pitched almost as high as a child's, hearing her swear was amusing, but I knew damn well to bite back my laughter. The woman was small but scary when provoked.

"What are they brewing, then?" she pressed. "More Velvet Leash? Or do you think they're making more of that crap they used on Tabitha and the other one?"

"I don't know. Pateme asked me to try to list the ingredients they have on hand, so I'll be watching for a while tonight. I'll keep you informed—"

"Please do. And where are the little darlings now, anyway?"

"They're still scattered, but Katin's back in Pigeon Forge."

"Do you know the nearest portal offhand?"

"Crossville, I'd think…"

"Yeah," she mused, "that makes sense. Okay. Any idea if the Hunt knows the way to their location?"

"Their cabin? Uh, doubtful. As for Pigeon Forge…I don't know about Wylan, but Annie might be familiar with it, or at least Gatlinburg. I can ask."

"Don't trouble yourself with that just yet," Kabno replied. "But do keep me apprised."

As I was shooting a text message to Pop—he was staying late at the office for reasons he'd declined to share with me, and I didn't want to interrupt him if he was also trancing—Yven poked his head into the studio. "Rosie, honey? Anything on fire?"

I looked up, grimacing. "Katin's about to start brewing,

Pateme wants to know what they're using, and I—"

"Let me get a sketchpad," he said before I could finish. "And put on fresh coffee. Give me ten minutes, and I'll help you."

Taking the chance to stretch my legs, I pushed myself off the couch and followed him into the kitchen. "What'd I ever do to deserve you?"

He kissed me before grabbing a filter from the cabinet stash. "Come on, this'll be fun. You draw what you see, I'll try to identify it, and then we'll work up what potions they're planning to make. It's like a puzzle, right?"

"You have a warped idea of fun, babe."

Grinning as he reached for the jar of coffee grounds, Yven said, "Don't tell me you're just now noticing that."

CHAPTER 14

The problem with trying to draw dried plant bits was that, at least to me, so many looked like brown confetti.

Yven did his best to come up with potentials, considering the few ingredients we could positively identify, but my intel-gathering left much to be desired on the plant identification front, and unhelpfully, nothing was labeled. What was even more frustrating was that the only potion the foursome began to brew that night was Velvet Leash, which called for barely a quarter of the ingredients on hand.

By midnight, Yven and I were exhausted and out of leads, as Katin had left Dirk to babysit the brew while she and the Tampa duo caught a few hours' sleep. I let Yven coax me to bed and collapsed beside him, barely lasting long enough to feel him spoon behind me before I crashed.

Saturday dawned gray and drizzly, and between the weak light and the soothing patter of raindrops on the windows, I could have remained snuggled up with Yven until lunchtime. But he rose first—his orchid fanciers club was holding their monthly meeting that morning at a quiet breakfast spot in Old Farm—and so I flopped onto my back in the middle of the bed, closed my eyes, and checked in on Cudda to see whether he was still snoring off his self-pity bender.

When Yven emerged from the bathroom with a towel around his waist, I was pacing the bedroom, my stomach pulled into a tightening knot. "Sweetheart?" he asked cautiously, staying out of my path. "Are you all right?"

"I can't lock on Cudda."

"He...got his blinding protection redone early?" Yven guessed. "Or does he have one of those rings like Ivari's people?"

"Neither," I said, and paused in my circuit. "I know what those feel like. He's dead."

"*Dead?*"

"Yeah. Shit," I muttered, and headed out of the room in yesterday's clothes. "Got to wake Pop."

The team from Laws was first on the scene, and they brought along a medical examiner.

"Initial impression is suicide," Kabno informed Pop via conference call around nine. "He left a bottle on his nightstand."

"A bottle of *what?*" asked Pop.

"Hang on..." I heard a burst of quick clicking—Kabno was, apparently, at her computer—and then she said, "The bottle was labeled as a sleeping potion, but tests show strong traces of cyanide."

"How would one possibly switch those labels? Who made the potion?"

"No markings—looks like a home brewing situation," she replied. "And I don't know anyone crazy enough to brew sleeping potions and rat poison simultaneously, do you? So, now we have a couple of theories. Maybe this is just a tragic accident...but what was your agent's mental state? Was he depressed, suicidal? Would he have kept something like that around in a decoy bottle?"

Pop looked troubled as he considered the phone on the desk between us. "I sent him home on administrative leave yesterday pending an investigation."

"Into what?"

"Professional misconduct, and I'll leave it at that for now," he said, earning a faint grunt from the other end of the line. "But no, I never knew Cudda to be suicidal. If he were, the agency therapists would have mentioned it."

"What was he wearing?" I asked.

"Uh…let me check…" After another few seconds of clicking, Kabno said, "He was fully dressed."

"Still had his robe and shoes on?"

"Yes…"

"Can you shoot us a picture of the scene as they found him?"

"If you like," she replied bemusedly. "Sending it…now."

Pop's phone chirped, and he opened the message for me.

"This was staged," I said, holding the phone close as I compared the image against my last view of Cudda the evening before. "He's exactly as I last saw him."

"Want to elaborate?" she asked.

"Sure. After Cudda left DOI, he went home and drank on the couch *all* day. Around dinnertime, he got a call from someone—his girlfriend, I think—and then he stumbled off to bed and face-planted, just like he is in the picture. Same clothes, same pose. He passed out, and I know he didn't drink a potion first. That bottle wasn't on the nightstand."

"Mm. Where did he leave his phone?"

"Coffee table."

"That would be his personal phone," Pop interjected. "I confiscated his agency phone before he left."

After a few seconds, Kabno said, "There's no mention of a phone in the report, and that's one of the things we look for. You're sure it was on the coffee table?"

"Yeah, the table in front of the couch in the den," I confirmed. "He dropped it there after he hung up. So, unless he woke in the middle of the night, found that potion, drank it, and then fell back into the same position…"

"Unlikely," she finished. "Which means that someone gave him the potion while he slept."

"What does the medical examiner say?" asked Pop.

"She confirmed death and gave us an approximate time, but that's all thus far. The body's gone back to the tower for autopsy, toxicology, and a potion scan. As for the scene, there's no sign of forced entry. He didn't set his alarm ward last night, but the door was locked." With a sigh, Kabno said, "Right, then. First call is to telecom to get his phone records. There's a girlfriend, is there?"

"So he said," Pop replied, looking at me, "but he wouldn't identify her yesterday. Unless Rose overheard something..."

I shook my head. "Negative."

"Then we'll try other avenues. Kabno, what was the time of death?"

"Uh..." she said, "looks like between midnight and two this morning."

"Thanks. I'll have my people take a look and see what happened. You'll be available later today?"

"Sure," she replied. "If someone's killing agents...yours, mine, anyone's..."

"Appreciated. I'll be in touch," said Pop, and hung up. With a grim smile for me, he said, "Time to ruin Ganti's Saturday."

"I'm sorry I didn't see it happen—"

"Rosie, for the tenth time, no one is upset with you," he said as he pulled Ganti's contact in his phone and dialed. "And this is fixable, yes? We have a timeframe, we have past-oriented farseers—"

"Boss?" came Ganti's tinny voice.

Pop put the call on speaker. "Good morning. I'm sorry, but I need someone I can trust. Are you doing anything right now that can't be put aside?"

"I mean, it won't be a matter of life and death if this oatmeal congeals," Ganti joked. "What's up?"

"Cudda's dead."

"Huh?"

"This morning. Presumably poisoned."

Ganti swore softly in *colorful* Low Elvish. "And you want me to look into it?"

"Please. Incidentally, do you know the name of his girlfriend?"

"I didn't know he had one," he replied. "Cudda and I weren't exactly friends outside the office…"

I didn't miss Pop's slight wince. While he counted Ganti among his closer friends—or whatever passed for such, given Pop's odd circumstances—there was zero overlap between their social circles. Calien, for instance, would have been appalled had she known that Ganti was a more than occasional guest at Pop's dinner table.

"Don't worry about it," said Pop. "If you could see what Cudda was doing after midnight, I'd appreciate it."

"Happy to check, but wasn't he protected?"

"Yes, but it had degraded far enough for Rose to see him. He was in Monday's batch—"

"Did Rose see him die?" he asked, his voice tensing.

Pop gestured to me, and I leaned toward the phone. "Hey, Ganti. No, I was dealing with the damn Golden Children until I went to bed, and I woke up and realized I couldn't lock on Cudda anymore."

"*Ah*. Good."

"I can handle death," I protested.

"That doesn't mean you should be handling it unnecessarily, youngling," he replied. "I'll see what I can find, boss. Give me an hour or two."

At ten-thirty, as I was watching Katin check her brew while Dirk and the others made a lazy pancake brunch, Pop shook my shoulder to snap me out of trance. "I've got Ganti here," he said, holding out his phone, and I mumbled a greeting as I sat up and blinked at my studio.

While Yven and I didn't make a habit of locking our apartment, Pop almost never entered without our permission—no further than the foyer, and then just to call for us if, say, the TV's volume was up too high for us to have heard his knock. I wasn't upset that he'd let himself in to find me, but the fact that he'd done so left me ill at ease about what Ganti would report.

"She's here," Pop said to the phone. "What did you see?"

"Not as much as I'd have liked," Ganti replied, "but I can tell you that Cudda was fucking murdered."

Though Ganti still sounded a little groggy from his own trancing, his anger was unmistakable. Friend or not, Cudda had been his colleague.

"He was passed out on his bed at midnight," Ganti continued. "Clothed, shod, drooling on the pillow. I found the alcohol bottles in the kitchen. Just after one, someone let themselves in through the front door."

"Someone?" Pop echoed.

"Yeah. Whoever they were, they're protected. Cudda was fuzzy, but with the newcomer, all I saw was an ambulatory blot."

"What *color* blot?" I croaked.

"Funny you should ask," said Ganti, though he sounded anything but amused. "Very dark gray."

"Not blinding potion, then, but—"

"One of those damn rings," he finished. "Whoever killed Cudda has a connection to the southern Halls."

"Not necessarily," said Pop. "Remember the missing rings?"

I knew that rankled Ganti. During their long years in hiding outside, each member of Ivari ti'Ammaas's group of refugees and their descendants had constantly worn a ring that blocked farsight. Unlike the whiteout I saw when trying to focus on someone protected by blinding potion, with the rings, the target appeared almost dead—there was a faint difference in the shade of black, a distinction subtle enough to have fooled Pop for centuries. If the refugees still wore their rings—well, the ones not on penal farms—I couldn't say, as I hadn't had cause to spy on them. But I did know that a few of the rings had gone missing from the DOL property locker, and when Ganti had investigated to look for the thief, he'd found that the culprit was protected by blinding potion, and the security cameras had been briefly hexed.

"All right, perhaps not," Ganti grudgingly allowed, "but whoever they were, they brought the potion with them. I didn't see the bottle until they finished in the bedroom—oh, and they took the syringe with them."

"He was injected?" I asked.

"Precisely. They put the empty syringe on the nightstand for a moment while they cleaned up. I don't know *where* Cudda was injected," said Ganti, "but I can tell you that he didn't knowingly take that potion. Death came quickly," he said, his voice lower. "His breathing grew labored, then ceased. I don't believe he ever woke."

"What about his killer?" I pressed. "What did they do?"

Ganti chuckled mirthlessly. "Good question. Once Cudda was dead, my vision ended, and I couldn't follow the other person. They were there until he breathed his last, I can tell you that much—probably watching to be sure the poison worked. But beyond that, I can't see anything."

"Did you see how they arrived at the house?" asked Pop.

"No," said Ganti. "Bastard parked too far away, outside my viewing radius. I tried to track their path down the street but couldn't go all the way to their vehicle—*if* they had a vehicle. For all I know, they live in Old Farm."

"A possibility," Pop allowed, "but I think it would be prudent nonetheless to get the Portal Authority involved."

I frowned at him. "There isn't a portal to Old Farm. If you're thinking of getting the data of everyone who came into Beukal yesterday…"

"Hardly," replied Pop. "There's a traffic camera installed along the main artery from Old Farm to downtown. The Portal Authority employs it primarily for weather conditions, but it's also a useful gauge for sporting events and such—when traffic out of Old Farm picks up, the wave coming from the inbound portals won't be far behind," he explained. "I want to know who drove in and out of there last night."

Ganti grunted. "Do you need my help, boss?"

"You've done enough, and I'm sorry for asking that of you—"

"Not the worst I've seen."

Pop stared at the phone. "There are few good deaths we're called upon to witness, youngling."

"Yeah, yeah. I'm fine," said Ganti. "Well, if something else arises, you know where to reach me. And I assume this is to be kept quiet for now, yes?"

"If you would, please. I'd like to speak with his family first."

Once the call had concluded, Pop told me, "I need to inform Kabno and start getting the traffic records. Are you okay?"

"Sure, fine," I replied. "I was going to keep an eye on the Golden Children, but if there's someone else you need me to watch…"

"Not yet." He patted my shoulder and started to leave, then glanced back. "Take a shower, dear. Clear your head."

I snorted. "Trying to tell me I stink, eh?"

"Never," he deadpanned, and let himself out.

I learned later Saturday night that Pop had intercepted Yven while he was racing home from his orchid meeting and strongly encouraged him to give me space. I was kicking myself over missing Cudda's murder, and to keep my mind from spiraling, I spent hours with the Golden Children, watching their little groups go about their business—eating at McDonald's, taking a walk around a pond, brewing God knew what—until Yven, who'd even taken a turn entertaining Tabitha and Stephanie, left the sanctuary of the greenhouse to fetch me for dinner.

By then, Ganti and I weren't the only ones who'd had our weekend ruined by Cudda's death investigation. Old Farm was large and popular, and as Pop had asked for the traffic data from four p.m. Friday until four a.m. Saturday, the list of potential suspects to clear was *considerable*. DOI's analysts had been on the project since noon, cross-checking vehicle registrations against addresses, but the herculean task would stretch at least until Monday.

That night, after ascertaining that Katin was just watching the brew with a paperback romance while Dirk and the others had gone to a dinner show in Gatlinburg, I took a break to continue the slow work of my parents' portrait. I'd finally decided to place them in our front yard, creating a reminder of the childhood home I couldn't cling to indefinitely, and I could almost hear them as I sketched the house in the background.

It's okay, Rosie.

You're doing your best.

You couldn't have saved him.

I studied my mother's face, smarting as I recalled that my final dress fitting was in the morning. Once again, I was reminded that I would never have the big wedding gown experience with my mom and a bunch of bridesmaids, trying on half a dozen white dresses until I found "the one" and everyone popped champagne. Sure, if I called Aunt Lily, I was positive she'd get up at the crack of dawn and make the drive from Briardale, but much as I loved my great-aunt, it just wasn't the same.

Besides, if Calien got snippy, I wouldn't have put it past Aunt Lily to throw hands. So what if her father had been lord of Hall ti'Cren? Liliol had spent decades tossing around bags of mulch and toting shrubs, and she was still protective of me. I could envision all five feet, two inches of her getting up in my cousin's face and delivering a backhand to knock Calien into the next week, and frankly, that wasn't an outcome I wanted to explain to Teolm, Pop, or Miral.

But Mom smiled at me out of the portrait all the same. I looked at the whitish-silver spot in the hollow of her throat: her little diamond solitaire, a gift from Dad for their tenth anniversary. It wasn't large or flashy, a round half-carat stone on a thin gold chain, but Mom had treasured it, and of all my mother's jewelry, it was the piece I loved the most. I planned to wear it on my wedding day.

There was no harm in wearing it to the fitting, too. After all, Mom would have wanted to be there.

I walked into Black Swan at eleven Sunday morning to find Calien waiting in a chair in a skintight magenta dress, eyeing me sourly. There was no sign of Tiami, but Jevva waved from the door of her office. "Be right there!" she called, smiling. "Let me get my kit. Go ahead and step into the dressing room, dear."

As I slipped behind the curtain to disrobe, Calien followed, loitering just outside. "You look awful," she muttered.

I pulled my T-shirt over my head and tossed it onto the chair. "Well, I've been up since three, and I haven't had a full night's sleep in days, so cut me a little slack."

"Huh?"

Idioms. "Go easy on me. I've got rogue brewers stretched over half the southeast U.S. and a murdered agent on my plate, and it's cutting into my beauty rest."

"You could always mask, you know. You're not the only one whose reputation takes a hit when you walk around looking like that."

"If Pop were offended, I'm sure he would have said something at breakfast," I retorted, unzipping my jeans. "Of course, he's busy right now, too, so we've both got more important problems to worry about than the state of my face."

Shortly after I got down to my underthings, Jevva bustled in, alteration kit in hand and my gown floating along behind her, its golden laces already loosening. "Oh, it's gorgeous," I said as it hung itself on the wall hook.

She beamed. "We did well, didn't we? Let's see how it fits. And don't worry about that bra, I built one in for you."

I let her lace me into the gown, holding it up as she cinched the waist, and despite my stress and exhaustion, I smiled at my reflection. Yes, I had puffy eyes and a messy bun, but the dress fit like a glove, and for the first time in my wedding preparations, I felt genuinely *pretty.*

Jevva helped me out of the changing room and onto the platform before the mirrors, giving me a better view of myself in near profile. "Stunning," she decreed, spreading the train with the twitch of a finger. "Absolutely stunning. Now, tell me about your shoes. I left a little extra length because we didn't talk about heels—were you planning to wear something taller?"

"Flats, definitely," I replied. My girlfriends who'd already been down the aisle swore by them. "Something unobtrusive—"

"That dress is completely out of fashion, you know."

I glared at Calien in the mirror, but Jevva turned to her before I could argue. "Child," she said with disdain, "that is a *classic* silhouette. It remains in fashion because it's a proven winner. But doesn't your cousin look beautiful?"

"Fine, I guess," she begrudgingly allowed. "For a sorcerer."

Jevva met my gaze in the mirror and rolled her eyes.

"If you're going with flats," the designer said, "then I'll need to take up just a bit of the hem. Stand still, please, so I can make this even…"

Though she knelt beside the platform to check her work, the pins flew into place by magic, forming a perfect line. I turned as Jevva requested, and in a few minutes, she had tucked and tailored to her satisfaction. "So," she said as I faced the mirror once more, "tell me about your jewelry."

"I've made an appointment with Veriarda," said Calien, interjecting herself into the conversation. "Had to beg and call in favors, but I got one for Wednesday evening. We'll find something to work with that dress, I suppose."

"Uh…thank you," I said, trying to sound appropriately grateful, "that's very kind of you, but that won't be necessary. I've already picked out my jewelry."

Calian's eyes narrowed. "What do you mean?"

"This," I replied, pointing to the diamond at my collarbones. "And I've got a pair of studs to match. They're the right size—"

"*Studs*?" she echoed, appalled. "We've been over this! You're not wearing earrings!"

I pointed to the holes in my earlobes. "Doesn't make sense to leave these empty."

"Mask them, you dolt!"

"You know," said Jevva, stepping into the breach, "that's not a look we typically see here, but I think it could work. Show me?"

I threw together a mask, creating the impression of diamond studs. "Like this. I wanted to wear my hair at least partially down…"

"Those do work well with the pendant," she said, and tapped one finger against her lips as she considered the effect. "What would you think about adding a bit of sparkle to the gown? Rhinestone accents? Very small rhinestones, nothing overpowering, just a little twinkle. May I demonstrate?"

"Sure!"

She gestured for a few seconds, and a spray of teeny rhinestones appeared along my neckline, followed the boning of the bodice, and dissipated over the skirt like stardust, nearly invisible until they caught the light. I gave it a twirl, admiring the effect, and grinned at Jevva. "This is lovely! You like it?"

"It's out of fashion!" Calien protested. "And you *cannot*

wear that necklace. It looks cheap."

At that, I finally saw red. "The necklace is non-negotiable," I snapped, turning to glower at my cousin. "My father gave it to my mother. I'm wearing it."

She sniffed. "*Why*? If you must have something old and used, surely Uncle has a better piece tucked away that he could loan you for a few hours."

"Maybe he does," I said, digging my nails into my palms to hold my temper in check, "but it's not about the size of the jewelry. You don't get it."

Calien crossed her arms and smirked. "Enlighten me, then."

The woman was pushing every button I had, but I kept my voice down. "Whenever you get married"—I refrained from adding, *If you find someone crazy enough to go through with it*—"your parents will be there. You're not in any imminent danger of losing them. But I won't have mine. The last time I saw them in person, I wasn't quite twenty-three, and I had to stand there at the funeral home and keep it together while all their friends and coworkers told me how sorry they were for my loss. Then I sat in the front row at the graveside service and got to throw flowers on their caskets. Roses, incidentally," I said, fighting the warning tightness in my throat. "They died on Valentine's Day, so at least the florists were well stocked. Small consolation," I muttered. "But they're not going to be there for the big day in June. At least this way," I said, lifting the necklace with one finger. "I'll have a small piece of them with me. Okay? Good enough for you?"

But she remained unmoved. "You're going to have your damn trees, right? Assuming your amateur officiant can figure out what he's doing."

It was Yven who'd called Calien to inform her that Teolm was taking over for her buddy Feon, and she'd been sulky about the matter ever since.

"I'm sure he'll manage," I said.

"Wonderful," she replied with feigned enthusiasm. "So,

you're already planning to flaunt the fact that you're a half-breed. Why rub it in further?"

"*Excuse* me," Jevva interrupted, but Calien plowed on.

"Anyone doing a write-up of the event will either comment on how small and cheap-looking your jewelry is—or tacky, if you insist on those," she said, tapping her unmarred ears—"or else they'll sniff out your little sob story about Mommy and Daddy and write all about that sordid affair. *Again.* You've dragged the Halls through the mud enough, haven't you?" she continued, her voice shrilling. "Mine *and* ti'Cren? Have you no shame at all?"

I stood there until the echoes of her near-shout had died in the mercifully empty shop, then took a long breath and swallowed my tears and anger.

How did Pop make it look so damn *easy*?

"The necklace is non-negotiable, Calien," I said. "Thank you again for making an appointment with your jeweler, but that won't be necessary."

"Don't be ridiculous. Veriarda is one of the hottest designers in the city, and she's a personal friend—"

"If I needed something," I said, speaking over her, "I would call Teolm and look through the ti'Cren vault, not patronize another of your bitchy little friends so you two can stand there and mock me."

She stepped back, huffing her indignation. "You are *such* an ingrate, and you'd be a disaster without me. Ti'Cren, *please.* Their pieces aren't fashionable."

Jevva's loud, incredulous laughter cut Calien short and left her scowling. "Since *when*?" she said. "Ti'Cren Designs has been the best jeweler in Beukal for decades. I've coordinated with them hundreds of times. Now, perhaps you and your friends prefer something a bit more…up and coming," Jevva allowed, "but there is nothing wrong with a ti'Cren piece. Nor," she said, gently tapping my solitaire, "is there anything wrong with subtle jewelry."

Finding no quarter, Calien straightened and grabbed her purse from the chair where she'd left it. "Well, I see you two have this under control," she said, then plastered on a smile that was nowhere near convincing and sashayed out of the shop without a backward glance.

Once the door had slammed closed, Jevva whistled low. "She's a fun one, isn't she?"

"What's the phrase?" I murmured, and switched to High Elvish. "Warm as a spring blizzard?"

She chuckled softly and replied in kind. "I didn't realize you'd acquired the old tongue."

"Useful for dealing with the southern Halls. The East Branch bunch got both varieties along with Pactish, but I think it would offend the New Yorkers' sensibilities to ever use Low Elvish. But hey," I added, brightening, "at least this means I'll understand my own wedding ceremony, right?"

"You'll be fine, dear," said Jevva, then gestured to my gown. "Now that we have the place to ourselves, let's finalize the design, shall we?"

CHAPTER 15

In my experience, interagency meetings—at least when the agencies in question were DOL, DPP, and DOI—tended to convene in the executive conference rooms at DOL or DPP. Both were spacious and offered lovely views of the city (though Laws never let the others forget that they had an extra ten stories on the DPP tower). But as this concerned the murder of one of DOI's own, Kabno and Pateme made the trip to Pop's windowless building for a change, and we met in Pop's office with the door locked and the wards engaged against eavesdroppers.

We filled his office's table at ten Monday morning, just the directors, Ganti, the two analysts who'd spent the weekend with the traffic data—Dienk Focan and Nim Gemellu—Yven, and me. Yven had come along at Pop's request, as apparently, I was about to have a busy week, and Pop thought matters would go more smoothly if the person who'd tasked himself with looking after my welfare knew what was happening. It was not the first such meeting Yven had attended in his role as Unofficial Farseer Babysitter, but no one seemed surprised when he took a seat beside me. In fact, Pateme had called late the night before and told Yven he was on leave until after our wedding, as he had a strong suspicion that Yven would be of little use to Regulatory for the rest of the month.

I'd had occasional dealings with the analysts, as they were lent out to the other investigative agencies as needed, and neither seemed well-rested. Dienk, a dark-haired faun who stood barely taller than five feet, had wearily shuffled his hooves as he approached the table, while his frequent partner, Nim, a lanky, gray-skinned metal nymph with long gray hair and piercing blue eyes, clutched his computer in one hand and a frighteningly large travel mug in the other. While the pair had thrown on formal robes that morning, neither man's robe had been anywhere in the vicinity of a steamer. Yven, as usual, looked presentable, and I'd pulled a robe from the closet after Yven had peeled me off my studio couch and coaxed me into the shower, but Ganti, who'd spent the rest of the weekend helping the analysts, had rolled up in jeans and a purple melee jersey from a team I couldn't name.

Someday, perhaps, I would learn the various leagues and teams of Beukal's favorite sport, but seeing as I'd never been great with sports back home, I had a *long* way to go.

Pop waited until everyone was unpacked and equipped with caffeine as needed, then nodded to the analysts. "Gentlemen?"

Dienk tapped a button on his computer, and a projector in the middle of the table flashed an ID photo of a female elf. She was pretty, a blonde with dark eyes and pouting lips, but I didn't recognize her.

"This," said Nim, "is Jillu ti'Non. Born in December 1950 in the southern Halls' New York compound. Currently receiving training in our banking system. I don't know what she did outside, but she seems adept with financial matters."

The view changed to a pie chart with several colored wedges. "Here's the traffic into Old Farm Friday night," Nim continued. "Seventy-three percent of vehicles that passed the camera did not leave again until at least dawn Saturday, and of those vehicles, seventy-one percent are registered to homeowners or listed renters in the neighborhood."

"And the other two percent?" asked Pateme.

"Subleases and romantic partners are our suppositions.

We have a separate list. None of them had any regular connection with Cudda." The biggest chunk of the projected pie went black. "Moving on, ten percent of the traffic was from delivery vehicles, none of which entered after midnight." Another sliver vanished. "Nine percent were shuttles and ride-share groups, the last of which left the neighborhood before eight that night, and three percent were DOL patrols. Director Erenani, we received vehicle data from the agents on shift in that area, and all are accounted for."

The two wedges blackened, leaving a red sliver of the pie.

"And these," said Nim, "are our weird ones. Friends coming over to socialize, people making quick stops."

"Hookups," Dienk offered.

Nim nodded. "There were a few known sex workers among this group, yes. But when we considered all of the possibilities, Jillu's concerned us most. She drove into Old Farm ten minutes before one Saturday morning, and she drove out at one forty-eight." He cocked his head and stared at the projection as it switched back to Jillu's face. "What was she doing for fifty-eight minutes in the middle of the night? And since the time frame coincides with Ganti's observations…"

"She's our killer?" Kabno asked.

"We didn't want to leap to conclusions, ma'am," said Dienk. "Especially because, on paper, there's nothing that would link the two."

The view changed, putting Jillu into an empty family tree.

"Jillu is married to Mirin ti'Ammaas," Dienk began, and a man's face appeared beside Jillu's. "Their records say the two joined in 1985…though I certainly don't know about matrimonial conventions in *that* group. They have two sons, Cefet ti'Non—he's almost of age—and Utien ti'Ammaas, who's about five." The children's pictures joined their parents'.

"Odd for the elder to take ti'Non," Pateme mused. "That's...what, a middling Hall?" he asked, turning to Pop.

"As I recall, yes. But more importantly, Mirin has been incarcerated since last March."

Kabno snapped her fingers. "I knew that name sounded familiar. He was involved in the North Lake kidnapping."

"His brother as well, I believe...Jeviel ti'Tola?"

"Sounds right," Kabno mused, frowning.

"Which still leaves the question of why Jillu and Mirin's elder child took ti'Non," said Ganti.

Pop grunted. "A moment," he said, tapping at his computer, and then he sat back, his mouth a tight line. "I have access to the records for the East Branch and New York groups—Hall assignments, familial data, and such. The boy was given ti'Non because Jillu is, or *was*, an heir to that Hall. Jeniel ti'Non was the lady when the southern kingdom fell. Her eldest from her New York marriage is her daughter Irrafta, whose eldest is her son Kerro, and his eldest is Jillu. Of course, that doesn't matter now because the current head of the Hall is...Zoe Black," he said, checking his notes, "who descends from Jeniel's firstborn from her previous marriage, Noah Church. But I digress—what caught my eye is that both Jillu and her husband are ti'Ammaas grandchildren. Jillu's mother is Dolia, who's Ivari and Farral's fourth child. Mirin's mother is Beani, Ivari and Farral's second. They're first cousins."

"The same issue East Branch had," murmured Yven.

"Yes. Let's hope their children outbreed," Pop muttered. "I'm sorry, Dienk, please continue."

The agent picked up with the family tree, adding the connections that led both spouses back to their incarcerated grandparents. "For the sake of completion," he said, adding two more faces, "Jillu has a younger sister, Obelli ti'Ammaas, and a younger brother, Rivi ti'Non. Now, we didn't see any immediate connection between any of these individuals and Cudda, but that was before we had the Portal Authority pull vehicle data for the last three months." Noticing my frown, he said, "The decal on your car tracks it through the portals, but it also pings on traffic cameras like the one in Old Farm. And here's what we saw."

A map of Beukal and its sprawling suburbs appeared in place of the family tree, and a pair of dots, red and blue, began tracing lines and loops around the city. As I watched, I noticed periods of synchronization appear with relative frequency.

"They were meeting up," murmured Kabno.

"That's what the data suggest, ma'am," Dienk replied. "And as you see, Jillu repeatedly visited Cudda at home."

"She doesn't live in Old Farm?" Pateme inquired.

"No, sir. She lives in an apartment in District 4. And before you ask, none of the New Yorkers live in Old Farm. Most are in District 4—all but some of Hall ti'Ammaas, and they moved together to Cirinti."

Maebe was the first of the new heads of Halls to build a proper house, and she'd done a heck of a job. Cirinti was far from Beukal, a fishing village sandwiched between the mountains and the western sea, and she'd built Hall ti'Ammaas on a fantastic cliffside property overlooking it all. I'd been out a few times with Jane to see the mansion's progress, and Maebe had every right to be proud of her home. Since its completion, much of the rest of her Hall had joined her—it was far less expensive than paying District 4 rent, and Maebe was eager to get to know the kinfolk nominally under her authority.

Kabno looked down the table at Pop. "With Mirin on a penal farm, do you suppose those two were having an affair? Is Jillu your agent's girlfriend?"

"I confess, I don't know," Pop replied. "There's evidence, certainly, but I don't have a firm answer. If she *is* Cudda's girlfriend, then I'm not surprised he kept her existence quiet. Born and raised outside, a century his junior…married with children…"

"If I may interrupt," said Pateme, looking at the analysts, "are we positive that Cudda's death wasn't suicide?"

Both nodded. "Autopsy report came in last night, sir," said Dienk. "Nothing suspicious in his stomach, and the medical examiner found the injection site in his neck."

"As I told you," Ganti mumbled.

"Just a thought," said Nim, glancing between Pateme and Kabno, "but assuming Jillu was in a relationship with Cudda, might the head of Hall ti'Non have any insight?"

Pop shook his head. "Zoe's underage, and she lives in the dorm at North Lake. There's no reason that she would be aware of this." To Kabno, he said, "The New Yorkers who weren't arrested—their protective rings were never confiscated, correct?"

"That's my understanding," she replied. "We'd have had no grounds to take their property. It's not like the rings are weapons…"

"No," said Ganti, "but it means that this Jillu could have been the person I saw kill Cudda…or rather, the person I *couldn't* see."

After a moment's contemplation, Kabno said, "It could make sense. Cudda and Jillu see each other quietly, she learns that the existence of their relationship has been exposed, and she sneaks over to kill him in order to prevent her husband from hearing of it."

"But assuming Cudda told the truth," I said, "why would Jillu convince him to help free the Golden Children? What's in it for her?"

When no one jumped to answer that, Pop said, "It's unclear as of yet, but the fact that she's a ti'Ammaas in all but name gives me pause."

In fairness, Pop had a legitimate grievance against Ivari ti'Ammaas, who had orchestrated his parents' assassination in an attempt to destabilize the northern kingdom. That the two former kings despised each other was no great secret. And given the number of Ivari's kin who'd helped massacre half of East Branch or kidnap the survivors, I couldn't deem Pop's unease groundless.

"So, what now?" asked Pateme, looking around the table.

In reply, Kabno cracked her knuckles one by one as she said, "I think we bring Ms. ti'Non to the tower for a little *conversation.* Any objection?"

"Not as long as I can watch," said Pop.

"Of course," she replied with a menacing smile. "How does your afternoon look, Diriem?"

Jillu ti'Non was an unreservedly attractive woman, a little taller than I'd anticipated, with the typical slim elven build and a light tan. Her blonde hair was pulled back in a glossy high ponytail, and her makeup was flawless, the work of a well-practiced hand. She wore a soft pink floral sheath dress with a white shrug and a string of dainty pearls—feminine but conservative by outside standards, though Calien surely would have deemed it unstylish. Personally, had I been stuck in banking training, I might have opted for something a bit more comfortable, but Jillu looked polished, and her kitten heels clacked on the hard floor of the interview room.

DOL's interrogation spaces came in two flavors, depending on the subject. There were plenty of rooms like those I'd seen in police procedurals all my life: a table attached to the floor, two or three folding chairs, a bolt to which handcuffs could be affixed if the subject got aggressive. The other style was far more welcoming—larger, for starters, with comfortable upholstered chairs and mats, wooden coffee tables, and often a small beverage fridge in the corner. These were the sort of rooms with coasters on the table and a box of tissues at the ready, often used to interview crime victims and non-suspect witnesses. But they were also a good tool to feel out potential suspects, less intimidating than the standard interrogation room and so more likely to put the subject off his guard.

Regardless of the style, though, all interview rooms were flanked with viewing rooms, spaces on the other side of one-way glass from which any number of agents, detectives, or other personnel might observe the proceedings. Those were fairly utilitarian rooms, soundproofed and often stocked with a coffeemaker but otherwise bare-bones.

I sat with Pop in a pair of mismatched chairs, trying to read Jillu's mood as I watched her make herself comfortable next door. Superficially, she was smiling and pleasant, but she seemed tense to me, her back a little too straight, her ankles crossed a little too tightly, her hands gripping her purse as if for comfort.

The detective with her was also an elf, Merrot ti'Gata, a well-seasoned member of the Violent Crimes unit with a long track record of cracking reluctant subjects. Tall, dark, and blessed with a deep but often gentle voice that put people at ease, Merrot had a quick smile and knew how to employ self-deprecation to great effect. I'd watched him work on many occasions—some in person, some via farsight—and I thought Kabno had chosen wisely.

"Thank you so much for coming, Ms. ti'Non," said Merrot as he closed the door. "Make yourself at home. Can I get you a drink?"

"Water, if you don't mind," she replied. Even my poor ear could tell how strange her accent was. Most elves spoke Pactish with a slight lilt, evidence of native fluency in Low Elvish, but Jillu's carried strong notes of Manhattan. Per Pop, most of the New Yorkers had opted only for Pactish in their language potion; *High* Elvish had been the language of the southern kingdom, an older and purer form of the tongue, and aside from some of the younger adults, most refused to sully themselves by learning the bastardized variety that had survived the collapse of the northern kingdom. But as High Elvish had become a ceremonial relic in the Pactlands, with few actual speakers, Merrot and Jillu were forced to conduct their conversation in Pactish.

"Of course." Tucking a manila folder under his arm, he pulled a pair of bottles from the fridge, then took the seat opposite Jillu as she opened hers. "I'm sorry for the interruption in the middle of your day, but my investigation is high on the director's priority list, and I couldn't very well ask her if we could schedule you for the weekend."

"Smart man," Kabno muttered beside Pop.

"No, that's fine. I understand," said Jillu, and took a sip. "Mind telling me what this is all about...uh, Agent?"

"Detective," he replied, grinning. "Very close. And certainly—I don't want to waste your time." He opened his folder and riffled through the contents, then passed Jillu a full-page color copy of Cudda's DOI photo. "Do you know this man?"

Jillu stiffened but maintained her composure as she took the picture from him. "No," she said, furrowing her brow. "I've never seen him—not to my knowledge, anyway. Could have passed him on the street or something, but I don't know who he is."

"Well," said Merrot, making no move to relieve Jillu of the photo, "let me help you out. That's Cudda ti'Ren. He was found dead in his bed early Saturday morning, and since he was a certified farseer, DOI is *invested* in this case."

"Not natural causes, I take it."

"No. There was an empty potion bottle found by his bedside—a poisonous draught," the detective explained. "But the autopsy showed that the potion was injected into Agent ti'Ren's neck. Highly unusual for a suicide...especially since the syringe wasn't recovered at the scene."

Her poker face wasn't quite as good as Pop's, but it was impressive all the same. "Meaning?"

"Between the physical evidence and the report from one of DOI's past-oriented farseers, someone entered the house in the middle of the night, injected the victim, and took the syringe away. The question is who."

Jillu offered him a calculated little shrug. "I'm afraid I can't help you there, Detective. As I said, I've never seen this man."

"Sure, sure," said Merrot, and paused for a drink of water, giving Jillu a moment to shift in her chair. "Let me see if you can assist me with another issue, eh?" He pulled two pieces of paper out and laid them on the table between their coasters, facing Jillu.

She leaned closer to read them, then sat back, startled. "Is that my car?"

"Well, it's registered to you. This is your vehicle entering the Old Farm neighborhood shortly before one Saturday morning, and this is your vehicle leaving almost exactly an hour later. Since Agent ti'Ren lived in Old Farm, we took a look at the traffic camera," he said in a conversational tone that was anything but. "Now, you live in District 4, do you not?"

"Uh...yeah..."

"Bit of a drive. Would you mind telling me what you were doing in Old Farm at that time of night?"

She blinked rapidly, then ran a manicured hand over her face. "There's a bar," she said quietly. "The Decanter. Sometimes, when I can't sleep or I'm stressed...you know, a drink will smooth out the rough edges."

Merrot nodded. "Of course."

"We've had a great number of...*changes*...in the last couple of years," Jillu continued. "Lost our home and our jobs, got a new home, training for new jobs, everything's in a foreign language except the imported programs on TV..." She shook her head. "My husband is incarcerated, did you know that? My older son lives with us, but my baby's not quite five. He keeps asking when Daddy's coming home, and barring a miracle, he'll be long grown before his father's a free man." She sighed and closed her eyes. "I'm trying to keep it together and set a good example for them. I don't want my boys walking into the kitchen for a drink of water in the middle of the night and finding me with a bottle of gin. So...The Decanter's nice. Quiet. Decent prices. Feels safe enough that I can have a drink or two and probably not end up...uh..." She frowned in consternation, then said, "*Roofied?* I don't know the Pactish."

"Drugged?"

"Sure, let's go with that."

He picked up his water bottle and took a long swig, then recapped it and set it aside. "What you just said makes sense, Ms. ti'Non, but for the fact that The Decanter has been closed for the last two weeks."

Jillu stared at him across the table, her face frozen.

"I live in Old Farm, too," Merrot added. "Been going to that bar for years. They closed to redecorate, remember? New floors, ripping out those awful bathrooms—well, I don't know what the women's is like, but the men's is gross. Whatever they've got in the plans *has* to be an improvement. So, seeing as you couldn't have been at The Decanter Saturday morning, want to tell me why you really were in Old Farm?"

Before she could answer him, someone pounded on the interview room door, and Merrot gestured it open. In came an agent in black, a gray-skinned, green-haired nymph, and just behind him, Eullan Bargem, his dark hair loose over his shoulders and his blue eyes steely.

"What's *he* doing here?" asked Kabno, squinting at the mirror.

The Golden Children's counselor was impeccably dressed in a silver robe with black embroidery, and he gripped Jillu's shoulder almost possessively. "Not another word, Ms. ti'Non," he said, staring at the detective.

Merrot slowly stood. "Counselor. I didn't know Ms. ti'Non was represented."

"She is, in fact," Eullan replied. "And I'm ending this interview. Jillu, let's go—"

"Not so fast." Holding the sorcerer's stare, Merrot said, "Ms. ti'Non, you're under arrest for the murder of Cudda ti'Ren."

"Based on what evidence?" demanded Eullan, puffing out his chest. "You have nothing on my client!"

"I'll have our file sent to your office this afternoon," he replied. "Now, if you'd be so kind as to take your hands off Ms. ti'Non, she needs to be processed."

Jillu turned wide, fearful eyes on the counselor, but he did as Merrot asked. "I will alert your elder son," he assured her. "The little one will be fine."

"But—"

"*Not another word*," he repeated over her protestations. "I'll see you tomorrow." To Merrot, Eullan said, "Tell your counselors to expect my motion for a probable cause hearing."

"I'll pass that along," the detective replied, "but you should know that the file has *two* farseers' reports in there."

While I was no expert on Pactlands criminal procedure, I'd learned a bit through my agency work. An arrested person had to be given a file containing the probable cause for his detention within twenty-four hours, which at least gave him an idea of the basis of the charges to come. Detainees *could* move the Tribunal for a probable cause hearing, but those were seldom granted; the evidentiary bar was low for DOL at that point in the proceedings, and the judge who considered the pretrial matters usually denied a hearing based on the strength of the file. On occasion, the lead investigator might be brought in, put under the truth spell, and asked questions about the evidence, but that was infrequent—and if a farseer's report was in the file, the odds of a hearing fell precipitously, which made Ganti's crew and me *very* popular.

"The deceased was a DOI farseer, was he not?" said Eullan. "I was under the impression that they employed blinding protection."

"Oh, they do," Merrot replied with a smile. "Apparently, Agent ti'Ren was due for reapplication when he was murdered."

Eullan didn't so much as flinch, but I caught Jillu's

flash of surprise before she locked down her face.

"Anyway," said Merrot, "we'll have that file to you, Mr. Bargem. Agent Commru, would you be so kind as to escort him back to the lobby?"

Once the counselor and his escort had departed, two agents who'd been on standby in our viewing room—another elf and a *large* troll—went next door, one holding handcuffs and the other a syringe. As Jillu eyed them like a cornered animal, Merrot calmly informed her, "The dampening potion is temporary, but it's for everyone's security. I'd advise you not to resist."

She glowered at them but didn't fight as the troll injected the potion into her arm. With that accomplished, the elf snapped handcuffs on her, then picked up her purse. "Did you bring any other property?" he asked. "Besides your vehicle. That will be kept in the garage for you, and you can authorize its release to another adult once it's no longer needed for the investigation."

"Uh…no," she muttered, "just my bag…"

"One moment," Merrot interjected, and gently lifted Jillu's hands. He slid a silver ring off her finger, then handed it to the troll. "Make sure this ends up in the director's drawer in the property locker, understood?"

As the troll walked out with Jillu's ring, I said, "Guess I know what I'll be doing tonight."

Pop patted my knee. "I'll see that Ranarma sends up snacks."

Without her ring, Jillu was wide open to me, but though she absently rubbed her naked finger, she otherwise seemed too preoccupied to care.

By the time I got home, the agents had finished processing Jillu and left her alone in a secure cell in the tower's basement levels. She was pacing in front of her bunk when I focused on her, twitching with nervous energy, and might have kept it up all night had an agent not come to the door to deliver her dinner...and a phone. "Here," she said, putting the tray and the phone on the little table bolted to the wall. "This is for you."

Jillu eyed the offering suspiciously. "You're giving me a phone?"

"In case your counselor needs to reach you," the agent explained. A sorcerer, she seemed at ease around Jillu, who wasn't cuffed any longer but was surely feeling the effects of the dampening potion. "We've sent him that number. Or if you need to call anyone else," she said, and took her leave, adding, "Lights out at nine."

Once the agent's footsteps had faded on the tile floor in the hallway, Jillu's first call had been to her older son, Cefet. I couldn't hear his side of the conversation—even if she'd put the phone on speaker mode, Cefet would have been blocked to me, thanks to those damn rings—but I gathered plenty from his mother's end of the call.

"There's been a terrible misunderstanding," she said in rapid English. "I'm okay—I've got a lawyer. A good one. But I need you to look after Utien until I get out of here, all right?" She paused, listening, then said, "I don't know, sweetie. As soon as I can. But please, *please* don't tell your brother where I am. He'll panic...I don't know," she mumbled, running her free hand through her hair. "Tell him I've got a surprise work project out of town for a few days. It was really sudden, and I didn't want to go, but it's very important, and I love him so much..."

When she paused that time, it was to blink back tears.

"I love you, too, baby. And thank you. I'll call tomorrow, let you know how things are going. Or you can call my lawyer—his name is Eullan Bargem...Yeah, weird, right? He was supposed to...oh, good. So, you've spoken with him?" She listened briefly, then said, "Well, he's supposed to be the best of the best, so I'm in good hands. You take care of yourself tonight, eh? And can you get your brother to daycare in the morning?...Thank you, son. I can always count on you."

Unfortunately for Jillu, Cefet was the only person to answer her calls that night. Until the lights went out, she tried to reach people, but every attempt ended in muttered profanity. At one point, she sat on her bunk with her head in her hands for a few minutes, taking deep breaths, before resuming her fruitless phone calls.

By the time the lights dimmed, with Jillu's dinner tray still untouched, I almost felt sorry for her.

Almost.

Then Jillu yelled for help. One of the agents, armed with a flashlight, came down to check on her, and Jillu explained, "My phone died. It's not working—"

"Because it's lights out," said the agent. "Your phone will work in the morning. Go to bed."

I heard Jillu's frustrated sigh as she sank onto her creaking bunk, and as I left her, I picked up on the faint sound of muffled sobs in the darkness.

At least Jillu got some sleep. I passed the night flipping between her and the Golden Children like the world's worst late-night insomnia channel surfing, focusing on Katin's brewing operation but checking on the others in case someone else was up to a little unauthorized magical chemistry. Her comrades seemed to be behaving, at least for the night, and I found no signs of brew equipment in any of the Golden Children's other hideouts...but that left Katin's operation, and I still couldn't figure out what she had cooking. Maybe someone experienced like Yven could have guessed, had he been able to take in all the nuances of the setup and the potion in progress, but I couldn't share my mental movie with him, and my sketches proved unhelpful.

Around three, he pried me off the couch, coaxed me into hydrating, and said, "I spoke with a friend of a friend who guards the cells. The lights won't come on until five-thirty. Bedtime, Rosie."

I relented but was up again in time to watch the overhead lights burst back to life in Jillu's cell. She groaned beneath her blanket, then sat up, wincing in her rumpled brown DOL-issued shirt and pants. Her hair was mussed, her makeup smeared around her eyes, and she massaged the small of her back, glaring at the morning. Once she'd gathered herself, she picked up the phone and dialed…and that time, someone answered.

"Where the *fuck* have you been?" Jillu demanded in rapid English. "Why didn't you take my calls last night? I'm in fucking jail!" She listened briefly, then snapped, "Oh, good. Nice to know that I can count on my son, even if my sister is useless!"

Sister. I leaned closer, trying to hear the voice on the other end of the phone, but I might as well have had my ears packed with dirt. Of *course* Jillu's sister would be blocked to me…Obelli ti'Ammaas, I recalled, that was her name.

"They took my phone," Jillu continued. "This is one of theirs. Said I could call my lawyer or anyone else…" Her eyes widened as Obelli spoke. "No one said anything about recording my calls. Wouldn't they have had to warn me?"

"You're not in Kansas anymore," I muttered, though Jillu couldn't detect me.

She huffed, then switched to High Elvish. "Better? They can't understand this. Morons," she said under her breath, and pushed her tangles from her face. "Look, I need you to talk to Eullan and—"

What followed from Obelli's end couldn't have been great, as Jillu reddened and pulled the phone slightly away from her ear. Finally, she got a word in: "I was not *sloppy*!" she protested. "I followed *your* damn plan! Kept your hands nice and clean, didn't I?"

Judging by the length of Jillu's silence that time, Obelli was unimpressed.

"I'm sorry, all right? I didn't have time to find another

car…Fine, yes, that was a mistake," she said testily, "but you've got to clean up this mess. Me getting shipped off to prison for *murder* wasn't part of the plan!"

Her jaw clenched as Obelli spoke.

"I don't know how I let you talk me into this shit," said Jillu. "You were the one fucking him—why did I have to get rid of him?" She listened to Obelli again for a moment, then said, "Just get me out of here. Do whatever it takes, I don't care, but I am *not* spending the next century on one of those damn farms, got it? And someone's coming," she muttered as footsteps crescendoed in the hallway. "Got to go."

A few seconds after she hung up, an agent arrived with her breakfast, and I pulled myself back to my body. I sat up on the couch, waiting for the momentary vertigo to clear, then stumbled to my feet and opened the studio door.

"Sweetie?" Yven called from the kitchen, where I could hear the coffeemaker percolating. "Are you okay?"

"Uh-huh," I mumbled, and grabbed the phone I'd dropped in the den on the way to bed a few hours prior.

Pop picked up on the first ring, sounding remarkably chipper for the hour. "Did you come looking for me? I apologize, I went to the office early—"

"Jillu wasn't Cudda's girlfriend," I interjected. "She's the one who killed him, but it's Obelli ti'Ammaas who's been with him."

"Mm. That's the younger sister, correct?"

"You don't sound surprised."

"Call it a hunch. I'll put in the request for more portal data—let's see where this Obelli has been going. And you're positive that Jillu is our killer?"

"I'm…more than confident," I replied. "Hey, those phones they give inmates in the DOL cells—are those calls recorded?"

I could hear the smile in Pop's voice. "Absolutely. Something Kabno should hear?"

"She's going to need a translation from High Elvish, but yeah."

"Well, now," he said, "I suppose I could assist. Go to bed, Rosie."

"I just got up—"

"And you barely slept. It's audible. Go on, rest," Pop cajoled. "You'll be needed this afternoon. Tell Yven to wake you for lunch, hmm?"

Yven seconded the motion when I gave him the update, and he turned off the coffee pot in favor of curling up in bed with me again. "This is nice," he murmured into my hair as I fit my body against his. "Almost like vacation."

"Ha."

He kissed the nape of my neck. "Two and a half weeks, and we get a real one. You, me, and the nicest little chalet in the Edolis."

"I hope so."

"And no phones," he said. "They'll have to get by without you for a few days."

"You say that, but if Interdiction needs me, watch Gentle Breeze track us down."

Yven snorted. "She can *try*. You still have that portal map Diriem sent you when we were hiding from Inade, right?"

I rolled over and found him grinning in the twilight of our room. "Yeah. What're you thinking?"

"I'm thinking that we never gave anyone the address of our rental house in Hitchens."

"Mm. You know," I said, "Maine's probably pretty nice in early June. Less muddy than it was in March."

"Even up east?"

"*Down* east, babe."

He sighed. "I still don't know what that means. Whatever. Tell you what, should Gentle Breeze or anyone else come knocking, we'll go back to Beukal, sneak out the portal, and drive north before they know we've slipped away."

I smiled at the thought. "You really want to honeymoon in Hitchens?"

"If it means I get time with you. No Golden Children, no novel potions, no crises—just us and *maybe* a few interesting pieces of furniture to test."

"Naughty boy," I said, and kissed him. "But I'm right there with you."

As I closed my eyes, Yven said, "With all the overtime you've been pulling, who's to say we couldn't do both? Edolis as planned, Maine on the sly?"

"Unauthorized trips outside the Pactlands?" I replied with a teasing *tsk*. "I've been a bad influence on you, ti'Ansha."

"Tell me Diriem wouldn't come up with a cover story to authorize it."

"Okay, *we've* been a bad influence on you. But I like it," I whispered, and snuggled closer to him to sleep.

CHAPTER 16

The meeting that afternoon was a conference call, with Yven and me joining from my laptop in our apartment. I'd spent a few hours in trance, jumping between Jillu and Katin, but Jillu was being quiet, and Katin was babysitting her brew with her romance novel—unsatisfactory all around. Shortly before four, Pop called and asked us to join, which was how I found myself trying to avoid the small picture in the corner of the screen showing my mussed hair and baggy eyes.

By comparison, Nim and Dienk seemed a little manic, and I suspected they'd been mainlining caffeine, Happy Juice, or both.

"Just look at the synchronization," Nim practically crowed as the screen switched to a map view. This time, the red and blue dots were joined by a yellow one, which moved in its own strange orbit. Nim zoomed out to show that the yellow dot was heavily traveling between Cirinti and Beukal. "Red for Jillu, blue for Cudda, and yellow for Obelli," he explained. "Now, superficially, we see more overlap between Jillu and Cudda, especially in the capital. But watch what's happened over the last two months."

At odd times, mostly in the evenings and on the weekends, Cudda took quick trips out of Beukal...and about three-quarters of the time, wherever he went, Obelli met him.

"They were trying not to be seen," mused Kabno. "Why?"

"Well, for starters," said Dienk, "Obelli is married. Her

husband is Eccenna ti'Gol, and he lives out in Cirinti in the ti'Ammaas mansion with her. One son, Yrel, eighteen. Obelli, like Jillu, is in financial training—that's what brings her into the city—but Eccenna is apprenticing with a luthier."

"Huh," said Pateme, rubbing his chin. "Guess he didn't care for banking…"

"And theirs is an odd match," Pop added. "Look at their Halls—she's a ti'Ammaas, her grandmother was Lady ti'Pul, and her father was the heir to Hall ti'Non, son of Lord ti'Merin and Lady ti'Non. Eccenna isn't the firstborn, and his parents are Lord ti'Gol and the younger sister of Lord ti'Vanil—much lower ranking."

Kabno smirked. "Translated?"

"Looking purely at Hall status, theirs isn't a marriage of equals, and he didn't bring much to the table."

Off camera, I found Yven's hand and squeezed it hard. He squeezed back, and I caught his brief smile in our feed.

"She didn't marry a close cousin, so she has that going for her," said Pateme. "Perhaps it's a love match."

"More likely one of convenience," Pop replied. "Their compound was like East Branch—the pool was very limited. Cudda was quite a bit older than Eccenna, and he was relatively good-looking. Maybe she decided to explore her options now that she had some."

"How do ti'Ren and ti'Gol compare?" Kabno asked.

Pop consulted his notes. "Ti'Ren is several degrees higher. Now, Cudda wasn't main-line, unlike Eccenna, but…" He shrugged. "Do you see Ivari's Manhattanite banker granddaughter with a *luthier*? Not that there's anything wrong with luthiers, but the earning potential isn't there."

"So," said Kabno, "Obelli has a boyfriend on the sly, Cudda keeps the relationship quiet, you confront Cudda, who tells you only that his girlfriend—no name—wanted the Golden Children to go free, and then Jillu sneaks in and kills him when he's passed out drunk?" Scowling into the camera, she said, "Something's missing. What were the sisters afraid of, that Obelli's husband would find out?"

"Afraid enough to kill?" Pateme added. "That seems unlikely. If Obelli was in a relationship with Cudda, then why would she want him dead?"

"And he was clear with her that he didn't say her name," I offered. "I watched that call. She had no reason to believe that Cudda would give her up."

Yven cleared his throat. "Question, if I may."

"Please," said Pop, gesturing toward his camera.

"Does it strike anyone else as odd that Jillu and the Golden Children have the same counselor? Considering that Obelli apparently pushed Cudda to have them released…"

"And Bargem got there pretty damn quickly yesterday," I said as his voice faltered. "Jillu or someone close to her would have had to alert him before she went to DOL for questioning, and since he's kind of a big shot—"

"They have a prior relationship," Kabno finished. "I was curious about that as well—good instinct, kid," she said with a little nod, and Yven flashed a grin. "Which leads to the question of *why*. What legal work has Bargem done for the sisters?"

"He wasn't involved in any of the citizenship issues," said Pop. "Nor did he defend any of Ivari's people. As far as I know, he's not represented them until now."

Kabno considered that. "It's *possible* that this is a fluke and Jillu called him on her way here because she saw what he did for the Golden Children…"

"But that would be one hell of a fluke," said Pateme, and Kabno nodded. "So," he said, "how do we play this?"

"Well, I don't know what DPP wants to do," Kabno replied with a grim smile, "but as for me, I'm sending my team to bring in Ms. ti'Ammaas for a friendly conversation. You're all cordially invited."

Jillu was pretty, but Obelli was a knockout, a tall, slender woman who wore her blonde hair in a thick plait over one shoulder. Her dark eyes were fringed with impossibly long lashes—whether a mask or extensions, I couldn't tell—and like Jillu, her lips were poised in an almost sultry pout, which she'd accented with a light plum stain. She strutted into the interview room in black three-inch heels, and while Merrot might not have taken note of their red soles, I couldn't miss them. The Louboutins accessorized a sleeveless black sheath dress that fell just above her knee—not on the cusp of fashion in Beukal but classy in my estimation. Set off with a considerable strand of white pearls, it was an ensemble that spoke of money, not a whisper but certainly not a shout.

And Obelli wasn't just a pretty face. Having learned from her sister's encounter with DOL the previous day, she came to the interview accompanied by good old Eullan, and the counselor shut down the questioning before the detective could do more than ask Obelli her name. By six, she was off to be processed on suspicion of conspiracy to commit murder, despite Eullan's claims of police overreach, but Merrot promised to pass along her probable cause file and sent Eullan on his way.

"Wasted trip, huh?" Yven muttered as we packed up to leave. He'd driven us in from Viratta, a drive made longer by the fact that most of the internal portals in Beukal had switched to outbound mode.

"I wouldn't say wasted—it was a nice break," I told him, shouldering my purse. "Need anything at the office, or should we head back?"

"Just a minute," Pateme interrupted, and stopped Kabno before she could leave the viewing room. Holding up his phone, he said, "The Roulette team wants to brief us tomorrow on the novel potion. Will ten work?"

Kabno and Pop agreed, and Pateme turned to me. "Why don't you bring the victims as well? They have a stake in this, after all."

I grinned. "Oh, I'm invited?"

He rolled his eyes. "You'll just watch remotely if I say no."

"In that case, I may bring a couple others. Annie's invested, and you know Jane's sensitive to anything concerning Ragged Gap."

"That's acceptable," he replied. "I'll tell security what to expect. And see if you can't watch the Golden Children tonight, hmm? If Obelli has a grain of sense, she won't touch any telephone in this building."

Pateme departed, followed by Kabno and the rest of Merrot's team, but before Yven and I could head for the garage, Pop quietly asked, "Yven, a moment?"

"Uh...sure," said Yven, and glanced awkwardly at me.

Pop nodded. "Rosie, stay as well. I..." He hesitated, then murmured, "Earlier today, I made certain comments about Halls and what various individuals were bringing to their relationship, and...I realized after that meeting that those comments could have been taken poorly. I meant no insult," he said, looking Yven in the eye, "but if I gave one, I apologize."

Yven, who looked a bit like a deer in oncoming traffic, quickly replied, "It's all right..."

But Pop was unconvinced. "I should have been more judicious, but I do hope you didn't take that personally. Believe me, if I thought you were a poor choice for Rosie, you'd have heard about it long before now, and not through some passive-aggressive aside."

His mouth twitched. "Fair enough. Apology accepted."

"Good. Please tell Ranarma I'll be about half an hour behind you two."

A minute later, as Yven and I rode the elevator down to collect his car, he said, "You know, if you'd told me five years ago that I'd be getting an apology from freaking Lord ti'Dana for vaguely classist comments..."

"He likes you a lot," I said, nudging him in the arm.

"And that is still slightly terrifying."

"Oh, come on. And hey, if we're going back five years, I didn't know elves *existed*, so I'm pretty sure both of our younger selves would think we were insane."

"Fair." He paused, then said, "I think that even ti'Gol outranks ti'Ansha. If you look at the old records—"

"You think I give a flying fart about that?"

He snickered. "Well, when you put it so genteelly…"

"I love you, station wagon."

A slow smile crossed Yven's face, and as the door opened, he took my hand.

It had taken Annie to convince Stephanie that returning to the DPP tower wouldn't land her back in quarantine. "I'm attending the meeting, too," she said as Stephanie stood in her guest room doorway, arms folded protectively over her borrowed bathrobe. "And if things get weird, I can have you out of there in the blink of an eye, okay? There's nothing in that building that can hold me."

Or so we assumed. No one had yet attempted to administer the dampening potion to a Huntsman, and Annie certainly wasn't volunteering. Knowing Wylan, he'd have raised holy hell had a research healer approached his wife with a syringe for science, and so the question of whether the Hunt's powers could be leashed remained open.

But that wasn't a matter that any of us mentioned to Stephanie, and after some heavy coaxing, she agreed to get dressed and ride downtown with Tabitha, Yven, and me.

Annie arrived on her own steam, as did Jane, who sat by Tabitha at Pateme's long conference table and exchanged bare pleasantries with Stephanie. Kabno and Pop walked in together, with Gentle Breeze and Syvin on their heels. Last to join us were the people we'd congregated to see, Vinla and Dante. Both seemed weary and murmured their thanks when Annie rose to offer them coffee.

Once they were provisioned, Pateme took his seat at the head of the table and nodded to the healers. "So, I understand you have news for us."

"Yes, sir," said Vinla, and Dante started the projection from his computer, revealing a test tube half-full of a familiar iridescent silver liquid. "This is the novel potion," she began. "We were able to extract traces from their blood," she explained, pointing to Tabitha and Stephanie, "and we reverse-engineered it from that."

"And what *is* it?" asked Pateme.

"Well, without providing a full ingredient list, the easiest answer I can give you is that it's based on Roulette."

"Come again?" said Kabno.

The healers nodded. "Not what we'd anticipated," Vinla told her. "But while it was built using Roulette as a model, it has significant differences. We've code-named it 'Elemental' for now because of the reactions we've observed."

"So…it's not deadly, then?" Annie interrupted.

Vinla made a face. "Sitting here this morning, I can't tell you. With Roulette, we had a sample of thirty-one from the initial exposure, and surely you recall how few of you experienced any side effects other than a long sleep. Three dead, two with a mutagenic response."

"They weren't the only ones exposed," I reminded the healer. "Uh…my neighbors smoked tainted marijuana, and one died. Her husband was unharmed. And there was George Hurley," I said, looking at Annie. "He died, Nick lived. So, the true sample size was at least thirty-five."

"I won't quibble with that," said Vinla, "but the problem is that here, we only have a sample size of two, so there's no way for me to say with any confidence that the pattern we've seen in the victims will continue. They may be outliers, and the potion *could* be deadly. We just don't know, and without a larger sample size—"

"Not an option," said Pateme.

"Of course, sir," Vinla replied, though I thought she seemed a mite disappointed. "What I'm trying to convey is that we can't accurately predict what effects Elemental would show in a wider population. Two humans aren't much to go on."

"Hey, you're doing your best," said Tabitha when Vinla paused for coffee, "and Stephanie and I appreciate it. Just curious, but now that you've got more of a handle on this thing, are we any closer to an antidote?"

The two healers exchanged glances, and Vinla took the lead once more. "So, uh...this may be a stupid question, but how much do you know about potions?"

Tabitha chuckled. "Well, I'm friends with a brewer, and he's slipped me a few healing potions, but that's about it. I mean, I've seen the *effects* of several others, but personal exposure? Minimal. I can't brew, of course, but I've got a solid background in biochemistry, if that helps."

Stephanie, whose idea of potions to that point had presumably been more along the lines of tinctures or dropping crystals into water bottles, could only shrug.

"Right," Vinla muttered, drumming two fingers on the table. "Well...potions intended to be consumed come in various strengths in terms of longevity. Some are fast-acting and quickly metabolized—invisibility is a good example. The effects are almost immediate, but it wears off in an hour or so."

"And the side effects go on for a few hours after that," said Dante, "but that's because so many of the ingredients are toxic. There's some, uh...violent purging that accompanies that potion."

I nodded emphatically, and the other agency personnel grimaced. Taking the invisibility potion was a standard part of training for any agent going into the wider world, and it could be useful in an emergency, but the aftermath made frat-party alcohol poisoning look like indigestion.

"Then there are longer-acting potions," Vinla continued. "Pain potions, healing potions, sleeping potions, and so on. They don't work indefinitely, but they last more than an hour or two."

"Something like Velvet Leash," Pateme offered, "the

one you made boil, Tabitha. It can last for days, but the effect weakens, and it requires re-dosing."

I glanced over in time to catch Stephanie's shudder.

"And last," said Vinla, "you have the potions that aren't naturally neutralized—memory potions, masking potions, the language potion…"

"The death draught," Pop murmured.

"Yeah, and that one," she said quietly. "Nasty stuff. Now, there are two ways to stop the effects of a potion if you don't want to wait or if the potion has an indefinite duration: broad-spectrum neutralizers like the one we use in decontamination or specialized antidotes. Neutralizers are good but imperfect. I gave you one, if you recall, and it did nothing."

Tabitha nodded. "Except empty my stomach."

"Not ideal, I know. We never had a chance to test neutralizers on Roulette, but given your reaction, I'd expect much the same."

"But Roulette has an antidote," said Annie.

"That it does," Vinla replied. "However…" She paused for a moment, then slowly said, "Not every potion has an antidote. The language potion can't be undone. Neither can the draught. It's an annoying quirk of certain potions, and some fantastic minds have been stumped by the problem."

When Vinla fell silent, Tabitha asked, "Are you trying to tell us that there's no antidote to this crap?"

"From what we've seen," said Dante, "it's highly unlikely. Elemental differs significantly enough from Roulette to push it into the class of permanent potions. We might find something, given more time to research," he added, "but the preliminary investigation suggests there's no way to undo Elemental's effects."

Before Tabitha and Stephanie could protest, Vinla jumped back in. "The good news is that we don't anticipate further mutagenic incidents—it's enough like Roulette that it shouldn't trigger additional changes, though it will maintain the ones you've experienced."

"Like when my antlers grew back," Annie mumbled.

The healers nodded. "Precisely," said Vinla. "And since you two appear to be stable, we can begin running tests to determine whether you can tolerate other potions and tools—masking jewelry first, I should think."

Stephanie bit her lip. "If that works, can we go home?" she asked in a small voice.

"If you can safely mask and control your new abilities, then I don't know of a medical reason why you should be kept here. *Political* reasons, however…" She cut her eyes to the directors. "That's a question for someone higher up the chain."

"We have no right to hold you once you're no longer dangers to yourselves or others," Pateme smoothly interjected. "Release is a question of *when*, not *if.* I understand that you've been practicing fairly successfully, yes?" he asked, and glanced at Pop.

"No major incidents," Pop replied. "They're making solid progress. Assuming they can successfully mask, then I would suggest they be returned home in…early June, perhaps? Two, three weeks?" he suggested, looking at Stephanie and Tabitha. "I realize you're eager to leave, but we do have a strong interest in ensuring that you can control your abilities…and hide them."

Stephanie's forehead wrinkled. "Hide?"

"Uh, *yeah*," said Gentle Breeze. "You've got to keep your powers under wraps."

"Why? I'm the one who was attacked by a crazy sorcerer! And I've been trying to cultivate real magic for so long—"

Jane pounded the table, startling Stephanie into silence. "Look around you, you dope!" she shouted, briefly slipping into English before reverting to the table's common language. "You think the Pactlands was built as some kind of secret clubhouse? This is a hiding place for refugees! If everyone out there knew that magic was real and this place exists, what do you think would happen? Peace, harmony, kumbaya around the campfire?"

"Humanity has a right to know about magic," she said primly. "Especially if there's a potion that can give you power."

She exhaled through clenched teeth, and I noticed the telltale dancing of tiny flames along Jane's arms. "You know Maebe? The aeromancer who hung out in quarantine with you?"

"Yeah…"

"She's one of the survivors of East Branch. Did she tell you how that community got started?"

Stephanie shook her head.

"Once upon a time, there were two elven kingdoms," said Jane. "One of them packed up and headed in here. The other mostly didn't. And in five years' time, humans had eradicated almost all of them who tried to stick around outside. East Branch was founded by the last *eighteen* survivors."

Pop nodded. "I was there. Jane speaks true."

"We've got *stories* outside about trolls and elves and fauns and centaurs and…and every other kind of person you find here," Jane continued. "They all passed into legend because they fled to the Pactlands to save themselves from humans—encroaching humans, religious zealot humans, whatever flavor of shitty neighbors they had. You want to put all these folks at risk, do you?"

"No," said Stephanie, "but *you* use your power back home! I've seen it!"

Jane rubbed her forehead. "I showed you when I was a stupid teenager, and my, uh…vigilante activities aren't exactly sanctioned."

"To put it mildly," said Kabno.

"Yeah, well, that's what happens when you grow up a bit feral," Jane retorted. "The folks I've helped and your little buddies know I'm the real deal, but they don't know the extent of what I can do. And they fear me."

Stephanie didn't argue with that.

"Fear is dangerous," said Jane. "Centuries of witch trials make that pretty damn clear, you know? I've kept my abilities quiet—it's not like I ran off to college and showed everyone this," she added, letting the flames on her skin erupt.

"Mind the upholstery, please," Pateme murmured.

She mumbled an apology and extinguished herself before her blue chair could be singed. "So, what do you think will happen if you go on TV in Atlanta and show everyone that you can vaporize?" she said to Stephanie. "Tell them you got this from a magic potion given to you by a real-life sorcerer? If people believe you, they'll panic. That's what mobs do. And if you're not hurt or killed by someone who, I don't know, thinks you're some kind of fucking demon, then you might just end up at a black site. Think about it, genius."

While Stephanie slumped in her seat, chastened, Dante spoke up. "There's no need to blow this out of proportion and scare her unreasonably. Haven't those two been through enough?"

Jane turned on him, brow arched. "Sorry, have you ever lived outside the Pactlands?"

"Uh…no…" he admitted.

"Then how the hell would you know whether I'm being unreasonable?"

"You said you used magic out there," Dante replied, "and you seem whole and healthy to me."

"I used it *very selectively*," Jane shot back. "In a small town, and largely around people who either believe in magic already or aren't the sort to run to the authorities. I used it to do things like chase spouse-beaters out of the county. Now, look," she continued, thumbing one hand toward Tabitha, "I'm not saying it's impossible for humans to do anything but panic when confronted with magic. Tabitha's been a real trooper. But individuals and mobs are two very different things, you know? You can't reason with mobs, and if history is any guide, allowing Stephanie here to start making videos to show off her new skillset would end in disaster." Turning to Stephanie again, she said, "I'm not trying to be a bitch. Honestly. I just don't want people getting hurt." Her mouth quirked. "Even you."

To my relief, Stephanie smirked back at her. "Gee, thanks, Fortune. But what am I supposed to tell everyone? They saw me disappear!"

"As little as possible would be ideal," said Pateme. "These associates of yours...they know magic is involved?"

"They know the vague contours," Jane told him. "And as long as Stephanie doesn't show off, they should be manageable."

"You don't think this is a situation in which memory potions would be effective?"

"Respectfully, fuck, no."

Jane, who'd been threatened with a memory wipe, was vehemently opposed to the use of the potion, and Annie, who'd almost lost all recollection of the Pactlands and Wylan via memory potion, was right there with her. If Pateme was looking for support from the culturally human end of the table, he was out of luck.

Before an argument could blossom, Tabitha asked, "What about the dampening potion—would that remove our powers? Keep us from accidentally revealing them?"

Vinla frowned as she considered the question. "*Possibly*. We'd have to test it. I mean, it works on nymphs, so there's a decent chance that it would work on Elemental. But that potion's effect is temporary, and you would need periodic redosing. If it works, we could use the procedure followed at the penal farms, but..." She spread her hands. "All I can offer you are hypotheses. There's *never* been a potion that creates talent, so we're in unknown waters. But what we might be able to do is offer you a permanent mask."

Tabitha's head cocked, spilling a few blue braids over her shoulder. "Explain."

"So, as I said, I'd like to start the experimentation with you two with masking jewelry. You don't need any particular talent to make it work, but there's always the risk of the jewelry being lost or broken. Stephanie, this isn't such a great concern for you, but Tabitha…"

She nodded. "How would you make it permanent?"

"There's a potion, and it's permanent unless you drink the antidote. Typically used in conjunction with the death draught for non-sorcerers—you can set up a mask that looks human and will age appropriately. If you wanted to take that—I mean, if your body can handle it, which is something we need to investigate—then we could restore your natural hair color."

"That'd be nice," Tabitha mused. "If I looked normal and didn't dissolve in public…"

"Uh, question," I said, and waited until the healers looked my way. "Do you have an ingredient list yet?"

"We think so, yes," said Dante, "but aren't you…"

"In remedial tutoring? Yeah," I finished, "but I'm not trying to make Elemental. Katin Waughnn is brewing *something* in her cabin, and I don't know what. If I had an ingredient list, then maybe I could compare that against the possibilities of things I'm seeing."

"Possibilities?" echoed Vinla.

I sighed. "The bottles aren't marked, and I'm doing my best, okay? Yven's helping me," I added, and he nodded. "We've got a running list of potentials for some of the ingredients she's using, but Yven doesn't recognize the potion. If you could give us the recipe for Elemental, we could check that against what I've seen."

As Vinla sent a copy of the potion formula to a printer in the hallway, Dante regarded me oddly. "You know where the Golden Children are?"

"More or less," I told him. "I can see glimpses. No street addresses or anything, but I've got a general idea of where they're hiding."

In truth, I'd snooped quite a bit more than that. Between my searches at the limits of my farsight's reach and some cross-referencing against mapping software, I had the hideouts virtually pinned down. But that was knowledge I'd shared only with the directors to that point, and until they gave me the go-ahead, I decided to keep my answers vague.

"Huh. I'll get that," he said to Vinla, then stepped out and quickly returned with the list for me. "There you go. Anything familiar?"

I pulled up a copy of my notes on my phone, and Yven, who was far more knowledgeable in that realm than I was, compared the two. After a long moment, he said, "Our mystery potion could very well be Elemental."

"How sure are you?" asked Pop.

"Not completely, but I think it's likely," he replied, holding Pop's gaze. "These combinations are too odd to be chance, and they're highly uncommon in standard potions. This recipe contains *multiple* obscure ingredients, and all of them are probably in that cabin, based on Rose's investigation."

"If she's brewing Elemental," said Vinla, "then why was she carrying so much Velvet Leash when she made her initial attack? I'm sorry, but I don't follow..."

"It's her old playbook," Jane explained. "The last time she was in Ragged Gap, she convinced a bunch of—"

Idiots, I suspected, was on the tip of her tongue.

"—unsuspecting folks to take Velvet Leash. She dosed them with Fingerflash and made them think that was just the beginning of unlocking their latent power, and once they trusted her, they willingly took the Velvet Leash she'd brewed. Once they were under her control, she and the other Golden Children took them to an isolated cabin and set them to work at their brewing operation."

As Vinla winced, Stephanie mumbled, "It was awful. They barely fed us, we never slept...they just made us drink more of that stuff."

The healer's eyes widened. "Wait, you—"

"Yeah. I'm not too fond of the Golden Children. Thanks again for letting them out," she added, folding her arms on the table. "For a bunch of folks concerned about secrecy, you had no problem plunking sorcerers in my hometown."

The table fell silent for a second before Kabno stepped in. "I understand your anger, Ms. Love. Believe me, we fought to keep them here, but..." Glancing at Pop, she said, "The information the Forum needed was corrupted...that, and they had a fantastic counselor."

"But back to Velvet Leash," said Vinla before Stephanie could argue with the director. "Considering the reaction the two of you had to Elemental, how was she planning to convince anyone to drink *Velvet Leash*?"

That time, Tabitha spoke first. "You've got to understand—the people she targeted *believe* in magic. They cast spells, use crystals, any number of things...but as you can probably guess, the effects aren't exactly immediate and concrete. Katin breezed into town with her magic oil, and it was *exactly* what her marks wanted. I mean, you can laugh at a bunch of dumb humans being fooled by Fingerflash, but put yourselves in our shoes. Rub in a little oil, maybe drink it, and suddenly, you can make your fingers light up like freaking E.T....uh, it's a movie," she added when Vinla's brow creased. "But *imagine* that. You've gone your whole life making charms and saying incantations and hoping the energy you put out into the universe is working, and now you can do something immediate and real."

"It was incredible," said Stephanie.

"And if I weren't so paranoid about unlabeled bottles without ingredient lists, I might have tried it, too," Tabitha continued. "You see what I'm saying?"

Vinla began to slowly nod. "I...think so, yes."

"Okay. Well, those folks she tricked into taking Velvet Leash woke up after their rescue with little memory of what actually happened, but since they'd been given a *neutralizer*, their magic was gone. Just about everyone blamed Jane and thought she'd driven Katin out of town from jealousy or spite."

Stephanie, I noticed, kept her eyes down and her mouth shut.

"So," said Tabitha, "when Katin reappeared, those people were thrilled, and Stephanie and I couldn't do much about it. If I had to guess, she probably didn't know how we'd react to Elemental. If we'd reacted better or shown something flashy, then everyone would have fought to be next in line...and she could bring out the Velvet Leash and rebuild her workforce. But because things went sideways for her, I'd bet we were the guinea pigs—she probably didn't realize how that potion would hit us."

"Guinea pigs?" asked Dante.

"Test subjects," Pateme clarified, then looked down the table at Tabitha. "I think you're on to something, Ms. Bradley, but assuming you're correct, that raises another question: why bother with Elemental when she probably could have coaxed your fellows into taking Velvet Leash again with more Fingerflash? That one is inexpensive and easy to brew—why use a novel, almost certainly untested potion instead of a sure thing?"

"Maybe she was mistaken about what Elemental would do," suggested Kabno.

"All right, next question: how the hell did the Golden Children get their hands on a potion built from *Roulette*? We've never released that formula," Pateme insisted. "It's protected."

"Well, *Laws* certainly never released it," said Kabno, and Pop shook his head.

Pateme sighed. "Which suggests that DOI isn't the only agency with a mole problem..."

At that, Yven, who'd been studying the ingredient list, cleared his throat. "Suggestion, sir."

"Ti'Ansha?"

Tapping the printout, Yven said, "Elemental includes white curraxit."

"Really?" He turned to Vinla and Dante, who nodded. "You're positive that it's *white* curraxit?"

"Absolutely," Vinla replied.

"And if memory serves," said Yven, "there's only one place to acquire white curraxit."

Pateme grinned. "Seven Stars. Well done."

"Sorry," I interrupted, "what's Seven Stars?"

"It's a private operation like Dashom Brothers," Yven explained. "Smaller, newer, but they make good product. Do you remember how Dashom calavaria is proprietary to that greenhouse?" When I nodded, he said, "Same with white curraxit. There are probably fifteen curraxit varieties—we grow many of them here—but the white strain is a fluke, and it's stronger. Your Aunt Lily buys it. I've seen her receipts during inspections."

"What does it do?"

"It's very good at stabilizing a few other plants that don't like to play nicely together," said Pateme. "And because those combinations often occur in psychedelics, white curraxit is highly regulated and only has a few legal uses."

"Awakening, for instance," Pop murmured, and winked at me.

Pateme huffed his disapproval. I'd only taken Awakening a few times as a baby farseer, but the stuff was face-meltingly potent.

"Hey, guys?"

The table turned to Kabno, who was scrolling on her phone. "Do you know who the owner of Seven Stars is?" she asked.

"Uh, sure," said Pateme. "Derringer Faln."

"*Derringer*?" Stephanie whispered.

"I'm more concerned about *Faln*," said Tabitha. "You don't suppose he's any relation to Ergal Faln, do you?" she asked the directors.

"Who the hell is Ergal Faln?" asked Stephanie.

"He's a member of an organization known as the Unity Plan," said Kabno. "Largely comprised of sorcerers. They want us to reveal ourselves outside, which most would agree is a poor idea."

"They could have gotten us killed last year," said Gentle Breeze. "Kidnapped a handful of us who can't naturally mask, dumped us outside, then released a hex in the system holding the Pactlands together. It was either risk the stability of the entire system to send search parties or else throw everything into lockdown. If not for people like Tabitha and Annie's parents…I mean, those cretins dropped *children* outside and sat back to watch the chaos unfold."

Frowning, Stephanie pointed to Annie. "Your folks know about this place, too?"

"*Oh*, yeah. Probably a good thing in retrospect," Annie added, glancing at Pateme, who grunted noncommittally.

"Ergal hid out in Tennessee with the key to breaking the hex," Tabitha told Stephanie. "He's a real piece of work."

"And now he's doing a century on a penal farm," said Kabno, then smiled mirthlessly. "He's also Derringer Faln's son. I remember the name from that case file."

An uncomfortable silence fell over the conference room, and then Tabitha said, "What if the Golden Children have joined forces with the Unity Plan? Stephanie and I didn't know what we were doing, but we manifested power within minutes of being injected. Now, if Katin's brewing more of that shit…"

She didn't have to spell it out. If unsuspecting humans vacationing in the mountains were attacked and suddenly found themselves sublimating or bursting into flame, with no control, no antidote…

Panic, certainly, and perhaps a problem too large to be covered up.

"So," said Kabno, putting her phone aside, "I believe we have work to do."

CHAPTER 17

DOL moved with haste, but they got their ducks in a row before they struck. Thus it was that I found myself in the viewing room shortly after five Thursday morning with Pop, Ganti, Kabno, Pateme, Syvin, and Gentle Breeze—and to my surprise, Merrot. I must have looked at the detective strangely, as he leaned past Kabno and explained, "At this point, it's a plant issue. Best to let the expert do her work."

The expert in question was Enva, who marched into the interview room where the arresting agents had left Derringer Faln in a swish of burgundy robe, clutching a thick folder in one hand and a nearly troll-sized travel mug in the other.

From behind me, Gentle Breeze muttered, "I *sincerely* hope that's not Happy Juice."

"She'd be dead if it were," Syvin replied.

"I don't know…that woman can go for days when pressed."

Enva closed the door behind her with her elbow, then settled in at the table. The interview room selected was not one of the nicer ones, and Derringer, unshackled but clearly ill at ease, watched with trepidation as she sipped her drink and opened her folder. "Good morning, Mr. Faln," said Enva, folding her hands on the table. "I'm Detective Enva Orafer, and I'm the head of the DPP liaison team here. Do you know why we've brought you in today?"

"No, ma'am, I don't. I thought everything's in order," he said in a rush. "My inspection with DPP was two weeks ago, and they gave me a good report—"

"Yes, well," she murmured, "DPP also doesn't tend to pull people out of their beds for regulatory mistakes."

At least the agents had let Derringer put pants on, I mused.

"I'll be frank with you," Enva continued. "White curraxit was identified as a component of a novel terroristic potion released within the last weeks. I need information."

His eyes widened, and he pushed back from the table. "Whoa, now, I don't know anything about terrorism—"

"Your son is Ergal Faln, correct?"

The elder Faln fell silent for a moment, then nodded and cautiously said, "Yes, he's my boy. I…don't agree with his decisions, but I can't deny him." He paused again, then asked, "Did the Unity Plan do something?"

"Possibly."

"I assure you, Detective, I'm not part of that organization. What my son did has nothing to do with me. I'm a legitimate businessman, ask DPP—my record's clean."

"Oh, we pulled your record," she replied in an almost pleasant tone, and patted the folder. "As you said, it's spotless. Commendable, sir. I've seen my share of records, and yours is among the best of the bunch. But." A dark eyebrow rose. "I need a list of individuals and organizations that purchased white curraxit within the last three months."

"I…I can get that for you, yes," he said. "Uh, if you told me more specifically what you were looking for, I might be able to speed this along. Most of my customers for that plant are institutions."

Enva flipped through the folder and extracted Katin's inmate photo, which she slid across the table to Derringer. "Do you know this woman?"

He frowned as he studied the picture. "Can't say that I do."

"Her name is Katin Waughnn. She's the presumed leader of a group of rogue brewers who call themselves the

Golden Children—"

"*Oh!*" he exclaimed, recognition dawning. "I remember their Forum appeal. Back in April, yes?"

"That's right. They were released on April sixteenth and set free outside the Pactlands. On May first, they attacked a group of humans several states away from their release point, and two were injected with the potion containing white curraxit. Now, I'm not at liberty to reveal the specifics of what befell the victims, but I *can* tell you that if this potion were used here, it would be considered terrorism. And I have it on good authority that the Waughnn girl is brewing more of the stuff as we speak. We know her group acquired supplies from the Tampa portal a few days ago, but our assumption is that she had sufficient white curraxit on her without restocking. I certainly don't need to tell you how difficult that plant can be to come by…at least through legal channels."

Enva let that hang, and even I could tell that Derringer was squirming.

"Mistakes happen," she said quietly after a long moment. "Sometimes, even the cleanest records are hiding dirt. You wouldn't be the first, Mr. Faln. And while neither DOL nor DPP condones…*inappropriate* sales, the fact that such a sale might have occurred is not our greatest concern right now. We need to know how your product got into the Golden Children's hands…and cooperation might cover a mistake, you know?"

Finally, Derringer cracked. "Business has been off. Ever since my idiot boy got wrapped up in the Unity Plan and…and helped kidnap those younglings, some of my customers have gone elsewhere. I've got a greenhouse to run, payroll to meet, creditors, two little girls still at home—you understand, right?" he asked, practically pleading.

The detective nodded. "You needed money."

"I *need* money," he corrected her. "Seven Stars has been hemorrhaging since winter. But…but she came with cash," he said, hanging his head. "Twenty-five thousand marks for a pound of white curraxit, no record of the sale. It was a ridiculous price, and I…I…"

"You said *she*," Enva probed. "Not Waughnn. She was removed from the Pactlands immediately upon her release."

Derringer shook his head. "No, not her," he said, tapping the photo. "I've never seen her in person, *never*. I swear it. The buyer wasn't a sorcerer, anyway. She was an elf."

That made the rest of the viewing room take notice, though Enva kept her expression still. "What was her name?"

"Avang ti'Gata," he mumbled. "Or that's what she told me, anyway. I didn't ask for identification. But there are security cameras all around the premises—I could pull them for you," he offered desperately. "Show you what she looks like."

Pop turned to Ganti, who nodded in response to the silent enquiry. Even if the buyer had come masked, her false image would give Ganti enough to focus on, and then he could follow her until she removed her disguise…assuming, of course, that the buyer hadn't taken precautions against farsight. Considering the amount of money she'd brought with her, that was a sobering possibility.

"That would be appreciated," Enva told Derringer. "How soon can you get it to us?"

"An hour or less."

"Very well." Sliding Katin's picture back into the folder, she asked, "Does anything else strike you as memorable about the ti'Gata woman? Her clothing, jewelry, something odd?"

He thought briefly. "Well…she's the first buyer I've ever had from Acori."

Enva frowned. "That little town in the Edolis? *That* Acori?"

"I wouldn't know. My wife and I are lake people, not mountain vacationers."

I'd been through Acori on a *painful* cross-agency training jaunt, as DOL had a facility up the mountain nearby. Acori itself was little more than a hamlet on a relatively flat spot. Tourists and hikers kept it alive, and I'd have been shocked if the town's permanent population numbered more than a hundred.

"If you didn't see her identification," said Enva, "then how do you know she was from Acori?"

"I asked," Derringer replied. "Her accent sounded strange to me—not the usual elven accent, but a little funkier. She explained that I was hearing the Edolis." Nervously, he licked his lips. "So, um...am I going to be prosecuted?"

Pop rose and smoothed his robe. "I'll be back at the office," he said to Kabno and Pateme. "Let us know when the security footage arrives, won't you?"

Pateme smiled tightly. "Fifty marks says she's not from anywhere near the Edolis."

Smirking down at him, Pop replied, "You know I can't take wagers like that. We *do* have a code."

"I'm correct, then?"

"I said nothing." Cutting his eyes to me, he added, "Rosie, keep your director out of trouble, won't you? This may be a long day."

DOL's first hit came in well before lunch Thursday.

There were only three Avang ti'Gatas in the Pactlands. One was a seven-year-old girl who lived in Beukal and attended North Lake with Maebe and the rest of the East Branchers. Her student ID photo was adorable—braided blonde pigtails and missing front teeth were a winning combination—and there was no way in hell that she was our mystery buyer.

Another Avang was of age—sixty-three, to be precise—but she lived way out in Cirinti and ran a popular tavern while her husband fished. I'd actually been there once with Jane, Annie, and Maebe, and the pastry-wrapped baked fish, perfectly seasoned with herbs and topped with a tangy berry-based sauce, was worth the trip. I recognized that Avang as the ruddy-cheeked brunette behind the bar with the braying laugh, who knew every patron but us on sight—not a difficult feat in a town the size of Cirinti. She'd passed by our table to check on us once, and she'd greeted Maebe with a smile and an, "Afternoon, youngling," which had suited Maebe *just* fine. Recently orphaned and newly wealthy and titled, Maebe was only twenty and bearing the weight of leading Hall ti'Ammaas, some of whose members had murdered half her family and tried to kill the rest. Ciriniti was *far* from Beukal, just a hamlet perched on the Pactlands' lonely western shore, and the locals had to have questions about the oddly accented newcomers living in the clifftop mansion. Since Maebe wasn't raised to put on airs, I wasn't shocked that she'd made the acquaintance of her neighbors, though I wondered about her affluent New York cousins.

The third Avang had a home in Old Farm not too far from Cudda's house, which had given the agents a moment of hope before they saw the data on her. This Avang was a little over five hundred years old and blind from birth, and her doting husband accompanied her everywhere to serve as her eyes. Research healers had long ago developed glasses for the blind that could magically interface with their minds, bypassing the injured nerves, but Avang, who'd never seen, couldn't make sense of the information the glasses tried to send her. Instead, she was a fixture in Old Farm, adept with a walking staff but usually strolling in the evenings with her arm linked around her husband's.

None of the Avangs lived in the Edolis, and it was unlikely that any of them was the mystery buyer.

Derringer's cooperation provided the second hit. While

one team checked names and addresses, another reviewed his security footage. Unfortunately, Derringer couldn't remember the *precise* date that he'd made the sale—the intentional lack of records didn't help DOL's efforts—but he could narrow the time span to a three-day window and provided DOL with all of his recordings for that period.

Around two that afternoon, as I watched Dirk decanting the Elemental batch into empty plastic Faygo bottles, Yven shook me back to my body and handed me my water. As I blinked, my eyes focused on him—working-from-home chinos and a blue polo we'd found on a sneaky weekend jaunt back to Richmond, blond hair slightly mussed, phone pressed against his shoulder. "You're wanted on a conference call," he announced. "Laws got a hit."

I set up my laptop in the den while Yven put on fresh coffee, and by the time I joined the call, Pop, Kabno, Pateme, and Ganti were waiting. "Heard they had luck," I said once my camera cooperated.

"Quite possibly," Kabno replied, and popped up a still image from the Seven Stars security cameras. "Here's our buyer, and that's about as clear a shot of her face as one could hope for."

She wasn't wrong. The woman had looked straight at the camera, and even without the helpful color footage, I could have recognized her as Obelli ti'Ammaas.

"*Wow.* Did she spot the camera, do you think?" I asked.

"Faln said he hid it in a decorative vase behind the main counter. The vase is studded with glass pieces, so no one would pay much mind to the flash off a lens," Kabno explained. "We've got her here, the camera shows her counting out marks from a large purse, and Faln identified the package he gave her as a pound of white curraxit. Pateme, I'm disinclined to prosecute him, but he's all yours."

"Oh, don't worry, he and I will be having a *chat* about the future of his licensure," said Pateme, steepling his fingers. "But let's prioritize. That's the ti'Ammaas woman, is it not? The one in your basement?"

Kabno nodded. "The younger sister, yes…or a convincing mask thereof. Agent ti'Van, can you confirm?"

At that, Ganti made a face. "If I can—and that's a big if, ma'am—it'll take days. She's protected, and I can't see through those damn rings. I could focus on Faln, and she'd be a blot. I'd only be able to follow the blot until she was a certain distance from Faln, and then I'd need a new focus…" He rubbed his temples as he contemplated the complexity of the problem. "Potentially doable but unlikely."

She grunted. "Rose, you're blind here as well?"

"My farsight is pretty narrowly focused on the present," I told her, "even without factoring the rings in. I'm sorry."

"You can't see through her protection? I thought there's a blood connection between ti'Ammaas and ti'Cren."

"There is," I allowed, "but the rings don't have the same weakness that the blinding potion does for blood kin. Besides, the more distant the connection, the more difficult it is to see through. Pop's not hard," I explained, "and Pateme is only marginally tougher, but they're third- and fifth-degree kin to me. I mean, I'm related to Maebe. We worked it out last fall, and we're, uh…"—I squinted as I recalled the answer—"fifth cousins seven times removed, that's it. I've got a ti'Ammaas connection up my ti'Cren side. If I could see through the rings, I'd have been able to help her find Ivari's crew and the East Branchers without Maebe resorting to bloodline potion over and over, but…"

"Just how many thrones *do* you have a claim to?" teased Ganti.

"Well, since all of East Branch is ahead of me on the ti'Ammaas side—"

"And this is purely academic," Pop interrupted, "since Rosie can't see the past. Let's think practically. How do we confirm that Obelli ti'Ammaas was the buyer if she's protected? Even assuming Ganti can't see the buyer, that doesn't mean it's Obelli."

The directors fell silent for a moment, but then Yven, who'd brought me a cup of coffee, leaned over my shoulder and said, "Just wondering, but does Seven Stars not have a camera on its parking lot?"

Kabno swore in what I assumed to be colorful Gnomic, and Pateme smirked. "*Thank* you, ti'Ansha," he said. "I suspect they do. Kabno, will you need our assistance?"

"No," she replied, reddening, "I'm sure we can manage."

The call quickly ended after that, and I sipped my drink and grinned at Yven, who seemed mightily pleased with himself. "Clever boy."

"That's why Syvin keeps me around," he said, and stooped to kiss my forehead. "Going back to work?"

I patted the cushion beside me. "Could do with a break first. Want to join me?"

"*That's* a given. Hold my seat," he said, hurrying to the kitchen to pour himself a cup.

The parking lot video offered, if not ironclad proof, at least considerable weight to the theory that Obelli was the buyer. Cameras tracked the woman into the building with the money and out with her package, and she hopped into a white Lexus sedan and sped off. Back in Manhattan, a white Lexus might not have stood out, but in Beukal, where most drivers preferred vibrantly colored vehicles, it was a rarity—and the fact that just such a car was registered to Obelli virtually sealed the deal.

By four that afternoon, when the conference call reconvened, we had more questions than answers.

Why did Obelli buy a large quantity of a highly regulated plant?

Could she have been the person who initially brewed

Elemental?

If so, then how did she get the base recipe for Roulette? Surely she hadn't come up with the formula by chance…

That suggested the possibility—nay, *probability*—of a mole within DPP, someone who would have had access to Roulette. But who would have given out the recipe, and why?

Or, assuming that someone at DPP experimented with Roulette to make Elemental, why would they give it to Katin and the Golden Children? To what end? And *how* did they get the potion to the Golden Children in the limited window between their release from custody and their return to Texas?

And there was the matter of the Golden Children's counselor, Eullan Bargem. He'd come immediately for the ti'Ammaas–ti'Pul sisters…had he been on retainer for them? Did they pay for him to represent the Golden Children? If so, *why*?

Then there was Cudda to consider. The evidence pointed to Jillu as his murderer, but Jillu's conversation with her sister suggested that Cudda might have been in a relationship with Obelli—and worse, that Obelli had masterminded his death. Assuming he'd been dating one of the sisters, why would they have convinced him to lie to Pop and the Forum in order to secure the Golden Children's release? And why had they killed him?

The pieces were on the table, but nothing seemed to be snapping together.

Finally, Pateme said, "Rose, this potion the Golden Children have been brewing—are you fairly confident that it's Elemental?"

"As sure as I can be," I replied, and Yven nodded over my shoulder.

"Then I don't know about you, Kabno," said Pateme, "but from my agency's perspective, they've brewed a dangerous quantity of a potion we've classified as terroristic, and to do so, they've acquired information known only to DPP and at least one restricted plant. I say it's time to bring them in."

"Agreed," she said, nodding slowly. "Do we have firm locations on them?"

I wiggled one hand. "Firm enough. Give me an hour or two to make some sketches and see if I can find pictures online, and that should suffice."

She frowned. "If you can get the addresses, we can go in from the nearest portal..."

"Or you could ask Wylan. He's been wrapped up in this mess since the night Tabitha was attacked—you know he wouldn't mind helping with retrieval. Heck, he'd probably enjoy it."

The directors considered that briefly, and then Kabno said, "I don't want to grow too accustomed to just calling the Wild Hunt every time we have a fugitive in the wind out there."

"Multiple fugitives, multiple locations, and they're all sorcerers, even if their training hasn't been superb," I reminded her. "The boys can attack quickly enough that they won't have time to warn each other. And they know not to use lethal force unless Wylan authorizes it," I added. "He can keep them on a leash."

"*Can* he?"

At that, Gentle Breeze, who'd joined the evening meeting, cut in. "Respectfully, ma'am, you weren't there when he took power. His brothers yielded *immediately*, every last one of them. I don't think Wylan would lose control of the Hunt."

"It *would* be faster than coordinating nighttime drives," Pop pointed out.

After another moment's thought, Kabno surrendered. "All right, fine. Who wants to invite Wylan to this party?"

Before she could change her mind, I called him and put my phone on speaker mode. "Hey," I said when Wylan answered, "sorry to interrupt. How would you like to take the guys out in the next few hours and bring in the Golden Children?"

Though his tone was distorted by the speaker, I could hear the smile in it. "*All* of the Golden Children?"

"Uh-huh. Katin's made herself a big old batch of Elemental, so DPP would like that as well. Evidence, you know. It'll look nice in front of a tribunal."

Wylan chuckled softly. "You want a bow on that, Rose?"

"I'd settle for handcuffs. If I can get you some reference pictures, do you think you can get the perps to DOL?"

"Oh," he replied, his voice dropping to a bass that made the hair on the back of my neck stand at attention, "that would be my *pleasure*."

The retrieval teams struck at four a.m.—Eastern, that is. Since the Golden Children had spread from Roanoke to Dallas, a few of them had an even earlier unpleasant awakening when the Hunt and a crew of agents from DPP and DOL swarmed their rental houses in the dark of night.

I'd done everything I could to make the landing easy and accurate, including pulling photos of the target locations off of vacation and real estate pages. The Dallas team caught a couple and their two children asleep in a long-stay motel, and with a few spells to minimize the noise, they got in and out without waking the other patrons. The Nashville team found another couple and their three kids in a rental house south of town, while the Roanoke team, faced with two adults and *ten* children to round up, brought along a group of agents accustomed to dealing with traumatized kids. The eldest boy of the bunch tried to make an escape out a window, only to be caught and yanked back by a Huntsman, who held him off the ground until he stopped kicking.

Which left Pigeon Forge, with four adults and way too

much Elemental to bring in.

Gentle Breeze led that team, including Pars and Annie, but Wylan was first through the door—and as I learned later, his wakeup method was rather rough. While a group of elves and sorcerers moved on the bedroom where the other couple slept, Wylan and Pars tag-teamed Katin and Dirk's room, and Wylan woke Katin by hoisting her out of bed by her neck. "Good morning," he growled. "You're fucked."

By five Friday morning, the adult Golden Children were split up in cells below the DOL tower, while their kids had been put in protective custody elsewhere in the building. When Annie called to give me the news, I retreated to my studio, quickly downed my coffee, and focused on Katin.

I caught her sitting on her bunk, still wearing her pajamas, and rubbing the spot on her shoulder where she must have been injected with dampening potion. She hadn't been given a chance to brush her hair, which snarled around her face and over her shoulders, and she glared at Merrot through bleary eyes shadowed with smudged mascara as he let himself into her cell.

"Katin Waughnn?" he asked.

"Shouldn't you know?" she retorted.

"Making certain. I wasn't involved in your prior prosecution—I'm a detective in Violent Crimes. Merrot ti'Gata," he offered.

She stiffened. "*Violent Crimes*? I haven't done anything—"

"That's questionable," he interrupted. "And my involvement at this point is rather tangential. There's a murder I've been investigating, and somehow, it seems to loop back to you and your…family? Friends? You know what I mean. Anyway, you're being charged with terrorism."

"What for?" she yelped, jumping to her feet. "We've been out there, right where you left us!"

"Not *quite*. Does the name 'Ragged Gap' mean anything to you?" he asked, pronouncing the name in heavily accented English.

"I...lived there once. Or near there."

"You weren't there, oh, two weeks ago? Injecting a couple of humans with a novel potion and attempting to dose others with Velvet Leash?"

Katin's mouth snapped shut.

"Here's the thing," Merrot continued, folding his arms. "That stuff you gave those humans—it's *nasty*. I hear that DPP can't find an antidote. And they're classifying it as a terroristic potion. Considering how much my colleagues found in that cabin with you..." He whistled. "I'd love to know what you had planned. And I do know you were the mastermind," he added with a faint smile. "There's a farseer who's had eyes on you since Ragged Gap, and she's made copious notes."

"Whatever she's told you, she's lying."

"Well, that's a matter for you and your counselor to discuss. You know farseers are put under the truthfulness spell during their testimony, yes? Maybe you're correct and she's been bluffing, but..." He shrugged as Katin's face paled. "Just something to consider. Now, you'll be properly processed later this morning, but for the time being, if you need to call someone, there's a phone for you." With a nod to the phone on the desk bolted to the floor, Merrot took his leave and locked the cell door behind him.

The detective was barely out of earshot before Katin let loose a volley of screamed profanity. Once she got *that* out of her system, she grabbed the phone and punched in a number, then glared at the wall while she waited. "*Hi,*" she said. "It's Katin Waughnn. If you get this, I'm in the DOL tower, and I need to see you. *Now.*"

CHAPTER 18

I wasn't surprised to find Eullan waiting when Katin, now sporting inmate brown, was led into a windowless room shortly after six that morning. He seemed dressed for work, wearing a deep green robe with ornate gold trim that probably cost a couple months' average wages, but his mouth was tight, and I saw none of the fire he'd exhibited when swooping in to save Jillu and Obelli. Instead, he merely nodded to the escorting guard as Katin took a seat, and the guard locked the door on his way out.

Katin glanced around the bare space, which seemed nearly identical to DOL's less welcoming interrogation rooms but for the absence of one-way glass. "Are they watching us?" she asked.

Eullan sat back and shook his head. "No. This is a private space."

Well…usually.

"What the hell happened?" she asked. "Not a peep from DOL in a month, not a sign of them, and then all of a sudden this morning…" She huffed and slumped in her chair, and while she'd been handed a brush after processing, her blonde hair hung in dirty clumps. "You've got to get us out of here. They snatched everyone, even the babies—"

"I'm afraid that's not an option this time."

Katin's eyes widened with alarm. "What do you mean? We did what was asked of us—"

"Tell me," Eullan murmured, "are you familiar with a game called chess? I understand it's popular outside."

"I…uh…" She floundered briefly, thrown by the non sequitur, then said, "We had a chess set growing up, yeah. I'm not *good* at it, but I know the basics. Why?"

"The objective is to protect the king at all costs, yes?"

"Yes…" she said, a drawn-out, suspicion-laden reply.

"The cause is the king," Eullan told her. "We are lesser pieces. Specifically, you and your miscreant band are pawns—you have limited use, and you've served your function, more or less."

"We are not *pawns*!" she yelled at him. "How dare you!"

The look with which Eullan regarded her was perhaps meant to be dispassionate, but his annoyance showed through the cracks. "You're correct. Pawns follow directions."

"We did!"

"Did you, now?" Leaning toward her, Eullan asked, "And what part of those directions said *anything* about returning to Ragged Gap?"

Katin stared sullenly back at him. "I did what I was asked to do."

"You were told to operate in a larger city. Dallas, Houston, Phoenix, perhaps Los Angeles. Instead, you returned to the one town where you should never have shown your face, and you decided to settle scores."

"I was trying to get *help*. Brewing at the scale requested needs manpower—"

"There are ten of you of age, are there not? Don't tell me you and your little boyfriend are the only brewers in your company."

"No," she allowed, "but with the kids to look after, and housekeeping, and trips for supplies—it takes a lot of hands to keep a big family running. Human assistance would have sped up production."

"And you didn't think anyone would notice if you returned to Ragged Gap and tried to use Velvet Leash again?" he snapped. "Had you followed instructions, no one here would have had cause to monitor you. But you went *there*, and you were stupid enough to attack the same group as before! Did you think it would go unnoticed?"

"They're just humans—"

"No." He pulled a file folder from his leather briefcase on the floor, then opened it to show Katin a picture of Tabitha—a photo that had run in Beukal's major newspaper following her testimony the previous fall. "You hit *her*. The human who literally stitched agents back together and helped rescue children. Did you not think the agencies would ride to her aid?"

"She was going to call the fucking Hunter!" Katin protested. "I had to do *something*!"

"Are you or are you not a damn sorcerer? You're telling me there was no other way for you to subdue a human than to inject her? You could have thrown her against a wall. Knocked her unconscious and made your getaway. But no, you turned her into a test subject, and you've been under observation ever since." Eullan pulled a stapled set of typed pages from the folder and slapped it on the table between them. "That's your probable cause file. DPP's pet farseer, the one who testified in all the Unity Plan tribunals last fall? She's been watching you. *Extensively*. The agencies waited to pounce until you'd finished brewing."

Katin sat silently for a moment as she skimmed the packet, much of which I'd written up the night before. "So…what do we do?" she mumbled, deflating.

Eullan collected the report and Tabitha's picture, and packed the folder away. "You're going to take the fall."

"*What?*"

"It's unfortunate," he said calmly. "You were given a second chance and squandered it, brewing a novel potion and testing it on humans—as is your wont. You returned to the scene of your defeat and took revenge. And you decided to make more of your new potion as part of your plan to right the imagined wrongs against you." As Katin sputtered, he said, "You're still young, and clearly, you're in need of more therapy than DOL provided last time. I'll try to work out a deal for ten to twenty years, seeing as the only victims were human and you were stopped before you could test your potion on someone who truly mattered. Go along with the plan, be contrite, and perhaps we can make a case that some of your fellows were less culpable."

"You...you can't be serious," said Katin. "You're supposed to be helping me!"

"The situation has changed," said Eullan, pushing back his chair, "and pawns protect the more important pieces."

"I'm not going down alone."

He chuckled faintly as he shouldered his briefcase. "I assure you that things will go far more poorly for you if you don't cooperate. Think about it, girl," he said, and knocked on the door to summon the guard. "Because if I don't fight for you, you'll spend the rest of your life on a penal farm. You can't *afford* to go rogue."

As Eullan left and the guard escorted Katin to her cell, I pulled myself back to my body and opened my eyes, only to find Pop studying the unfinished canvas of my parents. "Hey," I croaked, and reached for my water. "Sorry, been waiting long?"

"No. And the portrait is coming along beautifully," he said, nodding to the painting on the easel. "Well done, Rosie. I'm sure they'd be pleased."

"Thanks. What's up?"

"Just wondering what you'd been watching. Call it a hunch," he said, cocking his head. "Anything interesting?"

I took a long drink and wiped my mouth on the back of my hand. "Uh, *yeah*. Eullan Bargem is dirty. He told Katin to take the blame for Elemental, but I think she's balking. He said the cause is most important...she was supposed to go to a city, but instead, she went back to Ragged Gap, and he's pissed." Running through their conversation, I said, "Katin was released with marching orders from *someone*, and it sounds like they came through her counselor. What do you want to bet there was an arrangement? He helped the Golden Children with their appeal, and Katin did a favor outside." Frowning, I mused, "I think she was meant to release Elemental in a bigger city. She screwed up by going to Ragged Gap. But who would want her running around a random city with a potion like that?"

Smirking, Pop asked, "Are you aware that it's generally frowned upon for one to spy on counselor–client meetings?"

"Whoops," I deadpanned. "He told her I've been watching her. She should expect this, right?"

He gave me a look.

"Hey, people above my pay grade are saying this is a terroristic potion. I'm just trying to help in these challenging times."

"Naturally," said Pop, and though he rolled his eyes, he didn't chastise me further. "In that case, what would you suggest?"

"Who's going to interrogate Katin?"

"I'm not positive, but probably Detective Orafer, since she handled Derringer Faln." His mouth twitched. "Do you need her number?"

"Got it," I replied, and grabbed my phone. "Enva liaises with us, remember?"

"Of course." Pop glanced at the painting again, then said, "You captured Jocelyn's look well. That expression that suggests she's about to flirt with the line."

I grinned. "Is that so?"

"Mm-hmm. Then again, I suspect you could use a mirror for the fine details." Turning back to me, he laughed softly. "*There* it is. Never let it be suggested that you're not your mother's daughter, my dear."

"I'm pretty sure she came by it honestly."

"You might be correct about that," Pop replied, then winked and left me to call the detective.

Shortly past three that afternoon, having given Katin plenty of time to stew, Enva sat down with her in an interrogation room while Pop, Ganti, Pateme, Kabno, Gentle Breeze, Syvin, Merrot, Liogh, about a dozen other DOL agents, and I watched from next door.

Katin seemed wary, and Enva took a gentle approach as she began. "We meet again, Ms. Waughnn," she said, and offered Katin a little smile. "Something to drink?"

"Anything harder than water on offer?"

Enva chuckled. "I wish. Coffee, water, or I think I can find a can of fruit juice. That stuff's carbonated, it if matters..."

"Sure, that's fine. Thanks," she mumbled.

The detective stepped out and returned with two small cans of the stuff, which was sweet but too lemony for my taste. "There you go," she said, settling into her chair. "Now, just to remind you of the protocol, I have a right to ask you questions. You have a right to refuse to answer them. You have a counselor, and if you'd prefer, we can postpone this until he's available to join us...or we can proceed. If you choose to proceed, you may stop answering questions at any point. Do you understand?"

"Yeah."

"Would you like to proceed?"

"I think so, yes."

"Very well. If it's all right with you, here's what I'd like to do. I'm going to tell you what I know, and you just listen. After that...maybe we can come to an understanding. Okay?"

Katin nodded and cracked open her can.

After pausing for a sip of her own, Enva said, "I know your life hasn't been easy, Ms. Waughnn...or Katarina? Do you prefer that?"

"Katin's fine."

"Katin, then. Sitting here today as a detective, I can tell you why your parents and your friends' parents were taken into custody. Legally, DOL was in the right. But speaking as a person instead of a badge, I understand that the experience was incredibly traumatizing for you, and it should *not* have happened the way it did. We should have been more careful and realized you kids were out there alone."

"Why," Katin muttered, "so you could lock us up, too?"

"No, so we could take care of you. Educate you. Just as we did for your friends' children while you were incarcerated here. Believe me, I understand that growing up as a government ward isn't ideal, but we could have protected you while you were still kids. You should *never* have been left in charge at...what, sixteen? That was an awful burden laid on you and Dirk, and it shouldn't have happened. For what it's worth, I'm sorry."

"Did you snatch my parents?"

"No," said Enva, "I wasn't on that case. I've since used it as a training tool in hopes that a situation like yours never arises again," she added, "and the lead detective in that matter had a long, unpleasant talk with the director once your group came to light." Shrugging, she said, "Not worth much, I realize that, but I *am* sorry that DOL failed you."

"You could have left our parents alone, you know."

Enva flashed a brief half-smile. "Do you know why we raided your compound?"

"Because they were brewing illegally for some asshole named Silver," Katin replied.

She nodded. "And did anyone ever tell you about Silver?"

"No...did you lock him up, too?"

"Eventually. Silver was the...*business* name, let's say, of Inade ti'Cren. *Lord* ti'Cren, that is. Rich, powerful, and ruthless, as it turned out. We may never have a full reckoning of the people who were murdered at his direction. But one of his tactics was to keep small groups of growers and brewers outside, people who could reliably ship in product and who wouldn't be terribly missed if their facility blew up or he needed to silence a few wagging tongues. You were born into one such group," Enva explained, "and your family's imports were heavy on the heroin-laced potions. Your parents and the others are still alive because they never admitted that they were working for Silver, and because of the layers of intermediaries he used, I doubt they could have named him had their lives depended on it."

Katin's eyes narrowed. "So…where is he now?"

"Cavimet. He's got most of the next three centuries to think over his choices. Your parents are at other facilities," she assured Katin, "just as we kept you and your group away from Cavimet. He's on the dampening potion, but I don't trust him, all the same."

"Rich people always have an easier time of it," said Katin. "Pablo Escobar got to design his own prison, you know."

"Yeah, I've heard of him," said Enva. "But ti'Cren's not exactly living in luxury. His son was given the title and control of the Hall's finances, and the present Lord ti'Cren doesn't seem to have much use for his father."

"*That's* an understatement," Pateme muttered beside me.

"Anyway," Enva continued, "here's what I know about the last month. You were released on April sixteenth, in part because DOI couldn't render a unanimous opinion about your future dangerousness to the Forum. Now, DOI are a closed-lipped bunch on a good day, but I've been informed that there was a single holdout who said you wouldn't cause any trouble. On May tenth, that holdout was confronted and admitted he lied—he tried to secure your release at the behest of his girlfriend. Cudda ti'Ren. He was murdered in his bed early the next morning."

Katin stiffened but said nothing.

"But let's back up. On May first, you injected Stephanie Love and Tabitha Bradley with a novel potion. Ms. Love was a victim of yours from your last time in Ragged Gap.

As for Ms. Bradley…" She paused to check her notes. "Threatened to call the Hunter, did she?"

"Yeah."

"Well, since he helped bring her to quarantine, I'd believe it. Both women survived, incidentally," said Enva. "And their accounts match the farseer's. *She* just happened to check in on Tabitha and saw everything as it went down. She's been watching you ever since."

To be fair, I couldn't blame Katin for cringing.

"Once the research healers figured out the potion from the victims' blood, the plant nerds checked the ingredients off against what the farseer saw you using, and it was evident that you were brewing more of it. DPP has named it Elemental, I presume because of the effects. Do you know what it does? You left Ragged Gap before seeing the results."

"Uh…no."

Enva nodded. "Abilities almost nymphic in their direction but considerably stranger. Of the two victims, one manifested power over liquids, the other over gases. And both can phase, if you will, into their 'element' and back."

That took Katin aback. "They can *liquefy*?"

"Well, Ms. Bradley can. Ms. Love sublimates. But here's the interesting bit," said Enva, leaning closer. "DPP believes that Elemental is built from a potion called Roulette, but unlike Roulette, there's no antidote. In other words, congratulations—you've just given two humans permanent magical abilities. Now, I'm guessing that wasn't your idea," she said as Katin processed the news. "Considering your previous actions outside, that seems illogical for you."

After a long, awkwardly quiet moment, Katin mumbled, "We didn't know what it would do."

"That's what I figured, considering there's no way you could have acquired the formula for Roulette on your own. And I know Jillu ti'Non and Obelli ti'Ammaas are wrapped up in this, but I'm not entirely clear as to *how*. So, that's what I have," said Enva, and paused for a sip of juice. "What I want to know is why you would jeopardize your freedom by getting involved with Elemental, especially so soon after your release." When Katin sat silently, Enva said, "I'll be honest with you, youngling—you're in deep trouble. DPP has classified Elemental as a terroristic potion—"

"Why? If it gives power—"

"It did for *two* people. Roulette is variable in its response—some are unaffected, some grow new appendages, and some drop dead. We don't know if Elemental has a single reaction or if your two victims got lucky." Lowering her voice, Enva said, "There's no reason for you to spend the rest of your life on a penal farm if you weren't the mastermind here, and I don't believe you were. You'll almost certainly do *some* time, but five to twenty is much better than a life sentence, isn't it?"

Again, the silence stretched between them, and Katin nibbled her lip. Finally, in a voice barely louder than a whisper, she said, "My counselor said he'd help me if I took the blame."

"Your counselor is sacrificing you. I can get you a new one—a free one. Since your counselor is currently representing Ms. ti'Non and Ms. ti'Ammaas in their murder charges, am I correct in guessing that they hired him to work on your appeal?"

She nodded.

"Tell me, Katin," said Enva. "Help me, and I'll help you. You have my word on that—and in case you doubt me, these interviews are recorded. You can request a copy at any point."

"If I talk, you'll help the others, too?"

"All of the Golden Children, I promise. Just tell me what happened."

She swigged back the last of her juice and asked, "Could I have another, please?"

Enva left the room to retrieve a can, and Katin drained

at least half before she began, her voice soft and her tone resigned. "Late last year, when I was at Bebala, the Superintendent sent for me and said I had a visitor. It was Eullan Bargem."

"The counselor?"

"Uh-huh. He said it was a legal visit, so we went into a room alone, just the two of us. I didn't know him—I'd never seen him before—but he said he was a damn good counselor and willing to help us with our appeal. I told him I didn't have any money, and he said that was fine—I had *patrons*. That's the word he used. They were going to pay his fees, and he'd help us, and in turn, we'd do a favor for them."

Enva began making a few notes on a lined pad. "Did you ever learn your patrons' identities?"

"Not until March. Things were moving along with the Forum, but I…I didn't want to commit to this *favor* we were going to owe until I knew who was requesting it and why. When I balked, Eullan filled in some blanks. He didn't really *want* to, but I was ready to pull the plug, and I guess he decided he needed us as much as we needed him."

"Who was paying him?"

"Jillu and Obelli. I don't know shit about the Halls or whatever, but Eullan told me they were loaded."

The detective nodded. "And what did they want from you?"

"They wanted us to spread this new potion—Elemental, I guess. The plan was for us to get out, and they'd give us the potion and ingredients to make more of it. We were supposed to go to a city and randomly inject people. I asked what the potion was," Katin continued, "and Eullan said it would give the drinker actual power…in theory, at least. It'd never been tried. Guess no one here was stupid enough to swig it."

"So, that was the deal? They paid for your counselor, and you spread Elemental outside?"

"That, and they were going to give us a chunk of cash once we'd tried it on fifty people. One hundred thousand dollars. It wouldn't do us forever, but it'd go a ways toward getting us on our feet."

Enva's pen rapidly scratched across the pad. "Did you ever meet your benefactors?"

"Meet in person? No. I spoke to Obelli several times once we were free. Almost everything went through Eullan until we were out, but he promised they were good for the money as long as we held up our end of the bargain. That's why I've been brewing, see?"

"Sure. But what I don't understand is why they would want you to spread Elemental."

Katin laughed softly and finished her second can. "From what I was told, the goal was to sow chaos outside. Inject a bunch of people, and do it in a place with plenty of media coverage. Suddenly, you'd have humans exhibiting magical talent, and then..." She shrugged. "A freak-out, maybe? Riots? I don't know exactly what they had in mind—the goal was just to do something too big to cover up."

"You don't suppose..." Kabno murmured.

"And why would Jillu and Obelli want that?" asked Enva.

"Because they'd joined this group called the Unity Plan."

Kabno slapped her thigh. "*There* it is."

Enva kept her expression more guarded. "Are you familiar with that organization?"

"Eh." Katin wiggled her hand. "I know they kidnapped people and dumped them outside last year, and the dumbasses got caught. Some of them ended up at Bebala with me."

"Do you know *why* they did that?"

She smirked back at Enva. "Because they're idiots. Eullan calls it 'the cause,'" she said, her voice dripping and eyebrows rising with false gravitas. "I think the gist is that if we were to reveal the existence of magic, humans would back off and make room for us. Either live and let live, or else we'd subjugate them."

"And you don't agree, I take it."

A snort answered that. "*No.* Speaking as someone born and raised out there, the Unity Plan's predicted outcome is a pipe dream."

The phrase didn't translate well in Pactish, but I knew what she was getting at. No one with any experience in the wider world believed humanity would roll over if the Pactlands' citizenry were to appear among them. Sure, there might be chaos for a time, but the smart money was on the eight billion humans.

The Unity Plan was largely a sorcerer organization, however, so what were Ivari's granddaughters doing?

"Do you know why they approached you in particular?" Enva asked Katin.

"Funny you should mention that. I actually asked Obelli once we were home," she replied. "She said *she* couldn't easily get outside, but she knew that we could if the Forum would play along. Plus, since I was locked up for, you know, *brewing*, she thought I'd be competent enough to handle her new potion. I haven't tested the batch I made, but hell, I can follow a recipe."

Enva smiled. "I would say so. And I suppose Obelli didn't consider that you'd have scores to settle outside, did she?"

"Don't think it crossed her mind. Then again, since they've all hung me out to dry, I guess we all know how much consideration she had for me and my family."

"Apparently none. Do you want something else to drink?"

Katin waited, rubbing her temples, until Enva returned with a familiar red can. "Coke?" Katin asked, popping the top. "You've been holding out on me."

"Found it in the back of the fridge," Enva explained. "I thought that might suit you."

"Appreciated. This caffeine withdrawal headache is a beast," she muttered between long sips, then joked, "Worst part of lockup, right?"

Enva frowned. "I'll be right back," she said, and stepped into our room. "Okay," she said once the soundproofed door had closed, "who has a field kit?"

"I don't," said one of the female agents, digging in her bag, "but would this do it?" Extracting a tube of familiar pale green liquid, she offered, "Migraines."

"I'll pay you back," Enva told her, then took the potion next door and passed it to Katin. "Just a painkiller, but that should help."

Katin, who'd been steadily nursing her soda, flashed a genuine smile at the detective before downing the potion. "You know the feeling, eh?"

"Too well. But while we're on the subject of potions, can you tell me where Elemental came from? Who formulated it? I know one of the ingredients is a heavily restricted flower, and your associates were able to buy others near the Tampa portal—"

"Your farseer saw that, too, huh?"

"She's been a busy girl."

"True," I muttered, as Pop patted my knee. At least the Golden Children had given me an excuse to shirk some of my pre-wedding duties.

"But since the potion is based on Roulette," Enva continued, "either someone working with you had access to that formula, or else you were lucky to a statistically unlikely degree."

"Oh, there's a Unity Plan guy in DPP," Katin replied. "Probably several, but the one who matters is Dante."

I cut my eyes to Pateme, whose jaws had clenched.

"Dante?" Enva repeated. "Are you sure?"

"Yeah. Odd name—that's how I remembered it," said Katin. "When I was younger and thought that college might be a possibility—*ha*, no—I thought I needed to get a leg up, see? We were all homeschooled, and my schooling stopped once my parents were snatched, so I figured there were some gaps. I got my hands on a few high school and college book lists and thought I'd tackle some of the more interesting ones. Anyway, there's this Italian book, *Inferno*, and it's basically this guy, Dante, getting a guided tour of hell. *Weird* shit. It's got a couple of sequels, but I barely made it through *Inferno*. So, Obelli sent me the recipe, and I asked her who I could talk to if I had questions or problems with it, and she told me to call Dante. I've got his number in my phone, but I can't remember it offhand," she said.

"That's quite all right. And you're sure he's with DPP?"

"Positive. See, I called him the day after I got the recipe, just to make sure I was clear on things, and he was super-quiet on the phone and said he'd have to call me back. He reached out that night and said he'd been at DPP when I called, and so I'd need to call after hours. I asked if he worked there, and he said he's a researcher."

Before she'd finished, Pateme had turned to Pop. "Did you know?"

"I had my suspicions," Pop replied. "And she's right, he's not the only problem in your agency. I don't have a full list—"

"Then let's start with what we have." Grabbing his phone from his robe pocket, he quickly dialed, then said, "Good morning. Take Dante Perritin into custody and bring him to DOL. Cut off his system access *immediately* and confiscate his phone. Understood? I need everything preserved—"

While Pateme worked out the healer's arrest, I focused on the interrogation room. "The problem for Dante was that he couldn't make much Elemental—they thought it would take the Forum longer than it did for us to be released. So, he gave Obelli what he had, and Obelli got a ton of white curraxit from a supplier here for us, and they told us to brew more. But I knew that was going to take time and be a real pain in the ass, so I figured we'd go back to Ragged Gap and, uh...*recruit* some folks to help us. I mean, those idiots were dumb enough to drink Velvet Leash once, and I thought they might be convinced again, especially if Elemental worked like Obelli and Dante had told me. But it didn't."

"How so?"

"Well, based on what I saw, it hurt like the dickens. Stephanie and Tabitha started screaming almost before we got the needles out of them, and they both collapsed. And then Tabitha's hair turned blue...I mean, no one had mentioned *that* as a possibility. So, then I had a bunch of scared morons standing around, and I was trying to keep a happy face plastered on, but they were *not* excited about taking anything I was about to pass out. Before I could get Velvet Leash into any of them, my potion tubes started exploding—Tabitha's doing, I assumed."

Enva nodded.

"She's a tough bitch, I'll grant her that," Katin allowed. "Looked like she was in agony. But once Ragged Gap turned into a bust, we split up and laid low. I thought you people would be breaking down my door at any moment for the first few days, but no one came, and I...well, I guess I got overconfident. We found a place, got the last ingredients from Tampa, and started the brew."

"And you were planning to take it to a city and start injecting people?"

Katin nodded and sipped her Coke. "With a hundred grand on the line? Absolutely."

"Never mind the humans in your way, right?" Enva asked.

"They've never done much for me. But hey, you told me that Stephanie and Tabitha got talent out of the deal. If you look at it the right way, we did them a favor."

"Right," Gentle Breeze retorted from our side of the glass, "you stuck them with an unknown potion, and they didn't die. How *generous*."

While Katin finished her drink, Enva took a moment

to review her notes, then looked at another few pages in her file. After a time, she asked, "Does the name Cudda ti'Ren mean anything to you? You reacted earlier when I mentioned him."

"I never met him," Katin replied, "but I know *of* him. Once we were out, I asked Obelli how they'd managed to convince the Forum that we'd behave. She told me they had a friend at DOI, one of the farseers. I asked if he was part of the Unity Plan, too, and she said no—he was her boyfriend. So, I asked her if she wasn't concerned if they broke up or something, and she laughed. Told me that she had him wrapped around her finger, and he wouldn't dare. He was *smitten*. I mean, Obelli's married, and Cudda knew it, and he was still mooning after her."

"Do you know how those two got together?"

Katin shrugged. "Not exactly. But they're both easy on the eyes, and from what Obelli said, Cudda had money, too. She told him she'd divorce her husband and marry him if he could better himself at DOI."

"In other words," Pop murmured, "take my position."

"Sounds like you and Obelli were close," said Enva.

"Eh." Katin shrugged. "We understood each other, at least to a point. Neither of us wanted to be here, and we were stuck."

"Is that so? My understanding was that the elves who'd been hiding in New York joined us willingly…except the ones we arrested, naturally."

"Yes and no, or that's what Obelli told me," said Katin. "Some of the old ones were *really* into the idea of settling here, and they kind of strong-armed the holdouts into coming along. Obelli and Jillu want to go home, but they're trapped here now, and they're pissed at how things turned out."

"What do you mean?"

"Well, like, their grandparents and some of their other kin were incarcerated, and instead of having them or their parents in charge of the Halls, the Halls are being run by inbred bumpkins, most of whom are still kids," Katin explained. "Obelli bitched about a lot of people, but she really *hated* the guy who'd been king opposite her granddad...what's his name..."

"Diriem ti'Dana?" Enva offered.

"That's it. She thought he was behind all the shit that happened to her family—said it was revenge or something. Like, maybe her granddad did something to him a long while back, and he's been biding his time."

I glanced at Pop, whose face betrayed nothing.

By then, with her headache soothed and her caffeine level rising, Katin was on a roll. "So, at first, she wanted to find an in at DOI, you know, figure out a way to bring ti'Dana down. That's how she got wrapped up with Cudda, and I guess he didn't mind helping out."

"Bring down the director, advance in his career, and Obelli would marry him," said Enva.

Katin pointed finger guns across the table. "Bingo. And then Obelli heard about the Unity Plan and thought they'd be useful. I don't know exactly how she got involved, but she and her sister paid for Eullan to get us out, and Cudda screwed up the DOI prediction. So, Dante worked out the potion, and if everything had gone according to plan, there would have been too many Elemental incidents outside for you people to cover up. And we'd be sitting pretty...but you see how that turned out," she muttered. "You said Cudda's dead?"

"We have reason to believe he was murdered, yes," Enva replied. "By someone blocked from farsight."

Katin smirked. "Let me help you out, then. That would be Jillu."

The detective's eyebrow arched. "Oh?"

"Yep. That was the backup plan. In case Cudda ever got, uh...*squirrelly*," she said, using the English term, "Jillu was on standby. They have these rings that hide them from farsight, she claimed. Jillu got to know Cudda, too. Obelli was careful to keep things quiet, right, so her husband or anyone else wouldn't find out she was cheating, and since she was the one going to all the trouble of getting Cudda involved and keeping him in line, Jillu was going to kill him if it came down to it. Split the risk, as it were. So, if the person who killed Cudda was protected, and Obelli's got an alibi, I'd bet my life that Jillu did it." She paused, then asked hopefully, "There wasn't another Coke in the fridge, was there?"

There was, at is turned out, and as Katin slaked her thirst, Enva said, "Let me make sure I have my notes in order, okay? Starting from the top...Obelli ti'Ammaas had a grudge against Director ti'Dana and wanted to leave the Pactlands, so she convinced Cudda ti'Ren to both try to make the director look incompetent and help secure your release. She and Jillu ti'Non provided financial backing for Eullan Bargem to represent your group."

"Yep."

"Cudda wanted to marry Obelli, so he was willing to be useful to her. Once the director confronted him, I suppose the sisters deemed him compromised."

Katin nodded. "Sounds right."

"The Unity Plan wanted to create an incident outside that was too massive to be covered up, thereby exposing humans to magic and perhaps forcing us to reveal ourselves, if only to contain the chaos."

"Uh-huh."

"And you and the Golden Children wanted your freedom and a hundred thousand dollars, so you were willing to inject unsuspecting humans with a novel potion as part of a bargain for your early release. But you also had unfinished business in Ragged Gap, so you started in that town instead of a larger city and tested Elemental on two people you knew from your time there."

"That...doesn't sound great when you put it like that, but yeah."

Enva made a few more notes. "Katin, are you willing to swear to everything you've told me here today?"

"If you'll help us."

"You'll do prison time—there's no way to avoid it. You were active participants in a conspiracy that threatened the security of the Pactlands. But if you'll testify against the other participants, then DOL will pursue lesser charges for the Golden Children and recommend sentences on the lighter end of the range. Agreed?"

"Agreed." Katin thrust her hand across the table, and Enva shook it. "And look, a bunch of us were involved with the Ragged Gap incident, but only four of us have been brewing. Not everyone is equally part of this mess, you know?"

Enva regarded her briefly, then nodded. "That'll be taken into consideration. Bear with me while I get some paperwork together for you, and I need to bring in an assistant from the Tribunal…"

With the interview largely concluded, we began to pack up next door. "Any word on your healer?" Pop asked Pateme.

He nodded. "Already in this tower. I need to bring in Vinla and the rest of the Roulette team for debriefing. Tell me straight, Diriem—are any of them dirty?"

"Not to my knowledge, no." Turning to Kabno, he said, "My regards to your detective. I trust she'll be having a word with Jillu and Obelli? Or will this fall to you, Detective?" he asked, nodding to Merrot.

Kabno smiled grimly. "You know, I believe this will be a team effort. Clear your calendar for tomorrow morning, folks," she said, and cut her eyes to me. "Why don't you come as well, Rose? I realize you can watch remotely, but that doesn't mean I *like* it."

"Happy to oblige, ma'am."

She grunted. "Pateme, look after your people."

"I already have my hands full today," he groused, and patted me on the back. "Go home, youngling. I'll see you in the morning."

Kabno selected one of the nicest interrogation rooms, one with padded chairs and a rug beneath the seating area. It was set up with additional seating that morning, three chairs for Jillu, Obelli, and Eullan, plus another three for Enva, Merrot, and the director herself.

A few days in lockup had done nothing to improve the sisters' outlook on their situation or mellow the defiant looks they shot Kabno as she hoisted herself into her seat. Both had showered recently, but their hair was dull and snarled, the result of subpar shampoo and air drying. Obelli had developed a zit on her chin, one of the painful ones too far below the surface to pop, but with her talent dampened, she couldn't so much as mask it. Their counselor sat between them in a burgundy robe, alert and polished, and he eyed the detectives as they took their places flanking Kabno and pulled manila folders from their bags.

"Thank you for coming in on the weekend," Kabno began with a little nod to Eullan. "This really can't wait until Monday."

He faintly smirked. "Releasing my clients, are you?"

"Not exactly." She paused, then gestured to Merrot. "You've met Detective ti'Gata, who's investigating Agent ti'Ren's murder, and this," she said, gesturing to Enva in turn, "is Detective Orafer, the head of our DPP liaison group."

Eullan gave Enva a once-over. "What does DPP have to do with this matter? I thought the deceased was with Intelligence."

"He was," said Kabno, "but there have been…developments. Tell me, Mr. Bargem, these ladies aren't your only clients in our custody, correct?"

His face went very still, but after a moment's hesitation, he said in a normal tone, "No, they are not. You people seem to have arrested the Golden Children again. Did you not learn your lesson back in April?"

Kabno looked at Enva, who smiled across the table at Eullan and the sisters. "So," said the detective, "I had a talk with Katin Waughnn yesterday."

Eullan stiffened. "Without me present?"

"She wished to proceed without you…and after having spoken with her, I understand why. She explained her part in the Unity Plan's conspiracy to spread the novel potion known as Elemental outside in order to create a problem too large to be managed without revealing the existence of magic or the Pactlands. An *untested* potion, I should add. She said she was surprised by its effects on the two victims who received it. Since that potion was built from the restricted potion known as Roulette, there was a significant possibility that some individuals exposed to it would die." Turning her head slowly to take in the three of them, she said, "Even if you want to argue that the intended targets were just humans, that exhibits a gross indifference toward life. The two victims have been irreparably changed without their consent."

"What does that have to do with us?" Jillu blurted.

Enva smiled. "So glad you asked, Ms. ti'Non. See, Ms. Waughnn feels as if she's been rather poorly treated of late. Apparently, Mr. Bargem, you told her to take the blame for Elemental…conveniently leaving your clients here and *yourself* out of the conspiracy."

Jillu started to speak again, but Eullan slammed his arm in front of her to shut her up. "You can't seriously tell me you believe her," he said, focusing on Kabno. "She's a grifter, a liar, and now that she's caught, she'll say anything."

At that, Enva patted the folder in her lap. "She reiterated her statement while under the truthfulness spell. Administered by a Tribunal assistant and everything. And while Ms. Waughnn certainly has a history of crimes of deception…well, she didn't lie yesterday."

"But we wanted additional proof," said Merrot, "so we enlisted the aid of DOI—the past-seeing farseers," he explained with a little grin. "There's a whole team, you know? They typically only assist us in major cases, but seeing that one of their own was murdered in his bed…" His smile widened. "This is *personal* for DOI. So," he said, holding up a folder, "I have here a selection of reports from their investigation yesterday. They couldn't see your clients," he continued, pointing to Obelli and Jillu, "because they were wearing those blinding rings until recently, but they could see *you.*" He paused, letting that hit Eullan, then said, "Ms. Waughnn told us the truth. We've got confirmation from the farseers. And thanks to DOI's findings, when my team raids your office and your home in about"—he glanced at his wristwatch—"five minutes, they'll know where to look to find your Unity Plan files. Counselors and their backup copies, am I right?"

As Eullan's mouth flapped open and closed like a landed bass's, Kabno slapped a folder on the table between their groups. "Your probable cause file. Eullan Bargem, you're under arrest."

A couple minutes later, once the agents who'd been waiting outside the interrogation room had injected him with dampening potion and taken him downstairs for processing, Kabno turned her attention to the sisters, both of whom looked queasy. "For obvious reasons, ladies, Mr. Bargem will be unable to represent you in your criminal proceedings. If you don't have another counselor on retainer, we can arrange for the Tribunal to appoint counselors for each of you. That probably won't happen until Monday, but we'll give you the weekend in case you'd like to make your own arrangements." She stared at them for a moment, then murmured, "If I were you, I would think long and hard about my next moves. Ms. ti'Non, you're currently facing charges of murder and facilitating terroristic activity. Ms. ti'Ammaas, your charges include conspiracy to commit murder, facilitating terroristic activity, conspiracy to interfere with an official government function, and unlicensed purchase of a restricted botanical. Let me explain something to you, as I suppose you've not had a firm grounding in the Pactlands justice system. Sentencing takes into account the crime, mitigating circumstances, and the species of the perpetrator. After all, a life sentence for a sorcerer and an elf would be drastically different, and so the Tribunal endeavors to make sentences proportional. Understand?"

They nodded silently.

"Good. Now, as elves and nymphs don't die of natural causes, your sentences are the lengthiest. And considering the charges you face—charges that are supported by farseer testimony and Ms. Waughnn's confession, for starters—you two are looking at probably a couple centuries' incarceration."

"*Centuries*?" Obelli yelped. "But...but we..."

"Your actions were intended to jeopardize the safety of the Pactlands," Kabno calmly told her. "That is a serious offense."

"I've got a son!" she protested. "He's just eighteen—"

"I've got *two*," Jillu interrupted. "Cefet's grown, but Utien's a little kid. He needs me!"

Their pleas fell on deaf ears. "Your children have fathers, do they not? Including the one you cheated on, Ms. ti'Ammaas?"

Obelli's cheeks colored. "You don't understand—"

"I do, and you won't be the first mothers sent to a penal farm. Your children will be able to visit you, make calls, write letters...you won't be entirely cut off." She paused while the agitated sisters fumbled for a winning argument, then said, "Cooperation with our investigation would go a long way toward lessening your sentences. We could work out an agreement if you could provide us with helpful information and your eventual testimony."

"Like what?" asked Jillu.

"Well, you could start by confirming the identity of the individual at DPP who developed the potion you gave Ms. Waughnn for distribution outside. Ms. Waughnn has already pointed a finger, but we always like more proof. Or you could identify active members of the Unity Plan, others involved in this conspiracy beyond the two of you, your counselor, and the Golden Children. Help us, and we'll help you. You have my word."

"And...this will keep us out of prison?" pressed Jillu.

Kabno shook her head. "No, though cooperation would heavily factor into sentencing—"

"Just let us go home, damn it!" Obelli shouted. "That's all we want! You people ruined our family, stole our money, and stuck us here—let us go!"

The director was unfazed by her outburst. "Correct me if I'm mistaken, but you *petitioned* for citizenship."

"The olds gave us no choice. I *hate* this place," she spat. "Let me go, and I'll never bother you again."

"I'm afraid that's not an option."

I saw the flash of murder in Obelli's eyes an instant before she lunged across the table, probably intending to throttle Kabno. But raised as she was in New York, perhaps Obelli never learned what a terrible idea it is to fight a gnome. Sure, they're the size of kindergarteners, but they're incredibly strong and damn fast...and Kabno, who'd spent the best part of the last three centuries training at DOL, made a formidable opponent.

Pop and Pateme winced as Kabno slammed Obelli through the coffee table, then landed atop her and bent her arm into a stress position until the much larger elf screamed for mercy. "Poor choice," she said, straightening her robe as a pair of agents dragged Obelli out of the room. "I'll give you the rest of the weekend to reconsider. And you, Ms. ti'Non?" she asked, turning to Jillu and cracking her tiny knuckles.

The other sister went quietly, leaving the detectives to collect the scattered paperwork.

I walked through the DOL garage with Pop, as we'd carpooled into the city in his Porsche 911. "Tired, Rosie?" he asked. "You're quiet."

"Glad they're in custody," I replied. "Are the charges going to stick this time?"

He chuckled low. "You know I shouldn't answer that."

"But you *could*?"

Pop held his silence until he'd started the ignition, then said, "I wouldn't worry about the Golden Children causing any more mischief in Georgia."

"And Obelli and Jillu? Eullan? Dante?"

"The evidence against them is strong and mounting, and that's all I'll say, youngling."

As he pulled onto the street, I leaned against the window and sighed. "Now to figure out how to make things right with Tabitha and Stephanie."

"That's not an immediate problem. They won't be turned loose today."

"Then when?"

He reached across and patted my arm. "*Patience*, Rosie. And now that the conspirators are in Kabno's custody, don't you have a wedding in two weeks to worry about?"

I groaned.

EPILOGUE

Pateme gave me the next few weeks off. "You've been working long after hours," he said when he called Sunday afternoon, "and if memory serves, I gave ti'Ansha some pre-wedding vacation, too. Don't come back until you're married, eh? I'll see you at the ceremony."

I certainly wasn't complaining. After a few nights in which I didn't feel guilty for sleeping instead of spying, my head was clearer and my appetite better—maybe not the *best* thing in the home stretch to the wedding, but Jevva swore on Wednesday when I picked up my gown that the lacing would keep me comfortable if my weight fluctuated. She'd done a magnificent job, and without my darling cousin there to critique, I felt like a million bucks.

Perhaps not a *bride* just yet, but closer.

For the first time in days, I allowed myself to relax. Yven, who'd reluctantly agreed to keep my dress a surprise to him, was game for nearly anything—long lunches in Beukal, a walk in the woods at Green Lake, and even a sneaky trip back to Richmond with Annie and Wylan Thursday night when Maya called and said she'd had a rare late cancellation on a cheesecake order. We sat at a four-top in the corner, gorged ourselves, drank enough to make the world a brighter place, and talked for hours…and I just *breathed.*

"I needed this," I told Annie when we trekked to the ladies' room together. "Between the wedding and the Golden Children…"

"Prosecco is a hell of a drug," she joked, fishing a

blackberry seed from between her teeth. "Hey, what's the sitch with Tabitha and Stephanie? Do they need a change of space?"

"Nah, they're fine with us." Since Tuesday, the pair had been making daily trips to DPP for careful testing with the healers. Monday's visit had been scuttled because the team needed a chance to regroup and check their security after Dante's ignominious removal from the building, but while his betrayal had left them shaken, Vinla insisted that the Elemental victims come in for evaluations. "We *think* we understand the potion," she'd explained. "We need to be certain. And the more experimentation we can do, the sooner we'll know when we can safely return those two to Georgia."

Sure, neither woman was thrilled to still be stuck in the Pactlands—and Tabitha was no more enamored of her blue hair than she'd been when she woke and got a shock—but Pop had offered them the use of almost any car in the garage and a map, and Tabitha had been dragging Stephanie out to explore. They'd had dinner with Jane and Connor at Maebe's house in distant Cirinti that night, an outing Jane had orchestrated in part to give Maebe something to think about other than her incarcerated cousins.

Jillu and Obelli had made nuisances of themselves since the weekend. With help from Teolm, Maebe and Zoe Black, the young Lady ti'Non, had taken steps to have the sisters' finances partitioned on an expedited basis, giving them access to funds to retain counsel but keeping a larger percentage untouchable for the benefit of their husbands and children. While Jillu's husband, Mirin, was himself incarcerated, their son Cefet was nearly of age, and a judge permitted him to take emergency custody of his baby brother, albeit with Tribunal oversight. As for Obelli's husband, Eccenna the apprentice luthier, he'd already initiated divorce proceedings and moved for sole custody of their boy. Jillu and Obelli had then turned to their parents for assistance, but their father had washed his hands of them. Their mother, Dolia, had been gentler in her refusal but still firm. The poor woman already had both parents and a brother locked away, and from what I'd heard, she was disgusted with her daughters for dragging the family through the mud once more.

With only limited support, the sisters had opted to have counsel appointed. I didn't know whether they would take Kabno up on her offer for their cooperation, but for the moment, that wasn't my concern.

I woke late Friday morning and rolled over to find Yven still in bed beside me. "Hey, you," I murmured, smiling as I snuggled closer. "Overdid it last night, huh?"

"Not exactly," he said, adjusting his position to better accommodate me. "I just thought this would be a better way to wake up than sneaking off to the greenhouse at dawn."

I gasped. "You mean to tell me that I actually trump the orchids?"

"Sometimes." He kissed me, and I giggled. "They're beautiful, of course," said Yven, "but this view..."

"Not bad?"

"Hmm. Better than satisfactory, I suppose—"

I shoved him in the shoulder, and he laughed as he flopped onto his back. "Just for that," I said, "you can lie here and think about what you've done while I shower."

He rolled over again as I untangled myself from the blankets and stood. "Might you need assistance in the shower, by chance?"

I glanced back at him, and he waggled his eyebrows. "Down, boy," I said, bending to kiss him again. "Save it for the Edolis, eh?"

A hot shower was just what I needed to wash away the last of the evening's drinking, but as I began to wake, an unexplainable anxiety started twisting in my gut. Telling myself it was nothing, I finished up, dressed while Yven took his turn, and suggested we brunch at a cute little café in Viratta.

But food and caffeine did nothing to calm my nerves, and my unease deepened as the day went along. By dinnertime, I could only pick at my food—Ranarma's delicious roast chicken, to make matters worse—and after we ate, Yven followed me upstairs and gave me an impromptu shoulder massage once we'd turned on the TV. "Can you tell me what's wrong?" he asked as I grunted beneath his strong hands. "Wedding jitters?"

"I don't know," I mumbled. "I can't pinpoint it..."

"Could it be tomorrow's brunch?"

"Ugh. Maybe."

Saturday at eleven was the last of my major pre-wedding engagements with Calien, brunch at a trendy and overpriced restaurant in Beukal. Since I didn't have a bridal party, I'd assumed that the brunch would be for my girlfriends and perhaps some female relations, but no—this was a blowout event designed by (and let's be honest, for) my cousin and her society friends. Calien swore this was necessary. "You're too young to be presented," she'd griped, "you know no one, and you come from nothing. Don't you want to know your guests before the wedding?"

I didn't want to invite strangers in the first place, I'd wanted to retort, but I'd bitten it back and surrendered.

The brunch was meant to be spectacular, and I'd given Calien full rein to plan it to her specifications. On Tuesday, she'd happily announced that no fewer than *three* society writers would be in attendance...and she'd warned me not to screw this up.

At least her mother would be attending. If the other girls were awful, I could always talk to Miral, or failing that, sit in the corner and smile into my coffee.

Yven's hands migrated lower, and I slumped over as he worked out the knots. "Two hours, Rosie. And if you need me to, I'll pick you up afterward with a bottle of wine to dull the pain."

"What about some of Aunt Lily's special brew?"

"Ooh. Tell you what, you see how you're feeling once this mess is past, and if I need to drive out to Briardale to procure the good hooch, I will."

"I still don't know what I did to deserve you."

He bent and kissed the side of my neck, and then, in a tone I'd come to know *very* well, murmured, "What do you say we turn off the television and go to bed early?"

"And you distract me from thoughts of brunch?"

"Could be fun, right?"

He darkened the TV and the lights with a gesture, then scooped me off the couch and carried me into our room. "Let me brush my teeth first, okay?" I said as he gently deposited me on the bed. "There was a lot of garlic in the chicken seasoning tonight."

Yven laughed but promised to wait for me, and I stepped into the adjoining bath to freshen up and drop a few choice items of clothing in the hamper. When I returned, the bed was ready, and Yven, who'd preemptively removed his shirt, stared at me with the sort of naked hunger that does wonders for a woman's confidence. He'd been putting in a little extra time at the gym in recent months—his own form of wedding prep—and while he would never be stacked, his abs had taken on pleasing definition.

I wondered only for a second how I'd ever gotten so lucky before I was in his arms.

During our long engagement, Yven had become quite adept at distracting me in that particular fashion, and he gave it his all that evening. But while we both fell asleep satisfied, I woke less than an hour later, my anxiety stronger than ever. As I stared at the ceiling in the dark bedroom, I admitted to myself what I'd been dancing around all day: this was a nudge, a tickle from my talent.

What *now*? Surely no one was going to accidentally bulldoze our wedding venue…

I thought of stretching out on the couch in my studio and trying to track the source of the problem, but instead, I put a fresh canvas on an easel, set up some paints, and glanced over at my parents' unfinished portrait. "Wish me luck," I told them, then focused on the unspoiled whiteness in front of me and let my mind blank.

All farseers had their tricks and, when necessary, crutches to get into the proper headspace. For me, it was my art—painting Maya's mural, sketching Aunt Lily and the men who'd forced her to go on the run, even doodling under the influence of Awakening. I'd dropped into a flow state during my brief stay at the ti'Cren mansion and come out of it hours later to discover I'd painted my great-grandparents and all of their children, and while I hadn't realized it in the moment, my farsight had indicated the ones involved with Inade's criminal enterprise. While I'd progressed to the point that I could access my talent without a pencil or brush in my hand, my old habit could sometimes get me where I needed to be more rapidly than just closing my eyes and trying to power through.

And so, I painted. With my phone quietly playing instrumental music in its dock, I sat alone, illuminated by a single lamp, and might have kept working long into the next day had Yven not come in to check on me. "Sweetie?" he asked cautiously, jarring me out of my quasi-trance. "Are you okay? It's nine-thirty. Your brunch is at eleven, remember?" As I turned to him on my swivel stool and rubbed my head, he asked, "Have you been up all night? Is that…" He squinted past me at the canvas. "Is that Briardale?"

I reached for him, and he steadied me as I stood, then stepped back to take in the result of the night's farsight-driven flow.

Aunt Lily's home and garden nursery were built on the side of a mountain overlooking the town of Briardale, an

Appalachian outpost barely large enough to need its own police department. The downtown area, as it were, had largely been set up on a grid—the streets were numbered, while the intersecting avenues were named for trees—but past those few planned blocks, the roads turned winding as they snaked into the outskirts and up the surrounding hills. A few neighborhoods ringed the core of Briardale, but zoning was lax, and small businesses and houses shared space. Standing at the edge of the parking lot at Aunt's Lily's place, if the weather cooperated, one could see many of the highlights of Briardale: the steeples of First Baptist, Grace Methodist, and St. Peter's, the park with the gazebo and the baseball diamond near the little brick library, the gas station (still full-service if you honked for an attendant), and Mabel's Place, the oldest and best of three eateries in the town limits.

That was the view I'd painted, a scene of spring-green trees, narrow strips of asphalt, and a few pickup trucks—not Aunt Lily, not her hidden greenhouse, but Briardale itself.

What could be so important about *Briardale*?

"Let's get some caffeine in you," said Yven, helping me from my studio. "And food. Ranarma didn't prepare a big breakfast today, but I know there's coffee in the kitchen."

I shuffled out of our apartment with Yven by my side in case of wobbling, and we made our way downstairs, where we found Ranarma at work on a few loaves of bread. "Morning, Miss Rose," he called over his shoulder as he kneaded the dough. "Don't you have brunch plans?"

"She's been working," Yven explained, and left me on a barstool as he fixed my coffee. "Here, honey, drink that," he urged, putting the mug in front of me. "Ranarma, don't tell Diriem I'm raiding his snack stash, eh?"

Five minutes later, Pop joined us and found me staring into space with my hands wrapped around the warm mug, alternately sipping and trying to absorb caffeine via steam inhalation, an untouched bag of imported Doritos on the counter beside me. "Difficult night, Rosie?" he asked, frowning as he took me in.

I nodded. "Woke with a nudge. I painted to try to make it come into focus, but I'm not sure what I'm supposed to be seeing." Looking up at him, I asked, "Have you been getting any concerning flashes lately?"

Pop smiled grimly. "*Always*, my dear. Can you be more specific?"

"Something to do with Aunt Lily, maybe? Or Briardale?"

"I wouldn't know Briardale if I saw it," he replied apologetically, "and as for your great-aunt...not exactly."

"That's not a no."

"A feeling, that's all. Nothing defined," he said, folding his arms. "My recent flashes don't make much sense. Too many holes."

"Holes?" I echoed.

"Protected individuals."

My guts twisted afresh. More dirty agents? Forum representatives? Maebe's cousins?

"Why don't you show me your painting?" Pop suggested. "Perhaps I'll recognize something..."

His voice faded as a muffled ringing came from his pants pocket, and he pulled out his phone. "Kabno."

"Well, that can't be good," I muttered, as he took the call on speaker mode.

"I'm at home," Pop answered, not bothering with pleasantries. "What's wrong?"

"Prison break," Kabno replied.

For the briefest of moments, he looked stricken, then closed his eyes and swore under his breath. "Which one? How?"

"All three. It was coordinated, they had help from the guards, and some of the inmates—"

"Have already fled the Pactlands," Pop finished.

"*Yeah.* Want to guess who's missing? We're still compiling lists, and there are inmates running loose around the farms—"

Tuning out the conversation, I closed my eyes and willed my farsight to cooperate. Only a handful of the Pactlands' prisoners could have business in Briardale, and I feared I knew who might have run in that direction.

When my inner eyes opened, I punched through the fresh blinding protection around my *other* great-grandfather and found him riding shotgun in a black sedan. He'd exchanged his brown inmate uniform for a simple black shirt and matching pants—a look that could have passed for an agent's. He held up one hand, wiggling his fingers, and sparks flashed over the tips. He hadn't just taken the blinding potion—he'd been given the antidote to the dampening potion as well.

Inade ti'Cren was unbound and heading straight for his eldest daughter.

I couldn't tell who was driving the car or who the two people in the back might be—they'd taken the blinding potion as well—but Inade was danger enough. I stayed with the vision only long enough for the car to pass the painted wooden WELCOME TO BRIARDALE sign on the outskirts of town, then threw myself back into my body.

"Inade's on his way to Aunt Lily," I announced, interrupting Pop and Kabno.

"You saw him?" Yven asked.

"Yeah, and he's not alone. We've got to get to her," I said, staring at Pop. "*Now.*" Before he could argue, I was on my feet and grabbing for his phone. "Oilville is the closest portal. Briardale's about an hour and a half to the west. Tell your people to move."

"How many are with him?" Kabno asked.

"Three others in his car, but I don't know if they're traveling alone. Just hurry!" I said, and ran from the kitchen.

Yven caught up to me on the staircase. "What's the plan?"

"Gotta get to her," I said as I jogged, slipping into English as my exhausted mind raced. "Gotta get there…need a car…"

"Call Annie."

"*Annie.* Good. She's probably up, yeah? Do you think—"

Yven gripped my shoulders at the top of the staircase and squeezed until I focused on him. "Get your phone and call Annie," he said, and pushed me toward the south wing. "Run, Rosie. I'm right behind you."

ACKNOWLEDGEMENTS

So, uh…sorry about that cliffhanger. Don't worry, the story will pick right back up in *Unity*…

My thanks, as always, go to the Novel Chicks for the camaraderie, the feedback, and the support. Y'all are the best!

I also sincerely thank Adam Domby, who continues to squeeze time for these books into his schedule of Far More Important Things.

And yes, here's to you, Mom and Dad.

ABOUT THE AUTHOR

When not writing fiction, Ash Fitzsimmons is an appellate attorney and an unrepentant car singer.

Find her online:
www.ashfitzsimmons.com

www.ingramcontent.com/pod-product-compliance
Lightning Source LLC
LaVergne TN
LVHW050925080826
845145LV00001B/217

* 9 7 8 1 9 4 9 8 6 1 7 7 8 *